DAISY'S SECRET

Abandoned by her sweetheart and rejected by her family, Daisy Atkins feels she has no choice but to agree to being evacuated to the Lakes at the start of the war. Still grieving for the baby boy she gave up for adoption she resolves that he will be her secret, spoken of to no one, and she seeks consolation by taking under her wing two frightened little girls. When she meets Harry Driscoll it seems she will have a second chance at love; but her secret is about to come back to haunt her...

DAISY'S SECRET

DAISY'S SECRET

by

Freda Lightfoot

Magna Large Print Books
Long Preston, North Yorkshire,
BD23 4ND, England.

British Library Cataloguing in Publication Data.

Lightfoot, Freda
    Daisy's secret.

    A catalogue record of this book is
    available from the British Library

    ISBN   0-7505-2073-6

First published in Great Britain in 2003 by Hodder & Stoughton
A division of Hodder Headline

Published in Large Print 2003 by arrangement with
Hodder & Stoughton Ltd.

Magna Large Print is an imprint of Library Magna Books Ltd.

Printed and bound in Great Britain by
T.J. (International) Ltd., Cornwall, PL28 8RW

To Mim, number one fan, who loves to read my books when not watching Manchester United.

Prologue

Laura

'I thought I might stay on for a bit.'

'Stay on, in heavens' name what for?'

Laura glanced about the empty room, the last few people having said their farewells and departed, their faces sad, their condolences genuine and heartfelt. They'd made the customary offers of support, shaken her hand with polite formality, told her how proud Daisy would have been that she'd coped so well with the day. Laura had thanked them for coming and now they were alone, she and Felix, still with decisions to make, at least so far as she was concerned.

'Aren't there always things to attend to, after funerals?'

'Don't be childish. Do you imagine the family solicitor is going to turn up and read the will or something? They don't perform such silly melodramas nowadays, Laura, and we really should be getting back. What is so important that can't wait till we come and clear the house ready for the sale?'

She couldn't, offhand, think of a single thing, not one sensible enough to convince Felix. Her husband was always the one to deal with important financial affairs, keeping the wheels of their busy life oiled and endlessly turning. Yet she knew that she didn't want to leave and whatever he said, whatever arguments he put in her way, Laura resolved that she had no intention of doing so. On this occasion she meant to stand firm. She'd always felt stubborn and strong willed inside, but perhaps it was a side to her character she'd neglected to reveal often enough.

She stood at the window and watched the cars trundle out of the farmyard as loyal neighbours hurried homewards, their minds already turning to the next chore to be done, cows to be milked, sheep checked, meals to be made. This was a busy time of year for them with lambing about to start. It was amazing that so many people had turned out for one old woman, though she had lived in their midst for years and must have known them all well.

Laura felt suddenly chilled and out of place in her smart black town suit and high-heeled shoes, knowing she was the stranger here, not them. She could see a faint outline of herself mirrored in the glass against the deepening dusk of the sky, superimposed upon the scene beyond like a double exposure. Anyone could see that she didn't belong. She didn't have their healthy, country robustness; was too thin, too serious, too plain and unhappy for a woman in her early thirties, supposedly in the prime of life, an image not entirely the result of a long, rather stressful day. Even her long, dark hair lacked its usual lustre, scraped up tight about her head with barely more than a few wispy curls to soften the stark hairline.

It was wet and blustery out, typical weather for a funeral. Laura remembered many such days here as a child, with rain beating on the windows and the wind roaring in from the east over Blencathra with nothing to stop it in this barren landscape but the stone walls of the farmhouse itself. She used to lie in her bed high in an attic room, all tucked up cosy and warm and listen as it howled and whined with the ferocity of a wild beast, flustering the hens in the old outhouse, tossing wheelbarrows, harrows and other farming implements about the yard like corks, and hammering on the tightly fastened shutters as if somehow determined to gain entrance. But as so often happened in this mountainous region with its fickle weather systems, the following morning she would wake to a day that was blithe and bonny, the sun beaming benignly upon them all, the greens and golds and russets of the land luminous in the glow of early morning, like a freshly washed face.

How Laura had loved spending time here, helping to feed the hens and lambs, being spoiled by the guests who came to stay at Lane End Farm to enjoy Daisy's ham and egg breakfasts. And then for some reason she had never quite fathomed, the visits had stopped. There were no more long summer holidays in the Lake District, no more picnics to look forward to on Catbells, no more sailing on Bassenthwaite or long, breathtaking hikes over Helvellyn, and nobody would tell her why.

She turned to Felix now with a preoccupied smile, half her mind still clinging to this mystery and to recalling memories of a happy childhood, the rest attempting to find a way to exploit the situation to her advantage. The prospect of not returning with him to Cheadle Hulme was intoxicating, exciting. Would Daisy mind? Somehow she didn't think so. She tried to explain but he hardly seemed to be listening as he paced restlessly about the room, clearly anxious to depart himself.

'Daisy used to tell of this house being used as a refuge by so many people during the war. She likened it to a fortress, a bastion of strength against the man-made evils of the world. Isn't that a lovely thought?'

'Where's my cell phone? Did you borrow it, Laura, or put it somewhere?'

'She made the house available for those who sought shelter within its thick stone walls. A sanctuary. Don't you think that was a generous thing to do?' Yet there wasn't a war on now, except one conducted in bittersweet undertones between herself and Felix.

Felix stopped looking for his phone long enough to scowl furiously at her. 'Don't try my patience any further with this, Laura. We need to leave in the next half-hour to have any chance of getting home by eight. You know I still have the accounts to do and there will no doubt be a long tailback on the M6 as usual, so can we please get a move on?'

Laura began poking down the sides of the sofa, ostensibly looking for the phone, yet her mind still focused on the need for escape, the idea of barricading herself away from all the frustrations

14

of her life. From the moment she'd been told that Daisy had left her the house, she hadn't been able to get the idea out of her head. It was so tantalising.

'People – lodgers, evacuees, friends and family all came to stay here; all hanging together to get through the hostilities; all dreaming and hoping for a future when the war finally ended and they could start new lives. I once called it the House of Dreams but Gran had laughed and said more like a House of Secrets. I always wondered what she meant by that. Though I know of one secret she was forced to keep, it sounded as if there were more. Perhaps...'

'For God's sake Laura, you haven't even packed my bag.' Snatching up the empty suitcase he strode upstairs, the echo of his footsteps resounding in the empty house.

Laura looked up in surprise, as if she'd half forgotten he was there, then fell into a fit of stifled giggles. That must be a first. Packing his own suitcase. But the moment he came back downstairs, bag in hand, she went to him and kissed his cheek. 'I've definitely decided to stay on for a bit. You can manage without me for a little while, can't you, darling? There's so much to attend to here. Gran's things to go through for one, her clothes, books and other belongings, all the usual stuff. Someone has to do it.'

'You can surely leave all of that to the auctioneers.'

'No! She's my own grandmother, for heaven's sake. I'm not having strangers go through her personal things till I've at least checked them

15

first. It wouldn't be right. That's why I wanted to come in *my* car, in case I decided to stay.' As she talked, she went to the phone and rang for a taxi, having no wish to take him herself to the station and prolong the lecture still further; then began to collect up dirty cups and saucers, empty glasses and used napkins. 'I'll also need to see old Mr Capstick, the family solicitor; deal with any papers, deeds and suchlike, for the take-over of the house.'

'You can safely leave me to do that by phone,' Felix told her, sounding irritated as he tossed cushions aside and flung open cupboards and drawers, still looking for his phone. 'And next week is going to be a particularly stressful time for me, getting everything organised before the Gift Fair.'

'I know darling. I was rather thinking I'd give it a miss this year. I'm sure you don't really need me. It's not as if you ever take any notice of my opinions, now is it? Ah, there it is.' Laughing, she picked up the mobile and tucked it safely away in a pocket of his briefcase, then giving a quick frown, returned to the issue which so occupied her. 'Do you think I should let Dad have the farm after all, despite it being left to me?'

Felix gave her a startled look and his tone became clipped and sharp, punctuating his words as if he were speaking to a five-year-old child. 'Don't talk ridiculous! Sometimes, Laura, I wonder what you use for a brain.'

'It's just that it seems such a waste to sell it. I mean, we don't really need the money and he...'

'For God's sake, people always need more

16

money, and this isn't the time or place for philosophical discussions about your father and his numerous problems. Look, I have to go. Make sure you see that solicitor. Do something useful with your time here besides wallowing in nostalgia, and tell the dithering old fool to get a move on. Property prices are buoyant right now but who knows what might happen to the market in the next few months.'

'But what if I decide not to sell?'

Felix let out a heavy sigh. 'We've been through all of that and the decision has been made. We cannot afford sentiment, for God's sake.'

'No Felix. *You* have made a decision. *I* haven't. I said I needed time to think about it. So, I shall stay here for a little while longer and sort through Gran's things and do whatever is necessary while I give the matter some thought. Anyway, the rest will do me good. This peace is utter bliss.'

'Peace? Huh, deathly quiet more like. Your problem, Laura, is that you are a hopeless romantic.'

'Isn't that why you fell in love with me?'

'Damnation, that's my taxi, where's my bag?' He flung her a kiss a good half-inch from her cheek before charging off through the door. Laura ran after him with his overnight bag, quickly stowing it in the boot of the taxi, she gave a cheery wave as the taxi driver slammed all the doors and revved up the engine, just catching his final words, 'I shall expect you home by the end of the week, darling,' as it roared off at a cracking pace, no doubt under Felix's specific instructions.

Laura stood in the farmyard long after the taxi

had disappeared, relieved that he'd allowed her no time to respond to this latest instruction. She wondered if Daisy had felt this explosive burst of happiness when she'd finally broken free of her restrictive home life? But then Daisy's situation had been so different from Laura's. Only once had she spoken of the tragedy of her loss, the 'shameful secret' her strict parents had forced her to keep. How on earth had she endured it?

Daisy

1939

1

'Don't think for a minute that you can carry on as if nothing has happened. Not after behaving so shamefully. We're done with you now, Daisy Atkins. You're no longer any daughter of mine. As for your father, he's made it abundantly clear that he'll not have you set foot in the house. Not ever again. We might be poor with not much to call us own, but we have us standards. Make no mistake about that.'

Daisy looked into her mother's set face and saw by the pursing of her narrow lips and the twin spots of colour on each hollow cheek, that she meant every hard and unforgiving word. 'Then what am I to do? Where am I supposed to go?'

'You should've thought of that before you – well – before you did what you oughtn't to have done.' Rita Atkins sniffed loud disapproval and folded her arms belligerently across her narrow chest. Daisy noticed that she was wearing her best black coat and hat for the visit, the one that she wore for chapel and for all funerals and weddings in the family. It bore a faint sheen of green and smelt strongly of mothballs. 'I'll not have it. I won't. It's just like your Aunt Florrie all

19

over again.'

Daisy let out a heavy sigh, feeling a prickle of resentment by the comparison which had been flung at her more times than she cared to remember in these last, agonising weeks.

Aunt Florrie had brought disgrace to her family by running off with a man almost twice her age to live in the wilds of the Lake District. Daisy had no real memory of her, beyond the odd Christmas card but she'd always rather envied this adventurous, long-lost aunt who had escaped the boring inevitability of life in Marigold Court, Salford. She'd run away from broken windows, strings of washing and the reek of boiled fish and cabbage. And who could blame her? Certainly not Daisy. Whenever she'd ventured to say as much, she'd been slapped down by her mother, which Daisy didn't understand at all. She thought it would be the most glorious thing in the world to breathe clean, fresh country air and live where the grass stayed green and wasn't always covered in soot. Hadn't she long dreamed of just such an escape?

She'd thought she could achieve it by marrying her sweetheart Percy, who kept a market stall out at Warrington. He'd certainly seemed smitten by her, proclaiming how much he adored her halo of golden brown, corkscrew curls, which Daisy privately loathed, longing as she did for more sophisticated, smooth bangs like Veronica Lake. He'd told her frequently how her soft, brown eyes just made him melt inside, how he adored each sun-kissed freckle and he'd certainly been more than happy to kiss the fragile prettiness of her small, pink mouth.

He'd talked endlessly about his own hopes and ambitions for the future: how he aimed to have a string of market stalls one day, or better still, a whole row of shops, selling meat and fish as well as vegetables. She would listen to this extravagant fantasy, head tilted attentively to one side, eyes intent on his face, not wishing to miss a word.

'And will I be able to help you in these shops?' she'd enquire coyly. 'Or will it be some other girl?'

'Course it'll be you, Daisy,' he'd say, pulling her close. 'You're my girl. Always will be. You can serve behind the counter.'

'Happen I don't want to be your girl and work on a market stall or behind the counter of a fruit and veg shop. Mebbe I want a big house in the country.'

'Then you shall have one, Daisy girl. I'll build you the biggest house you ever did see, with a fine garage for the car, and stables for horses. 'Ere, I could run 'em in t'Grand National, eh? Come on, chuck, don't be mean, give us another kiss,' and Daisy would sigh with pleasure at the joy of being in love.

Sadly, these dreams had been dashed by discovering that the one and only occasion she'd foolishly allowed him to go 'all the way', she'd got caught. At first, in her innocence, Daisy had felt excited at the prospect of motherhood. They'd intended to get married anyway, she told herself, so it meant only that she could leave home even sooner and escape the claustrophobic restrictions her mother imposed upon her. She would marry

21

Percy and they'd find a pretty cottage in the country and while she minded the children, she'd also keep hens and grow flowers and vegetables which he could sell on his market stall. Oh, life would be just perfect!

All such foolish daydreams had been swiftly shattered.

Percy had been struck speechless with shock when she'd announced proudly that he was about to become a father. 'Nay, Daisy lass, that's bit of a shaker. I'm not old enough to be a dad, any more than you're old enough to be anyone's ma. Tha's only sixteen and I'm nobbut a couple of years older, fer God's sake.'

'Don't you love me?'

'Course I do. I'll allus love thee, but how would we manage? I've hardly any money coming in, nor will have for some long while yet. Can't we wait for a bit longer?'

'How can we wait? The baby's coming now.'

'Nay, I can't see how we'd manage. It's too soon.'

She'd argued against this point of view, naturally, attempting to explain how much they would love the baby, once it was born, and carefully outlining her plans for their future. Far from reassuring him, his horror had increased, and he started making all manner of excuses about why this couldn't possibly work. He couldn't live anywhere but Salford, he said. He only knew how to sell fruit and veg, not grow them, and he really wasn't ready yet to start his own business, particularly in a strange place where he wasn't known. Again and again he kept

22

repeating that he still loved her but that it was too soon, the timing was all wrong, as if the baby were an unwanted gift that could be sent back. And then one day he'd come to her triumphant.

'There's going to be a war, Daisy, so that settles it. I've volunteered to join the Navy. Tha'll have to get rid of it, or do as thee mam says and have it adopted. Best thing all round I'd say. There's plenty of time for us to start having babies, later, when the war's over.'

Daisy was filled with fear. She knew nothing about war. She'd been far too caught up with being in love, and the youthful exuberance of simply enjoying herself to even care, let alone understand what was going on in the wider world. If she'd noticed any rumblings on the wireless, or overheard worried comments from her parents, Daisy had ignored them, imagining that such things didn't concern her and certainly would not affect her life in any way. How wrong could she be? The war was taking her sweetheart away from her.

As if that wasn't bad enough, there had been one almighty row when she'd happily told her parents the news. Her father, as always, had simply looked mournful and said little, leaving it to her mother to rant and rave at her, though that was after she'd almost fainted with shock and needed the application of sal volatile to recover.

Daisy was their only child and Rita Atkins had never really accepted that her daughter had grown up. She believed in keeping her safe at home and never allowing her to have many friends beyond those she met each Sunday at chapel. Percy had been kept a secret as Daisy feared he might be disapproved of, his family not being quite so low in the pecking order as themselves since they were market stallholders, for all they lived only a few doors down. Daisy recognised instinctively that although her mother might have an inflated notion of her own worth and take on airs, this was simply her way of hanging on to her pride, a way of proving she wasn't quite in the gutter for all the lowly status of her husband's job. As a humble rag-and-bone man, Joe Atkins owned nothing more than the horse and cart which he drove around the streets of Salford, handing out donkey stones for rubbing doorsteps in exchange for other folk's cast-offs.

Rita told Daisy she'd never fit in with that stuck-up lot, and that she was far too young to wed. She scoffed when Daisy explained how she was in love, and that she'd intended to marry Percy anyway, saying that at sixteen she'd really no idea what love was all about. She was a strong-willed woman, and, in her opinion, there was only one way to do things: her way. She made it abundantly clear that Daisy had let her down by such loose behaviour.

Discussions on what should be done about 'the problem' had gone on interminably and neither parent, it seemed, was prepared to listen to a word Daisy said, or cared a jot about what she wanted. It was made clear to her, in no uncertain terms, that she must give up her precious baby the moment it was born.

She'd cried for weeks in the Mother and Baby

Home but no sympathy had been forthcoming. Her mother maintained she was fortunate to have family willing to help her; that they'd chosen a good Christian place and not a home for wayward girls, which was most certainly what she deserved. Though how they'd managed to afford to pay for it, Daisy didn't quite understand, since to her knowledge her parents had never had two halfpennies to rub together. Daisy endured countless sleepless nights agonising over the prospect of giving her baby away but whenever she tried to object, Rita would relate horrific tales of girls driven to having a backstreet abortion, or to taking their own lives rather than shame their families. She would listen to all of this with deepening dismay and no amount of argument would deflect her mother from her purpose.

Percy went off to join the navy, kissing her goodbye and promising to write every day. Since then she'd had only a couple of letters, telling her how busy he was and how exciting his new life was going to be; how he hoped she could sort out her 'little problem'. *Little problem!* Daisy felt deserted by everyone, as if there was no one at all to love her.

When the baby was born, a boy, who had slipped easily into the world and exercised his lungs almost instantly on a bellow of rage, Daisy cried with delight, not even noticing the pain. But within seconds, he was taken from her. The stern-faced sister who officiated at the birth wouldn't even allow her to hold him.

'He's not your child, Daisy. He belongs to

25

another woman now. Best you don't even see him,' and nor did she, not properly. She glimpsed a tuft of red-brown hair, just like Percy's own, before he was swaddled in a blanket and whisked from the room. She could hear his cries fading in the distance as the nurse marched him away down the corridor. It felt as if they had ripped her heart from her body.

At first, she hadn't even cried, quite unable to take in the full impact of what was happening to her. She'd sat up in the bed all day long in stunned disbelief, her ears tuned for the slightest cry she might recognise. Once, she sneaked out and prowled the corridors, hoping to snatch him up from the nursery and run off with him, but she'd been apprehended by a young nurse, duly scolded and marched back to bed.

It was then that the tears had come and once having started, Daisy felt they might never stop.

The next day her mother lectured her on how she must put this mess behind her and forget all about it.

'Forget? How can I forget? He's my baby. My child!'

'No he's not. He belongs to someone else now, like Sister said.'

'Who?'

'That's none of your business. He's being adopted. You've no say over the matter at all.'

'But I haven't even given him a name,' Daisy wailed.

'Nor must you. The very idea. It's not your place. His new parents will do that. All you have to do is sign the paper and it's all done and dusted.'

'But Mam...'

'No buts. You're lucky it's turned out as well as it has. A fine healthy boy is always easiest to place. It'll all be done privately, very hush-hush. But you must never mention a word of this business to anyone, do you understand, Daisy? Not a single word,' and she wagged a finger in her daughter's face, to emphasise the point.

Daisy stared at her mother, wide-eyed with shock. 'Never mention him? Whyever not?'

'Because it'll make you look cheap, that's why. This business could ruin your reputation. No chap would have you as a wife if this ever got out. Men don't like used goods.'

For once in her life Daisy was struck speechless. Such a prospect had not occurred to her. She'd never, in fact, thought beyond the moment of the birth itself, worrying about how she would feel when the baby was taken away from her. She'd given no thought to how her life might change thereafter.

Rita gave her a little shake, urging her to pay attention. 'This has to be our little secret. Do you understand, Daisy? It must never be mentioned, not to anyone. *Ever!* Is that clear?'

Eyes glistening with fresh tears, Daisy could do nothing but nod.

Perhaps she'd assumed, if she'd thought about it at all, that once the baby had been safely delivered to its new parents she might be able to visit it from time to time, and when she was old enough, get him back and take care of him herself.

But Daisy saw now how very naïve that dream

had been, both in allowing herself to trust in Percy's love in the first place, and in imagining she could in any way keep the baby. She'd behaved very foolishly and her only excuse was that she'd been young and innocent, had felt desperate for some breath of freedom away from Rita's stifling control.

Even after she'd signed the adoption papers, as demanded of her, Daisy wasn't about to be forgiven for her transgression. Nor would her father ever be allowed to speak to her again. Though why should she care? When had he ever cared about her? If he wasn't out on his cart, he'd be in the pub or with his mates. He'd never had much time for a daughter. A son would have been much more use.

Yet it seemed awful that she wasn't even going back home. How could she be sure of ever seeing Percy again if she was to be sent even further away. Daisy didn't care to imagine where she might end up. Tears spilled over and slid down her already wet cheeks as a lump of fear lodged painfully in her chest. The future looked bleak, more uncertain than ever, her dreams all crumbled to dust.

'Why can't I go home?' she begged one more time, desperation in her voice as her longing for Percy, for someone to love and care for her, almost overwhelmed her. She imagined him marching in, saying he'd changed his mind and they could get married after all. Then he'd carry her off to the pretty cottage in the country, baby and all.

'Because you can't. Anyroad, the exodus has

already begun.'

'Exodus?'

'The Great Trek, the evacuation, what d'you think I'm talking about? Stop arguing, girl. My nerves are in ribbons already, what with the war and everything, let alone worrying about you. Like I say, you're nowt but trouble, just like Florrie.'

'I'm not a bit like Aunt Florrie,' Daisy protested hotly. 'I haven't run off and got wed, more's the pity. I did as you asked, even though it's not *my* choice to have the baby adopted. I want to keep it. And why shouldn't I? I've nobody else to love. No one gives a tinker's cuss about me.'

Rita Atkins flicked out a hand and smacked her daughter smartly across her cheek, leaving an imprint of four red lashes where her fingers had made contact. 'Don't you *dare* use such language with me! I'll have none of your lip, madam. I've had as much as I can take. Now then, get your coat and hat on. It's time to go. I'll not be responsible for you a minute longer, not with a war starting. The bus leaves at twelve sharp.'

'Bus, what bus? Where *am* I going?' Tears stood proud in Daisy's eyes but she refused to let them fall, holding on to her defiance for as long as she could.

'Stop asking so many fool questions. I've told you already, I've no idea. You're fortunate they'll take you, great girl like you. Anyroad, I've fetched a few things from home what I thought you might need, and your gas mask,' indicating a cardboard box and the small brown suitcase standing by the bed which Daisy had taken to

29

mean that she was going home, until she'd learned different. Now she was being banished to goodness knows where, perhaps for ever. 'Don't sit there like a lump of lead, pack your night things and get yerself ready.'

Having issued this instruction, Rita herself began to fold Daisy's night-dress, then opening the bedside cabinet began to draw out the few personal items she'd brought with her to the home. Soap bag and flannel, brush and comb and a small satchel of handkerchiefs which she'd painstakingly stitched for herself, fussy madam. She followed this with a book and magazine Daisy had been reading, snapped shut the suitcase and hooked the strap tight.

'Right then. That's you ready for off.'

'But off *where*?' Daisy once more appealed, naked misery in her tone.

'How many times do I have to say it? *Evacuated.* Off to these pastures new you've always pined for. Well, now you'll get your chance to live in the country, though it's more than you deserve in the circumstances. You should thank your lucky stars you've got off so lightly. And remember, not a word about this business to anyone. Not ever!'

At the bus stop, Rita handed the case to Daisy, together with a bus ticket and instructions over what time she needed to be at London Road Station where she would be joining dozens of other evacuees, mostly children younger than herself. 'When no doubt all your questions will be answered and somebody in charge will tell you where it is you're to be sent.'

30

The bus arrived seconds later, the wheels churning through a puddle that splashed Daisy's clean stockings, coat and skirt, speckling them with spots of mud.

Rita clicked her tongue in dismay, spat on her hanky and began to rub frantically at the offending marks. 'Nay, why didn't you step back, you gormless lump? Why have you never any sense? It's time you took your head out of the clouds girl, and started to think about what you were doing. You can't go on being Daisy Daydream, you really can't.'

The bus conductor, watching this display of motherly fussing for some seconds with wry amusement, finally remarked, 'Do you do short back and sides an' all?'

Rita Atkins gave her daughter a little push, to urge her on her way. 'Get off with you. They won't wait all day,' just as if it had been Daisy holding up the bus, and not her mother at all. But now Daisy did hesitate, hopeful perhaps of a goodbye kiss, a fond hug, good wishes for the future, or even an assurance that her mother would write.

But Rita was busy tucking away her now grubby handkerchief in the big black handbag she always carried on her arm. Then with hands clasped tight at her waist, mouth compressed in its usual firm line of censure she took a step back, clearly mindful of a possible repeat of the unfortunate incident.

Reluctantly, Daisy climbed on board but even then stood clinging to the rail on the conductor's platform before finding a seat. 'I'll write, Mam,

31

when I get to wherever it is I'm going.'

The engine chose that very moment to rev up and roar as the bus jerked forward, and Daisy was never afterwards entirely sure whether she had heard her mother correctly, but it sounded very like, 'Don't bother. I'll not be answering no letters from you, madam. Your father neither. Not if I've any say in the matter.'

2

Daisy felt stunned by the speed of events, overwhelmed by the crush of children on the platform, many of them crying, others excitedly enjoying the novelty of a train journey into the unknown. All of them clutched tight to a suitcase, brown paper parcel or kitbag, a doll or teddy and of course their gasmask box strung across their chest where was carefully pinned a large label stating their name and age, just as if they might forget it in the trauma of events.

'Don't play with the doors. Take your seats quickly, there's a good girl.' A woman in a green hat skewered to her iron-grey hair with a long hat pin, issued these orders in a loud, crisp voice, anxious to make herself heard above the din of a platform packed with children; a false, cheery smile fixed on her face.

Tens of thousands would be leaving Manchester over the next few days, as well as London, Birmingham, Liverpool and cities right across the land. London Road Station seemed to be filled with people giving orders: police and railway officials, local borough councillors who'd come along to offer support plus dozens of teachers, nurses, members of the Friends' War Victims Relief Committee, and WVS ladies, all of whom had evidently responded to government posters to help with the evacuation process.

Now, at last, all the plans were coming to fruition and they were off, and everyone seemed excited by the prospect. Everyone except Daisy.

Daisy felt affronted at being evacuated with a host of children. She'd noticed a carriage full of pregnant young mums further along the train who'd been provided with their own midwife, just in case one of them should go into labour during the journey, she supposed. Daisy felt a burst of envy for them. They would all be allowed to keep their babies, of course, because they were married to husbands who loved them.

The woman with the green hat and loud voice permitted herself one censorious glance at Daisy before ushering her into a carriage and slamming shut the door on her protest, almost as if she knew her dreadful secret and had decided she deserved no better consideration than to be left with a bunch of noisy ten-year-olds. It made Daisy feel confused. What was she then, child or woman?

Perversely now, she'd no wish to leave home for the idyllic bliss of the countryside, or to abandon her beloved Manchester which was suddenly under threat of war. In any case, she'd miss all the excitement and really she should be doing something useful, not being spirited away as part of this 'Great Trek' or whatever they called it, to some unknown safe haven, however well meaning these bossy people might be.

'Don't cry, Trish. You know what to do, remember? Just like we practised at school. Stick tight to teddy and we'll be all right.'

'I feel sick.' The piping voice at her elbow brought Daisy from her self-pitying reverie to find two small girls at her side. The face of one, little more than four or five, was wet with tears and a river of mucus from each nostril. The other, older by a year or so, was attempting to comfort her and mop her up.

'Where's me mam? I want me mam?' wailed the smaller one.

'She's waving from the platform. See, there she is,' and the older girl attempted to hoist her sister up so that she could see out of the carriage window to view some unidentified mother amongst the crush of women waving and bearing brave smiles as they sent their children off into the care of strangers.

Daisy sprang into action. 'Here, let me hold her for you,' and she grabbed the child to hold her high at the half open carriage window where she waved frantically, her small face a heart-rending mix of joy at the sight of her mother, and pain at their parting. The other, older girl, hung out of the window long after the train had drawn out of the station, still waving when all sight of the crowd of sorrowful women had disappeared in a cloud of steam. 'Come on, love. Let me pull it up with the strap, or you'll get grit

34

and soot in your eyes.'

The two little girls sat huddled in the corner of the seat opposite to Daisy, skinny arms wrapped tight about each other. They were dressed in navy blue gabardines far too long for them, yet with several inches of skirt trailing below the hem, presumably to leave ample room for growth. Each of their small, round heads was covered with a large beret, revealing only a few tufts of brown hair which stuck out around the edges. Daisy almost suggested they remove them, and then thought better of it. Who knew what lurked beneath? Their faces were drawn and anxious, the skin a familiar pallor that Daisy knew well, but then there wasn't much sunshine to be had in the back streets of Manchester. They looked so thoroughly miserable that she attempted to jolly them into conversation by asking them their names.

'I'm Megan,' the older girl solemnly responded. 'And this is Patricia, although we call her Trish for short.'

'Mine's Daisy,' said Daisy. 'And I'm happy to make your acquaintance.' They both exchanged weak smiles. 'Do you, by any chance, know where we're going on this train?'

Megan shook her head. 'I expect the King does.'

'Oh, I expect he does,' Daisy agreed. She glanced again at Trish who was still suffering from hiccuping sobs and seemed far from reassured by this news. When the tears finally subsided she curled up into a tiny ball, cuddled against her sister, popped her thumb into her mouth and went to sleep. The only time she perked up was some hours later when Megan drew out a packet of sandwiches, one for each of them.

Feeling a pang of hunger herself, Daisy reached down her case from the luggage rack and searched through it for a similar thoughtful gesture by her own mother. She found nothing. Embarrassed by this lack of attention, she quickly snapped it shut and returned it to the rack.

'Didn't you bring no food? We were told to fetch enough for one day.'

'It's all right. I'm not hungry.'

Unconvinced by the lie, Megan held out her packet. 'It's only fish paste, but you're welcome to have one. Mam allus makes plenty.'

'Thanks.' The fish paste sandwich went down a treat, followed by a second offered by Trish who even managed a shy smile, and thus their friendship was born.

'Weren't you given a list of what to bring? We were.'

'I don't know. It was all a bit sudden and – er – unexpected.'

'Mam had a bit of a job finding some of the stuff. We had to have a toothbrush, one *each*, spare socks and plimsolls, and a warm jersey. We've never had owt spare before, have you?'

'And a macktosh,' put in Trish, now bright-eyed and filled with vim and vigour after her sandwich.

'Mackintosh,' Megan corrected. 'Did you have to buy a new one, Daisy? We did. Well, new to *us* that is. We got them on the flat iron market.

Look, aren't they grand?' she said, smoothing down the lapel with pride.

'And I've got a face cloth. A blue one,' Trish added with some importance.

Daisy admitted that she'd no idea what was in her suitcase since her mother had packed it, and the pair looked at her askance, evidently having taken great interest in the treasures their mother had collected for them.

'D'you think we'll see the sea? Mam said we might.'

'I don't know.' Daisy shook her head and tried to smile in response to Trish's bright gaze. The little girl was rallying, seeing it all now as the adventure her mother had promised. If only she could view it in the same light. Oh Percy, where are you? If only you hadn't let me down. If only there hadn't been a war. If only I hadn't been so foolish as to get pregnant, or if only they'd let me keep the baby, then everything would have been so different. So many if onlys. If none of it had happened, she'd have been happy to go on this train today and steam away into the unknown. It would've been a new beginning. Instead, she'd been ordered to shut all that 'shameful' part of her life away, just as if it had never happened and her baby boy had never been born. Daisy turned her face to the window so the children couldn't see her tears.

It had seemed, while they had waited inter- minably in London Road Station, as if the journey would never start, now they thought it might go on for ever. The train would chug along

37

for a while, and then stop, back up into a siding and wait for seemingly hours until some express or passenger train had thundered by, before edging slowly forward again. Dusk fell and at each station after that the carriage lights would go out just as the train drew into a station which made it difficult to read the signs on the equally dark platform, and then twenty or thirty children would get off and troop out to the buses usually lined up on the street nearby. The 'exodus' seemed to be very well organised and just a little alarming. Daisy had realised they were heading north, which cheered her and made her think of Aunt Florrie again, though they could end up in Scotland, which would be no help at all. When finally it was their turn, they were released, late in the evening, on to a small, unknown, country platform seemingly in the middle of nowhere. She felt stiff and nervous, certain they must have been travelling for days, though it was probably a little over seven hours.

'You're a very lucky girl to be here at all,' was the frosty response when she dared to ask the woman in the green hat why it had taken so long. 'Evacuee trains can't be given priority over the normal service. People still have to get to and from work, you know. Now, more than ever.'

This all seemed rather odd to Daisy. Why evacuate them at all if it wasn't an emergency? And if it was an emergency, then why not give the trainload of children priority? As things stood, it not being a corridor train, desperate little boys had been peeing out of the window, and little girls quietly weeping over the state of their knickers.

Poor little Trish had been in floods of tears since this was apparently the first time she'd ever worn knickers in her life and they were brand new. It had been a great relief to escape the stink of the stuffy carriage.

Green Hat was speaking again, in an even louder voice this time as hundreds of confused, tired children milled about the rapidly darkening platform. She clapped her hands smartly together, to bring them to attention. 'Since we've arrived much later than expected, the dispersal officer isn't here. Probably gone back home, assuming we'll arrive tomorrow instead. However,' she continued with forced brightness, 'our spirits are undimmed, are they not? We shall sleep tonight in the station waiting rooms. Boys in the gents. Girls in the ladies. Now stand in line and make your way in an orderly fashion. No pushing and shoving.'

They were given a hot drink of Bovril made on the station waiting-room fire and bread and butter, by the ladies in smart uniforms, and afterwards, blankets were handed out. Daisy, Megan and Trish huddled up together for warmth beneath one but the September night was cold, the waiting-room floor hard and Trish kept sniffling and sneezing while Megan got a fit of coughing, which worried Daisy. Eventually they slept fitfully, woken with a jerk in the early hours by a cry of alarm that quickly spread, creating panic when the word 'gas' was heard.

The ladies in charge acted quickly. Whipping off all the children's blankets, they fled to the lavatory where they soaked them in water and then hung them at all the doors and windows for protection. The night was even colder after that and the three new friends gave up all hope of sleep though they were grateful at least for Megan and Trish's 'macktoshes', their only protection against the blast of cold air that roared under the waiting-room door every time a train went through.

As the children stood about in a ragged group in the cold light of early morning, a trickle of local women began to appear. Green Hat told them that the women came not only from the local villages, but also from nearby Penrith, a town in the northern Lakes and Daisy felt a burst of hope. Wasn't it somewhere round here that Aunt Florrie had come to live? Desperately she tried to remember her married surname but for the life of her couldn't bring it to mind. All that had ever been written on the infrequent Christmas or birthday cards was *'Yours, as always, Florrie'*.

Bullied by the dispersal officer, who had finally arrived, the village women made their selection, and all Daisy could do was search their faces to see if any one of them resembled her own mother. None did.

'I'll have this one.'

'I'll take her.'

'I'll have that little lad over there.'

One woman put a hand on Trish's collar and was about to haul her away when Megan made a grab for her, loudly protesting. 'No! Our Trish stops with me. Me mam said we had to stay together. Daisy too,' she added for good measure,

40

casting a quick glance in her new friend's direction. Daisy did not protest. The decision seemed to have been made without the need for words during the long, cold, miserable night. No matter what, they meant to stay together.

Unfortunately, this proved to be asking rather much of the good ladies of the Lakes. Many were glad to help the evacuees, some did so out of a sense of patriotism or duty, while others took the attitude that having to take one child was bad enough, two was an imposition, and three quite impossible. It became alarming, and then frightening to see the other children marched off one by one, and still be left hanging about on the cold platform with a diminishing number of possible hosts, or 'foster parents' as they were optimistically described.

'Does nobody want us, Daisy?' Megan asked, a slight wobble to her voice.

Trish tugged at Daisy's skirt. 'I feel sick.'

'Don't think about it, then you won't be.'

'Shall I be sick in me beret, only me mam told me not to take it off.'

'No, no, your mam's right. Leave it on, love. You won't be sick, I promise.' And, by a miracle, she wasn't.

In the end, there were only the three of them left, and Green Hat came over to inspect them. 'Really, this determination of yours to stick together isn't very helpful. How would it be if everyone adopted such stringent rules?'

The three stared up at her, uncomprehending. At last Daisy felt obliged to respond, since she was the eldest. 'They're only young, four and

41

seven, and Trish is just getting over a bad dose of flu, so they need special care. I've promised to help since their mother had to stay and look after elderly relatives.' Daisy had heard the whole sorry story during the long night, about the entire family going down with the flu, grandpa dying and their grandmother still poorly with pneumonia. The two children, Trish in particular, were feeling homesick already.

Eyebrows arched quizzically. 'Oh, so you are not related then?'

'They are. To each other, I mean. I'm not, but...'

'Ah well, that changes everything. You should have said,' the woman responded briskly. 'In that case, you shall go with that old gentleman over there, and the two little ones with Miss Pratt. There, that's settled you all nicely. A good job well done.'

Daisy and Megan exchanged glances of dismay while Trish let out a great wail of protest and flung her arms about Daisy's leg, as if she might never let go. But there was no hope of escape. Abruptly disengaged from her hold, the weeping child was smartly handed over to a tall, thin, elderly woman with whiskers on her chin who was regarding the two little girls as if she'd never set eyes on such creatures in her life before.

'Can't I go with them? Please?' Daisy gasped, as the pair were dragged away.

'No indeed. You will go to the billet selected for you. Mr Witherspoon? She's all yours.' Within seconds there was no sign of a WVS uniform or large hat of any colour or description left on the

42

platform. Daisy swivelled about in panic, took one glance at the haggard, unsmiling face of the old man beside her, then turned tail and ran after the wailing children.

'Miss Pratt,' she yelled. 'Miss Pratt, please wait a moment.' She caught up with the woman out on the station forecourt, quite out of breath and keenly aware of Mr Witherspoon bearing down upon them, like the devil incarnate. 'I'll do anything, clean your house, do the washing, anything. I'll make myself really useful and promise faithfully to keep these children out of mischief and off your hands. You need me, you really do. Young children are a great deal of work, and I don't eat much, I swear.' This last was quite untrue, but she thought perhaps the elderly woman might be worrying about feeding them all. She was certainly looking preoccupied.

'That is not a consideration at this juncture. I have a large garden and produce much of my own food, and naturally I have someone come in to do for me, though I do wonder if Gladys said she might be going to her sister's in Edinburgh.' Her eyes took on a vague, troubled look. 'But perhaps you may have a point with regard to the children. I have other commitments after all, and certainly could not tolerate any bad behaviour.'

Daisy held her breath. So far, in her own short life, she'd made a frightening number of mistakes, managing to ruin her entire life at just sixteen. Now, some half-formed idea in her head was telling Daisy that perhaps by helping these two children through their own troubles it might compensate in some way for the baby she'd lost, and that the pain in her own heart might somehow reduce.

After a moment, Miss Pratt swung around and called across the forecourt to Mr Witherspoon, still shambling towards them, his breathing laboured. 'I've decided to take the older girl as well, Mr Witherspoon. If it doesn't work out, I'll let you know.'

He paused, lifted one hand and waved to her by way of conceding defeat. It was difficult to tell if he was relieved or not, as only his flowing beard was visible beneath a widebrimmed hat that completely obliterated the rest of his grim face.

To Daisy it seemed like a reprieve.

Her relief was short lived. Almost at once Daisy began to experience grave doubts. Miss Pratt's house, only a short walk from the station, was a gaunt, rather forbidding greystone property with tall, ornamental chimneys, mullioned windows, and a date – 1644 – carved over the lintel. It stood in a large walled garden overlooking the street, the kind of house once occupied by a notable packhorse owner, a carrier of merchandise between the North and London, York, Kendal and Edinburgh. Not that Daisy would have recognised it as such, nor be able to imagine for one moment what it must feel like to own such a place.

Despite the evidence of new measures put into place for the sake of the war, splashes of white paint on kerbs, walls and railings so that people could find their way in the blackout, a poster stuck to a nearby lamp post urging women to offer their services to the local council for evacuation work, and stacks of sandbags everywhere, the tiny village seemed to be an embodiment of all her dreams. Its neat, grey-stone cottages with their bright gardens surrounding a wide expanse of village green was like something out of a picture book. The setting of the house was stunning. The panoply of blue-grey mountains that enfolded it, gleaming benignly in the early morning sunshine, quite took Daisy's breath away. Never had she seen such a glorious place, such splendour, so much space! There were sheep grazing on the village green by an old, grey-stone church that must have stood there for centuries. It was a beautiful, magical scene.

Oh, but she was tired, a dragging ache low down in her belly serving as a nagging reminder that she'd only recently given birth, hardly slept the night before and her knees felt all wobbly, as if they might buckle under her at any minute. How she longed to lie down in a bed and just sleep and sleep. The two bedraggled children beside her were, however, wide awake, mouths agape, hardly able to believe their good fortune. 'Is this where we're going to live?' Megan asked in awed wonder. 'In this big house?'

'Where's the sea?' Trish wanted to know. 'Is there some sands an' all?'

Miss Pratt was opening the front door with a large key she'd taken from the pocket of her tweed suit but paused to consider the child, as if her words had indicated some sort of criticism. 'No, we are nowhere near the sea, and have no sands for you to play on.'

45

Trish looked crestfallen. 'Me mam said we'd be able to buy a bucket 'n' spade.'

'My family has lived here for centuries and never felt deprived by the lack of a beach.'

Daisy intervened swiftly. 'Oh, she wasn't complaining. They're just a bit stunned by their good fortune, that's all. We all are. We – we're not used to anything so – so grand.'

Miss Pratt let out a bark that might have been laughter and marched off down a central lobby. 'Grand? Stuff and nonsense. This house isn't in the least bit grand. Needs a few repairs here and there but nothing I can't fix, given time. It's a big, draughty barn of a place, and I can only hope that you won't be bothered by damp, nor the odd ghost or boggart. Part of its country character, don't you know? Certainly doesn't bother me. You'll just have to cope without any fuss. No patience with fusspots.'

'Oh, we'll be fine,' Daisy assured her. 'Don't worry about us. Not at all.' Living with damp she fully understood. There'd been plenty of that in the tenements of Salford, and however much in need of repair this place might be, it certainly couldn't be in as bad a state as the two miserable rooms she and her parents had occupied in Marigold Court off Liverpool Street.

'What's a boggart?' Megan enquired tentatively, still hesitating to cross the threshold, Trish still clinging on tight to the belt of her sister's mackintosh.

Miss Pratt marched smartly back and with an impatient flap of her hand, urged both children to hurry up since she didn't have all day. 'It's a

46

naughty imp or elf that is always up to mischief. I hope you two aren't going to be naughty?'

The pair gazed up at the old woman from beneath the rim of their large berets, eyes wide with fear and, wordlessly, shook their heads.

Again Daisy rushed to intervene, gathering them in her arms and drawing them along the lobby. 'They're very good children, really.'

The woman looked doubtful and began to mutter to herself as she cast a critical eye over them. 'Glad to hear it. Still, brainwave of yours to come along. Know nothing about bairns. Never married, d'you see? More into dogs myself. Had to make the offer though to take a couple of vacees. Got to do my bit, no choice really. They'd have billeted some on me whether I liked it or not.'

Is that what they were? 'Vacees'! Some sort of disease to be foisted upon people? This wasn't at all how she'd imagined it would be, Daisy thought. Oh dear. How complicated life was. And how would she ever find Aunt Florrie now?

Laura

3

Laura had been awake for hours, had watched the sun come up through the narrow window of her lofty bedroom, seen the first rays light the yellow flowering broom into a glorious blaze of gold, and on the distant horizon a dazzling glint of snow crusting the summit of Helvellyn. By seven she found it impossible to stay in bed a moment longer, pulled on a pair of clean jeans and sweater and, padding to the kitchen in her woolly socks, made herself toast and coffee which she ate standing on the doorstep, marvelling at the view and revelling in the sensation of clean, fresh air that tingled on her face and sparkled like champagne in her lungs.

The night before, once everyone had gone, she'd trawled the house like a lost soul and then, like a homing pigeon, found herself up in the attic, the room she had always slept in as a child. The blue and white gingham curtains still hung at the window, though they were now somewhat faded from the sun; the patchwork bed cover that Daisy herself had stitched out of scraps of old curtains, still covered the bed. On impulse, Laura had run back downstairs for her wash bag and nightshirt, slipping with a sigh between sheets that smelled slightly musty, of a different age and old lavender, yet dry and soft against her skin. She knew it was sentimental of her, but she'd always felt safe there, cosy and strangely secure, and quite blissfully alone. With a pair of socks warming her cold toes and her night-shirt tucked firmly around her knees she'd soon thawed out, for all the wind was howling and rattling at the windows and the rain still hammering on the panes of glass.

It must have played out its temper during the night for the morning brought one of those rare, unexpectedly sunny days of spring, perhaps heralding a good summer to come. It was far too wonderful to waste by eating inside. Up on the higher slopes she could see the sturdy, dark Herdwicks, heavy with lamb. Perhaps the weather had lifted their spirits too for they seemed almost frisky as they browsed for new young grass shoots. And who could blame them, having carried their progeny through the long, grim months of an endless Lakeland winter, with freedom from their labours almost in sight.

Some said the Herdwicks had come to Lakeland with the Armada, others that it was the Vikings who had brought these small, sturdy sheep to these shores, darkly beautiful with their hoar-frosted faces. Or then again, it might have been the Celts who'd first appreciated their hardiness, unless of course Daisy's theory had been correct, that they'd always been here, walking these barren passes long before even man attempted to tame this landscape.

Finishing her toast, Laura brushed the crumbs from her hands, tugged on a warm jacket and boots, for the breeze would be cold higher up, and set off up the smooth slope of Blease Fell. It was a long and tedious climb but fresh air and exercise, she decided, were the perfect antidote to stress. By the time she reached Knowe Crags her heart was pounding but there was the view as recompense for her effort. She sat on the slope to catch her breath and look back upon a chain of mountains, only a few of which she could name: Wetherlam and Black Sails, Helvellyn of course, Crinkle Crags and Scafell Pike. The glint of Derwentwater to her right and the grey huddle of houses that was Keswick. And further away still, in the far distance, the hills of Scotland and the Solway Firth.

The grandeur of the scene had a marvellous effect upon her, seeming to fill Laura with a joy as heady as wine. There was much still to explore on the mountain itself, which would have to wait for another day. Daisy had always called Blencathra a proud mountain, a benevolent giant who kept watch on the cluster of white walled cottages that formed the village of Threlkeld in the valley below. Its shape, being that of twin summits linked by a curved depression, had tempted the Victorians to give it a new name: Saddleback. Daisy hated this pet name. If it had originally been named Blencathra, then Blencathra it must remain. Strong, indomitable, lofty, rather like herself in a way. She'd loved living here, claiming that the Lake District, and in particular this mountain, had captured her heart from the first moment she'd set eyes upon it, and Laura could only agree.

Daisy had stayed for the rest of her life but how long could she stay? Was it pure fantasy to even consider such a prospect? Living under the harsh conditions that were common in these climes, wasn't something to take on lightly. In the upper reaches of Lakeland, summer and autumn could be magical but winters were long, and spring more often than not little more than wishful thinking. Could she cope?

As she sat there, a lone walker passed by several feet below her, acknowledging her presence with a cheery wave. Perhaps he was staying at the

50

Blencathra Centre further down, the
Victorian buildings that had once hou
Sanatorium and was now a Field Study
The mountain was certainly busier th   ...
Daisy's day, with its procession of walkers
heading for the summit via various ascents,
Wainwright in hand; but still lonely, still empty
for much of the year.

How much easier it would be for her to decide,
if Daisy herself were here to talk to and share her
troubles. Laura's eyes filled with a rush of tears.
Yet she could guess what she might say. 'Do what
you must, girl, but remember men are delicate
creatures. Tread softly. Make your point, aye, but
don't go at it like a bull at a gate.'

And Laura could only agree. Felix was not one
to let go easily.

'Don't argue with me all the time, Laura, it's an
irritating fault of yours,' he would say whenever
she attempted to put forward her own opinion on
a subject. Or, if she expressed a desire to go
somewhere: 'You're far too attractive to allow out
of my sight for a moment. One sideways glance
from those soft brown eyes of yours and any man
would be putty in your hands. I certainly am.'

It wasn't true of course. She had never been the
one to look outside the marriage for her
pleasures. Besides, in Laura's estimation she
could only pass for pretty after a great deal of
effort and expense, not to mention hours in the
bathroom, titivating. She saw herself as entirely
unprepossessing with long, dark brown hair
which showed an infuriating tendency to curl,
pale skin and a far too slender, non-voluptuous,

gure. Even her legs were long and gawky, and her feet too big. It never ceased to amaze her that Felix had chosen her, above all the other girls desperate for a date with him. Was it any wonder if he strayed from time to time with such an unexciting wife to come home to?

Yet, besotted by his charm, his good looks and ambitious, go-ahead style, as well as being anxious to be a good wife to him in the new house he'd bought for them in a fashionable part of Cheshire, Laura had dutifully gone along with all his high-flown plans and done everything she could to make him happy.

Chin in her hands she recalled how, as a new bride, she'd so looked forward to spending their days working together, building a business to be proud of. But then the rules of the game had been made properly clear to her and excitement, and hope, had slowly faded.

Laura was not, after all, to be allowed to actually work at Felix's Fine Arts Gallery. It dealt only in specialist material, he'd explained, needing a particular expertise, so he'd hired a young, attractive graduate called Miranda, for the task. When Laura had readily volunteered to attend classes in modern art or interior design, do whatever was necessary to enable her to be a useful member of the team and perhaps, ultimately, a partner in the business, he'd appeared highly amused.

'Stick to answering the telephone and making appointments for me, darling. You can't do much damage there. As well as making those delicious lemon cheesecakes, of course. There isn't anyone who could resist doing business with me, having tasted one tiny sliver of your delicious desserts.'

'But it seems so little, just to cook and entertain for you. So unimportant.'

'It is not in the least unimportant, my darling. Food, next to sex, is a vital ingredient of a happy marriage.'

And certainly the sex they'd enjoyed together had been good, at least in those early days, for when he was not actually working, they'd spent the time largely in bed. She'd been captivated, at first, by this evidence of his need for her, and of how he appreciated all she did to create a lovely home. And if, as the years slid by, he spent more and more time at the gallery and less with her, wasn't that only to be expected when he was so successful? She learned not to complain about the eighteen-hour working days, the times when he rang to say he couldn't make it home as he had to dash off to the outer reaches of Yorkshire or Derbyshire at a moment's notice to view a Lowry or whatever. He never recognised evidence of his own neglect, because he considered that she had sufficient to occupy her, looking after him.

Laura had endured his bossiness and tolerated his need for control largely in silence over the years; even been amused and flattered by his unwarranted and foolishly obsessive jealousies. On the whole, she'd shown exemplary courage and patience above and beyond the calls of wifely duty. But she'd discovered there were limits, even to her patience.

Nurtured by a stubborn determination to rescue herself from miserable oblivion, somewhere, at the back of her head, an idea was taking shape. Laura wasn't sure when it had nestled there, but it seemed to be settling in nicely, fighting off all attempts to brush it away. And where was the harm in giving this crazy notion an airing? Wasn't that why she'd wanted to stay, to give herself time to think, to dream.

All she had to discover was whether she could find the strength to carry it out, whether she could match the kind of fortitude Daisy had shown during her own troubles.

The house at Lane End Farm was large and rambling and old, probably built some time during the seventeenth century with slate walls nearly four feet thick, a storm porch at the front to keep out the worst of the Lakeland weather, and a confusing array of circular chimneys. Its most historic feature was a priest hole off one of the upper rooms that Laura remembered Daisy saying had once been used as the family chapel, as well as some rather nice linen-fold panelling in the dining room.

The sound of her footsteps sounded hollow on the uncarpeted stairs and upper landing, throwing open doors as she went along. The silent, empty bedrooms, of which there were six, not including the attic, were furnished in a somewhat outmoded, nineteen-fifties style. It was like entering a different world. There must have been eight at one time but two of the smaller rooms had been turned into bathrooms. Nevertheless, Daisy had done well here in her day, particularly taking into account that she'd started with absolutely nothing, and most of her youth had been blighted by war.

But it was the atmosphere of the house which moved Laura the most. It wore a sad air of abandonment. Wheelbarrows, harrows and a myriad of other farm tools rusted quietly away in the huddle of broken-down outbuildings, from which issued no happy squawking or other farmyard sounds. The house itself seemed to weep and mourn, wearing a shroud of sorrow for the woman who had loved it and lived within its four walls for more than half a century, generously sharing her home with all who wished to find sanctuary here; a place to nurse wounds, dream dreams and mend broken hearts.

Today, it was Daisy's own granddaughter in dire need of such care and it seemed to be opening its arms to her, offering her peace, almost like a warm embrace as a solution to all her troubles.

Wouldn't it be good to repay that generosity by bringing the house back to life?

Wouldn't it be fun to open up the guesthouse again, Laura thought. To do up the faded rooms and welcome a new generation of walkers and lovers of the Lakes. She certainly had no fears about producing good food for them. Even Felix had nothing but praise for her dinner parties, and she did love to cook.

Of course it would be hard work. There would be beds to make, bathrooms to clean, and very little privacy with guests coming and going all the time. She'd need help of some sort, and money to get started. She would have to advertise, yet it was a popular route for walkers and those stressed out by their jobs in need of peace and fresh air, as well as folk who didn't care for air travel or beach holidays. Many people loved to escape to a place like this, so was it such a crazy idea? Could she make it work?

Laura went back to the kitchen and made herself a mug of coffee. Cradling it in her hand, she sat at the kitchen table and thought about this plan with mounting excitement. She could surely refurbish and update the place without spending a fortune, though she'd need to make one or two of the larger bedrooms en-suite by installing shower rooms. And the entire house would need redecorating, of course. After a while she abandoned the coffee half drunk to continue with her exploration, moving restlessly about the house, picking things up, putting them down again and going on to the next room. And all the time turning the idea over in her head, examining it from every angle, weighing up likely costs and finally admitting that if she went for it, she would effectively be declaring her marriage to be over. She would have to leave Felix.

Was she ready for that?

The thought doused her enthusiasm and brought back the depression, as if a cloud had passed over, blotting out the sun. She had loved him so much. Why had it all gone so badly wrong? And would he even notice she was gone? For all his claims to jealousy and constant declarations that he needed her to be there for him, he was rarely at home. He spent almost every waking hour working either at the gallery, meeting clients, making contacts, or travelling.

Laura flopped on to a sofa. Perhaps it might have been different if they'd had children, but Felix had made it clear quite early on that they were not to be a part of the picture. Laura's wishes on the subject were, apparently, to be ignored.

Felix had one daughter already: Chrissy, the child of his first marriage who had brought nothing but worry and anxiety into his life, so he'd no wish to repeat the experience. Chrissy was fourteen and lived with her mother, Julia, who claimed to be a diligent and caring parent while generally seeming to be in a perpetual state of dissension with her rebellious child. Reminding Felix if Chrissy had a birthday coming up, or of a school function he must attend, was one of Laura's chief functions in life, although there were occasions when she was required to stand in for him. In theory, Felix was expected to take most of the flak when things went badly wrong; in practice whenever he was summoned to unscheduled meetings with the girl's despairing teachers, he was more often than not mysteriously occupied elsewhere and so the task would fall upon Laura's shoulders.

But then Laura's main roll in life was to smooth the way for Felix: to remove unnecessary obstacles of stress which seemed in danger of wasting his valuable time, or causing undue annoyance. To say she resented this fact was putting it mildly, but then she'd come to privately resent a good many aspects of her life.

If the gallery was ever overloaded with work

because of an upcoming exhibition, Laura would be permitted to deal with simple correspondence and any non-specialist matters considered too trivial for Miranda's expertise. She would be the one expected to ring the press and marshal interest; the one who kept fretting artists at bay when they rang constantly to see why their work wasn't selling quite as well as they'd hoped. And when everything proceeded smoothly as a result of her efforts, it was generally the lovely Miranda who took the credit.

'She's such a marvel, that girl. How would I manage without her?' Felix would say.

Laura knew, instinctively, that he was unfaithful. She tried to be adult about it, modern and forward thinking, but it hurt her deeply. She'd given Felix her all, every scrap of her being, her love and loyalty, and yet whenever she'd confronted him with her suspicions he'd simply laughed them off, accusing her of being over-emotional, as if she were unstable in some way, which usually resulted in Laura apologising for not trusting him, as though she were the guilty one.

But then he never took her 'little rebellions' seriously.

Now, at the back of her mind was the worry that perhaps he'd given in to her whim to stay on at the farm rather too easily. Placating or ignoring her was what he excelled at, and no doubt he did indeed expect her to come crawling home by the end of the week.

So what would happen if she didn't?

She really mustn't allow it to matter what Felix

58

did, what Felix thought, or what he planned. She couldn't build a future on a sense of misplaced loyalty. It was time to give more thought to herself. All that was important now was what *she* wanted, what *she* decided to do with her life.

By leaving her the house, it was as if Daisy had offered her a glimpse of the freedom she so longed for and needed, and it was irresistible. Laura knew that if she didn't grab this opportunity, she might never get another.

Daisy had been an ideal grandmother, of whom she'd been inordinately fond. Bright and fun, unfussy and surprisingly go ahead, full of energy and with a wry sense of humour. Laura could see her now, her wildly curling hair like an aureole of white about her head as she busied herself about the house and yard, always seeming to be in a tearing hurry, setting off on some new scheme or other, never still for a moment. She felt an increasing curiosity to discover more about her. What had happened to her as an evacuee? How, exactly, had she come to Lane End Farm? And how had a girl from the slums of Salford come to own such a fine house?

What had caused her to deprive Laura's father of his heritage? A situation which filled her with guilt, though she'd no wish to hand it back. Losing the house was the last thing Laura wanted, for hadn't she always loved it, even as a child?

It was tragic really, that Gran and Dad never properly made up their quarrel, whatever had caused it in the first place. Both too stubborn and hot-tempered, she supposed, and determined always to be right. He never even spoke of his own father who had died when he was about seventeen, the year after Robert had left home to join the navy, so it would appear that memories of him were painful too. How very sad!

What was at the root of it all? she wondered. Following the enforced estrangement, Laura had begun visiting her grandmother again during her years at university, the moment she was free of the restrictions placed upon her by Robert. Sadly, they'd lapsed again during her marriage to Felix. She felt guilty about that too. Yet despite the enforced absences between visits, she and Daisy had remained close.

Which was more than could be said about Laura's relationship with Robert. That had always been difficult, particularly since the death of her mother. Twelve was a difficult age for a girl to lose a mother and they'd spent much of her teenage years at odds. Even the question of her education had been a source of conflict between them. Her father had actively prevented her from attending a *cordon bleu* course in Paris by telling her that there were no places left, when, in fact, he'd never made any attempt to book her in. He'd secured her a job in the bank instead and, naïvely, Laura had believed his story. It had been Felix who had laughingly told her the truth, years later. The only thing she had ever done which her father had approved of was to marry Felix, whom he'd considered to be quite a catch.

She glared at the phone, willing it to ring. Why did he never call her? There were times when

Laura believed that if she didn't take the trouble to ring, she might never hear from him again. Why didn't he ring to apologise for missing the funeral, or at least ask how it went, how she'd coped with it? Right now, she could do with some support. Every time she rang him, she hoped that he'd break a lifetime's habit and offer some.

With a sigh, Laura picked up the phone. Nothing would be gained by allowing pride to stand in the way, as had happened between Robert and Daisy. She certainly had no intention of treating her father with the same kind of cavalier neglect that he had used upon his own parent. That wouldn't improve matters one bit. 'Hi Dad, it's me. Laura.'

'Of course it must be you, Laura, who else would call me by that infernal name?'

Her heart sank. Clearly in one of his moods again. She felt her hand tighten on the receiver, even as she tried to put a smile into her voice. She'd discovered long since that reacting to his black humour only made matters worse, yet conversation between them was always difficult at the best of times. 'I just thought I'd ring to see how you were.'

'How do you think I am? I'm not quite senile yet, you know.'

Oh, definitely on good form. 'So, you're quite well. Good.'

'Last time I looked I was still alive. Hale and hearty in fact.'

'Excellent. I began to worry you might be ill.'

'If this is a criticism about my not turning up to that dratted funeral, you can save your breath. I'd

61

never any intention of going and Daisy would not have expected me to be there. A hypocrite I will not be.'

'She was your mother, and she's dead.'

'Well, I rather assumed that, since they were burying her.'

Laura stifled a sigh. 'Whatever happened between you two, is over now.'

'You have a sad talent for stating the obvious, Laura. Look, if you've only rung to castigate me for my lack of filial duty, you could have saved yourself the bother. It was my prerogative to decide, not yours. No doubt you're ringing from some airport or other, on that damned fancy mobile of yours. Where is it you're gadding off to this time?'

'No, no, I'm still at the farm. Anyway, I'm not the one always gadding about, that's Felix. I'm the little pig who stays at home, remember? The one who keeps the home fires burning, except that I'm not any more.'

'Stop talking in stupid riddles, Laura. If you've anything to say, say it in plain English.'

She took a deep breath. 'OK, what do *you* say to my starting up Daisy's guesthouse again? Wouldn't that be fun?' The sound of breathing echoed loudly down the wire like the rattle of gunfire. 'Dad, are you still there?'

'I think there must be something wrong with this line, I thought you said you were going to start up Daisy's guesthouse again.'

'That's right, that's exactly what I'm going to do. What do you think?'

Again a short silence, followed by a sound very

62

like a suppressed explosion of rage. 'Does Felix know about this?'

'Not yet, but I mean to tell him.' Just as soon as she'd plucked up the courage, or got matters so far advanced there was nothing he could do to prevent it.

'Ah, well he'll soon put a stop to such nonsense. Really, Laura, what a child you are. Fancy ringing me up in the middle of my post-prandial nap to prattle on about some stupid fantasy you're having.'

'It's not a fantasy. I mean to do it. I intend to find out as much as I can about Daisy, then follow in her footsteps.'

'I'm coming over.'

'What?'

'You've clearly taken leave of your senses. I'm coming up. Not to that dratted farm. I'll take a taxi from the station and you can meet me at the Golden Lion. I'll buy you lunch.' He named a date and time and before Laura had time to say whether or not this was convenient, she found herself talking to the dialling tone.

Daisy

4

The room allocated to them was next to the kitchen, which itself was a surprisingly dark, cold room with tiny windows set high in thick stone walls and a huge pine table taking up much of the available space. When Miss Pratt had flung open the door, Daisy had tried not to show her surprise. It smelled strongly of dogs, though there wasn't one in sight. A cat rubbed itself against her legs, either by way of greeting or hopeful of some dinner. Along one wall was stacked a pile of wooden boxes in which were a variety of plant pots, string netting, bamboo canes, old pairs of boots and other gardening items. It seemed odd to store such things in a bedroom and Daisy guessed that that was its real purpose – for storing *things,* not children. There were no curtains at the narrow windows, no rug on the stone floor, simply a tatty piece of straw matting. There were only two beds in the room, for which Miss Pratt did not apologise, merely commented that she'd prepared for two vacees, not three.

'Oh, we can manage, thank you.' Daisy had expected to be taken upstairs where there must surely be half a dozen bedrooms, though perhaps this was how the old lady lived, all on one floor, even in a big house like this. Miss Pratt's next words explained everything.

'It's not much but I dare say it's better than you're used to, so you won't notice. Can't have you sleeping in my best beds, dear, though I accept it's not your fault if these children are verminous and semi-literate. So would anyone be, coming from the slums.'

The remark brought a flush of annoyance to Daisy's cheeks, and for some reason recalled her mother's comment, 'We might be poor but we have us standards.' She cast down her eyes, willing herself not to reveal these thoughts. The old lady was opening up her home to complete strangers, after all.

'There aren't *really* any ghosts are there?' Megan enquired timorously, a slight frown puckering her brow. The two children were hovering at the kitchen door, unwilling to venture in any further, remove their coats and berets, or even set down a single bag until these concerns had been dealt with. Trish's mouth had taken on the shape of an upside-down U as if she might burst into tears at any minute.

Allowing no time for Miss Pratt to open these floodgates with horrific tales of headless horsemen or clanking chains, which would surely give the children nightmares, Daisy barged in with, 'Course there aren't. You'll be nice as ninepence here, won't they miss, once they've settled in?'

'I've certainly come to no harm living in this house, child. No harm at all. And if you hear any odd noises in the night, pay no attention.'

Megan said, 'What sort of noises?' and Trish gave a little whimper but this was apparently as much sympathy as they were going to get.

Daisy had half expected some dragon of a housekeeper to emerge, such as those who occupied the pages of the penny novelettes she devoured from Boot's Library. Or Gladys, the woman who 'did', if she hadn't gone to her sister's house in Edinburgh. No such person had appeared and Daisy's longing for a mug of hot, sweet tea was becoming overwhelming. She ached to put up her feet and rest, feeling bone weary after the sleepless night and the long walk from the station. She could feel a sticky residue of blood between her legs and thought even more longingly of a hot bath and clean underwear. Not that she dare mention any of this, of course, but at least they'd arrived at last and soon these needs and longings would be attended to.

Trish gave her sleeve a little tug, pulling Daisy down to her level so she could issue a fearful whisper in her ear. 'You won't ever leave us on us own here, Daisy, will you?'

Daisy squeezed her hand, as much to reassure herself as the child, and exchanged a cheery smile with Megan. Both little girls looked nervous but at least they were moving about more freely now, as if they couldn't quite make up their minds whether to be excited by this unexpected turn of events, or turn tail and run home to their mam. Deep inside, Daisy felt much the same way.

That first day had been a nightmare. They

stowed their personal belongings in a wooden trunk with a heavy lid that stood between the two beds. It was not ideal since it smelled of mildew, but there was nowhere else.

'What now?' Megan asked in fearful tones, voicing all their thoughts.

'Oh, I'm sure Miss Pratt has done her best to make us comfortable, and we must be grateful and make the best of it. She just didn't expect quite so many of us,' Daisy remarked brightly, wishing she felt as confident as she sounded.

There came a chorus of excited barking from the back garden and all three clambered up to peep out of the window to see what was going on. They couldn't, unfortunately, see anything beyond a tangle of weeds and shrubs but they could hear Miss Pratt's strident voice clearly enough. She was talking to the dogs, calling them to her and then after a few minutes all went quiet.

'She's happen giving them some dinner,' Megan whispered.

'Can I have mine now?' Trish piped up. 'I'm hungry.'

Moments later they heard the old woman pass by the kitchen door, muttering to herself as she strode back along the lobby, followed by the slam of the front door.

'P'raps she's gone shopping.'

As they sat huddled together for warmth on one of the beds, waiting for her to return with food for their dinner, it slowly began to dawn upon Daisy as the minutes and then an hour, and then two hours ticked by, that she might not return at all, or if she had, she'd entered through a different door and they hadn't heard her come in. Either way, she seemed to have forgotten all about them.

'Come on,' Daisy said at last, her voice sounding strained and over-bright as she rallied the drooping children. 'She's made me responsible for you both, so that's what I'll be. Responsible!' Surely, she thought, with a quaking sensation in the pit of her stomach, she hasn't taken me at my word and left me to cope with these children on me own? 'Let's raid the kitchen cupboards and see what we can find.'

They could find disappointingly little. A large bag of flour, one of oatmeal and a smaller one of salt. Further explorations revealed a larder with slate shelves upon which Daisy located a tray of eggs and boxes of potatoes, onions, leeks and other vegetables. 'Oh, look at these. Treasure indeed!'

She quickly set about gathering the ingredients for an omelette, but was then confronted by the next challenge. How to cook it. Faced with a stove that might well have been put in at the same time the house was built in 1644, judging by its rusty appearance, it proved, as Daisy suspected it would, depressingly difficult to light. By the time they'd finally got it going, driven more by their intense hunger rather than any notion of the correct procedure, not only had the morning passed by but much of the afternoon as well. By which time Megan was almost in tears, Trish was curled up on a piece of sacking with her thumb in her mouth and Daisy could easily have eaten the eggs raw.

At last, however, grit and determination paid off and some small measure of heat began to filter through. Daisy found a frying pan, a knob of beef dripping and soon an appetising aroma of frying onions was filling the kitchen, making young mouths water and eyes shine with anticipation. Then she beat up six eggs in a jug and tipped those over the onions into the hot fat, smiling in delight as the mixture bubbled and frothed. They all felt much better after the meal, washed down by a pint of tea each. There was even a little bit of milk left over for the cat. But then came the realisation that the autumn day was drawing to a close and dusk was falling with no offer, thus far, of the much longed-for hot baths.

In the circumstances, this was unfortunate in the extreme. It had soon dawned upon Daisy that although she herself came from one of the worst parts of Salford, her mother's puritan strictness had ensured stringent cleanliness, even if she rarely bestowed upon her daughter the smallest scrap of love. Young Trish and Megan, though more blessed in that department and assured of their own mother's love and concern for them, could not, by anyone's estimation, be considered clean. Each child bore the telltale, sweet-sour smell of stale urine and, once the berets were finally removed, hair crawling with head lice was all too plainly revealed. They were, as Miss Pratt had rightly predicted, verminous. There were also ominous looking scabs and cracked skin between their fingers which looked in sore need of attention.

Using some of the warm water from the kettle she'd boiled, Daisy washed the children's hands and faces with a large bar of carbolic soap she found in the pantry. The necessary attention to their hair would have to wait till tomorrow, she decided, as they were far too tired tonight. Besides, something stronger than carbolic would be required to solve that particular problem. Daisy made a mental note to find Miss Pratt first thing in the morning and ask if she would get them something from the chemist, or perhaps from the dispersal officer.

That would also provide a good opportunity to mention one or two other matters which were troubling her. There were only a few eggs left in the tray, and the Bovril jar was empty so there was nothing for supper. If she was to be responsible for these children, Daisy needed to know who would do the shopping. Daisy was outraged at being so ignored. There should have been postcards for the children to write and send home to their mother, to let her know where they were. And apart from the very essential matters of food and general care and cleanliness, there was also the question of school for the two girls, and work for herself.

She tucked them up together in one of the beds and sang them a lullaby, and it came to Daisy in that moment that she should have been singing to her own child this night. Tears sprang to her eyes as she wondered in whose arms her little son was cuddled at this precise moment. The image brought a stab of pain to her heart and she struggled to block it out. Dwelling on her loss wouldn't help one bit, and she'd been assured that he was safe and well, that he'd been found a good home with parents who would love him as their own. In the circumstances, it was the best she could hope for.

When tired eyelids began to droop with sleep, Daisy crept from the room, poured fresh warm water into the bowl and began to wash herself. The soap and water felt good against her skin. After that, she scrubbed all their stained underwear as best she could, and left them to soak in salt water as her mother had taught her, before crawling into the other bed. Just before she slipped into a deep sleep, she told herself that at least they were safe from Mr Hitler's bombs, and there was surely nothing wrong with their billet that couldn't be put right in the morning.

Daisy used the last of the eggs to boil for breakfast, since there was little else in the larder, and tried not to think about what they would do for dinner. She felt thankful that she'd at least thought to bank up the stove with coke so that it had stayed in overnight but she'd also need to investigate later where the rest of the coal store was, and if there was a better way of getting hot water other than by boiling kettles? These, and various other important matters were in dire need of attention.

Since early morning she'd heard stairs creaking, doors banging, dogs barking, Miss Pratt muttering to herself as she moved about the place, and had every hope that soon she would come to see

71

how they were after their first night. Daisy had initially meant to ask for a more comfortable bedroom than the one they'd been allotted but now that the stove was warming it up a little, and supposing she could find extra supplies of coke to refill the big coal scuttle, she was having second thoughts about that. It might be even colder elsewhere in the house.

Yet no one could consider the arrangements satisfactory and Daisy worried that Trish might start up with flu again, or Megan's cough get worse. Like herself, they were more used to an overcrowded, sheltered, city life, where the close proximity of other people at least helped to keep you warm. Here, there seemed to be nothing but draughts, wide open spaces and bitter cold. Surely the dispersal officer would call eventually, to check they were all right?

It proved easy enough, in the event, to find the coal cellar and, together, the two children and Daisy shovelled sufficient coke into the huge coal scuttles to last them throughout the day. It was less easy to carry them back up the stairs into the kitchen, but with a great deal of gasping and heaving, puffing and blowing, they finally managed it between them.

'I still need to talk to her though,' Daisy said.

'Perhaps she'll be in the garden, giving the dogs their breakfast,' Megan suggested.

To their dismay, they found the kitchen door locked. Megan went pale with fright. 'We can't get out, Daisy! Will we have to stay locked in here for ever?'

'What, till we die?' Trish wailed.

'Not if I can help it.' Daisy was so appalled she could feel herself actually start to shake with fury. How dare the woman lock them in? Heaven help us, no one should treat children in such a manner. Making a game of it, she urged the children to search for an alternative way out but the only exit, in the end, proved to be through a pantry window.

'Ooh, what fun. Go on, Trish, you first. I'll give you a boost up.'

It felt good to be out in the autumn sunshine but Miss Pratt was not, after all, in the garden. Nor were the dogs. 'Looks like she's taken them out for their morning walk. Let's have a scout around and see what else we can find.'

They found the hens and on seeing how frantic they went at the sight of the three of them, all running about and flapping their wings, getting very excited, Daisy concluded that their hostess must have forgotten to feed them as well. A search in a nearby outhouse supplied the necessary mash, and she put some in their metal hopper while Trish filled up the water dish and Megan carefully collected three fresh, warm eggs.

'Well, we won't starve, that's for sure. Though we may end up clucking a bit,' Daisy joked.

There was little else to see. The garden was wild and neglected with nothing but an old crab apple tree, practically bare of fruit and even that was sour, judging by the one Daisy risked trying, not realising they weren't meant for eating straight off the tree. Beyond the dry-stone wall at the bottom lay a wide expanse of ploughed field that

73

looked as if it was growing something, though what it might be, Daisy couldn't guess, knowing nothing of such matters. It started to rain so, mindful of Megan's cough, she hurried the children back inside and boiled the kettle for yet more tea, though sadly without milk.

'Mam used to make soda bread sometimes,' Megan said, looking at the big bag of flour. 'Perhaps we should try,' but since none of them had the first idea how to begin, that idea quickly foundered.

The three girls patiently waited throughout all of that day and the next, for Miss Pratt to call in and check on them. They somehow weren't surprised when she didn't. Daisy did her best to keep the children amused by telling them stories, or teaching them little songs and nursery rhymes. There were no books, nor even pencil and paper in the kitchen so it was hard to devise games beyond I-Spy, and they quickly tired of that one. The house had become strangely silent and they preferred being out in the sunshine. Playing in the garden helped to fill the empty hours and they made sure the hens were well taken care of. They lived on eggs, mashed potato and fried onions. But the children were badly missing their mother and Daisy was growing increasingly uneasy. This wasn't the way to look after children, vacees or not. She felt overwhelmed by the responsibility, quite out of her depth. If she hadn't been considered capable of looking after one tiny baby, how could she possibly care for two little girls?

The third night they were disturbed by the dogs

howling. The sound was so alarming, they all ended up cuddled together in one bed.

'Was that a boggart d'you think, Daisy?'

'Or a ghost?'

'No, it's just the dogs, disturbed by the wind I expect. Go to sleep.' Easier said than done. It was a fine night, with not a breath of wind and Daisy lay wide-eyed throughout, her ears pricked for the slightest sound.

By eleven o'clock the next morning with still no sign of their host, and with not even any eggs left for breakfast, Daisy felt they'd been patient long enough. She instructed the two little girls to stay put in the kitchen, while she went to search further afield.

'No, no, don't go Daisy,' Trish begged, wide-eyed with fear.

Megan added her own plea. 'What if the boggarts come again, Daisy?'

'Don't be silly, they weren't boggarts, only the dogs and they're quiet now.' That was another odd thing. They hadn't seen hide nor hair of a dog in days. 'I must find Miss Pratt and if I can't find her, then I shall look for the lady in the green hat, or some other official. There must be *somebody* responsible for us "vacees". I mean to find out who.'

But she had reckoned without Trish who refused, absolutely, to let her go.

Mouth downturned into the familiar curve, cheeks awash with tears, it would have taken a harder heart than Daisy's to prise the child's fingers from their fierce grip upon her skirt and simply walk away.

'All right then, we'll all go. But wrap up well.'

The navy gabardines and berets were put back on, scarves tied into place, and the inseparable trio set off together. 'Just like the three Musketeers,' Daisy joked. 'We'll soon find Miss Pratt and get this all sorted out.'

They walked the length of the village street knocking at every door, but an hour later, were no closer to finding her. Many of the neighbours expressed their concern, urging Daisy to call again if they didn't find her.

'She has got a bit odd lately,' one woman admitted. 'Taken to walking them dogs for hour upon hour on the hills. But she loves her garden and her hens. She'll be back soon, I'm sure.'

Eventually, one kindly shopkeeper took pity on them and suggested they take the bus into Penrith and try the town hall 'T'isn't right, you children wandering about the place with nobody to look after you,' she said, quite outraged at the very idea. Daisy could only agree with her.

'How much is a bottle of milk?' she enquired politely, counting out the few pennies her mother had given her for the journey.

'Oh lord, don't tell me you haven't even any milk? I allus knew Miss Pratt were a bit eccentric like, and she's been going more and more peculiar lately, but by heck, this takes the biscuit. Ah, that's a thought. Biscuits. Now, I've some nice garibaldis somewhere.' The kindly woman began to rummage on her shelves and soon handed over a packet of biscuits, together with the milk, waving away the six pennies Daisy had managed to get together. 'I'll put it on her bill. Anything else you need? Bit of bacon? Slab of cheese? Dab of butter?'

All further searches for their missing hostess were postponed as the three gleefully watched the shopkeeper fill a brown paper bag with these goodies and gathering up their prize, scampered back to the kitchen. Afterwards, stomachs stuffed with food, they lay down on their beds and fell into a sweet, dreamless sleep.

Laura

5

Lunch with her father was every bit as disastrous as Laura had expected. Over the soup he castigated her over her obstinacy in staying on at the farm after the funeral, instead of going home to her husband like a good little wife, presumably. During the fish course he reminded her how her own amateur efforts at cooking couldn't be compared with this sort of professional cuisine. And finally, when the cheese was served (her father didn't eat dessert and made the assumption that his daughter wouldn't require one either), he warned her of the perils of defying her husband's wishes to sell.

'Lane End Farm will fetch a good price, and Felix is so much more skilled than you in such matters. You must be guided by him.'

'Why must I? The house was left to me, not Felix.' As soon as the words were out of her mouth, Laura regretted them, since they sounded so arrogant, almost as if she were bragging. 'I didn't mean that quite as it sounds. It should be yours, of course, and...'

'Don't twist yourself into knots over this, Laura. I don't want the damned farm. Never have. Wouldn't touch anything of Daisy's with the proverbial bargepole.'

'Oh, for heaven's sake, what was it with you two? Why didn't you get on? You've never properly explained it to me.'

'I don't see that it's any of your business.'

'Well, I think it is. She was my grandmother, after all. I mean, why did she leave the house to me, and not to you?'

'Because she knew I wouldn't accept it and she wanted it to stay in the family.'

'So tell me, what was the problem? Something silly, I'll be bound.'

'We didn't agree on what was important in life, that's all. We had a completely different set of values. I believe in honour and openness, Daisy the complete opposite. No doubt as a result of being dragged up out of the gutters of Salford.'

'That's rather an unfair attitude, not to say a most provocative remark, and completely untrue from what I've learned about her, even in this short time. Her neighbours and friends here seem to think she was lovely. A charming, cheerful soul always ready to help others. They say she was generous to a fault.'

'Oh, she was that all right, in more ways than

one.' He dug the cheese knife into the Camembert and cut himself a large portion.

'What is that supposed to mean?'

He placed a portion with painstaking care upon a cracker and, noting how entirely focused he was upon eating it, refusing, absolutely, to respond, Laura gave up and ordered coffee. They took it in the lounge, in a strained, uncomfortable silence and it wasn't until after the bill had been paid when he was shrugging into his overcoat, that he again referred to her plan to reopen the house to guests.

'I hope you'll put an end to this nonsense forthwith, opening guesthouses and the like. Utter tosh! In any case, how could you afford to?'

'I shall use the money Mother left me. It might just stretch to a few renovations.'

Robert snorted his disapproval and changed tack. 'Neither will I have you prying into Daisy's life. Sell the dratted farm and have done with it.'

'I don't think I can do that.'

He glared at her, the expression in his grey eyes hard as flint. 'Are you deliberately defying me, Laura?'

She shook her head, desperately trying to curb her impatience. 'I'm simply trying to understand the woman who left me a house she loved, presumably because she thought I would love it too. And I'm not sure I deserve such generosity, since I feel I neglected her shamefully. My own grandmother!'

'For which you blame me, I suppose.'

Laura sighed. 'I'm sorry you found it necessary to cut me off from her as a child but I wouldn't dream of blaming you. How can I, since I don't have a proper explanation of what went wrong between you? If anything, I blame myself.' She kept her eyes downcast as she began to button up her own coat, deliberately avoiding the chill of his gaze. 'I should have stood up to you more as I got older, and to Felix. I intend to do so now.'

'Damnation, Laura, is there some man involved?' he roared, making heads turn in the lobby and bringing a flush of embarrassed crimson to her cheeks. Snatching her arm he drew her into a corner where he could snarl at her in comparative privacy. 'Is that what this is all about? Some sort of silly revenge against Felix's indiscretions? Because if so, it won't do, Laura. It won't do at all. Dammit, I won't have you shame me, or Felix.'

Laura stared at him in disbelief. 'For God's sake, what are you implying?' She might have laughed, had not the notion that it was perfectly acceptable for Felix to have affairs but not herself, filled her with cold rage. Was she of such little consequence that she had no rights at all? Or was he suggesting that no man would be interested in her? It might also be worth starting an affair, she thought, just to prove she was equal to the challenge.

'You want to know exactly what grievance I had against my mother? She was a *whore!* Nothing less. There, now you know, and if you cheat on Felix then you will deserve exactly the same contempt that I gave her.'

Laura was stunned. 'What a terrible thing to say. What on earth are you suggesting? In what way was my grandmother a whore? Surely you're not saying that Daisy had an affair? Oh – because she had a baby before she married, is that it?' Her frown cleared. 'Oh, for goodness' sake, Dad, don't be so old-fashioned. No one bothers about such things these days.'

His face turned a dark red and for a moment Laura feared for his health. The last thing she wanted was to induce a stroke. She hastily began a halting apology, hand raised in supplication but his roar blotted out every pacifying word.

'I am *telling you,* nay – *ordering you* to stop all this prying into Daisy's life. It's over and done with. Past history. *Leave it alone!* There's absolutely nothing to be gained by digging up old hurts and miseries. So be a good girl, go home to your husband and stop being so damned interfering.'

As she drove back to the farm, Laura railed over why she'd never thought to ask questions when Daisy was alive, or paid more attention to what little her grandmother had told her. Why had she allowed herself to remain happily ignorant of the facts until now, when suddenly it seemed vitally important that she discover them. Laura no more believed that Daisy had cheated on her husband than she herself would cheat on Felix, despite being given plenty of provocation. Daisy simply wasn't the type.

And why should she give up her quest to find out more about her?

She found herself drawn like a magnet to Daisy's bureau but the little desk produced nothing more exciting than a drawer stuffed with bills, most of them fortunately paid, as well as old accounts from when the farm was fully functional during the war. She was bitterly disappointed. She'd been banking on some sort of diary, however small, to reveal more about the woman who had occupied this house before her.

Even so, she spent the next two days going through the bureau with meticulous care, obstinately refusing to give up. There were several smaller drawers tucked beneath the roll top, and a number of pigeon holes, all filled with a detritus of paperwork: auction details, programmes for the County Show, orders for hen pellets. Laura felt a burst of excitement as her hands closed over a bundle of letters. Tucked right at the back they were tied up neatly with pink string, the kind farmers call binder twine. She smiled at this practical touch, so typical of Daisy but which also seemed to indicate that the letters had been read recently, since such material surely hadn't been available during the war. Perhaps Gran had put her affairs into some sort of order before her death.

Laura pulled out the first one. It was short, but clearly a love letter, and was addressed to a mother and baby home. It was the one from Percy and had clearly been read many times for it was coming apart at the folds and the paper had gone brown with age. Laura slipped it carefully back inside its envelope.

Tucked behind, interleaved between this envelope and the next were two or three sheets of blue lined paper pinned together at one corner with a rusty pin, each filled with closely written handwriting which Laura recognised as Daisy's own.

The first was headed with the somewhat outmoded phrase: *'To whom it may concern – The way things were!!!'* Laura was enchanted, particularly by the exclamation marks but, as her eyes swiftly scanned the contents, saw that it was not the diary she'd hoped for, more a chronology of events with short explanations and comments of their effect: the date the first bomb was dropped in Manchester; of folk watching dog fights in the skies during the days of Blitzkrieg; the collapse of France. The list went on to include details such as when rationing had been introduced, together with a droll comment that she'd like to see the government survive on such a meagre meat ration. There were instructions on how to turn a pair of flannel trousers into hot water bottle covers and some fairly pithy remarks outlining her despair over how they would manage to get any eggs at all, now the hens could only be given household scraps. 'What scraps!' she had written, and Laura could almost sense her indignation. More pragmatically, it was followed by a recipe for using dried eggs.

Laura smiled to herself and put the pages to one side with the rest of the letters, to read more fully later.

She glanced quickly through a book which listed purchases and sales of livestock, no doubt in order to keep a record of their movement and progress. The latest recorded date appeared to be 1958. Were records no longer needed by then? Or was that when it ceased to be a farm and the land was then let off? If the latter, what had occurred to cause this change?

There was also a visitors' book from when the house had operated as a guesthouse, starting with the first lodgers during the war and the later pages going on well into the fifties and sixties. Laura sat on the floor to glance through it, her back propped comfortably against the bureau.

'Miss Geraldine Copthorne,' Laura read out loud. 'I wonder who she was? Sounds rather grand. And what was her reason for being here during the war?' She'd written a few lines by her name in a carefully curving script. *'Home from Home. I shall never forget you Dear Daisy and how you made me part of your family.'* Laura read some of the others: Ned Pickles – *'Not much cop in the Home Guard, untidy guest, but a lifelong friend for you Daisy.'* Tommy Fawcett – *'Best day of my life when I landed up here. Shall never hear* Lady Be Good *without thinking of you all.'* There were any number of others. So many names. Pages and pages of them: couples, families, maiden ladies with their companions, lone walkers coming to explore the mountains, all saying what a wonderful time they'd had, how they'd loved the Lakes, the walks, the view of Helvellyn, Daisy's cooking. Would it be possible to trace any of them, after all this time? Probably not. Laura smiled to think she might have acquired her own culinary skills from her grandmother. Most of all she felt a fresh kindling of excitement. Perhaps that's why Daisy had left her the house, so that she could carry on where she had left off. The rooms were still here, after all. Intriguingly, inside the front cover of the book was a short dedication written by Daisy herself:

To Florrie, who allowed me to take over her kitchen and carry out my crazy ideas, often against her better judgement. To Clem, for being the father I'd always wanted, counsellor and best friend. And most of all to my dear husband, for always letting me have my own way, even when it would have been wiser not to.

'I should think he had no option,' Laura said out loud, chuckling softly. 'You were ever one with a mind of your own, Grandmother dear.'

'I'd say that was a true assessment of Daisy's character, bless her heart.'

Laura dropped the book with a clatter, so startled was she by the interruption. She'd thought herself quite alone in the house, as well as in the void of empty countryside around, and it came as a huge shock to look up into a grinning face, one eyebrow raised in quizzical amusement as a perfect stranger picked up the book and handed it back to her. She felt thoroughly unnerved by the encounter, and quite unprepared to be challenged by an unknown male in what was now her own home, let alone one so flagrantly pleased with himself.

'I didn't hear the front doorbell?'

He threw back his head and roared with laughter. 'I announced myself with a shout from the back door. That's the usual method here in the country. You must have been too absorbed to hear me.'

For several long moments each considered the other. He with curiosity, she with open animosity. Laura recognised at once that he was exceptionally good-looking, which rather seemed to undermine her confidence all the more and she found herself rubbing her dusty hands over her jeans, now rather grubby themselves after days of scrabbling about in attics and old cupboards. She even found herself tidying away a few straying wisps of hair. He was about her own age, in his mid-thirties, and with an unruly thatch of black curls that flopped over a wide brow. Beneath this were winged eyebrows that were still quirking most irritatingly upwards as if amused by some private joke, and long curling lashes over wickedly teasing, light blue eyes. The whole set in a face that bore the kind of chiselled features usually seen on male models, if sufficiently weather-beaten to indicate a life spent largely outdoors that in no way detracted from his charms.

Laura felt herself becoming slightly flustered by the impact of this blue-eyed scrutiny and levered herself quickly to her feet, setting the visitors' book carefully among the bundle of letters on the bureau as she did so.

'Interesting is it, reading other people's love letters?' Before she had gathered her thoughts sufficiently to answer that one, he went on: 'Perhaps you like your own way too, to be prying so swiftly into her affairs. You won't find any hidden share certificates or premium bonds, I'm afraid. I don't think Daisy believed in saving for a rainy day. Always claimed she'd had plenty of

86

practice dealing with those in the past. I think she gave away more money than she ever spent on herself.' When still she didn't reply, he frowned and asked more politely, 'I take it you are the granddaughter?'

Laura stared blankly at the hand thrust out before her, making no move to take it as she struggled to damp down the hot curl of anger spiralling up inside her. Eventually he slid it back into his pocket with a shrug. He was wearing jeans and a blue checked cotton shirt open at the neck over a white T-shirt, despite the cold wind that had sprung up again outside and was now blasting its way through every crack and cranny. It crossed her mind, inconsequentially, that if the house didn't have some sort of heating system, it would cost a fortune to put in. But was that a good enough reason to return to the home fires of Cheadle Hulme?

'Hello? Anyone at home?' He interrupted her thoughts with a quizzical smile. 'Would you like me to go out and come in again? I seem to have lost your undivided attention.'

'I don't think you ever had it. Who the hell are you, anyway?' Laura switched to attack because she knew, instinctively, that her cheeks had gone quite pink, though really she'd no reason to be embarrassed as she'd every right to be going through Daisy's papers. 'I'm trying to deal with my grandmother's affairs. And I still haven't caught your name, which is?' Asked in her frostiest tones.

'Sorry. Remiss of me.' Again he thrust out the hand. 'David Hornsby, your nearest neighbour, and lessee of the land.' The smile might have been considered encouraging, or simply vague, for his gaze had moved back to the bundle of letters which Laura had left propped on the drop-down lid of the bureau. 'Never seems quite right to me, to pry into a person's life just because they are dead.'

Laura took a moment before answering, quietly drawing in a calming breath. 'My grandmother was seventy-nine, old enough to have decided long ago which material she wished to keep and which should be consigned to the fire. I feel safe in assuming that any letters or other papers she has left, she is quite happy for me to read.'

'OK, good point. Hadn't thought of it that way.' A slight pause and then he added. 'Anything interesting?'

It was on the tip of her tongue to say she wouldn't tell him if there were when he picked up the guest book she'd just been reading and flipped it open. 'Ah yes, I remember her showing me this once, telling me about some of these people.'

'She talked to you about them?' Despite her initial antipathy to the guy, Laura couldn't disguise her surprise. She was instantly intrigued, wanting to know more.

He glanced up, recognising the interest in her voice. 'Sure, why not? We were near neighbours for almost ten years, and she was on her own, so enjoyed a bit of a gossip. I was very fond of Daisy.'

'I didn't see you at her funeral.'

He gave a sad little chuckle. 'She gave me firm

instructions not to come. Said she hated the things, had been to more in her lifetime than anyone ever should and too many folk either wept and mourned with little sincerity, or started sharing out the household silver before the incumbent was reclining in her grave.'

They both laughed and Laura admitted there was some truth in the comment.

'Genuine grief, Daisy said, should be carried out in private, and I was to drink a toast to her instead, and get on with my life. Her philosophy was to live for today, and let tomorrow take care of itself.'

'There are some who might consider that to be a dangerous policy.'

'Not Daisy.'

'I wish I'd known her better,' Laura burst out, suddenly envious of this man's inside knowledge of her grandmother.

'If you want to hear more, I'd be happy to tell you. Why don't you come for supper tonight and I'll tell you everything I know, as much as I can remember anyway.'

Despite her curiosity, Laura instinctively backed off from the speculative light she recognised in his eyes. She really didn't need any further complications in her life right now. Not until she'd finally made up her mind what to do about Felix. She shook her head. 'Thanks, maybe another time.'

He looked disappointed. 'Oh, I thought you were genuinely interested in Daisy, and not just in whatever it is she left you.'

Again Laura's cheeks started to burn, and the

tone of her reply was stringent. 'I am.'

'Well then, come to supper. You have to eat after all, and it is a Friday, which is as good a reason as any.' He glanced at the book and stabbed a blunt fingertip on a name. 'I could tell you how she met Harry Driscoll for instance, the love of her life.'

'Harry? But that wasn't my grandfather's name. At least – I don't think it was.'

'Was it, or wasn't it?'

For the life of her, she couldn't remember. Had she ever been told his Christian name, or simply not paid attention? He'd died before she was even born. She knew a great deal about her maternal grandparents, who were sweet and supportive and had recently retired to Torquay. But of her father's family she knew less than nothing, which wasn't at all surprising. What she did know was that her father's surname, her own maiden name wasn't Driscoll. 'Where did she meet this Harry Driscoll, and if he was the love of her life, why didn't she marry him? Was he killed in the war?'

'Oh dear, you really don't know anything at all, do you?' Laughing, he shrugged his wide shoulders and swung away from her, back towards the door. 'But, if you're not hungry, either for food or information right now, I'll leave you in peace. Give me a call if you change your mind.' And to her utter fury and frustration, he strolled calmly away.

After he'd gone Laura headed for the shower, hoping to take the steam out of her temper.

90

Almost at once she began to regret that she hadn't accepted his invitation. I mean, what else did she have to do but wash her hair and eat a limp salad? Maybe that's what she needed in her life, a little more impulsiveness. A touch of recklessness. And he was rather gorgeous. She'd really lost touch with how to handle such delicate matters, though perhaps it was just as well. She was still a married woman after all. Laura groaned and stepped under the jet of hot water, letting it do its work.

Later, wrapped in a huge towelling robe, she forsook the salad and sat on the sofa eating crackers and cheese, kicking herself for the missed opportunity. He was probably her best contact to find out more about Daisy, and she'd blown it. Accepting the simple offer of supper, off the cuff as it were, would have meant she could have gone in her jeans, cobwebs and all, with easy informality, just to be neighbourly. Now, although she was burning to hear what he had to tell her, nothing would induce Laura to ring and ask if she could come over. It would seem too contrived, too artificial, almost like asking him for a date. He'd think her a control freak who must do everything her own way, in her own time.

She switched on the TV, then turned it off again. The sound of it was too startling in the empty room, seeming to emphasise a loneliness she hadn't previously noticed, but then the ensuing silence folded disconcertingly in upon her, which was worse. They'd had quite a set-to, she supposed. She certainly hadn't been very

91

polite to him, or welcoming. Laura couldn't help but compare the sparks that had flown between them, two perfect strangers, to the conversations she'd had recently with her husband. Felix always shied away from confrontations, rode over tender feelings and sensitivities that he had no wish to acknowledge, just as if they weren't there. Laura had learned early on the fruitlessness of revealing her softer side, for he only trampled on it.

Nothing mattered to Felix except cutting the deal; making the big bucks. He'd even found time on the day of the funeral to read through some papers he'd brought with him, sneaking off into some quiet corner while Laura handed round the sherry and accepted everyone's commiserations. She'd made no comment but, deep down, had been hurt by such insensitivity.

Surely he hadn't always been that way. He'd once been so full of enthusiasm, so animated about his plans. 'This is just the start, Laura,' he'd say. 'The first of a chain of smart little galleries all over the country. Once we're established we can franchise the idea and make a small fortune.' Laura had listened, spellbound by his passion, at first perfectly in tune with his ambition to make something of his life. Being the son of an unemployed miner had left him with the need to prove that he was as good as everyone else. She'd admired that in him, at least until that need had grown into a huge chip on his shoulder.

Nowadays their relationship was too tired, too predictable to bring any excitement into their lives. And Felix was very much his own master. No one could make him do anything he had no wish to do. She was fortunate, Laura supposed, that he'd agreed to come to her grandmother's funeral at all, which probably had more to do with wanting to assess the value of her inheritance than to pay any last respects.

Why was she so harassed by infuriating men? No wonder Robert approved of Felix, they were alike in so many ways, both obstinately determined to have their own way and be in control.

Her father's parting words following that dreadful lunch came back to her with haunting clarity. 'Be a good girl and go home to your husband.' It told her so much about herself.

Perhaps the fault was entirely hers in a way, because she'd allowed him to control her. Is that why she'd never asked questions, never liked to pry into her father's life or emotions? Because she'd wanted him to love her, for him to see her as a good girl? He'd certainly done his level best to govern every last detail of her life, even to keeping her from her own grandmother. The result had been that it had left her a prime candidate for marriage to an equally controlling husband. Laura had never properly appreciated that fact until now. If this were true, then it was long past time she decided what she meant to do about it, because it was what *she* wanted from life that was important now. She'd been a good girl long enough.

Having stirred up her sense of injustice to a suitably high pitch, she picked up the phone and called her new neighbour to accept his invitation to supper. Though of course, only because she wanted to hear more about Harry.

Daisy

6

Daisy and the children slept the clock round, waking late the next morning. It being a Saturday, still with no sign of their host, and facing the prospect of an empty larder for the entire weekend, Daisy made the decision to go into Penrith. She and the children joined the queue at the bus stop with every intention of finding the town hall and making a complaint, or at least a polite enquiry. This was not at all what they had expected by being evacuated. It didn't seem right that someone, beyond Daisy, wasn't available to look after these children. Fond as she was of them, the responsibility worried her. There was a war starting, after all. What if something happened to her parents, and she had to dash home for some reason? Who would look after the two children then?

Her more immediate concern, of course, was what on earth had become of Miss Pratt. The old lady had indeed seemed odd, and quite unused to children. Even so, it was most peculiar just to go off with the dogs and leave them, not even think to call in from time to time to see how they were.

So engrossed was she in her own troubles, and adjusting the children's berets and scarves when it started to rain, that it was only when the bus drew up some minutes later, that Daisy paid proper attention to the queue ahead of them and realised it comprised entirely airmen and soldiers. When it was their turn to get on, the conductress put out her hand to prevent them climbing aboard. 'Sorry, this is a special services bus, no civvies allowed.'

'Oh, isn't it going into town?'

'Aye, but like I say, it's for services personnel only. You can allus walk, young, fit girl like yourself.'

'But how far is it? I don't know the way.'

'Stranger to these parts, eh? Thought so.'

'How long before the next bus?' Daisy asked.

'There'll no doubt be one along in the next hour or so.'

'An hour or so?'

'Aye, well, there aren't so many buses these days. Short of drivers, d'you see. There is a war on, tha knows.'

'But it's so cold and wet, and the children haven't been well.'

'Nowt to do wi' me. Not my place to molly-coddle children,' and she reached up to ring the bell but her hand didn't quite make it. Her wrist was caught and held, a grip so uncompromising it prevented the conductress from moving an inch.

He was tall, almost six foot, in RAF uniform like all the rest, square-jawed and with a wide, smiling mouth, his forage cap tilted at just the right angle over neatly clipped brown hair. His face was more what you'd call homely than handsome but to Daisy it was the most cheerful, the most friendly face she'd encountered in a long while.

Harry Driscoll had been watching this little exchange with interest, and had decided to put in his four pennorth. He hated bullies, particularly female ones. Besides, the young girl was quite pretty. 'She's with me.'

'I beg your pardon?' The conductress was furiously attempting to pull her arm free, blotches of scarlet gathering high on her cheekbones. 'If you don't take your flippin' hand off me this minute, I'll call the driver and have you all thrown off.'

He released her with a small bow. 'Nevertheless, she's with me. This coffee and bun fight we were all treated to at the village hall, she helped organise it, so you can let her on. Can't you see them nippers are soaking wet through already. Have a heart, love.'

'I don't get paid to tek civvies on this bus.'

'We'll have a whip round. Either you let them on, or we all get off. Then we'll be late back and our CO will want to know why. Ain't that right lads?' A rousing cheer echoed from behind him, most of the men not having the first idea what the dispute was about but ready enough to support a mate. Seeing herself defeated, the conductress's stance crumbled and, moments later, Daisy and the children were being found a seat in the depth of the warm bus and being chatted up by at least a dozen servicemen.

'Thank you,' Daisy said, having eyes only for her rescuer who stood grinning down at her.

'That's the first good deed anyone has done for us in an age, though that was a fib you told. I didn't have anything to do with the bun fight at the village hall.'

He shrugged. 'So what? Good deeds are all in a day's work for us hero types.' He held out a hand. 'Harry's the name. Harry Driscoll.'

'Daisy Atkins.' She put her hand into his and felt the warm strength of a firm grip. He made no effort to release it as he looked straight into her eyes, his gaze steady and direct and both of them fell silent, each shyly considering the other. His eyes were a greeny-grey, quite the nicest eyes Daisy had ever seen. The next instant Harry became aware of being studied by two other pairs of eyes, both blue, and laughingly released her hand. Daisy felt bereft, wanting to hold on to him.

'They're surely not yours?' He jerked a chin at Trish on her knee, and the older girl leaning against it. Was that a shade of anxiety in his voice as he asked the question? Daisy smiled and shook her head. 'Do I look old enough to have kids like this?'

But she did have a child. She did! She did! A shameful secret she must never tell. Daisy pushed the thought away.

'You don't look old enough to be out on your own, let alone be getting a free ride with a bus full of service personnel.'

'We're evacuees, from Manchester,' she offered, by way of explanation. 'Are you a pilot?'

This innocent remark was met by a roar of laughter. 'They wouldn't let him loose in a plane.

He gets lost with no road signs to help him, let alone no roads.'

'Anyway, his hair's too long. It'd get in his eyes when he was flying.'

'And his mam don't like him being out at night.'

Daisy laughed along with them, enjoying the banter. They seemed a cheerful bunch, and at least it was warm on the bus. They were certainly eager to chat, telling her how they were undergoing training at the RAF base in Longtown. Also on the bus were men from the tank corps stationed at Lowther, though what exactly they were up to, they were not at liberty to say, they explained. All very hush-hush! Several offered to take her out, give her a conducted tour of the area or fill her in with more details of their life history, strictly in private of course. Nor did they forget the children, who were presented with a variety of sweets, and even a cough drop for Megan. It was all so good-hearted and fun, Daisy was soon wiping tears of laughter from her eyes, which made a change from the other sort.

She would like to have stayed on the bus for hours but in no time, it seemed, the conductress was calling out her stop and she was getting to her feet and ushering the children off. As a way was made for them along the aisle, Harry grabbed her hand again.

'Where are you billeted?'

She told him, but quickly added. 'It's not very good. I'm hoping they might relocate us.'

'Move along the bus please, we don't have all

98

day,' the conductress shouted, determined to maintain some control over this obstreperous crew.

'Aw, stop moaning, woman. Give 'em a minute, fer God's sake.'

Galvanised into action by the conductress's ill temper, Harry began to desperately search his pockets. 'I need a pen. Somebody find me a pen.' There was a flurry of activity, more laughter and joking as the entire busload searched pockets until a pen was finally found and Harry began to write his address on the back of her hand. Once more he looked deep into her eyes. 'You can't lose that. Write to me.'

Daisy glanced down at the scribbled words, a mere blur through the stars in her eyes.

'Are you getting off or not? I've a few more runs to make today, if you please,' the conductress snapped.

As Daisy struggled through the crush of servicemen, she strived to keep her gaze upon him, couldn't bear to tear it away. There were plenty more offers of addresses but the children were being helped down from the platform, the conductress was dinging her bell with grim determination this time, and if Daisy didn't hurry the bus would leave and she'd still be on it. As it was, she jumped off just in time before it jerked forward.

'Don't forget! See that you write. A letter to that address will find me, wherever I am,' he yelled.

As she gathered the children about her, Daisy plucked up the courage to call back: 'I will write.

I won't forget. I promise.'

She wasn't even sure if he'd heard. As she walked away, heart pounding, keeping a lookout for anything likely to be the town hall, Daisy wondered what right she had to make such a promise? None at all, not with her shameful secret.

The visit to the town hall turned into a quagmire of questions and bureaucracy, of being passed from pillar to post, nobody quite being prepared to accept responsibility until, at last, they were taken to an entirely different office, in a separate part of the building where they finally met the billeting officer, a large woman with a sour face. She looked down her nose at the trio as if they really had no right to be there and even after listening to Daisy's story, denied that any such thing could happen on her patch.

'Our billeting hosts are most carefully chosen, *most* carefully, and Amelia Pratt is a dear friend of mine.'

'Then perhaps you can find her. We're at our wits' end. In the meantime, these children need breakfast, but just make sure it isn't eggs.'

Some long hours later, investigation proved that the poor woman had not, in fact, abandoned them. She'd died quietly in her sleep, her dogs gathered protectively all around her.

Daisy was shocked. 'Oh, poor Miss Pratt. No wonder they were howling. How dreadful!'

Megan tugged at her hand. 'Does that mean there weren't any ghosts after all?'

'Yes love, that's what it means.'

'But if the lady has died, isn't she now a ghost?'

Daisy stifled a smile at the innocent question, since this wasn't the moment for explanations. 'It doesn't quite work that way.'

'Why doesn't it?' Megan was annoyed that Daisy should think her stupid. Everyone knew ghosts were dead people, and Miss Pratt was now dead, wasn't she?

'Hush now, I'll explain it to you later. Meanwhile, I think we need a new billet, and some medical attention for these two children.'

To Megan's complete horror, quick as a flash, the billeting officer took a bottle from her desk drawer, whipped off the girls' berets and poured an evil smelling liquid over both their heads. Trish started to sob and Megan was hard put to it not to give the woman a smack in the eye.

Megan had no wish to be 'vacee'. She'd had enough. It wasn't at all the adventure she'd been promised. It was boring and alarming and frightening. She wanted to go home to her mam. Whenever Mr Hitler dropped his bombs, she'd run away as fast as her legs could carry her and miss them all. If her mam and gran could stop at home when they didn't run half so fast as her, then where was the problem?

'Can't I go home? I want to go home?' she wailed, but Daisy only made a shushing sound, and the woman ignored her completely. Megan didn't like being ignored, so tried again, 'How will Mam know where we've gone?'

'Don't worry, you'll get a postcard this time so you can write and tell her.'

They were handed over to a middle-aged

couple who already had two children of their own. The boy was a year older than Megan and the moment they were left alone 'to make friends' he pinched her hard and called her awful names like 'Smelly' and 'Pee-wee'. Megan thumped him hard and he started to yell. His sister was younger and she kicked Trish in the shin, which made her tune up in unison.

Megan could tell this was going to be a disaster and she was absolutely right. Even though the couple had agreed to take Daisy as well, and Mrs Hobson claimed to be the motherly type, she was furious when Megan accidentally smeared blackberries all over her white sheets. Megan didn't see what all the fuss was about. Serve her right for putting sheets on the bed in the first place. They always used blankets at home, although she knew that her mam did keep one sheet in a cupboard, in case someone should die and need covering up before they were buried in the ground. It had been used for an old aunt once, and Megan had kept careful watch, just in case the old lady wasn't really dead at all, and might rise up beneath it.

Anyroad, she'd been hungry, and had gone out into the garden at first light to pick a handful of the blackberries she'd spotted earlier, which she'd eaten under cover of the sheets so that no one would know. It wasn't her fault if she'd happened to drop a few without noticing and then fallen asleep on top of them, squashing them flat.

Megan thought it equally unfair that she was blamed for breaking the best sugar basin at breakfast, when it was the nasty son who'd handed it to her and then let go before Megan had quite taken hold. It'd just rolled off the table and smashed to the floor, scattering precious sugar everywhere. An hour later they were back before the billeting officer.

Their next billet was with a vicar and his wife, who were very kind but a bit vague. The first thing they did was to offer them a bath. Megan was horrified and point blank refused to get into it. It stood like an enormous white pot basin on six legs and a witless fool could see by all the water inside it, that she'd drown. Then when the stupid woman lifted Trish into it, despite her screams and Megan's pleading, she very nearly did drown. Megan was appalled to see her little sister go right under the water as she went completely stiff in some sort of hysterical fit.

Worse, Megan and Trish's room contained a night commode and after waking one night to find the vicar enthroned upon it, she decided that enough was enough.

The next day the vicar's wife sent her on an errand to the corner shop. Megan insisted on taking Trish with her, explaining how they must never be separated. But instead of buying bread they got on a bus and used some of the money to buy two tickets to Preston. Here they changed buses to one bound for Manchester. It was pretty full, but the other passengers made room for them and one lady even gave them a few sweets. Hours later, while everyone was no doubt still frantically searching every corner of the village for them, Megan and Trish walked into their

103

house in Irlam, telling their startled mother that they were back.

It upset Megan that instead of giving them big hugs and kisses, Mam was cross. She shouted at her, calling her terrible names like selfish and naughty and irresponsible.

'You've risked your life, and that of your little sister, in the most dangerous way. What were you thinking of to do such a daft thing?'

Tears sprang to her eyes. 'But there's been no bombs dropped yet. Daisy says so.'

'Who's Daisy?'

'Her what looks after us.'

'Well you should have stayed with Daisy.' Then Mam softened slightly, seeing the tears, Trish's stricken face and the wobble to her lower lip. 'I can't keep you here, love, much as I'd like to. I love the bones of you both but it's dangerous here. There's a war on and I have to work. I've got a job in the munitions factory.'

'Who'll look after Gran if you go to work?'

To her dismay, Megan was informed that her grandmother too had died, of the pneumonia, and life suddenly seemed desperately fragile, what with everyone dropping down dead all the time. Mam wouldn't even let them share her bed, as she'd used to do. There was a sailor in it now, called Jack, and he wasn't moving out for no one, he said, certainly not two little whippersnappers who should learn to do as they were told.

Worse than all of this, the very next day Mam begged a day off work and took them straight back to the Lakes.

A new place was found for the two little girls, this time with a Mr and Mrs Marshall, who were a policeman and his wife. They had no children but Daisy took to them on sight. Megan and Trish, however, were understandably nervous.

'Will she make us take a bath and have a commode in our room?' Megan asked, feeling it best to know how things stood from the start.

'Not if you don't want to, though I think baths can be quite good fun if you don't have too much water in them,' Daisy explained, deciding to make no mention of their more usual benefits.

'Will the lady lock us up and leave us on us own?' Trish wanted to know.

'No love, she won't ever lock you up.'

'But what if she dies too?'

'She won't die. She's quite young and healthy.'

'Has she any boggarts?'

'Or ghosts?'

Daisy gathered them close. 'Listen. This is a nice lady. She has no ghosts, no boggarts, not even any peevish little boys to pinch you. What she does have is a warm bed for you both, plenty of food in the larder and she's promised faithfully not to leave you alone for a minute. The only thing...' Daisy hesitated, feeling emotion block her throat as she came to the difficult part. 'She can't take me as well.' As the protests started, tears spurted and Trish's mouth did its upside-down act again, Daisy did her best to mollify them, kissing their cheeks and trying to mop them dry all at the same time. 'No, no, don't worry. It's all right. I shall be close by in a neighbour's house, at least until I'm sure you two are all right.'

'Will we see you every day then?'

'Every single day.'

'Promise?'

'Cross my heart and hope to die. Oh no, sorry, I didn't mean that.' But even Megan managed a crooked smile at her mistake. 'Oh, and Mrs Marshall says she has a dog, a little cocker spaniel which you can take for walks, if you like.'

They glanced at each other, still uncertain but their little faces had brightened. The idea of walking the dog was winning them over.

Megan took a deep breath. 'All right then. We've decided we'll go, haven't we, Trish?' And Trish nodded her agreement.

The elderly couple with whom Daisy was staying just next door, were kind enough, if set in their ways and unused to having a young person about the place. She could tell this by the way Mr Chapman stared at her sometimes, as if he was trying to dig under her skin and find out what she was thinking. But then he was so old, in Daisy's estimation at least, being well into his fifties, that he'd probably forgotten what it was like to be young.

He was a solicitor and very generously found a job for Daisy in his office, opening letters and addressing envelopes, the post boy having volunteered for the navy. Within a week Daisy envied him his escape, dangerous though the seas were at this time, for this was the most boring job imaginable, working all alone in a dusty corner of the mail room. Mr Chapman did his best to make

106

things easy for her though, by popping in to see her at frequent intervals to explain anything she didn't quite understand, such as the way he liked the stamp book kept, or the deeds tied up. He would pat her kindly on the shoulder, see that she took regular tea breaks, and once brought her a cushion when she complained of the hardness of the chair she had to sit on all day, tucking in her skirts for her as she settled it in place. He really was most kind and attentive. Her own parents had never shown such care and she thanked him for his thoughtfulness.

'We simply want you to be happy with us, Daisy. If you ever feel lonely, you must say so. You're so very young to be sent away from home, and such a pretty girl, not at all the usual sort of evacuee that we get here who hail from the dregs of society. You are special, my dear, I can tell, and we feel privileged to have you. Consequently we must make an extra special effort to see that you are well taken care of.'

Daisy rather enjoyed the notion of being considered special and pretty, but then he was only trying to make her feel at home, which was nice of him. She'd heard enough horror stories from some of the other evacuees to feel grateful for her good fortune and if her life seemed rather dull with a sameness about it, at least she was warm and well fed. She thanked him warmly, thinking what a charming old fusspot he was. Mrs Chapman stayed home to keep house and make the meals, and although there was always plenty to eat, they too were sadly predictable. You could guess what day of the week it was from the food put before you on the table. Bacon and mashed potatoes on Mondays, which was wash day with no time for cooking. Welsh Rarebit on Tuesdays. Cottage pie on Wednesdays. On Thursdays it was invariably liver and onions though sometimes they might have heart, which Daisy loathed. And on Fridays – a nice bit of fish. Daisy looked forward all week to the home-made pie that Mrs Chapman baked on a Saturday, and the roast on Sundays which they ate in silent splendour in the front parlour to celebrate the sober importance of the day.

Daisy had a room to herself in the attic. It contained one narrow bed and a chest of drawers, a bentwood chair and a cupboard built under the eaves into which she hung her few clothes. The only view from the tiny window was of a chimney pot but at least nobody told her what time she must go to bed, though early rising was essential.

The couple's motives for taking Daisy in soon became all too apparent. Mrs Chapman suffered ill health, in truth she revelled in it. Each morning, before leaving for the office, it had apparently been Mr Chapman's task to take breakfast in to his wife on a tray while she reclined in bed; a duty he quickly delegated to Daisy. Likewise in the evening, she was expected to wash up the dinner things, and give the kitchen a wipe over before doing any bits of ironing Mrs Chapman had not felt well enough to tackle during the day.

'You don't mind helping with the odd chore, my dear, do you?' Mrs Chapman would enquire in her timorous voice. She was a fragile, birdlike creature with grey hair fashioned into tight little waves all about her head. She always wore a plain grey skirt with a twin set, also in grey or a serviceable blue, and a single strand of pearls.

Daisy assured her that she did not mind in the least. 'I'm only too happy to help, since you're offering me a safe billet.'

'We thought that would be the case. Counting one's blessings is so important, I always think. And of course you must be so grateful to be out of Salford and off the streets,' making it sound as if living in the slums automatically branded her a prostitute.

Daisy could do nothing but nod in mute agreement before running to her room to laugh herself sick.

7

Daisy soon discovered that there were more chores to be counted than blessings, an increasing number each week in fact. She would be asked to prepare the vegetables each evening ready for the following day, to clean Mr Chapman's shoes, the fire grate each morning and the household silver once a fortnight. Cushions had to be kept nicely plumped, newspapers folded away into the rack and beds promptly made. And if she fell short of Mrs Chapman's high standards, that good lady would gently point out her deficiencies.

'I realise you don't know any better dear, but I do prefer the napkins to be folded into triangles. A square is so common, don't you think?'

And although Daisy had no objection to doing her share of household tasks, she had not come to them as a housemaid but as an evacuee, and she was fully aware that the Chapmans were being paid to accommodate her, partly by the government, and partly by a contribution from her own parents. The Chapmans were legally obliged to open their home to someone, and it really wasn't Daisy's fault that there was a war on, so constant proof of her gratitude shouldn't be expected of her.

But Daisy said nothing, uncomplainingly bearing the burden of more and more chores each evening, despite having spent a long day addressing envelopes for the various secretaries and clerks Mr Chapman employed, while Mrs Chapman sat in her comfy chair and read *Woman*. She told herself that she didn't mind the extra work, as it gave her something to do and kept her mind fully occupied.

It was the quiet moments alone in her room that were the worst. Those were the times when she thought of what might have been, of how things could have been so different if Percy had not let her down, if she hadn't had her lovely baby taken from her. But where was the good in self-pity? It only ever ended in Daisy sobbing into her pillow, which left her red-eyed and exhausted the next day and did her no good at all.

Yet it was hard not to feel abandoned. Despite

all her valiant efforts to keep cheerful and to cope, Daisy was lonely.

Sometimes she even found herself thinking fondly of Marigold Court with its back entry cluttered with dustbins, groups of gossiping women pegging out threadbare washing and men hanging around street corners smoking dimps, hoping their each-way bet on the dogs would come up. Daisy hated to admit it but, like Megan and Trish, she was homesick for the familiar streets and markets, for her ineffectual, ever-silent, hen-pecked father who'd never stood up to his domineering wife in his entire life, not even when his own daughter had been shown the door.

To her shame she didn't miss her mother one bit, but, one evening alone in her room, Daisy wrote a letter to her parents, giving her current address and telling of her adventures to date. She cried as she wrote it, for all it made her feel better afterwards when she'd popped it into the postbox. Perhaps, one day, her father at least might send a reply. It would be something to look forward to.

In the weeks following, she watched every morning for the postman but no letter came for her and Daisy strove to accustom herself to her new life, pondering on how easily promises were made – and broken. Percy's promise to love her for always had certainly meant nothing. He'd been a mistake, a bad one, and she would take much more care in future over where she bestowed her love.

The image of a pair of steady grey-green eyes

111

sprang instantly to mind. Harry Driscoll, the young airman she'd met on the bus.

She'd once considered writing to him. Daisy had carefully copied out the address he'd written on her hand because, after all, if it hadn't been for him she might never have got into town that day and they'd have been forced to spend another night in that awful house with poor Miss Pratt dead upstairs. Unfortunately, she'd never quite plucked up the courage to actually put pen to paper, which made her feel a bit guilty about breaking her promise.

But where was the point, she asked herself? He would no doubt be sent out on ops soon, or whatever they called them, and she might well be moved again herself. Daisy still dreamed of finding her aunt. If only she knew where to look, and under what name. You'd think her mother would be prepared to help her there, but no, not a word.

Her own parents' obligation of love and care had failed her too just when she needed them most. Daisy was quite certain, deep in her heart, that she would never have made that dreadful mistake and fallen pregnant, if her mother had properly explained to her the facts of life. It had been her own ignorance, in comparison to Percy's obviously superior experience, which had been her downfall.

Even poor Miss Pratt, who'd promised to 'do her bit' and look after them, had broken her word through no fault of her own. But then that was the problem, wasn't it? How did anyone know what was going to happen next? You could cross your heart, spit on your hand as they'd used to do in the school playground, write a promise in your own blood and nail it to a tree but lightning could strike the tree, or someone in higher authority could simply pick you up and move you, just as if you were an insect to be plucked from one place and dropped somewhere entirely different. It was really most alarming how very little control Daisy had over her own life.

And those two little ones, homesick for their mam, must feel even worse. She was glad that at least she'd been able to do something to help them.

In the event the two children settled in remarkably well. Mrs Marshall was a kind-hearted woman and although at first she was alarmed and distressed by the state of them, in no time at all she persuaded Megan into the bath with the lure of a rubber sailing boat, and soon had the pair of them shining clean, their hair cut and glowing like a pair of polished chestnuts. Each day as they walked the dog Trish would describe, in painstaking detail, every scrap of food they had eaten and Daisy would ask Megan about school. She still wasn't the most forthcoming child, but she was getting better and sometimes could be quite entertaining.

'The other children say we talk funny, so I said they did too. At least we don't ask someone, "Are you gaily?"' and she did a fair imitation of the Westmorland accent.

'So how would you ask someone how they were?'

She thought about this for a minute and then said, in her broadest Lancashire. 'Hey up? Howarta?' and then collapsed into a fit of giggles. Trish put her hand to her mouth and giggled too, though she wasn't entirely sure why or what she was laughing at.

Daisy joined in with the hilarity, mainly because it was good to see the children happy for once, and tried to think of more silly words. 'What about lish for lively? Or thrang for busy? They say that too round here.'

'Mrs Marshall calls her bread knife a gully. I thought that was the same as what we would call an alley,' Megan said. 'And porridge she calls poddish. That's the silliest word I ever heard.'

'I know a sillier one. How about powfagged?' Daisy said, wiping tears of laughter from her eyes. 'My grandma complained of being that all her life.'

'What does it mean?' Trish asked.

'Weary, which is what I am now after this long walk. Come on, let's see if Mrs Marshall can supply some lemonade.' And she hugged them both, feeling a huge relief and sense of satisfaction that all was going well with them at last.

Megan thought the war was overrated. There were no aeroplanes dropping bombs on them and flattening their houses, no tanks thundering through the village streets. They never had to run for their lives to an air-raid shelter, only creep down into a dark, damp cellar where there were spiders and goodness knows what else. Not even any enemy soldiers invading to take them prisoner or shoot at them, as she'd been led to expect. War was boring.

Everyone was calling it the phoney war and Mr Marshall said that more people were being injured falling over in the black-out than by enemy action. 'The common bicycle is turning into a lethal weapon,' he mourned, as he went out every morning on duty.

Each night they all had to listen to the news on the wireless and a man had talked about an aircraft carrier being torpedoed by a U-boat. It was called *Courageous* which Mrs Marshall said was a most appropriate name.

Megan had asked if this meant that the war would end soon, and Mr Marshall assured her that hostilities would all be over by Christmas.

Megan was glad to hear it. Perhaps then she could go home and stay at home. Many of the evacuees in her class at school had started to go back already because they were missing their family too much. Megan was annoyed that she wasn't allowed to go too, for not only did she think the war boring but so was living in this village with nothing more exciting to look forward to than collecting newspapers for the Armed Forces, though how the soldiers would find time to read them with all that fighting and shooting they had to do, Megan couldn't imagine.

Soon, they were going to have something called a Weapons Week. Megan had got quite excited about this at first, thinking that at last she might get to see some real guns, or even have a go at shooting with one. But then Mrs Marshall had explained that it meant they were to hold a rummage sale and coffee morning, and do other things like pay to guess the weight of a pig in order to raise money for the war effort. Megan had lost interest at once.

For months she'd been moved about from pillar to post, with nobody really wanting either her or Trish, calling them 'little nuisances' or dropping dead on them. And then they'd landed up here, stuck in the dullest place on earth.

On that first morning they'd stood together, she and Trish, in the school hall along with a load of other vacees from Tyneside while they'd been allocated classrooms and given instructions about not trespassing into the next-door farmer's field, and to remember always to bring their gas mask to school. One day Megan forgot and Mrs Crumpton, their teacher, made her walk all the way home again to fetch it. It felt like miles! What a waste of time, as if the Germans might suddenly decide to land on that particular morning. Megan hated her gas mask. It smelled funny and made her feel sick every time she had to put it on during gas mask drill. It was red and looked like Mickey Mouse but Megan wasn't fooled. She knew perfectly well that if she wore it for too long, she'd stop breathing all together.

The week before Christmas something exciting did happen. Megan had been looking out of the window when she suddenly gave a yelp of joy. 'That's Mam. Look, it's our mam. She's in the street outside.'

Trish instantly burst into tears and Mrs Marshall didn't know whether to pick her up and cuddle her, or dash outside to bring the poor woman in, since she seemed reluctant even to approach the door. Megan solved her dilemma by flinging open the front door and careered across the street to be swept straight up into her arms.

When all the hugs and kisses had been exchanged and Trish was safe and warm on her mother's knee, a cup of tea before her on the kitchen table, the tale of her nightmare journey began. 'The train were that full of soldiers, airmen and civvy workers, I had to stand up most of the way, squashed up in a corner of the corridor. We stopped at every set of signals, broke down near Preston when we all had to get off and go on to another train. Then we were rerouted to Wigan for no reason I could see. Eeh, I thought I'd never get here. Still, it were worth it to see my little lambs again.'

All of this was related later to Daisy, together with how Mrs Marshall had brought out her best biscuits as well as a Dundee cake, and then had left them quietly on their own so they could talk. To her shame, Daisy felt a burst of envy at their good fortune. 'Mam stayed nearly two whole hours,' Megan told her, breathless with excitement. 'It were wonderful.'

'And she give us Christmas presents,' Trish added.

'Which we mustn't open until Christmas Day,' Megan warned her sternly. 'I saw you trying to peep, our Trish, so I gave them to Mrs Marshall. She'll make sure you don't, so think on, you behave. Right?'

Trish nodded slowly, looking suitably chastened.

'And how did you feel when she had to go back home?' Daisy enquired gently.

Both little girls exchanged a glum look before, eyes cast down, Megan gave a little shrug of her thin shoulders and admitted quietly. 'I cried, and our Trish was sick. But I'm glad she come, Daisy. I am that. I'm right glad she come to see us. We know she's all fine and dandy now, don't we, and she's given that sailor his marching orders she says, because he was a mucky bugger.'

'Don't say that Megan. It's not a nice word.'

'And me mam's promised she won't die, hasn't she our Trish?'

Trish nodded solemnly.

'Of course she won't die,' Daisy said, shocked by the very idea. 'Whatever made you think such a thing?'

'Well, that other lady died, and me gran did, though she were old, and Kevin Lupton, a boy in my class said that when the Germans start dropping their bombs, we might all die.'

'What a very silly boy he must be.'

Trish was nodding again but her little mouth was turning down all the same and Daisy judged that it was time to change the subject, the conversation having taken a somewhat morbid turn. 'Well then, we'd better give this little rascal his walk. He must have felt a bit neglected today, what with the Christmas preparations, and all these tea parties going on.'

The two little girls ran for the dog lead, eager to cast their worries aside. And, because they were

118

children, that's exactly what they were able to do. Daisy could only envy them their innocence.

Christmas came and the two children had a marvellous time with presents from Mr and Mrs Marshall in addition to the small gifts their mother had brought. Neither of Daisy's parents came near, nor even sent her a present. She received a card, of course, with the simple, unsentimental message, *Hope this finds you well, as are we,* in her father's best handwriting but nothing more. Mrs Chapman gave her a pair of knitting needles and some wool so she could knit balaclavas for the soldiers.

'How very kind,' Daisy said, thinking quite the opposite.

Daisy helped Mrs Chapman cook a small goose for their Christmas dinner, which they ate in reverent silence in the parlour with properly folded napkins, and crackers to mark the importance of the day. Afterwards, Mr Chapman insisted they play a few hands of canasta, which he seemed anxious to teach Daisy, helping her to play the right card and hold them correctly in her hand. After that, Mrs Chapman made a pot of tea and cut them each a thin slice of Christmas cake.

'Who knows when we may get another, what with rationing threatened in the New Year. Dear me, this war is getting most unpleasant.'

'War usually is, my dear,' Mr Chapman murmured, giving Daisy a huge wink, just as if only the two of them could properly understand what was going on.

Daisy escaped as soon as politeness allowed, slipping next door to spend the remainder of the evening with the Marshalls, Megan and Trish. Trish had got thoroughly overexcited and even Megan couldn't stop talking about the wonders of the day, her blue eyes shining with happiness. They'd stuffed themselves with so much good food it was perfectly clear they'd never had a Christmas like it.

It was on Boxing Day that they experienced the biggest thrill of all. It was a bright, sunny afternoon, if rather crisp and cold and Daisy was out with the children walking the dog as usual when the sky suddenly seemed to darken. Glancing up she saw it was filled with parachutes.

'Crikey, we're being invaded!' Daisy stood rooted to the spot with shock. Everyone else seemed to be reacting in just the same way. There had been no air-raid siren, so perhaps even the authorities had been taken by surprise. Daisy felt overwhelmed, terrified by what might be about to happen. The sky seemed to be filled with dozens, if not hundreds of men. Is this how the war will end, she wondered in alarm, with us being murdered by Germans dropping out of the sky?

Moments later men were hitting the ground, rolling over the wide expanse of grass and, finally coming to her senses, Daisy grabbed the children's hands and began to run. She wouldn't give in without a fight, oh dear me no!

'Why are we running?' Megan gasped.

'Will they dead us?' Trish asked in sheer terror,

her small legs pumping like pistons as she desperately tried to keep up.

'Not if I can help it.'

And then, miraculously, out of the blue, she heard her name being called. *'Daisy!* Daisy for God's sake stop running and slow down, I can't keep up with you, not with all this gear on.'

Slithering to a halt she turned to find an apparition in leather helmet and flying suit rushing towards them, a silken parachute dragging behind him. Trish gave a frightened scream, yelling something incomprehensible about ghosts and hid behind her skirts, which Daisy didn't really wonder at. This was the nearest to a ghost she'd ever encountered herself. Only Megan seemed to have her wits about her.

'It's that nice man from the bus,' and pulling herself free of Daisy's hand, ran towards him. 'Harry, Harry! Are you in a tangle?'

He laughed. 'You could say that, sweetheart.'

Daisy could feel her cheeks flush with pleasure. She'd found him again, or rather, he had found her.

The next minute he was standing before her, that famous grin splitting his face from ear to ear. 'Well, this is a fine how-do-you-do. I don't usually have to put on a parachute and jump out of a plane in order to get to see a girl but if that's what it takes, who am I to object?'

Daisy, at a complete loss for words, was having trouble even catching her breath. She hadn't expected to ever see Harry again, let alone in this startling way. Hadn't she only recently repeated her vow to have nothing more to do with fellas?

Seeming to recognise her confusion, Harry took charge and started chattering away, happy to answer a string of questions from Megan about whether he had hurt himself and how he'd come to be falling out of the sky, and if he'd be doing it again.

'I expect so on another day and yes, I'm fine, thanks. This is nothing to worry about kids, just a training exercise. Christmas or no, our CO likes to keep us busy. And he thought it might give you good folk of the Lakes a feeling of comfort to know how swiftly help could be summoned, if needed. However, since it is Christmas, what about a hot potato as a treat, eh? Nothing better, I've always thought, on a cold day. Or perhaps a lollipop? If I can get my hand in my pocket, I'm sure I must have a few pennies here somewhere.'

Within seconds, or so it seemed, the two little girls had helped him delve into his flying-suit pockets, extracted the pennies and run off in the direction of the cart with the big black stove and tall chimney at the edge of the green, where the hot potato man had optimistically set up business for the day.

The moment they'd gone, Harry grabbed both of Daisy's hands, holding them tight and warm in his own. 'I've got maybe five minutes at best, probably less. Where are you living now Daisy? Are you all right? Are the children OK? Is there any chance that I could see you again?'

She felt dazed, utterly stunned by events. One minute she'd been reflecting, yet again, on her lonely state, the next, happiness had literally dropped out of the sky, bringing an unexpected sudden ray of sunshine into her life.

He seemed to be watching the thoughts spinning in her head. 'Please don't keep me in suspense. Say you will.' He glanced anxiously back over his shoulder and for the first time Daisy noticed that his comrades were swiftly gathering up their parachutes and hurrying over to a truck standing not far off. People were hindering their departure by thumping them on their backs, pumping their hands in vigorous handshakes, as if anxious to thank them for the risks they were about to take. 'I'll have to go in a minute. Please, Daisy, say yes. I've got an evening off next Thursday, how would that be? There's a dance. I could pick you up. God knows how long we'll be at Longtown. We could get our new posting at any time.'

She looked at him properly then, her eyes focusing upon the eagerness in his young face, the anxiety in his grey-green eyes and she thought, why not? Perhaps she was too young to give up men for life, after all. They couldn't all be as heartless as Percy, surely? And he seemed harmless enough. A nice young man, honest, cheerful, but not as handsome, nor so full of his own self-importance as Percy had been. A girl could surely feel safe with Harry Driscoll. Besides, he wasn't at all the sort of chap she could ever go crazy about, or fall head over heels in love with. 'All right,' she said. 'Why not?'

He gave a whoop of delight, picked her up and swung her round so fast and furious, the pair of them got hopelessly tangled in the cords of the

123

parachute and tumbled to the ground together, all trussed up like a chicken. Daisy could barely speak for laughing as they both struggled to release themselves from the muddle. Eventually, she found both breath and voice. 'You're quite mad, Harry Driscoll. Do you know that? Stark, staring crazy.'

'You're absolutely right, Daisy, I am. Crazy over you. I love your bright, brown eyes, and the adorable way you tilt your head to one side whenever anyone speaks to you. I love every freckle, I adore...'

'Shut up, you clown, and get me out of here.' She might have managed to untangle herself if she hadn't been so fully occupied wiping tears of laughter from her eyes.

'Oh, I don't know. I've really no objection at all to lying on this grass with you, cold and damp though it undoubtedly is. I can't think of anyone I'd rather be tied up with, and would happily stay here all day, if it weren't for the fact that I'd probably get court-martialled.'

'Well, I *do* object. Stop acting the fool and behave yourself,' but there was no disapproval in her voice. She was still helpless with laughter, her sides aching with it. He really was a card, was Harry Driscoll. Going out with him would certainly be fun, if nothing else.

Finally, and with great reluctance, he helped her back on to her feet, but even then didn't quite let her go. He gathered her small face between his two large hands and said, 'Happy Christmas, Daisy. You've made my day.' Then he kissed her. It was a light, friendly, unromantic sort of kiss but yet filled with tenderness, and strangely moving. The sort of kiss that kept Daisy awake half the night remembering it.

Laura

8

Laura was entranced by the tale, soaking up every word and the meal had been good too. A simple pasta dish, but delicious. They'd enjoyed a surprisingly companionable evening, just the two of them and talked for hours afterwards over an excellent Chardonnay, curled up on old comfy sofas before a blazing log fire.

'It's all so sad. Daisy couldn't have married Harry in the end, since he was called Driscoll, and Daisy's married name was Thompson.'

David shrugged. 'She could easily have married twice.'

Laura's eyes widened. 'I hadn't thought of that. Damn, I was so occupied fending off my father's anger, I never did ask him the first name of my grandfather. Did Daisy ever mention it to you?'

He shook his head. 'Not that I recall. She only ever talked about Harry. Harry, Harry, Harry. As I said, he was undoubtedly the love of her life.'

'Do you think they married and then something terrible happened to him in the war? Was that it? He surely wouldn't leave her once he learned of her secret child, or get a divorce, would he? Oh, I want to know so much more. What happened at the dance, for instance? When did Daisy realise she loved him? Did she ever tell him about the baby? Oh, it's so frustrating. I want to know everything about her. I hate my father for cutting me off like that.'

'Did you tell him that? Is that why he was angry with you, or shouldn't I ask?'

Laura screwed up her nose, not quite sure how to respond. 'He took me out to lunch to give me one of his little lectures on how I should organise my life. He's stubborn and dogmatic and uncommunicative. No wonder he and Daisy fell out.'

'So this search into her past is some sort of guilt trip, is it?' David tossed another log on to the fire and a shower of sparks flew up the wide, inglenook chimney. Outside, for once, all seemed to be quiet, the wind having died away.

Laura gave a rueful smile. 'In a way, but there's more to it than that.' She felt perfectly relaxed here, replete with good food and wine, thoroughly mellow so didn't take exception to the question. Besides, she'd discovered that she quite liked this man. He'd been perfectly frank about his own life, the difficulties of running a farm in today's economic climate, yet how determined he was to hang on. His uncle had left it to him about ten years ago because, like David himself, he'd remained a bachelor and had no children of his own. Beckwith Hall Farm had consumed him all of his life, as it now possessed David, leaving him little opportunity to socialise or look for a wife. If he didn't make a fortune working it, then so be it. His needs were small, he explained, with only himself to think about.

Laura said, 'I find Daisy fascinating and genuinely want to understand her. But there was some silly quarrel between her and my dad, so I didn't see as much of her when I was growing up as I would have liked. And he's furious with me for "interfering", as he calls it, for trying to find out more about her.'

'How old were you when this quarrel took place?'

Laura frowned. 'Maybe about seven or eight.'

'Well, I can understand you being under your father's control for some years after that. But you've been a big girl for a long time. Time enough to make your own decisions about who you see or don't see.'

Again she felt herself flushing, feeling the need to justify herself without divulging all the complicated intricacies of her marriage. 'True, but ... there were other reasons why I didn't get in touch as often as I should, even after I left home.'

Felix had seen little point in wasting valuable time visiting relatives. He'd once driven Laura up to the Lakes to see Daisy and complained bitterly about the mud which had splattered on to the underside of his brand new Mercedes. He'd refused, absolutely, to take a walk, claiming it would likewise ruin his highly polished shoes, nor would he borrow a pair of old boots, probably because they would look odd with his smart new suit. He'd also objected to country smells, messy animals and Daisy's plumbing, as well as her lack of fitted carpets and central heating. He'd never come again. Not until the funeral.

But how could she properly explain any of this, without making him sound a complete prig? Nor had she any wish to go into the fact that he'd objected to Laura coming on her own. She'd fought a battle every time she wanted to visit her grandmother so, in the end, had opted for the easy course and stayed away, thinking there'd be time to try again later when Felix was less tied up with the business and had got over his silly mood. Only there never had been enough time.

Explaining none of this, she confined her comments to, 'My husband doesn't much care for the country.'

'Ah, I see. It takes some people that way. All this fresh air and space. Is that why he's not here with you now?'

'He's a busy man, with a business to run.' If David Hornsby wished to read more into that, let him.

'Of course.'

Laura felt certain that he noted how she was avoiding his shrewd gaze. She could sense him considering her more intently, as if he'd like to ask her another question but apparently changed his mind at the last moment and offered her more coffee instead, which she refused politely. He gave a little deprecating shrug. 'OK, so I'm nosy. Living here, one grabs one's gossip where one can.' He grinned at her and made to top up her wine glass but she quickly put her hand over it.

'No, no, it's late. Heavens, yes, it's nearly midnight.' Laura stood up. 'I really must go.'

He didn't press her to stay longer or make any silly jokes about her changing into a pumpkin on the stroke of midnight. He simply collected her coat and offered to walk her back up the fields. Laura shook her head. 'I have my torch, and I came properly shod.' Slipping off the indoor shoes she'd brought with her, she pushed her feet into a sturdy pair of boots. They looked rather clumsy against her long blue evening skirt but would keep her feet dry, and what did glamour matter out in a field in the middle of the night? 'Thanks for a lovely evening. Most enlightening.'

'Glad you came?'

She glanced up at him, at the relaxed way he stood before her, hands in pockets, his smile warm and friendly. 'Yes,' she said, finding to her surprise that she meant it. 'I am. You must come to me next time. I cook pretty good too.'

'There is going to be a next time then?'

A small pause. 'I expect so. We'll have to see, shan't we?'

'I shall look forward to it.'

It was as he opened the door on to a still and cloudless night that he asked her the question that had clearly been on his mind all evening. 'What about your husband then. Doesn't he object to you having dinner with strange men?'

Laura busied herself fastening buttons and tying on her scarf so that he couldn't see the troubled expression in her eyes. 'Oh, probably, but he isn't here, is he?' and stepped over the threshold into the yard before he could pursue that particular line of conversation any further. 'Look at all these stars. Aren't they magnificent?

We can rarely see them in town these days. Too much light pollution, I suppose. It's good to know they're still there, keeping watch over us.'

'Perhaps Daisy is one of them now, keeping an eye on us all.'

Laura turned to him with a lopsided smile, 'What a lovely thought. Thanks again for the delicious meal. Perhaps we can talk again some time, about Daisy.'

'Of course. There's lots more I could tell you, I'm sure.'

She let out a regretful sigh. 'If only she'd left a journal, as the Victorians used to do. It would make things so much easier.'

'I suppose it would, but sometimes a little effort can be so much more rewarding, don't you think? Goodnight, Laura.'

Laura's morning walks became a regular routine, a wonderful way to allow the fresh air to cleanse her troubled mind, sort out her confused thoughts, and ensure that she fell asleep like a baby the minute her head touched the pillow.

She was used to spending time alone, hours and hours of it in the big empty house in Cheadle Hulme, but this was different. This was a special kind of solitude: invigorating and refreshing which brought with it a sense of enormous peace and well-being. She delighted in the bloom of purple heather, the sight of a lone curlew circling in an infinite sky polished to a brilliant lapis lazuli blue, the sound of a rushing beck and she could never grow bored with the ever-changing dance of the clouds on the mountains beyond. Laura

130

felt as if she were rediscovering the world, rediscovering herself.

As she strode out along the path she would list her assets, ticking them off one by one in her mind. She was strong, stronger than Felix gave her credit for, and self-willed. She was intelligent with many skills at her fingertips, and also capable of learning new ones. She wasn't afraid of hard work. She was still young enough at thirty-four to make a fresh start. Most of all, she was perfectly capable of coping without him. It had felt marvellous simply to refuse to go home, and although nothing had been finalised between them he rang daily to remind her that he still expected her to return soon. Laura knew that he could manage perfectly well without her, for all he may claim otherwise. No doubt the miraculous Miranda would move in and cook for him, if she hadn't already.

Laura giggled at the thought, no longer troubling to feel jealous as she speculated on whether the poor girl would be quite so keen when she realised all that was involved in being Felix's wife, rather than his mistress.

As always after one of these self-therapy sessions, she returned from her walk feeling cleansed and light-hearted, as if she had scoured off a mask of troubles, looked the devil in the face and survived. A fanciful notion but could she survive here through the aching cold of a long winter without the undoubted comforts of life that her husband could provide? Could she build a business and make enough money out of it to provide for herself?

Back in the kitchen she toed off her boots, made herself a coffee and carried it into the living room. There were surprisingly few chores to be done. Daisy had spent her last weeks in hospital during which time the house must have been standing empty but someone had stripped the old woman's bed, washed and ironed the sheets, left her bedroom all spick and span. She rather thought it might have been David and had tackled him on the subject when she'd encountered him once in the lane.

He'd shrugged her thanks aside. 'Someone had to do it. It was no big deal.'

In the days following the funeral, Laura folded and packed up clothes which most obviously needed to be disposed of. At first it had felt like an intrusion but she shook aside any sense of shyness since at least she cared about Daisy, and wasn't some unknown auctioneer simply listing her belongings in a dispassionate way. She opened every cupboard and drawer, all of which appeared to be stuffed with linen and clothes which must have lain neatly stored there for years, reeking of mothballs or old lavender. Some of the linen was so beautifully embroidered, or made from such deliciously soft Lancashire cotton, that Laura couldn't imagine ever disposing of them.

But then she didn't have to. They would come in very handy if and when she opened the house for guests. She spent a couple of days making a full inventory, counting every cup, saucer, plate and table napkin, anything which might be useful in her new business. After that she gave the

132

kitchen a thorough clean and threw away packets and tins which had passed their sell-by date. Now, there was nothing more to be done than sit down and relax: to do a little thinking and perhaps doodle a few notes about her plans.

She ate only when hungry, and then something simple like an omelette or a cheese sandwich. Nobody called and she felt quite alone in the world, free to stay in bed all morning if she so wished, or get up at dawn and walk over the mountain, or down through the lanes and fields for miles. On her return, Laura would feel so soporific that she would frequently fall asleep over whatever book she happened to be reading from Daisy's collection. Free of Felix's endless demands for the first time in years, she was at last able to think properly with blissfully few interruptions. And apart from his regular telephone call each evening, the phone didn't even ring.

As the time for his call approached, she would pour herself a glass of wine, ready to brace herself before picking it up. 'Hello darling,' she would say, as brightly as she could.

Felix, as always, would come straight to the point. 'How much longer are you going to be away?'

'I thought perhaps you might come up here on Friday evening. If you brought some more of my clothes, we could make a weekend of it. I can't recall when we last spent some free time together, must be a couple of years now. And the weather is glorious, you'd love it.' She could then choose her moment to reveal her plans and talk through their problems in a civilised fashion.

'I'd hate that Laura and you know it. Besides, I have to pop over to Toledo for a couple of days. Something about a picture which might be a Greco.' Felix was always dreaming of finding some undiscovered work of art which would make him a fortune. Laura paid this no attention.

'Well, don't expect me home quite yet. I'm having a lovely time being lazy and spoiling myself rotten. Don't you think I deserve to once in a while?'

She heard his exasperated sigh hiss down the phone line. 'It sounds inordinately selfish to me. Stop wallowing in nostalgia and come home where you belong. The sheets need changing, there's nothing in the fridge, and the house is like a morgue, I can hardly bear to be in it.'

'But you rarely are in it anyway, darling, even when I'm there.'

'Are you trying to be deliberately provocative, Laura? If so, I'm not amused. I work only for your benefit you know, to provide you with a lovely house, clothes, etc., etc.'

'So you keep saying, and I keep asking you to allow me to work with you so that I wouldn't be so bored and you so overstretched, but somehow I don't believe you're listening.'

'I don't intend to turn this call into another marital argument. I shall be catching an early flight home on Monday morning. I shall expect you to be at the airport to pick me up.'

Laura took a deep breath. 'Sorry, darling, no can do. I – I have an appointment to see the solicitor on that day.' The appointment was for Tuesday but the last thing she wanted was to rush home, spend the weekend cleaning up the house, restocking the fridge and then dashing to the airport to pick up Felix at the crack of dawn on Monday morning. Nevertheless, Laura could feel herself flushing at the deliberate lie and put her hand to her cheek, almost as if she were afraid he could see her guilt over the phone.

'Tell him you need to bring it forward. Or better still cancel it and I'll deal with the blithering old idiot by phone.'

'I could always come with you to Toledo. How about that? I wouldn't mind a romantic weekend somewhere warm and sexy. Then we could both fly back together on Monday morning and I'd nip back up here to see the solicitor.'

'I'm going to be busy all weekend. You'd be thoroughly bored. Stop arguing and do as you're told for once, Laura.'

'I always do as I'm told. Perhaps I'm growing tired of it. Anyway, there'd be the evenings, and the nights together. Is Miranda going to be there?'

'Monday morning, Laura. My plane lands at six-thirty. Don't be late.' There was a click and he was gone, subject closed, as abrupt and imperative as ever. She noticed that he'd not answered her question about Miranda. Laura stuck out her tongue at the now silent instrument and, finding the wine bottle empty, went to pour herself a drop of port from a bottle she'd found in a cupboard. Sly old Daisy had clearly enjoyed a tipple herself now and then.

On Saturday morning, when she knew that Felix

135

would be away, Laura drove down to Cheadle Hulme, let herself into the empty house and packed a couple of suitcases with clothes and a few personal items she needed. The fridge was indeed empty with nothing more than a bottle of sour milk and a lettuce that was running to liquid in the chill tray. Closing the door again, she made no move to clean or restock it.

She checked through the mail lying on the mat but left it there unopened. She rarely received either letters or bills and could see nothing beyond a bit of junk mail. She did risk taking a few of her favourite CDs from the rack, guessing that Felix would be no more likely to notice they were missing than he would think to check her wardrobe. By the time he did both, it would no longer matter. She would have made up her mind and come to a firm decision about her future, one way or the other.

She paused to linger for a moment and gaze at their wedding photo on the dresser, recalling with painful nostalgia the hope she had felt on that day. It was a close-up of the happy couple, cheek to cheek, with their arms about each other, Laura looking young and desperately in love. Felix was wearing his embarrassed, 'I'll be glad when this pantomime is all over' expression. Had he ever loved her? she wondered. If not, then why had he married her? Because she'd suited the image he had in mind for a wife? She was reasonably attractive, good in bed, and could cook. An excellent CV for matrimony. And was apparently willing to fit in entirely with his wishes and do exactly as he told her to.

Not any more.

Laura carefully locked up the house again and drove back to the Lakes. It really had proved to be incredibly simple to break free. By the time she was past the Blackpool turnoff and the motorway traffic eased, she felt quite light-hearted for the first time in months, as if she had rid herself of a great weight.

On Tuesday morning, Laura set off bright and early to drive to Keswick. She took Daisy's clothes to a local charity shop, then explored its miscellany of shops and narrow streets, hidden courts and yards, past the Moot Hall and market place, pausing only to eat lunch in a tiny café and buy food to take back with her to Lane End Farm. She considered taking in a play at the new Theatre By The Lake but decided against it and settled instead for a visit to the museum and art gallery in Fitz Park where she studied the original manuscripts of Southey, Ruskin and Walpole, among others.

At three-thirty prompt, she kept her appointment with the family solicitor, not old Mr Capstick but his son Nicholas, who turned out to be surprisingly young and smart, his office filled with a battery of computers. Even Felix would have been impressed.

He told her to call him Nick, said how pleased he was to meet Daisy's granddaughter at last, then expressed his regrets on hearing she was planning to sell. 'It's not a good time to sell. Farms aren't fetching high prices right now and Lane End is little more than a smallholding now.'

He chewed on his lower lip for a bit. 'Trouble is, because it's so remote, it will only attract a particular sort of buyer. It's unique. A fine house in many ways and you would sell it eventually, but it could take a year or two.'

'A year or two? Heavens, I think Felix was thinking in terms of a couple of months.'

Nick gave a hollow laugh. 'No chance. Not the way things work with this type of property. If I were you, and it's really none of my business, but unless you're strapped for cash I'd hang on for a bit. View it as an excellent investment for the future.'

Laura sat back with a satisfied little sigh. He couldn't have said anything guaranteed to please her more. Now she had some real ammunition with which to fight Felix. 'Thank you for your advice. I'll tell my husband what you suggest.'

He nodded, punched some keys on his computer and, after a moment, said, 'Apart from that, everything is progressing nicely so far as the probate is concerned. The land doesn't come with the house, you do understand that?'

'Oh yes, that was made clear.'

He nodded. 'You're the only beneficiary so there shouldn't be any complications. Not that there's much actual cash. The house was her main, well – her only remaining asset.'

'That's fine. The house is wonderful.' Laura got up to go. 'Oh, my grandmother didn't leave any papers with you, did she? Letters perhaps, or a diary?'

He frowned slightly while he considered this. 'Not that I know of. I believe we only have her

138

will. She kept all her papers, such as there were, in her bureau at home, including the deeds of the house. We offered to store those for her too but Daisy enjoyed browsing through them from time to time, because it was the story of Lane End Farm. She said everything had a life story, the house, the mountain, even the stones in the road.' He smiled fondly. 'Old folk get that way, a little fanciful in their declining years. But she loved that house, and why not? She didn't have much of a start in life, I believe, so deserved her bit of good luck.'

Laura had sat down again. 'You'd have thought then, if she believed a house had a story to tell, that she'd be happy to tell her own.'

'In my experience people very often say one thing and mean another. Hard to fathom at times. Have you spoken to David? David Hornsby, your nearest neighbour. They were great friends and I'm almost sure he encouraged her to do something of that nature.'

Laura was flabbergasted. 'He never said. I had supper with him the other night but he denied all knowledge of a diary.'

'Oh, I could be entirely wrong. Don't quote me. And Daisy was far too active to sit still for more than five minutes, let alone keep a diary. That much I did learn about her in the few years I knew her. If she wasn't mending walls, she was reroofing the barn or whatever. She felt an enormous pride in keeping the house up to scratch, and a great sense of responsibility though it got too much for her in the end. Clem had been determined that the property be left to her and not to Florrie, his wife. She would be Daisy's aunt, if you remember, who'd lived at the farm since they married. A bit before my time but they were an odd couple apparently.'

'In what way, odd?'

'Oh, something to do with him being a good bit older than her for a start, Florrie being one for a good time and Blencathra not really having its fair share of night spots. I think she found it rather lonely up there. And then there was the loss of their child, which didn't help.'

'Oh, how dreadful. What happened?'

He shook his head. 'Bit of a mystery and a long time ago, of course. The pair blamed each other, I believe. Did their relationship no good at all.' The telephone rang and he picked up the receiver with an apologetic smile. Seconds later he put it down again. 'My next appointment, I'm afraid. Well, it's been good talking to you, Mrs Rampton.'

'Laura, please.'

He smiled. 'I hope you come to enjoy living in the house as much as Daisy did. You may even change your mind and decide not to sell after all.'

'You never know. I'm certainly curious to learn more about her life, and anyone else who occupied the house before me.'

He led her to the door. 'You should talk to my father, retired and taking life easier now but he would have been around when Daisy was here, even if not when Clem was making his will. He may know something about it. Memories live long in these parts. Certainly my dad is sharp enough for anything that happened forty or fifty

140

years ago; ask him what he had for his lunch yesterday and that's another matter.'

'Thank you,' Laura said with a smile. 'You've been most helpful.'

On her drive back from town the sky grew heavy with snow, grey and threatening, the surrounding mountains seeming to retreat gradually and vanish in the gloom. A late snowfall would play havoc with the lambing and no doubt with her own plans. She took the precaution of stopping off at a supermarket for further supplies, mindful of the warnings of blocked lanes. The idea of being snowed in was not unpleasant, an excuse to postpone the inevitable confrontation with Felix but she'd no wish to be marooned without sufficient sustenance. Not that Felix could be ignored indefinitely. If she was going to turn Lane End Farm back into a guesthouse, she should tell him of her decision sooner, rather than later. She must face it at some point, and delay would only make his temper worse.

She bought meat, chicken, flour, herbs and spices, unsalted butter and other delicious ingredients together with a new cookbook she'd been promising herself for ages. She meant to take advantage of the respite by trying out some of the recipes. Laura also purchased a large notepad, in which she meant to start making lists and outline her plans for the house. She enjoyed making lists, was never happier than with a pencil in her hand organising something, that's when she wasn't up to her elbows in flour of course. She would restock the freezer and invite David

Hornsby round to act as guinea pig for some new dish or other. It would give her the opportunity to ask him again about a diary, and whether he had, in fact, succeeded in persuading Daisy to keep one, had perhaps been holding out on admitting as much and making her work for it.

She also bought such items as paint, brushes, turps, nails, screws, sandpaper and other unexciting but essential items. She meant to get started with the refurbishments just as soon as she'd spoken to Felix.

With the solicitor's advice to back her up, she felt a surge of new confidence, a tiny nub of excitement burning in the pit of her stomach.

The snow didn't look like it would stick, fortunately, but David Hornsby happily accepted her invitation when she came across him late that afternoon in the lane. She challenged him about the diary but to her disappointment, he repeated his belief that Daisy hadn't kept one. 'It's true that I did try to persuade her but, as I told you before, failed utterly.'

They leaned on the dry-stone wall looking out over towards Skiddaw Forest, chatting amicably: Laura explaining how she intended to try out a new recipe and David speaking of his concern for his ewes whenever the weather took a turn for the worse. 'The sky still looks heavy with snow. The last thing we need are blizzards to coincide with lambing. January and February are bad enough in these parts. But then you'll probably be gone by next winter.'

He cast her a sideways, speculative glance and Laura hesitated only momentarily before launching into an explanation of her plans to turn Lane End Farm back into a guesthouse. 'I've never done anything of the sort in my life before, and could easily make a complete mess of it.'

His face became alert with interest. 'I'm delighted to hear that you might be staying on, though I can't imagine your making a mess of anything, not for a moment. Daisy too was practical, a capable, no-nonsense, non-fussy type, and I'm quite sure you must be the same.' An odd sort of compliment which nonetheless brought a schoolgirl flush to her cheeks, more from the look in his eyes than the words themselves. Then he was continuing with his story of Daisy and Harry, and as Laura became totally absorbed by it, as always, everything else vanished from her mind. She forgot all about her cooking, and about ringing Felix to tell him what the solicitor had said about the house.

Daisy

9

When Thursday came round, Daisy was in a dither of indecision. What should she wear for her first date with Harry? She had very few clothes and no money to buy any new ones. Yet for some reason she felt torn in two, anxious to look her best, wanting him to like her while at the same time being unwilling to give the impression that she'd made any special effort. Mindful of the disaster that her first love affair had led her into, Daisy was afraid of making a mistake, and reluctant to take any similar risks, or encourage him in the slightest way.

In the event, in the hours before he was due to arrive Daisy was kept so fully occupied she didn't have a moment to think, let alone study the contents of her meagre wardrobe. To start with she was late home from work, then the moment she came through the door, Mrs Chapman sent her straight out again to join a queue she'd heard was forming at the butchers, though she hadn't the first idea what it was for. Daisy stood impatiently stamping her feet against the winter cold, fretting and worrying about how long this ritual might take and when, an hour later, she returned bearing the prize of half a dozen pork sausages, Mrs Chapman tartly remarked that it had hardly been worth the effort.

'If only you hadn't been late, and had joined the queue earlier, then you might have been more successful.'

Daisy gritted her teeth against the desire to defend herself by saying that Mr Chapman was the one to blame for her being late, by asking her to tidy the stationery cupboard quite late in the day. He'd then hindered the process by keep popping in to interrupt and check on how she was getting along. She knew he only meant to be kind but there'd been one moment, when he'd squeezed into the cupboard with her, that Daisy had felt quite claustrophobic, trapped by his bulk in the confined space. He was a large, stocky man and when he'd reached up, quite unnecessarily, to bring down a box for her to sort through, the smell of sweat from under his armpits had made her feel quite nauseous.

'You don't have to stay,' she'd told him. 'I can get a stool and manage very well on my own, thanks.' She didn't like to say that there wasn't room enough for the two of them in the narrow space.

'No, no, I'm happy to help. I'll hold you up, shall I?' To Daisy's alarm, he'd grasped her by the waist and lifted her off her feet so that she could reach the next box. She could feel his plump fingers digging into her ribs just below her breasts and went quite hot with embarrassment.

She'd been saved by the arrival of one of his clerks who came to tell him a client had arrived for their appointment. He appeared not in the least nonplussed to find his employer lurking in the stationery cupboard with the post girl, nor did he seem to notice how flustered Daisy was. But it was this small incident which caused her to experience her first doubts about Mr Chapman and his veneer of kind generosity.

As if this wasn't enough, she was further delayed by Megan and Trish who were waiting for her at the garden gate full of excitement over some news they were bursting to tell her.

'What d'you think Daisy, Mrs Marshall is going to have a baby.'

Daisy was startled. She hadn't realised ladies as old as Mrs Marshall could still have babies. She must be very nearly forty, if not that already.

'Really, how do you know?'

'We heard her telling the cleaning lady. She said how they'd been trying for years and had given up all hope. Isn't that good, Daisy? Trish and me like babies. P'raps they found the right place what sells them.'

'Yes, perhaps they did,' Daisy agreed, but even as she nodded and smiled, promising to meet up with them later for their usual early evening doggy walk, there was a smidgen of worry at the back of her mind. Would Mr and Mrs Marshall still be prepared to keep the two little evacuees once they had a baby of their own?

But all of these concerns melted away as anticipation of the evening ahead tightened in the pit of her stomach, making her feel very slightly sick. She couldn't get the image of Harry's cheerful face out of her mind as she set about her nightly chores with extra vigour, eager to get them done quickly then she could be on her way.

Daisy cleaned the kitchen, polished Mr Chapman's shoes and sharpened a batch of pencils for the holder on his desk, not forgetting the promised walk with the children and the dog, which left her just enough time to quickly wash her face, drag a comb through the tangled corkscrew curls and pull on the first clean blouse and skirt that came to hand. So much for studying her wardrobe.

Even though she flew down the stairs the moment the doorbell rang, pausing only to grab her coat, by the time she reached it Mr Chapman was already standing in the hall, holding the door wide open. 'There appears to be someone here

146

for you, Daisy.'

'Yes,' she agreed, slightly breathless from her headlong dash and from the blast of cold wind that roared up the lobby. 'Hello, Harry.'

Looking exceptionally smart in his blue uniform, he saluted her deftly. 'Evening.'

'Aren't you going to introduce me to your young man, Daisy?'

She did so, hearing her own voice sounding all stilted and embarrassed, stumbling over the words although why it should affect her in that way, Daisy couldn't imagine. It was really no business of Mr Chapman who she went out with, and, strictly speaking, Harry couldn't be called her 'young man' at all, only a friend who happened to be male. But Mr Chapman was frowning at Harry in a curiously critical way and she was anxious, suddenly, to be off.

'I won't be late,' she called, grabbing Harry's arm and pushing him out on to the step, in readiness for a quick exit.

'Indeed I should hope not. That wouldn't be right, not on such a short acquaintance. It would be most unseemly of your young man to return you home much beyond nine.'

'Nine?' Daisy was appalled. That barely gave them more than a couple of hours together.

Harry remarked bravely, 'We're going to a dance, sir. I could have her back by ten.'

Mr Chapman appeared to consider. 'Very well then, ten o'clock. Not a moment later. We are responsible for you to your parents, after all, Daisy. What would they think if I absconded on my duty?'

Daisy made no response to this as she hurried Harry quickly down the garden path and along the street, though she could feel him bristling with anger. 'Who does he think he is to lecture me about what's right or wrong? Does he imagine I'd do something to hurt you? Silly old cove. Anyway, how does he know how long I've known you, or what your parents would think of me?'

Daisy knew for certain that her mother would jump quickly to the conclusion that Harry wanted to have his wicked way with her, as Percy had done. If she'd been here, Rita would have warned her to make no mention of her dreadful secret, not if she wanted to keep her reputation intact, nor be taken advantage of. Not that Daisy had any intention of ever telling anyone about the precious, nameless baby who'd been taken from her, though for a very different reason. It was a subject far too painful to discuss with anyone, let alone a new acquaintance. Giving no indication of these troubled thoughts, she smiled brightly up at him. 'Take no notice, Harry. Like he says, he is responsible for me, in a way, since I'm an evacuee. And I am only seventeen.' She was properly grown up now that she'd had another birthday.

'And I'm only twenty-two. Too young to be fighting in a bloody war. But if I'm old enough to die for my country, I'm old enough to take out any girl I fancy.'

Daisy cast him a sidelong glance from beneath the sweep of her lashes, her mouth pursing upwards into a teasing smile. 'So you do fancy me then, eh?'

'I fancy you rotten, and don't pretend you don't know that already.'

The dance was being held at the village hall, put on specially for the 'boys in blue' by grateful locals who feared for what these young men might soon be facing, wanting their last memories of this small Cumberland village to be happy ones. Outside, the helm wind might blow across the tops with its usual fervour, guns might be sounding in far distant places, but here, within these four walls, all was merry and lighthearted. The music was loud, the room packed with air crew and starry-eyed village girls; a substantial supper of pork pies, sandwiches and home-made cakes to satisfy healthy young appetites during the interval. No one spoke of the war, or where they might be tomorrow, or the day after that. Here, for one night at least, everyone could feel safe and warm, happy and free to simply enjoy themselves.

Daisy was having the time of her life. She danced every number with Harry, even the square tango and the Boston Two Step at which they were both so hopeless they fell over each other's feet and very nearly ended up in another tangle on the dance floor.

'Oh lord, me mam allus did call me a clumsy oaf,' Daisy mourned and, for the sake of the other couples still dancing, suggested that perhaps they should sit the next one out. 'Otherwise we might get ourselves arrested for causing an obstruction.'

They sat on a couple of the hard, wooden

149

chairs set around the perimeter of the room, Daisy sipping a lemonade while Harry quaffed a welcome beer. She could feel the heat of his body pressing against hers and this somehow seemed strangely intimate. Smitten with a burst of shyness, she couldn't think of a thing to say throughout the length of two more dances. The long silence was nevertheless a contented one and it was Harry who broke it by saying it was getting late and perhaps they ought to be starting the long walk home. 'In any case, I don't know about you, but I could do with a breath of fresh air.'

The January night was crisp and frosty, with a horned moon riding high amongst the stars in a clear, bright sky. All around were the undulating folds of the Northern fells, filling the horizon, deceptively benign, their smooth faces blanked out by the darkness, it was here that the RAF aimed their dummy bombs. Daisy had watched them practise day after day, flying in low, searching for the wooden arrows on the ground which marked their target. Some time soon their target would be a real one, and not quite so passive. Tonight though, all was silent, save for the crack and splinter of ice underfoot as the young couple walked along the rough track. Harry tucked up the collar of Daisy's coat. 'Are you warm enough?'
'Yes, thanks.'
He put an arm about her and hugged her close to his side, just to make sure, he explained. Daisy didn't object. She liked the feel of him beside

150

her, warm and strong, solid and comforting, and the pressure of his hand moving up and down her arm was bringing small shivers of excitement deep in her belly. The more time she spent with Harry, the more she liked him.

They walked for a long time in silence, and then he said, 'Back home, in Manchester or Salford, wherever it is that you live, is there anyone special?'

'Special in what way?' Daisy asked, knowing full well what he meant, but needing time to consider her answer.

'You know in what way.'

'Well – there was once.' She knew she sounded hesitant and unsure, unwilling to speak of it.

'But not now?'

For one mad moment she almost told him. She could simply say: I was young and foolish and got myself into trouble because I thought we were in love. Except that instead of marrying me, as I'd hoped and longed for, he joined up and left me to deal with the consequences on my own. Yet how could she? She was scarcely much older even now. A wave of sickness hit her, and she was back in that Mother and Baby Home, arguing with Mam, pleading with her to let her keep the baby, crying for Percy to come for her.

Daisy realised that in a way, perhaps her mother had been right. She had indeed been far too young to care for a baby at sixteen. How could she even consider herself a responsible person when here she was, a matter of months after losing both Percy and her precious child, falling in love with someone new. Didn't that prove how fickle she was? How she was 'no better than she should be', as her mother was so fond of accusing her. How terrible to have to admit such a thing, or to confess that she'd recklessly lain with a boy without giving any thought to the consequences. What would Harry think of her then? Daisy couldn't bear to explore these thoughts any further and pushed them firmly to one side, saying only, 'No, not now. There's no one special at all.'

'I'm glad.' He stopped walking and drew her into his arms. 'If it weren't for the war, Daisy, I'd come happily courting you for weeks, take you out and about, see you whenever I could, letting us slowly get to know each other. But who knows how long I'll be at Longtown. Not much longer, I dare say. We could be given our new postings at any time, any day now. The training must soon be over and God knows where I'll end up. We might not see each other again for weeks, months even.'

Her heart was thumping like a mad thing as she thought about this, about not being sure of when she might see Harry again, of knowing that he could be somewhere high in the sky shooting at enemy aircraft, and worse, being shot at, maybe even killed. Fear coursed through her at the unknown horrors ahead of them both, waiting to snatch all hope of happiness at the very moment they had found each other.

When he kissed her this time, Daisy put her arms about his neck and held him close, pushing her fingers up into his hair, pressing herself against him, wanting the kiss never to end. His cheeks were cold against hers but freshly shaved and smooth, smelling beguilingly of soap and clean, frosty air. His mouth was warm and demanding, searching and exploring her own with an intensity that frightened her even as it burst open that tight bud of excitement within. She sensed his vulnerability coupled with the fire of his need, and felt an answering need in herself. She wanted him, no doubt about it but whether that meant she was in love with him, or Harry with her, was another question entirely.

This thought somehow brought her to her senses and Daisy broke free from his embrace. What was she thinking of to let him kiss her with such abandonment? Delicious though it was, and despite longing for it to go on and on, she pushed him away gently. It was far too soon. Hadn't she suffered burnt fingers already for loving too easily? 'I really think we should be getting home. Mr Chapman will be waiting up.'

Harry was gazing at her, his eyes dazed with emotion yet with a hint of puzzlement in them, not quite understanding her reaction. 'Yes, of course, you're right. Oh, Daisy, I've never met anyone quite like you. I'd really love it if you'd say that you'd be my girl, if you'd write to me – when I'm posted. Will you do that?'

How could she refuse, when he was going off to war and might never come back, when even now, despite all the sensible thoughts in her head, she just longed to kiss him again? Her throat had gone all dry, choked with emotion. Daisy told herself that it would be unkind not to write, that whatever reservations she might feel inside he deserved that at least. And it didn't mean that she was committing herself to him, not in any way. If he did survive to return to her in one piece, and God help him that he did, there would be time enough to reveal her dreadful secret but not now, when the poor boy had enough on his plate. So Daisy nodded, her heart a vortex of hope and fear and need. 'Oh I will, Harry. Every day.'

'Aw, that's great!' He was still holding her in his arms, smoothing the curls from her cheek, kissing her pert nose. 'So what about next week? We could go to the pictures. I'll see what's on. Not that it matters what's on, I just want to be with you, Daisy, and to hold you. You must know by now how I feel about you. I believe some people are meant for each other, don't you?'

Daisy sighed with delight, little tremors of passion running through her as he again kissed her on the mouth, a mere butterfly kiss this time but so tender she could have wept. 'Oh, I'd like to think so, Harry, I really would. It would explain everything.' She meant that it might all have been worth it, having Percy reject her, even losing the baby if Harry could love her for ever, as she so longed to be loved.

'I felt that way the minute I saw you standing at that bus stop, looking so lost and forlorn in the pouring rain. When this blasted war is over...'

She stopped whatever he might be about to say with a gentle touch of her fingertips. 'Let's take it a bit more slowly, shall we? As you say yourself, who knows what tomorrow might bring?' Suddenly Daisy felt afraid, realising what she risked by falling in love again. If she lost Harry, she didn't think she'd recover half so well as she had from the other tragedy in her life.

He walked her home, pausing only briefly on the doorstep of the Chapmans' house to give her one last lingering kiss to which Daisy did not respond with quite her former enthusiasm, being acutely aware of twitching curtains in the front parlour.

They said their goodbyes and she waved to him as he walked away, her heart aching for him, yet how could that be? she asked herself, a sudden rush of tears blocking her vision so that she fumbled for her key in the dark. Hadn't she lost all faith in love? Hadn't she sworn never to trust a man again, and it was certainly true that the coming of war, with its impetus to make and seal friendships all in a rush before the loved one was snatched away, made it even more difficult to judge which love was fleeting and which would last the test of time. Oh, why did it all have to be so confusing?

As Daisy finally found the keyhole and was about to push in her key, the door was flung open, flooding the path and street beyond with light. She barely had the words out of her mouth to remind Mr Chapman about the black-out, before he grabbed hold of her wrist and pulled her quickly into the hall.

'What do you think you're doing, showing us all up by kissing your young man in full view of the street? Have you no shame?'

Daisy gasped. 'We weren't doing nothing wrong. Anyroad, who was there to see us in this black-out? Nobody, at least not until you put the searchlight on to us. Harry got me back by ten

155

o'clock, like you told him to, didn't he? It's only a quarter to, in point of fact, so I'll be off to me bed now, if you'll excuse me.'

She marched away from him but at the foot of the stairs he caught her again by the elbow. Daisy could hear how his breathing was strangely laboured, coming in jerky, shallow bursts, as if there was something wrong with his lungs and they weren't quite working properly. He'd taken off the jacket he wore to the office and replaced it with a cardigan, but he'd not removed the formal black tie from beneath the stiff white collar, firmly pinned in place with a gold tie pin. Daisy fixed her gaze upon it, hoping he would release her arm soon, for she hated him to come too near. He still smelled oddly, of stale sweat and old wool, and she longed to go up to bed and relive every moment of this lovely evening.

'You mustn't mind me, Daisy. I was worried about you, that's all.'

'Well, there's no need to be,' she remarked huffily.

His grip slackened and he gave a little sigh, as if alarmed by her tone. 'You aren't angry with me, are you? I'd hate you to be cross with me. You know I want only what's best for you, Daisy. I want you to be safe. It's quite a responsibility looking after a young girl, particularly one as pretty as yourself.'

She glanced into his face and saw how stricken he was, and her anger melted away instantly. He was, without doubt, an old fuddy-duddy but harmless enough. There'd been no creeping about at night, no fiddling with her bedroom door knob or attempts to touch her in an inappropriate way apart from that time in the stationery cupboard, which had no doubt been entirely accidental, she was sure of it. He was, as Harry rightly said, a silly old cove who enjoyed her youthful prettiness.

Perhaps seeing her go out with her young man this evening had upset him, made him realise that his own days for courting pretty young girls were long gone. But that was his problem, a fact of life that he must come to accept whether he liked it or not. 'Don't worry, Mr Chapman,' she said, pushing him gently but firmly away. 'I can take care of myself, thanks all the same,' and so saying, marched up the stairs.

Oh, but was it true? Could she indeed take care of herself? Daisy reflected ruefully. She certainly hadn't succeeded in doing so thus far.

Daisy saw plenty of Harry in the weeks following and life was sweet but then the bombshell dropped. Not a physical one, although it seemed equally devastating to Daisy. She was walking home from the Saturday market when Mrs Marshall called her in for a quick cup of tea and regretfully informed her that due to her delicate state of health and the need to take extra precautions and lots of rest, having lost two babies previously, she'd been forced to ask the billeting officer for Megan and Trish to be moved.

'We've written to their mother, of course, and although the poor woman has expressed her sadness that the girls have to move yet again, she understands perfectly.'

Daisy was filled with concern for her young friends. They'd been through so much together it was as if she alone, and not their mother, were responsible for them. 'But where will they go? They'll want to stop near me.'

'I'm sure they will, dear, and I'm equally sure that the billeting officer will do his best to ensure it. I did mention their fondness for you and he promised to do his utmost to keep them in the area.'

Knowing the difficulties of finding a good billet, Daisy was less convinced and made a private vow to call in at the office and put in a word on her own account. Perhaps Green Hat could help, though how could she ask for her, if she didn't even know the woman's real name? Serve her right for not paying proper attention. 'Do they know yet?'

Mrs Marshall shook her head. 'We thought it best to wait until we'd found a new home for them. Make it easier.'

Daisy could only agree with this assessment, though how she would manage to keep the devastating news quiet, she really didn't know. They'd already been in enough different billets, and had settled in here so happily. It broke her heart to think of them being moved, yet again. She understood the Marshalls' reasons, but was nonetheless concerned. All Daisy could hope to do was ensure that they went to a good place, near enough for her to visit them regularly.

She might have visited the billeting officer that

very day, had it not been a Saturday, and for what happened next. Daisy had no sooner gone next door and put away the Saturday shopping when she was called into Mr Chapman's study.

'I've taken the liberty of contacting your father. I hope you don't object, Daisy, but I was concerned for your moral welfare.'

'Moral welfare?' Daisy stared at him dumbfounded, hardly able to believe her ears. This was too much. The foundations of her world seemed suddenly to be shaking to pieces yet again. 'What are you talking about?'

'I'm talking about what you get up to with this young man of yours. I've been watching you these last weeks, kissing and canoodling at every opportunity.'

Daisy felt mortified at being spied upon in this way, and her Salford accent was very much to the fore in the tone of her reply. 'We don't get up to owt, not anything we shouldn't anyroad.' Not that it's any business of yours, you dirtyminded old bugger, she longed to add but managed not to. Instead she retreated into her usual bitterness where her parents were concerned. 'What would Dad care anyroad? He gave up on me years ago. He's never been particularly interested in what I do. He's always left my "moral welfare", as you call it, to Mam, so why should he start to take an interest now?'

'I thought he should come and talk to you, that you were in need of some parental help and advice.'

Daisy made a little tush sound deep in her throat, scoffing at the very idea. 'He'd not take

159

the trouble to walk to the bottom of our back yard to help me, let alone catch a bus or train to come up here.'

'Well, that's where you're wrong, Daisy. He did come. He's sitting in the parlour at this very moment, even as we speak, very much looking forward to seeing you.'

It was some seconds before Daisy could find her voice. 'Dad? In the front parlour?'

'Yes Daisy, so run along and talk to him, there's a good girl. I'll give you half an hour, then I'll have Mrs Chapman bring in tea and sandwiches. He'll be peckish after his journey, I dare say.'

'Aye, happen he will. Tell her to put arsenic in them.'

10

Joe Atkins was a quiet, self-effacing man, though some might describe him as weak and ineffectual. Never one to push himself forward, or offer his opinion on anything, he preferred to take the easy route and leave all the major decisions in life to his wife, which included the rearing of their only child.

He spent his days collecting folk's cast-offs in his cart and selling them on to other dealers for a bob or two. Scrap metal was on the up and up at the moment. He'd happen do all right out of this war if he played his cards right. The work required more instinct than skill, which suited him perfectly. In the evenings he would eat the supper Rita had prepared for him, keeping his head down while she ranted on over something or other, then he'd escape to the pub, or a race meeting. If he'd had a bad week and he'd no money, Joe was happier standing on a street corner talking to his mates than stopping in with his family. He avoided trouble and his wife, with equal dedication, and, as Daisy grew into a young woman and began to rebel against the strictures set by her mother, his only response was to stay out even more.

Joe was well aware that he'd neglected his only daughter, that being out of the house so much had left him with not the first idea how to talk to her. If she'd been a lad, happy to come fishing with him, or stand him a pint, it might have been different. He would've liked a son but, after Daisy's birth, Rita had made it abundantly plain that there would be no more babies. Most men would have stood up to Rita's bossiness, maybe even clocked her one now and then to bring her into line, but that wasn't Joe's style. He'd opted for a different course. Not once, in all the years of their marriage, had he ever contradicted her in anything. Some might judge this as weakness on his part, but then they hadn't seen the way she treated her own sister, or her dying mother for that matter. No, Joe didn't see his behaviour as weakness, he looked upon it as his best means of survival.

Now she'd sent him to do her dirty work, as was her wont. Not that he'd had owt to do with that other business, refusing to take any part in it.

He'd been disappointed, angry too in a way that Daisy, a child of his, should behave so wantonly but he'd said nowt to anyone about the matter. Only once had he come close to expressing an opinion to Rita on the subject.

'I'm not happy about this business,' he'd remarked mildly.

'You're not, eh?'

He'd seen the challenge in her eyes. 'Not that it's owt to do wi' me. If'n you want to give away our Daisy's babby, then you find it a home. Don't ask me to do it. That's women's work.'

'Aye, and we know what men's work is,' she'd told him, her mouth twisted in that nasty way she adopted whenever she spoke to him. 'To take their pleasure and leave us holding the babby. Oh, I'll find it a home right enough, in fact I reckon I've found one already. So you keep yer trap shut. No prattling to yer mates if I tell you whose it is.'

'No, don't tell me. I don't want to know.' And he'd walked out of the house to avoid hearing the details.

After the child had been born, and it was a boy, a part of him wished he'd let Daisy bring the kid home. It might've been nice to have a babby about the place again, the boy he'd always longed for. But then, it would never have worked. Rita would have made all their lives a misery from dawn to dusk. So happen things had worked out for the best after all.

He glanced up at Daisy now as she came into the room and was filled with a rush of pity for her. He'd forgotten how pretty she was with all that mass of bright golden brown curls. No wonder the chaps all fell for her but she wasn't a bad lass, only a bit daft and dizzy, as many were at her age. She'd grow out of it, as they all did. She looked better, in fact, than he'd seen her look in a long while: lost that pastiness about her skin and was positively blooming. Happen it suited her, living here in this Cumberland village.

Daisy stood awkwardly at the door, reluctant to enter, fingers grasping tightly to the brass knob; the very shadows of this rarely used room seeming to reflect the sombreness of her mood. She expected to be faced with the inevitable questions, the silent expression of disappointment for ever evident in her father's face. Yet all her life she had only ever longed for him to love her.

When Daisy entered, he'd been sitting on the edge of Mr Chapman's armchair, straight-backed and awkward, probably wishing he'd never agreed to come or that Rita hadn't made him. As she approached he leaped to his feet and came to her with hands outstretched. 'Eeh, our Daisy, tha's lookin' reet well, all pink-cheeked and blooming.'

From his words, anyone would think he was pleased to see her, yet the truth was revealed in the way he dropped his hands before he reached her, attempted to put them in his pockets, then remembering he was in his best suit letting them hang loose at his sides, not quite sure what to do with them. It was a relief to Daisy that he made no attempt to kiss her, merely stood a few feet off, considering her, as if she were an unknown exhibit in a museum. They'd never been close. In many ways he was like a stranger to her and, in

Daisy's opinion, it was far too late to change things now.

'This is a surprise,' she said, for want of something to say.

'Aye well, when we got Mr Chapman's letter, Mother thought I should come and, er – um, have a bit of a chat like.'

'Why didn't she come herself?' Now that would have been no surprise at all. One whiff of scandal and Rita Atkins was usually on the trail like a bloodhound.

'She's not been too well lately, to tell you the truth. Not at all herself. In fact, I were glad of the excuse to come. That's why I'm here really. The fact is, Daisy, Mother wants you back home.'

'She what?' This was the last thing Daisy had expected to hear.

'She wants you to come home. Most of the evacuees are back by now, since nowt seems to be happening in the war like, so it wouldn't look odd, and that other business – well, nobody knows nowt about that, save for them involved. It were all quietly and privately arranged. Least said, soonest mended, eh? Like I say, Mother's not been so good lately and she wants you back so, in the circumstances, happen it'd be fer t'best.' It was a long speech for Joe, and left him breathless.

'In the circumstances?'

He shifted his feet, looking trapped. 'Well, we don't want any more – haccidents, now do we?' He pronounced the word with an aitch in it, as he always did when wanting to emphasise a word. 'Nay, I'm sure you've learnt from your mistakes

164

in the past, and wouldn't dream of repeating them. I told Mother as much, but she said it's better to be safe than sorry.'

'What's that supposed to mean?' Daisy could feel the usual sense of injustice fuelling her anger inside and she obstinately refused to show any sign of understanding her father's words. Why did her mother always think the worst of her? If he'd something to say, let him come right out and say it, instead of all this nonsense about Mam not being well.

Joe again shuffled his feet, glowering down at the polished toes of his Sunday best boots. He thrust his hands in his trouser-pockets and pulled them as quickly out again. Nay, but this was a bad business. Why did women have to be so blasted difficult? If she'd been a lad, he could've come straight out with it, given him a leathering, and that would've been the end of the matter. A girl was more canny, good at saying one thing and thinking another, and this lass of his was as slippy as a wet herring, more like her mother than she cared to admit. 'You know very well what she means. This young chap what you're seeing. Best you put a stop to all that nonsense, afore it all gets out of hand like. Anyroad, what with the way she's feeling right now, like I say – she needs you back home.'

'Are you saying she wants me to look after her?'

'Aye, that's about the way of it. She's done her back in, d'you see, summat to do with a slipped disc, and she can barely move an inch. Nay, she's in a proper pickle, lass, having to stop in bed all day, and sleep on a board. She needs you to look after the house, mek the meals, do the washing and so on. So here I am, to fetch you back home,' and he beamed at her, just as if he were doing her a favour.

He'd stretched the truth of course, as had Rita when she'd told him what to say. She'd strained a muscle, lifting something she shouldn't, but every disc in her spine, as with every cell in her cunning brain, was fit and strong and working well.

Truth or lie, he could see the tale wasn't working. Daisy was looking at him as if he were out of his head. 'You think I'd come back after you told me never to darken your doors again? After you threw me out and gave away my baby? You think I'd even want to stay in the same house as you? Don't make me laugh. Things haven't been easy since I left home, but life is a darned sight better than it was before and I'm certainly not leaving here now, not when I'm just settling in.'

Not when she'd just met Harry.

His face became, if possible, even more sombre and his voice adopted a doleful, censuring note, for the idea of returning to Salford without Daisy, as instructed, didn't bear thinking of. Rita would never let him hear the end of it. 'Don't let us down again, girl. I told Mother you wouldn't. Don't prove me wrong.'

Daisy's eyes filled with a rush of tears, though whether with temper or anguish she couldn't rightly have said. She blinked them away angrily. 'Oh, for goodness' sake, why can't either of you trust me? Why can't you show some faith in my

166

common sense?'

'Because you haven't got any, Daisy. You're a dreamer. Daisy Daydream that's what you are, what you've always been.'

'That's not true. You know it isn't.'

'Oh aye, it is, Daisy. You act straight from the heart without even stopping to think, that's what you do. Always did.'

'Well there are times when showing a little affection and care is no bad thing. I'd certainly have benefited from a bit more of that from you two. Mam calling me a daydream is her way of avoiding her share of the blame. How could I know about babies and suchlike if she didn't tell me? And what I did learn from my friends was mainly old wives' tales and not to be relied upon. I was an innocent, just waiting to be taken advantage of, and she knows it. All right, so I made a mistake, a bad one as it turns out but for heaven's sake I've paid a high price for it. And how many times do I have to apologise, eh? Why don't you both just leave me in peace?'

Daisy thought he might see how upset she was and put his arms about her to comfort her. But in the awkward silence that followed this impassioned little speech, Joe Atkins stood, cap in hand, awkwardly wishing he'd gone and played dominoes with his mates and not got himself mixed up with women's business after all. He certainly wouldn't again.

Mrs Chapman, listening at the door for an appropriate moment to make her entrance, chose this moment of obvious silence to come sailing in, without a knock and quite unannounced.

Daisy turned away quickly to stare out of the window, her vision of the street outside blurred by unshed tears. 'Ah, there you are dear. I do hope you are having a lovely visit with your father. I've made tea and sandwiches for him. Go and fetch the tray from the kitchen, Daisy, there's a good girl.'

The pair of them stood in the street as Daisy explained with a calm and measured firmness, why she wouldn't be returning with him to Salford. The last hour had passed with painful slowness with Mrs Chapman performing her social role of hostess with an increasing desperation, doing her utmost to maintain a flow of polite conversation while Joe responded in awkward monosyllables and Daisy had simply wished the floor would open and swallow them all up.

Daisy was saying how it was far too late to play happy families. 'You both had your chance and you let me down, every bit as badly as you seem to think I failed you. Let's be honest, neither you nor Mam ever had much time for me, and were probably glad to see the back of me. Let's just leave things as they are, shall we?'

Joe looked disconcerted by such plain speaking and, as usual when confronted with an un-palatable truth, avoided responsibility by placing any blame firmly in Rita's lap. 'It weren't my idea to give t'child away and you know how there's no stopping your mother, once she's getten an idea in her head.'

'Don't I know it.'

'But she wants you home now, to keep an eye on you properly like. If I go back without you, she'll say that it's not your place to decide what's best, that you're still under age and should do as we tell thee. Mother has only ever wanted to do what's right for you.'

'What's right for her, you mean.'

'That's an unkind thing to say Daisy, and unworthy of you.'

Daisy looked upon this self-righteous stranger who was her father and felt a deep sadness inside. Why wouldn't he face up to the truth and take some share of the responsibility for the mess they were in. Rita had never given consideration to anyone but herself, and Joe had never stayed in the house long enough to challenge her word of law.

'All Mam really cares about is what the neighbours would think, what people might say. That has been her yardstick all along, not my welfare, nor the child I gave birth to.'

The familiar choking sensation blocked Daisy's throat as again she ached to know where her son might be at this precise moment. Whose arms were holding him, who was kissing his soft baby cheek, changing his nappy, giving him his feed? Consequently, her tone acquired a hard edge in her parting words. 'Tell Mam I'm sorry she's not well, if that's really true, but I don't need anyone to keep an eye on me. I can look after meself these days, ta very much, and I've no intention of making me life any worse than it already is by giving in any more to her whims and fancies. I've broken free of her domineering ways and mean to remain so. Tell her that!'

Joe looked shocked. 'Nay, lass. She'll not like that. She'll not like that one bit.'

'Just tell her, that's all.'

'Eeh, well, I'll do me best,' he said, the mournful note back in his voice. 'I'll do what I can for thee, lass, but don't bank on her agreeing to leave you here. Don't bank on it at all.' If Joe knew anything about his wife, she'd never stop her scheming ways, not till they were hammering the coffin nails in.

He swung about and began to walk away, shoulders hunched, hands sliding thankfully into his pockets, as if his duty had been done and he could be himself again, at last.

It was as he turned the corner of the street that the thought came to Daisy, and she ran after him to catch him up. 'Aunt Florrie – remember? Doesn't she live here in the Lakes somewhere?'

'Aye.'

'Do you know where?'

'Near Keswick, so far as I can recall. I've no idea of the address.'

'And what's her name, her married name?'

'Pringle. She's called Florrie Pringle.'

'Thanks.' She'd never called him Dad, and she didn't now. The moment had been missed long ago.

Silence descended once again as father and daughter stood awkwardly facing each other, each wondering how to end the misery of this meeting. Joe settled the matter by jerking the neb of his cap in a gesture of farewell, muttered something about not wanting to miss his bus, then sidled away, his pace quickening with each step, as if he couldn't escape quickly enough. 'Ta ra then. We'll see you soon, happen.'

'Happen,' Daisy agreed, both somehow aware that this might be the last she ever saw of either of her parents.

Daisy didn't linger to watch him go but turned on her heels and hurried inside. She flew upstairs to her room, closed the door and leaned back against it with a sigh of relief before promptly bursting into tears.

Daisy's natural inclination was to turn to Harry for comfort, but how could she? That would involve explaining why Joe was so concerned, how he expected her to misbehave because she'd already done so once before, which would never do at all. She'd no wish to take any risks over losing Harry. She needed him too much. Finally Daisy acknowledged, to herself at least, that she was in love, but, instead of being ashamed of getting over Percy so quickly, as she should be, she felt positively brimming with excitement. Just being with Harry filled her with joy and happiness and with each passing day he became more and more important to her, the dread of separation growing ever greater for them both.

So why would she risk spoiling that by telling him stuff that would only upset him?

He was being trained to fly Tiger Moths, but even that couldn't last for ever. Some day soon, he'd be off, and then what? Daisy worried about this as she lay in her bed every night. Whenever he could wangle a day off to take her out, she'd feel sick with anticipation beforehand in case this was the day he would say goodbye. She loved him so much but sometimes she'd wonder where it was all going to lead? Would they ever get together? Would the war ever end? He loved her too, she was certain of it. Well, almost certain. But how would he feel if he knew the truth about her? What would his reaction be then?

Hadn't her mother made it clear that a man wasn't interested in second-hand goods and that he'd discover any lies she'd told him, on her wedding night. Daisy believed all of this as a matter of course, that in this respect at least, Rita must be right. It filled her with fear that Harry might find out about her murky past and decide she wasn't the girl for him. Men got funny ideas in their heads yet she didn't believe it was possible, or right, for her to keep her secret for ever.

Often, on the days they were together, happy and loving, she would scold herself for only looking on the black side, for not trusting him and only expecting the worst. After all, he'd never asked for more than she was prepared to give him. A kiss and a cuddle seemed to be enough whenever they walked out in the countryside, or when they sat in the back row at the pictures together, even when he walked her home afterwards in the black-out. This seemed to prove that he respected her, and Daisy loved him for that too.

If only she could keep that respect, even after she'd fully confided in him. Then she would know that he truly loved her. And surely he would appreciate how very young and naive she'd been at the time? All she had to do was to work out the best way to tell him.

'Have you ever had any other girlfriends, before me?' she asked him one day. 'Serious ones, I mean, where you – you know. Did *it!*' Her cheeks flushed bright crimson, yet Daisy didn't regret asking the question. This might be the very opening she needed to confess her own terrible secret.

He glanced at her, then quickly away again, shrugging his shoulders, trying to look casual and manly, but when he caught the querying look of hope and anticipation in her eye he misjudged it completely and gathered her close in his arms. 'Aw, don't look like that, love. I know chaps are supposed to have loads of experience before they settle down but, to be honest, I haven't had much at all. I've never done it with anyone, any more than you have, eh?'

The smile in his eyes as he looked down into hers was almost more painful than she could bear, for he clearly expected a negative response, and that's what he got.

'Course I haven't. What kind of girl d'you think I am? It was only that, like you say, chaps are supposed to spread their charms and get in a bit of practice first.'

'Well, not this one. I was saving myself for the right girl. Aren't I soppy?'

'Oh no, I think that's lovely.'

'And after meeting you, Daisy, I'm that glad I did.'

And her heart just melted inside at the thought

173

that he'd saved himself specially for her. Harry couldn't understand why she burst into tears.

Daisy couldn't remember a winter as cold as this one. Rivers froze over, pipes burst, roads became blocked by snow and utterly impassable, and the dreaded rationing started in earnest, cutting down on supplies of bacon, sugar, butter and other fats. It didn't lessen her own happiness one bit but Mr and Mrs Chapman rarely stopped complaining about how bad things were. Finland fell in March, Denmark was occupied in April, the blame for which Mr Chapman put squarely upon Neville Chamberlain's lap rather than Hitler's, as they'd got everything wrong from the start, in his opinion. He would explain this to them at great length each evening, as they sat with the black-out curtains drawn, listening to the wireless.

'If they'd shown more sense, we wouldn't be in the mess we're in now.'

'Yes, dear,' said Mrs Chapman, barely pausing in her knitting of balaclavas, save to correct Daisy in the mistakes she was making with her own effort, or pick up yet another stitch that she'd dropped.

It was in April too that Harry finally got his posting, to Silloth, just along the coast. He wasn't expected to be there long but it was the best news they could have hoped for, as it meant they could still see each from time to time, if not perhaps as regularly as before.

'You won't forget to write, Daisy? I'll be watching for your letters.'

174

'Every day, like I promised. And you'll write to me too.'

'Aye, but if you find your Aunt Florrie, you'll let me have the address of where you move to, won't you?'

'Oh, Harry, course I will. You'll always be the first to be told everything about me.' Well, she thought with a gentle sigh, almost everything. She'd been so much in love, so engrossed with the excitement of looking forward to her next meeting with Harry, that she'd forgotten all about her earlier determination to find Aunt Florrie. It no longer seemed quite so important. Seeing Harry, that was all that really mattered.

Mr Chapman expressed himself highly relieved when, in May, a coalition with Winston Churchill was formed, and not a moment too soon as it was swiftly followed by the fall of Holland and Belgium. A call sent out via word of mouth for whatever small craft could be made available, conveyed the frightening message that British troops were very possibly trapped with the sea in front of them and the Germans behind. Later, when pictures of the Dunkirk rescue emerged, together with stories of wounded and war weary soldiers being dramatically plucked from the beaches, it seemed that the war wasn't phoney any more. And far from boring. Defeat now seemed a terrifying possibility, making even Megan determined to do her bit.

'I've told Mrs Marshall that if she'll let us stop on a bit longer, I'll not be naughty no more. And our Trish says she won't cry in the bath never

175

again, even when she has her hair washed.'

'That's good, Megan. That's very good indeed, and what did Mrs Marshall say?'

'She said she'd ask Mr Marshall.'

So all their lives were still hanging in the balance, even the children's although Daisy hoped and prayed she could keep them safe. So far, she'd managed to stave off the proposed move by persuading Mrs Marshall to keep them on the promise that she herself would go in every evening, after work, to help put them to bed. And, being equally concerned for Mrs Marshall's health, she offered to do some heavy chores for her, in addition to the ones she did for Mrs Chapman.

Mrs Marshall protested that Daisy had enough work to do already, not being unaware of the situation in the Chapman household.

'I don't mind, really I don't. They love being here with you, and I get to see them every day.'

'But only if you have the time, Daisy.'

'I'll come whenever I possibly can, I promise. So you put your feet up and look after yourself. Just try to hang on a little bit longer. Please! You never know, they might be a real boon when the baby comes, another pair of hands you know.' And because Mrs Marshall loved children so much, and had grown quite fond of these two imps, as she called them, she'd agreed to let them stay a few more weeks. But the time for her confinement was drawing near.

'When I must finally decide what's to be done.'

It was the best Daisy could hope for.

Mrs Chapman expressed an opinion that her

neighbour was misguided and Daisy a saint. 'You're wasting your time trying to save those children, my dear. Such creatures are beyond redemption, nothing but a trial having already polluted dear Mrs Marshall's carpets and mattresses. Their mother seems to be quite unable to raise them properly, devoid of any sense, and bone idle to boot. Oh, do put the kettle on dear, I'm gasping for a cup of tea. We would certainly not have taken on anyone younger than yourself, dear Daisy, however much the authorities may have insisted.'

Daisy said nothing. Obligingly, she put on the kettle, made tea and brought it to her landlady, together with the biscuit tin. Mrs Chapman always enjoyed a wafer biscuit late in the afternoon, so long as Daisy was there to fetch it for her.

'And for what, I ask myself? For eight shillings and sixpence a week? Why, we couldn't feed a kitchen maid on that, should we be fortunate to have one,' she remarked tartly.

Daisy thought that she really had no need of a kitchen maid, not while she had her. But then Mrs Chapman invited her to sit down, help herself to a biscuit and tell her all about her day, and Daisy remembered why she liked her. She was lonely and tired, that was all. Who knew what old age would bring for any of us, Daisy concluded generously, and went to fetch herself a cup.

Laura

11

Lane End Farm kitchen had a flagged floor, now sealed but which in the old days would need to be scrubbed on a daily basis; an old fashioned range with a rocking chair beside it and a dippy rug in front of the hearth. A hinged bar still swung out over the fire from which would once hang a kettle or pan to heat water. The baking would have been done in the side oven and Laura could imagine her grandmother baking scones and pastry first when the heat was at its most intense, followed by the lighter baking and then the bread, and last of all when the oven was 'falling', the favourite tatie pot or casserole for supper. In later years, Daisy had been professional enough to install an electric cooker and it was this that Laura used for her own cooking.

Laura made a new version of chocolate mousse, the traditional sticky toffee pudding and some sourdough bread. She also tried her hand at oatcakes, or haverbread, as it was more properly called. With a little flour added for greater elasticity, it would have been eaten with every meal at one time, rolled up with hot bacon, or dipped in stews or gravy, filling hungry stomachs and supplementing meagre rations. Laura wasn't sure whether her own was quite crisp enough, and decided to roll it out thinner next time.

Tired, but satisfied with her first efforts at traditional Cumbrian fare, she headed straight for the shower. The water was blissfully hot and refreshing, soothing frayed nerves as well as tired muscles. Afterwards, she lay down on the bed and must have fallen asleep because when she woke it was quite dark, and she hadn't the faintest idea what time it was. It took a moment before Laura realised someone was banging about downstairs. An intruder, and there was something about the sounds coming up the stairs which made his identity plain. At one time her husband might have woken her with a kiss and some passionate love-making. Now, he apparently achieved the same effect by bashing pans together in her kitchen.

'Felix, this is a surprise.' She'd brushed her dark hair loose over her shoulders, quickly applied eye make-up and lipstick and slipped into a long skirt and silk shirt. Though Laura would have loved to simply slop about in jogging trousers and T-shirt after her long tiring day, Felix hated to see her anything less than smart and her current rebellion didn't stretch to annoying him any further, not until she'd achieved her object. 'How did your trip go? Get what you wanted?' She kept her tone light deliberately.

He was bashing the ice tray against the sink, hence the noise, had clearly downed one whisky already and was about to pour another. She took the tray from him and ran it under the tap, fixed the drink just how he liked it and handed it to

179

him with a smile.

He took a large swallow. 'The trip was a total waste of time and money. Complete fake. And I really don't have time for all this nonsense, Laura.' His voice sounded as brittle and cold as the ice that chinked against his glass.

'All what nonsense?' Laura leaned back against the sink, considering him, something she hadn't done properly in ages. He'd put on weight, was beginning to look positively paunchy and flabby about the face, almost florid. He'd never been the most patient of men but now his temper seemed to be growing increasingly irascible, his movements jerky and abrupt as if he was having trouble keeping control. 'I'm afraid I don't quite understand what you're talking about. The trip, or something entirely different?'

'You know damn well what I'm talking about. All this dashing back and forth up the motorway to the damn Lakes. And you said the weather was glorious. Look at it, freezing cold and starting to snow. It's a miracle I arrived in one piece.'

'Don't exaggerate Felix. The roads are all perfectly clear, I've driven out myself most days. You haven't dashed back and forth, and this is only your first visit since the funeral more than two weeks ago.'

'And my last. Get your bags packed. We're going home right now.' He shot back the whisky in one, slamming the glass down on the sink with far more force than necessary. When Laura gave no indication of moving, he continued in tight, clipped tones, 'Would you like me to do it for you?'

180

'At any other time in our marriage, help with the packing would have been welcomed. But not now, Felix. It's far too late. I'm not leaving, you see. I'm staying. Not just for a week, or for a month, but for as long as I feel like it.' This wasn't the way she'd intended to tell him but he'd driven her to it.

'I beg your pardon?' His face was not florid now, but puce, darkening to a deep crimson even before her eyes. 'Is this some kind of joke?'

'No joke. But it is certainly going to be better fun than my life has been for the last several years, with you. I've done quite a lot of thinking this last week or two, and I've made up my mind. I intend, by early summer, to reopen Lane End Farm as a guesthouse, to take over where Daisy left off when she retired all those years ago. I've thought it all through. I'll need to refurbish of course, bring the rooms up to date, have the necessary inspections done, register with the tourist board and so on, and hopefully be ready to open by early June.'

'Have you gone quite mad?'

'I don't think so. It seems an eminently sensible plan to me. I'll admit I haven't settled the finer details yet, found plumbers or whatever, but intend to do so over the next few weeks.'

His face seemed to have set like stone, rigid with temper. 'I've already made it perfectly clear to you, Laura. We are selling this house.'

Even now, when she'd finally made her decision to end her marriage, it still hurt that he didn't express any regret over the fact that she was leaving him, that his first – perhaps his only

181

thought was for the money he would lose by not selling. She blinked and turned away, took a packet of minced beef from the fridge and started to heat some olive oil in a pan. 'I don't think so, Felix. Selling wouldn't be a good idea right now.'

'So you mean to bankrupt me, do you?'

'Oh for goodness' sake, your sense of drama is magnificent. Any hole you are currently in is, I am sure, temporary. You've wriggled out of every other. Besides, I spoke to the solicitor and agricultural property isn't selling well right now, so putting it on the market wouldn't be an answer. It could take years. It would be a far better investment, he told me, to hang on to it for as long as we can.'

'What the hell does an old fuddy-duddy solicitor in some backwater know about the property market?' The sarcasm had gone and he was shouting, reaching again for the whisky bottle as if needing to refuel his anger.

Calmly Laura dropped the meat in the hot oil and began to sear it, turning it gently. 'A great deal actually. And he isn't an old fuddy-duddy but quite young and with it.'

'Ah, fancy yourself with a toy boy, eh?'

'Now who's being ridiculous?'

'I told you to leave everything to me. Didn't I say it would be a mistake your staying here? Now, on the word of some tin-pot local brief, you've decided against selling and got some foolish fantasy into your head about going into business. You imagine opening a guesthouse is the answer to your mid-life crisis, do you? And what about

182

me? I'm supposed to just smile and say fine, yes dear, do as you like dear?'

'I don't really think it is any concern of yours what I do. Not any more.' Laura selected a knife from the rack and began to chop onions.

Felix pushed his face to within inches of her own, not lowering his voice one decibel as he raged at her like a mad thing. 'Your head is *empty*, Laura, except for the cotton wool that comprises your brain. Don't overtax it. Stick to your cooking.' He was jabbing a finger hard at her skull.

Despite how her head was jerked by each stabbing motion, Laura studiously ignored it, continuing to chop onions until finally he ran out of breath and stopped. Calmly, she set the meat to one side in an earthenware casserole, and tossed the onions into the pan.

'Are you *listening* to me?'

She was finding it hard to breathe although her voice, when she finally found it, sounded remarkably calm. 'I rather thought that a guesthouse would be a good idea, and I'd enjoy the company. I get rather lonely stuck at home, all on my own the whole time.'

'Is that meant as some sort of criticism? Are you implying that I neglect you?'

'Heaven forbid! Felix, our marriage hasn't worked in years, for many reasons. It might have helped if I'd been allowed to work at the gallery. I would have loved that.' She scattered two or three mild chilli peppers on to the meat, her hand shaking slightly, hoping he wouldn't notice. She wanted him to simply accept what she had to say, and go.

'And *you* know how hopeless you would have been, far too gawky and clumsy. You'd have dropped a priceless vase, broken a valuable picture frame or some such.'

'You sound just like my father.'

'Perhaps because he and I show sense, and you don't.'

Laura could feel the tension tightening inside her, a coiled spring of emotion that threatened to break free and let fly. She knew he was deliberately attempting to provoke her. So often, in their rows, she was the one in a rage of tearful frustration who wanted to throw something, and Felix cold and manipulative.

Now, the tables had been turned and she was the cool one, outwardly at least, calm and composed about her decision, and supremely rational. She'd no intention of dissolving into tears so that he could mop them dry and tell her this was what happened when she started dreaming foolish dreams and expecting the impossible; reminding her how well he looked after her and kept her safe from harm. Of course he did. Locked up in luxurious but rigid seclusion while he got on with living his life, Laura thought. No, no, she couldn't go on any longer. Not any more. Imagining him with Miranda or some other young girl he currently fancied while she waited by the phone for him to say when, or if, he was coming home. Where was *her* life? *Her* needs? *Her* desires? Not to mention her pride and sense of self-worth.

She drew in a deep, calming breath. 'I believe

what I'm trying to say is that I'm leaving you. It wasn't an easy decision to make and it's come as something of a surprise to me too, that I've actually found the courage at last. Perhaps being left this house has helped.'

'Don't talk stupid!' Flecks of spittle from his fury spattered across her face. 'Absolutely no question of you doing anything of the sort! You can't stay here, and you certainly aren't leaving me. I won't allow it.'

Laura laughed, though there was little humour in the sound. 'And how do you propose to prevent me? You don't keep a wife by issuing an order, or sending her a fax to that effect. You do it with love and care and attention, all those things you've tended to ignore over the years. As for the house, it may have slipped your notice Felix, but it's mine. Not yours. So the decision of what to do with it is mine, and for the moment at least, I've decided to keep it.'

Laura thought, for a brief moment, that he was going to hit her and experienced a jolt of unexpected fear. Perhaps she'd finally driven him to the limits too. She moved quickly away across the kitchen, ostensibly to fetch a tin of kidney beans from the cupboard but wanting to put some distance between them, fervently wishing that she hadn't chosen this precise moment to reveal her plans. What with the threat of snow and him heading once more for the whisky bottle, it would mean he couldn't drive, so he'd be forced to stay overnight, a situation she did not relish. He might well continue in this fashion, ranting and raving at her until, finally exhausted and desperate for peace, she'd repent and back down from her stand.

Exactly as her father had done, he claimed to have misheard her. 'I'm not sure I quite got that, Laura.'

She mustn't let him bully her. Hadn't she stood up to Robert firmly enough, and could do the same against Felix if she held her nerve. Laura knew it was the only way to survive. Going back to life as she had known it at Cheadle Hulme, after catching a glimpse of what it could be here at Lane End Farm, was quite out of the question. 'Oh, I think you did. Daisy left the house to me. *Me!* I don't want to sell it. Which is my choice to make.'

He was spluttering with fury, pacing the kitchen like a caged lion, pausing occasionally to fling some fresh insult at her, about how stupid she was, how ineffectual, how she could never cope without him, how she depended upon him entirely. 'Hell's teeth, I'll not let you get away with this. You'll ruin my reputation, my *business* for God's sake, with your childish act of rebellion. You think you can go over my head as if this house has nothing at all to do with me, when we've been married all these years?'

'You know that I'm always interested in your opinion, Felix, but my decision is made.' Laura put on her brightest, hostess smile. 'Now, to more practical concerns. Have you eaten? Would you like some dinner? Oh, and if you were thinking of staying the night, due to the whisky and the worsening weather, I could make up a bed in one of the spare bedrooms. Otherwise,

186

you might care to call a taxi, while the roads are still reasonably clear.'

'You're selfish, do you know that?' he roared. 'Always were. It's *me, me, me*. That's all you care about. You haven't the first idea what you've done, have you, Laura?'

'Oh yes, I know exactly what I've done, and what I'm going to do next.' Laura was reaching for a jar of basmati rice but managed to withhold the quip that she'd just made some chilli con carne and now intended to make the rice. This wasn't the moment for silly jokes.

Perhaps he guessed her thoughts from the light-hearted tone of her voice for he snatched the jar from her hand and threw it with all his might. It hit the kitchen dresser which stood against the opposite wall, where it smashed into a dozen pieces, scattering shards of pottery all over the flagged floor, taking with it several broken cups, saucers, plates and other items.

'Dear God!' Laura put her hand to her mouth, heart racing with real fear this time.

Swinging round on his heel, he grabbed her by the arm and shook her violently, like a dog. For an instant she thought that he was about to fling her in the same direction when a voice from the door paralysed them both.

'I think it's time you left, don't you? Don't worry about the mess. I'll clear it up.'

Laura could hardly believe her eyes but she'd never been more pleased to see anyone in all her life. David Hornsby stood in the open door, looking perfectly relaxed, and as if he had every right to be there. His sheepskin coat was covered with a light scattering of snow which now he began to unbutton casually. He tugged the woollen hat from his head and unwound the loose scarf knotted about his neck but the benign smile on his face was entirely at odds with the light of grim determination in the blue eyes.

She whispered his name in a mixture of wonder and relief, at exactly the same moment as Felix yelled: 'Who the hell are you?'

David merely smiled and dumped his wet clothing into the utility room opposite, giving the impression he'd been doing that for years, which he probably had, Laura thought, whenever he came to see Daisy. Ignoring Felix completely, he walked calmly over to Laura and remarked amiably, 'Hm, something smells good. I did come on the right night, didn't I? Only, with seeing the car outside, I did wonder.'

Laura somehow managed to swallow the bolt of hysterical laughter that had come into her throat. He was telling her that he'd seen the car, been concerned, and, as before, had walked in bold as brass, just to check she was OK. In any other circumstances she'd have called that arrogant. 'Yes, yes, of course. Dinner won't be long. This is my husband, Felix. He's rightly anxious about the threat of snow which looks as if it's started already. Is it bad?' Felix still held her wrist in a punishing grip but, shaking herself free of his hold, she moved back to the cooker to check on the chilli.

'Quite a covering up on the high fells but the main roads are still clear, for now. I certainly face a cold night ahead, checking on my stock.'

It was all so civilised it was almost laughable,

were it not for Felix seething quietly beside her it might well have seemed like the start of a pleasant dinner party. Laura turned to him with a smile, determined to maintain the charade. 'I assume you'll want to be on your way then, Felix, before it gets too bad. You won't want to risk not being able to get to the gallery in the morning. Oh, sorry, I was forgetting. This is my neighbour, David Hornsby. He rents, or owns, much of the land around here and has promised to help me find out more about Daisy.'

David acknowledged the introduction with a brisk nod but did not offer to shake hands. Laura could tell by the narrowness of his gaze that Felix had been weighing up his options, toying with the notion of planting a fist on David's jaw but had begun to reconsider. Bullying a wife was easily within his grasp, tackling a fit, well-muscled male would not, perhaps, be quite so wise.

Ignoring the introduction, he strode to the door. 'Stay on for a while longer then, if that's what you want, and see where it gets you. A few months in this freezing hell-hole with only the company of peasants and you'll be begging to come back to me and civilisation. You'll come to your senses Laura, I know it.' He slammed out of the house, gunned up the engine and roared off down the lane at cracking speed. Laura had to sit down, she was shaking so badly.

'Feeling better? Or do you need more of this?' Dinner was over, although Laura had found her appetite quite gone and eaten very little. They'd demolished one bottle of wine already and David

189

was holding up another, a quirk of one eyebrow asking her consent to open it.

'Why not? Drowning my sorrows sounds like quite a good idea.'

'I'll allow you another glass only if you eat up your dinner like a good girl.'

'Don't call me that.'

'I'm sorry.' He looked startled by the snappy response to his joke, as well he might. It was so unlike her.

Laura stared gloomily down at her plate. 'I'm sorry too. It's not you that I'm angry with, so I've no right to take out my bad temper on you.'

He set the bottle to one side and sat down beside her. 'You're not in a temper. I couldn't imagine you ever being, but you are upset and have a right to be so. Any man who treats his wife in that fashion doesn't deserve to have one.'

'Nor will he have for much longer. That's what made Felix so angry. I told him about my decision to stay, which of course will mean divorce.'

'So be it! You deserve better.'

She turned and looked into his eyes. They were the palest shade of blue outlined with a rim of darker blue around the iris, looking at her with such an intensity that Laura found it impossible to break away. Even when he did so, it was only to allow his gaze to move over her face, her hair, seeming to take in every detail of her appearance, as if forming a picture he never wanted to forget, finally fastening on her mouth. 'I can't think of anything to say except something truly naff and clichéd like: did anyone ever tell you how lovely you are?'

'Why don't you say it then? Maybe I like those sort of clichés.'

Did she? Did she want this? Was she ready for it? Despite the undeniable attraction between them, was she prepared to break her marriage vows just because she'd finally decided oh a divorce? Mind whirling and emotions spinning out of control, in that moment Laura couldn't have answered her own questions. She knew only that for the first time in years, she truly wanted a man other than her husband, to kiss her.

Yet to even start along that path would lead to disaster. It was far too soon. Turning away abruptly, she couldn't prevent a small sigh of regret escaping the tightness of her chest.

Perhaps he heard, or was sensitive to her feelings for he smiled, 'Maybe I should be on my way before I run the risk of taking advantage of the situation.'

'What situation?' Eyes suspiciously bright, she found the courage to face him.

'Your delicate emotional state, and increasing inebriation on an empty stomach.'

He got up to go and for the space of a second she very nearly cried out in protest but thankfully managed not to. What on earth was happening to her, behaving like a schoolgirl? Laura followed him to the door, the warm feeling inside growing and spreading like a fever as he buttoned the sheepskin jacket, turned up his collar and hooked the scarf she handed to him, loosely about his neck. Despite her best efforts, her eyes were betraying her, revealing how very much she wanted him to stay; how she longed to forget the weather, the sheep, Felix, everything but this unexpected and indefinable need.

There was no sign of a smile now as he gathered her face gently between his hands and kissed her, a soft sweet kiss with the barest hint of passion in it. In that moment she ached to respond, to reach her arms up around his neck, may well have done so but the next moment he was stepping away from her with a small shake of his head.

'If, or when, we do get together, you and I, and I certainly hope that it is the latter, I want it to be when you've had time to give proper consideration to the implications. Goodnight, lovely Laura. Lock the door after me, and take extra-special care of yourself.'

12

Britain responded to the deepening crisis by taking down signposts, painting out names on railway stations and other hoardings, and issuing a list of instructions and new regulations.

Daisy was particularly alarmed by the one which said that 'All persons could be required to place themselves, their services, and their property at the disposal of the government.' Did that mean she too might be moved, whether she liked it or not? She wasn't concerned about leaving the Chapmans particularly, but desperately needed to stay in the area to be close to

Megan and Trish, as well as not wanting to move too far away from Harry.

Not that she'd have minded in the least if the government had decided to move her to a different job. She hated working in Mr Chapman's office. He still insisted on coming in to see her in the post room at frequent intervals, fetching her a warming mug of tea or leaning close over her shoulder, breathing down her neck while he checked that she was addressing the envelopes correctly. Often he would ask her to stay on to help him with what he termed 'a few end-of-the-day tasks', on the premise that she could be taken home in style, in his Morris car, afterwards.

There was something about the prospect of being confined with Mr Chapman in a motor car which did not appeal and Daisy always refused, saying she had to hurry home to do her chores for Mrs Chapman, so that she could then go and help look after the children next door.

'You've taken on far too much, Daisy dear. You'll wear yourself out.'

'No, no, I enjoy it. I like working about the house. I wouldn't do it otherwise.'

But one day, finally beaten down by his persistent persuasion, she agreed to stay behind. She was helping everyone else, why not Mr Chapman? Daisy spent an extra hour or more at the end of her normal work shift, cleaning out his desk and tidying his filing cabinet, which wasn't easy with him still using them. If she opened a drawer he would suddenly appear at her elbow, pressing up close as he reached in the cabinet for a file. She only had to move an inch in the wrong direction and he would choose the exact moment to move too and they'd collide, which was unnerving, or she'd trip over a pile of files and scatter them everywhere and he'd then have to help her tidy them all up.

His size seemed to grow alarmingly in the small, cluttered office, and the smell of his sweat became overpowering.

'You're a good girl,' he told her. 'But I believe you're tired. Let's go home and you can finish this job tomorrow.'

The thought of another late session in his office was depressing but it was with a vast sense of relief that Daisy watched while he locked the office door and they finally headed homeward. Except that the car wasn't waiting for him outside the office, as it should have been. After several telephone calls, Mr Chapman was hugely affronted to discover that it had been driven away by the police, all because he'd left it parked on the street all day without locking the doors, also leaving the key in the ignition.

'I have been leaving it there for years,' he shouted at the young constable who had the misfortune to inform him of this fact. 'No one would dare to steal *my* car.'

'Well, happen a German soldier might, Mr Chapman, him not knowing how important you are,' the young constable commented tactfully.

They then had to go down to the police station and Mr Chapman had to fill in a great many forms, produce several documents to prove ownership of the car, and listen to a long lecture by the desk sergeant. By the time they finally did arrive home it was to find Mrs Chapman in a fine paddy, and neither one of them dared to complain about the fact that their dinner was cold.

Laura spent most of the following morning again searching the house for any sign of a marriage or birth certificate, or diary of some sort. She found a bundle of deeds for the house which kept her happily occupied for a good hour or more struggling to decipher the old handwriting, none of which added anything further to her stock of knowledge on Daisy. Could Daisy have deposited some of her private papers with a bank? It seemed hardly likely. Laura wondered if her father had any in his possession because, if so, there was little hope of persuading him to let her see them. He had most firmly put the past behind him, determined to blot Daisy out of his life, and out of Laura's too.

The implication that she'd been generous with her favours sat oddly with everything else she'd learned about her grandmother. Daisy didn't at all seem to be the sort to have an affair.

Laura sat back on her heels and closed her eyes. There was a time when she might have said the same thing about herself, and yet last night... She put her fingers to her lips, recalling the tender moments of David's kiss. The snow had melted with the morning sun, almost as if it were part of some magical fantasy, a strange mix of dream and nightmare. Felix storming about her kitchen while she calmly made chilli and then David doing his knight-in-shining-armour bit. It had taken on a surreal quality. The meal together after Felix had roared off had been delightful and exciting. Laura had indeed wanted them to be snowed in so that he would stay and the good feeling could go on and on.

There was no denying that she'd ached for him to make love to her. Was that what she wanted? And would it have led to an affair? Or simply a one-night stand? Either way, it might well have made it more difficult for her to gain a divorce, so she really ought to take care and show more sense. She was staying on here to build herself a new life, create a new independence and for that she needed income, which meant getting the guesthouse going. Soon. It would certainly not be conducive for clear thinking to fall into bed with the first good-looking male who happened along.

Perhaps Daisy had fallen for someone in just the same way. Perhaps Daisy and Harry had married too quickly, because of the war, and discovered they weren't suited quite so well as they'd imagined? Or he'd never come back at all.

'Oh, but that would be so sad.' Laura found that she'd spoken the words out loud. She wanted Daisy to marry her sweetheart and live happily ever after, have some time together at least.

Perhaps she'd fallen for Clem, as well as his house. Was that why he'd left it to her? No, no, far too mercenary. Yet if something had happened to Aunt Florrie, it might have left Daisy and Clem living dangerously intimate lives alone at Lane

End Farm. But none of this seemed at all likely and so, in Laura's opinion, her father's condemnatory attitude towards his mother must be because of a foolish, youthful mistake, which anyone could make. What was it about men that drove them to cast the blame entirely on the woman when it quite plainly took two people to get into that sort of mess?

Laura still wondered if Daisy had some other dark secret, and, if so, how it could be discovered. If only walls really did have ears, and could speak as well, what a tale they would have to tell.

Looking in despair at the jumble of papers spread all over the rug, she tidied them away hastily and reached for the phone. Time to see old Mr Capstick. The best person to tell her about Daisy's documents was Daisy's old solicitor.

It was half past nine by the time Daisy went next door and rattled Mrs Marshall's letterbox. The door was opened by her husband.

'Oh, hello Mr Marshall, I'm so sorry to disturb you but I just popped round to say that I'm sorry I wasn't able to come and help tonight but I...' Her explanation was stopped in mid-sentence as Mr Marshall cut in with the blunt words that his wife had been taken off to hospital.

Daisy paled. 'Oh no, she isn't losing the baby, is she?'

'They're hopeful that the problem is nothing worse than simple exhaustion. There's no bleeding this time, thank God, but she has some pains in her back so just in case, they've taken her in to keep her under observation overnight. I

197

called the billeting officer and the children have been taken away.'

'Taken away?' Daisy was mortified.

'I packed their things myself. My wife is far more important to me than two waifs from Salford.'

'But...' Lost for words she took a deep breath and started again. 'Couldn't you at least have waited till I got home, Mr Marshall?'

'I'm sorry, Daisy, I know you're fond of them but as you said yourself, you weren't here and I didn't know whether you were coming later or not. Had you been, I might well have spoken to you about it, though it wouldn't have made the slightest difference. Generous as you are with your time, you can't be with them every minute, can you? You have your own work to do, after all. I'm not an unfeeling man but those two little live wires are more than Mabel can cope with right now, for all she's done her best.'

'Oh, I know she has. I know.'

'The little one, Trish, screamed the house down when I tried to explain to her that if we didn't send my dear wife away for a rest, the baby might die.'

'Oh dear, she probably thought that it was all her fault,' Daisy said. 'She's very sensitive about death, having already lost her gran, and Miss Pratt.'

'I can't help that. I must put my wife and my own child first. Megan thought at first I was saying there'd be no more room for them here, after the baby came, so she offered to sleep under the table. And when I said nobody will sleep under the table in my house, she said that it didn't bother her because she was used to it. That's where she'd slept at home when her mam had got a sailor in her bed. Really Daisy, I can't have such children around, not with a young, vulnerable baby to care for.'

'No, no, I do understand, and I'm not blaming you at all, Mr Marshall. It's just that... Did the billeting officer say where he was taking them?'

Mr Marshall shook his head. 'He said he'd find somewhere.'

Daisy felt too sick at heart to be able to respond to this without dissolving into tears. Since she'd lost her own little son, she seemed to have turned into a proper cry baby but she'd so hoped to keep the little girls close by her, where they felt secure and happy, and she could keep an eye on them. 'I'll go to the town hall tomorrow and ask where they are so that I can at least visit.'

Daisy felt sorry for Mr Marshall. The poor man was only trying to do his best for his wife, after all. The last thing they all wanted was for her to lose the baby. And Daisy was so concerned for Mrs Marshall, as well as being worried about Megan and Trish going to yet another unknown billet, that she felt quite unable to sit in the living room and listen to the wireless as she usually did at the end of the day, let alone sit and knit balaclavas and listen to Mrs Chapman's aimless chatter. She made the excuse of a headache, saying she wanted to go straight up to bed.

'Do you want a Beecham's powder, dear? Help yourself, you know where they are.'

'I'll be all right, thanks, nice as ninepence after

a good night's sleep.' No, she wouldn't, Daisy thought. She felt devastated by the loss of her two little friends, and desperate to think of some way to help them. She lay awake for hours, shedding quite a few tears into her pillow, struggling to find a solution until exhaustion finally claimed her.

Laura found old Mr Capstick living in sheltered accommodation, not at all the doddering old man she'd expected but lively and alert or, as he said himself, 'still bright-eyed and bushy-tailed'. He claimed to be one of the useless males of his generation who couldn't cope once his wife had died. At a guess he was well into his eighties so she told him he deserved a little tender care and attention after a lifetime of hard work.

'It's certainly a treat to be visited by an attractive young woman. I'm sure there must be more to it than my ageing charms. What can I do for you, my dear?'

Laughing, Laura explained who she was and how interested she'd become in finding out more about Daisy. 'Admittedly all due, in the first place, to an enormous sense of guilt. I neglected her rather, for various reasons. Now I'm absolutely gripped, keen to learn anything I can about her. I was talking to your son, Nick, and he told me that it was through trying to locate Aunt Florrie that she came to Lane End in the first place. And apparently it's Uncle Clem we should thank for the house, since he insisted on leaving it to her and not to Florrie.'

'Oh yes indeed, that is very true. Clem

wouldn't have it any other way. I'm afraid he and his wife didn't get on.'

This seemed to fit in uncomfortably well with her theory that Clem might have been Daisy's lover, and Laura wondered how to phrase her next question but, blushing slightly, decided to risk it. 'He wasn't a blood uncle though, was he? You don't think there was – well, anything between them, and that's why he chose Daisy in place of his wife?'

Old Mr Capstick put back his head and let out a great belly laugh. The chuckle rumbled from deep inside his plump stomach and soon Laura was laughing too. It was hard not to, as she'd clearly said something highly amusing. He took off his spectacles to wipe tears of laughter from his eyes, gave them a good rub with his hand-kerchief before continuing, 'Sorry to disappoint you, my dear, but nothing quite so melodramatic. Anyway, I doubt Clem would have had it in him. No, no, Florrie was a miserable old bugger and they didn't have a particularly easy marriage. Nothing suited her and she moaned from dawn to dusk about absolutely everything. As we say in these parts, she was never happy unless she had something to complain about. Daisy, bless her generous heart, was the only one who could deal with the woman.'

Laura was intrigued and yet disappointed all the same. She'd thought perhaps that this might be the answer, the secret that Daisy had kept to herself all these years. She was quite convinced that there must be another, besides the illegitimate child she bore, otherwise why call it a house of secrets? Plural! Why would her own son hate her with such a vehemence? Laura wasn't convinced this was simply because of the baby. 'Was that because of the child they lost? Nick mentioned something about it. That was perhaps why Daisy got on so well with her, because she too had lost a child.'

Old Mr Capstick glanced at her quizzically, eyes narrowing into a little frown. 'You know about that then, do you? About the child?'

'I know she had one and that he – I don't know all the details but I seem to remember when once she briefly told me the story, Daisy letting slip that it'd been a boy – and that he was given up for adoption against her will. Evidently her parents insisted that she keep the matter a secret, just as if it were something to be ashamed of.'

'That was certainly the way of it in those days, my dear. I'm afraid I can tell you nothing about the child, or about Daisy's personal life. It wouldn't be right. I acted for her in a legal capacity from time to time and maintained her confidentiality in life, therefore it is not for me to break it now that she is dead, not unless she had left strict instructions to the contrary. She was a very private person, living in seclusion up there on the side of the mountain. Though I can tell you that yes, you're right, it was a boy.'

'Thank you for that anyway.'

At that moment, a woman with a bright smile bustled in carrying a tray. 'What's this, Doris, ah tea? A gin and tonic would be more welcome.'

'Get away with you, it's only four o'clock. Not past the yard arm yet, or whatever you call it.

You'll have to make do with tea and a bun for now.' Then she gave him a wink and promised him a shot of whisky later.

'I shall look forward to it, dearest Doris. Prompt at six.' The sparring had brought a fresh twinkle to his faded grey eyes and he seemed to soften slightly as Laura poured out the tea and handed him a slice of cake. 'Daisy was lovely,' he continued, a fond smile on his wrinkled old face. 'I was very fond of her. Always ready to help others with their problems, even when she had more than enough to deal with on her own account as well as running that boarding house which kept her on the go from morning till night, I can tell you that much.'

And he did, singing Daisy's praises at great length, chattering on for some time about how she helped do the place up and took folk in, at first as if they were strays in need of care, and then for more businesslike purposes; what a wonderful cook she was and how she still found time to help on the farm, selling her eggs on Keswick market.

'She confessed to me that once she'd come close to walking out, even to packing her bags and standing them in the hall. I think this was when the place was packed full with lodgers, every bed occupied and all with their own worries and troubles about the war, and so on. "Frightened them all to death, I did" were her exact words. Can't remember what had driven her to such a course of action but she threatened to up and leave.' He laughed. 'Very determined woman, our Daisy, for all her sweet nature. Not

203

that she ever would abandon them, too soft-hearted, and they probably knew it. But she wouldn't hesitate to give them a good telling off from time to time if she thought them in need of one; sharpen their ideas up a bit.'

Laura chuckled, 'And would they behave any better afterwards?'

He smiled fondly. 'I should think so, for a little while at any rate, until their innate selfishness shone through again. But Daisy would forgive them. She was a saint that woman. No, that's not true. Everyone thought she was a saint, which isn't quite the same thing, and actually a greater responsibility.'

Frowning, Laura asked politely what he meant by that.

He blinked a little, drained his cup and set it down with care. Laura felt quite convinced that he was about to explain, but then said something quite different instead. 'In reality, I think Daisy had rather a sad life, certainly a hard one, but you would never have guessed it. Not for a moment would she allow anything to get her down. She was good at making the best of things, of doing what suited her and living for the moment. So long as she felt it to be right, it didn't matter to her whether others agreed or not. She was even prepared to put up with the gossip, for all she hated it with a venom. Daisy would simply shut her ears to it and draw more and more into herself, into her little kingdom up there.'

'What sort of gossip?'

'There's always gossip in a small community.'

'I suppose so.' Laura was intrigued. 'My father

and Daisy fell out, quite badly, when I was about seven or eight. Do you know anything about that?'

'I really couldn't say.' He frowned in thought for a moment. 'You won't remember old Clem. Died in the mid-sixties I seem to recall, probably before you were born. He reached a good age, eighty-two or three.' The old man smiled, 'But there was no hanky-panky between him and Daisy, sorry to disappoint you. He looked upon her more as a daughter.'

'I confess I would've been surprised and more disappointed, if there had been. From my own memories of my grandmother, I believe her to be an honest, upfront sort of person, except that love can have the strangest effect on people, make them do wild, unpredictable things. Anyway, whatever went wrong between her and my father perhaps makes him try to justify himself by blaming Daisy entirely.'

'Very possibly.'

'I mean, he's not an easy person for *me* to get along with, for heaven's sake. The other day he even accused *me* of having a man tucked away somewhere, as if that were the reason I was staying on.'

'When really you want to find out about Daisy?'

'Yes.' Laura thought for a moment. 'What happened about the baby? Did she ever tell Harry about him? I've been trying to find Daisy's marriage certificate, or the baby's birth certificate, so far without success. I know you say you can't talk about her personal life but I

205

wondered if there was any other place she might have stored her papers, besides the bureau? Or if there is anything more, anything at all, you can tell me about her.'

The silence went on for so long this time that, for a moment, Laura thought he might have dropped off to sleep. Then the old solicitor sat up and, perhaps refuelled by the little nod-off or the tea and several cakes he'd consumed, suddenly he seemed to brighten. 'I could tell you about Florrie. Miserable old goat that she was and a bit of a gadfly by all accounts. Utterly selfish.'

Laura agreed that would be most interesting. Unfortunately, they were interrupted in their cosy chat by Doris bringing his whisky which he routinely enjoyed before his dinner at six-thirty. Laura hadn't realised it was so late and got up to go. 'May I come again?' If hearing about the dreadful Florrie was the only way to discover more about Daisy, then why not? It might all add to the picture.

The old man looked pleased and gratified by her interest, clearly not averse to her calling again. He probably didn't get many visitors and still missed the company of his wife, so he enjoyed a bit of a gossip about the old days. They arranged a date for early the following week and Laura took her leave.

She drove home thinking of all she still needed to ask. Names, dates, whys and wherefores. Friendly as old Mr Capstick was, he had his boundaries beyond which he was not prepared to go. Evidently he was of the old school of solicitors who considered client confidentiality as tantamount to an oath of honour; one this old gentleman would never dream of breaking. Therefore, Laura needed facts, and if she couldn't get them from him, and she certainly had no wish to again ring her father, she could always contact the Public Record Office for copies of Daisy's marriage certificate. Perhaps she should have done that in the first place but it had seemed an unnecessary expense when someone probably had the simple information she needed, or it was lying about the house somewhere, perhaps in a drawer.

She drove past Beckwith Hall Farm, her gaze scanning the darkened windows for any sign of occupation, then sweeping over the empty fields for sight of him but David was nowhere to be seen and Laura felt vaguely foolish, like a schoolgirl peering over into the boy's playground for a glimpse of some fourth former she'd got a crush on.

The telephone was ringing as she walked through the door. It was Felix. 'Feeling better?'

'I beg your pardon?'

'After your little tantrum the other night.'

'*My* tantrum?' Only Felix could create mayhem and lay the blame squarely on her. Laura took a careful swallow. Losing it now wouldn't help at all. 'I'm very well, thank you. Never better.'

'Ah, lover boy came up with the goods, did he?'

'Don't be vulgar Felix. It wasn't at all that sort of dinner. I invited him out of politeness in order to be sociable and, as I've explained, because he knew Daisy.'

Having successfully ruffled her feathers, he blithely changed the subject. 'Some clients of mine are interested in the house. They're coming over to view it next Friday afternoon. We've agreed a price, assuming they like it, which will save us any estate agency fees.'

'*What?*'

'I'm sure you can arrange to be in. You've little else to do up there.' At which point the line went dead and Laura was left swearing at the dialling tone.

After a hot shower and a soothing bowl of home-made soup, Laura gathered up the bundle of letters and took them to bed to read. She'd glanced through some already, now she meant to read more. Anything to keep her mind off what she would like to do to Felix. She certainly had no intention of allowing him to bully her into selling the house.

Most were from Harry to Daisy but a few of Daisy's letters were there too. Not in any particular order, they were generally filled with plans for a future they dreamed of having together after the war. In almost every case a letter would contain some evidence of concern for others.

'*I'm worried about the girls. I haven't heard from them in ages. I'm afraid they might be unhappy again.*' They must be the two little evacuees Daisy had taken under her wing. '*I wish I could have them here with me. Should I ask Clem, do you think?*'

Many were little more than short notes

208

arranging a meeting, declaring that she still loved him, that she'd see him soon. Laura read slowly, savouring the sweet missives. Others were from Harry begging her not to get too friendly with the men who came to the farm. Would they be guests, Laura wondered, or hired workers? *'What would I do if you fell for someone else?'* was the heart-rending plea and despite her brave words to David Hornsby, Laura did feel it intrusive that she should be reading these intimate exchanges.

She could hardly wait for her next visit to old Mr Capstick and indeed he was eagerly waiting for her when she appeared at his door at the appointed hour, tea and cakes at the ready.

Carefully Laura led him back over old ground, relating what she had discovered herself from the letters, and from David Hornsby, and then reminded him gently of his promise to tell her about Aunt Florrie.

'Ah yes, indeed. The most irritating thing about the woman was that she could have helped Daisy, her own niece, right from the start, had she been so inclined and saved her a deal of misery, perhaps even further tragedy.'

'What sort of tragedy?'

'The tragedy which led to Daisy finally finding Lane End Farm.'

'Oh, do tell me more.'

13

Something must have woken her. It was still pitch dark and although Daisy felt sick with exhaustion and lack of sleep, she was wide awake and could almost swear there was someone else in the room. But how could there be, unless Mrs Chapman had popped in to see how her headache was? Wasn't that the sound of someone breathing, quite close by? And then she smelled the unmistakable scent of stale sweat and wool.

Daisy froze. Even before the covers were lifted and a heavy body slid into bed beside her, she knew who it was. She tried to move but an arm clamped itself tight around her, fat fingers starting to stroke her throat, moving slowly down to her breasts. 'Don't fret, little Daisy. I saw you were upset and I've come to give you a cuddle. Nothing like a cuddle to make a person feel better. You can cry on my shoulder, if you like.'

Daisy lay petrified, not knowing whether to scream and risk upsetting Mrs Chapman, hit out at him which could result in him turning violent and hitting her back, or suffer the soft pawing of his groping hand in silence. She opted for the latter in the hope an opportunity might present itself for her to make an escape. She wasn't optimistic. The weight of his overwarm body against hers was suffocating. Daisy could feel the pounding of her heart in her ears and her skin start to crawl as his hand lifted the hem of her nightgown, the stubby, ink-stained fingers now walking up her leg as he chanted a little nursery rhyme in her ear.

'Incy-wincy spider climbed the spout one day.'

She shot out of bed faster than a bullet and flew to the door, fumbling with the handle in her frantic anxiety to get out, until finally she wrested it open and almost fell out of the room, a jabbering Mr Chapman hard on her tail. 'It's all right Daisy. It was only a *little* cuddle. Be a good girl, there's a love, and don't make a fuss. Mrs Chapman wouldn't understand.'

'Nor do I, you dirty old bugger!'

'Daisy, please. Let me just explain...'

What it was he might have said, they were never to discover. As Mr Chapman came blundering out on to the landing, Mrs Chapman appeared suddenly at the top of the stairs in her long nightgown. Perhaps she'd come to check on Daisy's headache, or else to see what all the noise was about. It was quite by accident, in the heat and rush of the moment, that the pair collided but, for the rest of her life, Daisy would never forget the expression of total surprise on Mrs Chapman's face as she tipped backwards down the stairs, arms and legs flailing like a rag doll, her last image on this earth that of her husband prancing about stark naked on the landing in front of her evacuee.

Florrie Pringle took the letter from behind the clock where she'd tucked it more than a year ago and reread it with close attention, even though she knew the words off by heart already. She'd recognised the handwriting the moment the letter had arrived, even after all this time, and had guessed that it would carry no loving message. She'd been right, of course. Not a word of forgiveness, not even an apology for the years of silence, let alone for the bitter, cruel words that had driven her from home in the first place.

Ever since their mother had died and Dad had walked out on the arm of another woman, Florrie had spent her adolescence being bossed by her elder sister, furiously resenting the authority she insisted on exercising as of right. To be fair, Rita had probably found it hard to deal with a young girl who thought herself a bit of a flapper and liked to dance, listen to jazz and flirt with every young man in sight, and most shocking of all, smoke.

Florrie now considered where that piece of rebellion had got her. Out of stinking Marigold Court and the tenements of Salford certainly, far away from the harping criticism of her elder sister, but what had she gained in its place? A life of misery and back-breaking toil. Not at all what she'd had in mind when she'd kicked up her heels recklessly and run off with Clement Pringle, seventeen years her senior and owner, or so he'd boasted, of a large historic house in Cumberland that had been in his family for four centuries, together with nigh on seventy acres of land, not to mention grazing rights on several hundred acres more.

Florrie had imagined a Georgian mansion with a deer park, formal gardens, a wine cellar, and perhaps a housekeeper or a servant or two to answer her every need. It wasn't that Clem had actually promised her these things, nor lied to her in any way. It was more a case of leaving the finer details unexplained. She'd made the mistake of not asking specific questions, had been so desperate to escape that Florrie had never thought to take off her rose-coloured spectacles long enough to question his bragging more closely.

At thirty-seven, he'd been quite handsome in his way, funny and attentive, kind and supportive, his robust, stocky figure giving the illusion of stature and power, an instant allure to an adventure-seeking nineteen-year-old. She'd been utterly captivated. And it's not as if there were a great many suitors to choose from. Many of the young men she'd grown up with had been killed during the First War so was it any wonder that she'd snatched at the chance he offered, without pause for thought?

She still carried a clear memory of the day she'd arrived. Florrie could see herself standing in the middle of the kitchen in her high heels and the smart little frock and coat she'd bought for going away in; the entire modish ensemble completed with the very latest cloche hat in a matching periwinkle blue. Her hair had been cut in a stylish bob, her scarlet lipstick thickly applied, but instead of sitting down to a delicious dinner cooked and served by a fawning housekeeper, she was faced with a cobweb-strewn, damp wreck of a house with a leaky roof and smoky chimneys.

'Good God, when did you last take a duster to

this place?' she'd asked, her horrified gaze taking in the stack of dirty dishes left mouldering in the stone sink, the filthy towels hanging on the rack above the inglenook, and the dippy rugs all moth-eaten and caked with mud. The only tidy bit of the room amongst the clutter, was a row of filthy boots, not at all the kind of image she'd had in mind.

Clem had scratched his head and thought for a moment. 'Not since Mam were alive, I reckon.'

Through tightly clenched teeth she'd politely asked when that had been, thinking he'd say twenty years, or at least ten. It would surely take all of that time to create such mayhem. He'd thought for a bit before responding with, 'Three months last Tuesday. Mind you, she hadn't been herself for months.'

If it hadn't been so dreadful, Florrie might have laughed. Instead, she replied, 'Well, she could've washed up before she left.'

He'd been hurt, of course, by the caustic comment, had done his best to hide the wound, the first of many he would be forced to endure in the years ahead. Right then he'd tactfully explained that, as his wife, it would naturally be her task to look after him, and do all the housework. 'Isn't it like that in Salford?'

'Course it is. Don't talk so daft. I just thought ... I mean I rather expected...' But it was no good. Putting her dreams into words would only make her sound foolish and naïve, so Florrie had set them aside, along with the fancy hat and the scarlet lipstick, donned a pinny, rolled up her sleeves and set to work. It was almost like being

214

back at home and, to her utter dismay, Florrie found herself wishing she was.

The silence of the fells weighed heavily upon her. She couldn't bear the emptiness of the landscape. Their nearest neighbours were a couple of miles down the lane in the little village of Threlkeld. No one had been foolish enough to build above them, which was presumably why the house had been named Lane End Farm. Save for Blencathra Sanatorium, a bleak Victorian monstrosity for all those poor sick folk with TB forced to sleep in freezing bedrooms with the windows wide open in all weathers. They did not encourage visitors, not that Florrie would ever go near, it gave her the shivers, seeming to embody her hatred of this place.

The presence of the brooding mountain, rearing up behind the farm buildings she found overpowering and unsettling. Florrie would wander from room to room, gazing out over the empty fields below in the hope of seeing someone pass by, perhaps a local exercising their dog, then she would rush out and beg them to come in for a cup of tea and a chat. But this was too rare an occurrence to rely upon; Blencathra's austere beauty was seldom challenged save by a few crazy hikers in high summer. And Florrie would feel a desperate longing for a rain-sodden Manchester street, for the sound of children happily playing with skipping ropes and swinging round a lamp post, as she had used to do as a child, the women gossiping on their doorsteps. There was no chance of such social chit-chat here.

If she'd thought Rita to be a cold, unfeeling

woman, that was before she'd tried living with the silent, frugal Clem, who had turned out to be the most taciturn and grumpy of men, stuck in a routine which had remained unchanged for centuries, and in a house that should long since have been razed to the ground.

Florrie stared again at the letter in her hand. It amazed her that her sister had even troubled to write, let alone ask for her help. Astonishing! Rita firmly believed God had given her the right to stand in judgement over others, dealing particularly harshly with members of her own family who had, in her puritanical opinion, in some way transgressed. So it had been with Florrie in her day, and now, apparently, with her own daughter. Perhaps, Florrie thought, that was why she'd kept the letter, out of pity for the poor girl, understanding exactly what she was going through.

She tugged the sleeve of her cardigan over her hand and used it to rub a smear of dust from the oval mirror set in the mahogany mantle. The face which looked back at her was that of a stranger. It certainly showed no sign of the young woman who had once flouted convention. Florrie trailed a finger over the bruised circles beneath blue-grey eyes that had long since lost any glimmer of hope; smoothed a hand over pale, sallow skin which no longer glowed with youth, and tracked a contour of lines that pulled down a discontented mouth which did not flaunt the scarlet lips men had found to be utterly irresistible.

'You always said I'd come to a bad end, Rita. Mebbe you were right. Though I'll make damn

216

sure you never find out just how much of a mess I have made of me life.'

No, no, best she continue to do nothing about the letter, nothing at all. What other option did she have? She'd no wish to bring her tyrant of a sister back into her life, let alone drag young Daisy into the midst of this silent war zone.

Resisting the urge to tear it to shreds, she folded the letter carefully, slid it back inside its envelope and returned it to the dark recesses of the dusty mantelshelf, well hidden amongst a wad of bills that Clem never touched.

Now that had been another disappointment. The lack of money. Florrie had assumed, from the way he'd so zealously courted her, taking her out to dinner and buying her little trinkets that he was quite well placed and comfortably off. Sadly that had not been the case. It'd been all show. He'd needed a wife to help him on the farm and with no hope of finding one in this remote spot, he'd saved hard for months, then headed for the city determined to 'buy' himself a bride. Florrie had fallen for it all, hook, line and sinker.

She drew in a deep calming breath as she glanced at the clock, listening to the echo of its tick in the empty room and wondered if Clem had met with problems which made him so late home from the weekly auction mart, or whether he'd stopped off for a drink with his cronies. Not that it mattered to her one way or the other, Clem was far too careful with his money to ever have more than half a pint. His dinner was keeping warm in the oven, and she'd be off to bed

217

soon, the warmest place to be on such a cold, blustery night. However glorious the rest of the country, this little corner of Lakeland always managed to have a weather system all its own.

As if echoing her thoughts, she heard the kitchen door crash back against the wall, caught by the vicious wind no doubt. She made no move to go to him. Nor did he call out to her, or announce his arrival in any way. Why should he? No one else would be mad enough to be out on a night like this, so who else could it be but him? She could almost hear the wind chuckle with devilish delight at having gained entry at last, and a final whoosh of disappointment as Clem slammed shut the door, forcing it back outside where it belonged. She put a match to the fire she'd laid ready for his arrival and walked briskly into the kitchen.

'I'll fetch your supper.' Florrie had no intention of asking him about his day, though there were times when for no reason she could fathom, he'd readily tell her. This was apparently one of them.

'Them yows fotched good prices at the mart,' he said.

Florrie didn't trouble to reply. They either did fetch good prices, or they didn't. It was all the same to her.

She noted how he carefully put his cap to keep warm on the hook over the old kitchen range, how his boots had been placed on a piece of newspaper by the back door; odd little touches for such an unfussy man. She took the plate from the oven and placed it on the table before him. Clem picked up his knife and fork without comment and began to eat an overcooked steak and kidney pie.

Tucking lank strings of bleached blonde hair behind her ears, her one remaining vanity, Florrie stood and watched him for a moment, staring at his grey head bent to the task of eating, noting how his once handsome face was now crazed with lines, like a dried-up river bed; his proud shoulders hunched and stooped. Whatever had made him the man he was had died along with their darling Emma, and Florrie could find no pity in her heart to spare for him; she needed it all for herself.

This was the other, more poignant reason, why she hadn't written back agreeing to Rita's request. Because she'd no wish to have a baby around the place. That wouldn't do at all. An unknown child sleeping in Emma's cot? Florrie felt a shudder run through her at the very thought, knowing she could never bear it.

Don't think about Emma, she told herself. Not today. Not just now.

It was fortunate really that the modern young flapper inside her had died too. Otherwise, she'd have gone quite mad, as would Daisy, if she came here. This was no place for a lively young girl.

Then as if to make sure that she didn't weaken, Florrie snatched the letter from its hiding place and tossed it into the fire. When every last scrap had been consumed by the flames, she turned and went upstairs to bed, leaving her husband to his own company, as she did every night.

Laura began the redecorating with the smallest

219

bedroom, in case her first attempt wasn't too good. It took a full day simply to strip the paper from the walls and give the whole room a thorough scrubbing, then a further two to paint and paper it. Nevertheless, she was pleased with the result when it was finished.

'Not so useless after all, Laura old girl,' she told herself, admiring her handiwork with justified pride. 'Right, only five more to go. On to bedroom two.'

The prospective buyers came to the house prompt at two o'clock on Friday afternoon. Laura was waiting for them, not that she'd made any special preparations, as advocated by television programmes on 'how to sell your house'. She'd stripped the wallpaper and coated the old plaster of the second bedroom with size, preparatory to repapering. It gave off a pungent aroma. As she heard the car draw up outside, she calmly set down the brush on the edge of the can and only when the front doorbell sounded, did she wipe her hands on a cloth and go to let them in.

They were a middle-aged couple in their late forties, the woman with a thin, sallow complexion, not a hair out of place and lips painted a bright cerise pink. She was smartly dressed in a navy trouser suit and boots that had walked on nothing more taxing than tarmac. The man wore tweeds and brogues, as if he thought this to be appropriate gear for a day in the country. Laura smiled brightly at them. 'Mr and Mrs Carr? Ah, do come in. I was expecting you.'

The moment they stepped over the threshold

the woman wrinkled up her nose, hard. 'Is that paint I smell?'

'Indeed it is, I must confess. And size, for the wallpaper you know. It's a never-ending job isn't it? Particularly in a place as old as this.' She gave a trilling little laugh as she led them to a small room at the back. Once used as an office, clearly it hadn't been touched in years: wallpaper peeling off the walls, a torn green paper blind hung at the window and paintwork dingy and thick with grime.

The couple looked upon the room in open horror. 'Is that fungi on the ceiling Mrs Rampton?'

'I believe it must be, Mr Carr. As you will appreciate, this is an historic house in a cold area. You don't mind the cold I assume, Mrs Carr? I'm afraid it does necessitate a good deal of attention, because of damp you see. And no matter how many times I paint it, it still shows through in no time, all black and horrid, and then I have to start all over again.'

She put her hands together in mild supplication. 'Oh dear, you don't mind my describing the house, warts and all as it were, do you? I mean, I'd hate you to think I was being anything but entirely honest.'

'No, no, please proceed, Mrs Rampton. We appreciate your candour.'

Laura continued with the tour. The front parlour, once inhabited by the guests, was a little better if with a slightly musty smell to it. She'd made no effort to do any cooking today and had let the range go out so the kitchen was not only cheerless but freezing cold. Laura smiled apologetically. 'One has such problems with these old ranges, doesn't one? Still, you could always throw it out and put in central heating.'

She could see from their shocked expressions they had not budgeted for such a vast expense, and were far from impressed. They'd clearly had the cosy warmth of a modern Aga in mind.

'We were led to believe that this was a fully restored property. Completely habitable.'

'Habitable, oh indeed it is, yes, if you don't mind roughing it a bit. But to be absolutely honest with you, Mr Carr, I've just inherited this property from my grandmother and it has been sadly neglected over the years. However, as I say, with a lick of paint and a few refurbishments such as a bathroom here and there, once you've eradicated any possible dry rot and woodworm, that is, and you'll have a bargain on your hands. An absolute bargain.'

She caught the expression of panic exchanged between them as she moved them briskly along the passage. 'Now, here is the utility room, or wash house as my dear eccentric grandmother probably dubbed it. Pay no attention to the old boiler, it doesn't work, and it was only the wind which broke the panes of glass. I shall get it fixed directly, meanwhile it's securely boarded up.'

'Wind?'

'Indeed, we get positive howling gales up here, being situated on the side of the mountain, as we are. Oh dear, I wouldn't recommend you trying the taps Mrs Carr, the drain is blocked, unfortunately, at present. There seems to be some problem with the plumbing but I'm sure it's nothing that can't be remedied. Perhaps it is vermin stuck in the pipes. You know, a field mouse or rat, or...' She frowned. 'Or it may be the septic tank, I suppose, assuming there is one and not just a soakaway.'

'Soakaway, Mrs Rampton?' whimpered Mr Carr.

'Mice? Rats?' wailed Mrs Carr.

'I'm sure it's nothing at all to worry about, nothing a good plumber couldn't fix.'

'At a price,' mumbled Mr Carr as they lumbered back into the hall.

'Now, shall we go upstairs, or would you prefer to view the outbuildings, and the privy out the back?' Laura smiled upon them both beatifically.

'*Privy?*' The man barked. 'Damp? Dry rot! Woodworm! Vermin! I believe we have seen enough, Mrs Rampton. Thank you so much for your time.'

It was ludicrously satisfying to see how very quickly they escaped to their car. Laura had to sit down she was laughing so much. 'Oh dear, forgive me Daisy for maligning your memory but I hope you understand it was necessary, in the circumstances.' Wiping the tears of laughter from her eyes, she picked up her brush and went on with the painting.

'I shall finish this wall, then I'll relight the stove and cook myself a large steak for dinner. And I might open a bottle of wine. Why not?' She deserved it. No doubt Felix would ring later, and it wasn't going to be a pleasant experience.

Laura was absolutely correct in her supposition. Felix demanded a full briefing on the prospective buyers, refusing to accept her bland comments that they seemed slightly put off by the isolation and maintenance required with such an old property.

'You put them off deliberately didn't you?'

'Felix, what a thing to say.'

'What did you tell them?' He was shouting down the phone so loud, Laura had to hold it some distance from her ear. 'That it had rampant dry rot, I suppose?'

'How did you guess?' she said sweetly. 'Don't send anyone else, Felix. Remember what I said: the house is not for sale. And if you are so foolish as to try, I'll see them all off in exactly the same way.'

'Are you threatening me?'

'Of course not, darling. Simply being entirely honest, open and frank, as I was with the Carrs. Believe me I find it tiresome to have to keep repeating myself, but until you start listening, I must continue to do so. The house is not–'

'I'm not done yet, Laura. Don't think you'll beat me, because you won't. I'm not giving up on our marriage and unless you intend to ruin me, neither am I giving up on selling that damned house.'

After he rang off, Laura wondered why she didn't feel pleased that he wasn't giving up on their marriage, only deeply uneasy.

On Sunday, David took her out for a pub lunch. They drove to Borrowdale along the eastern shore of Derwentwater, taking a detour to visit Watendlath by way of Ashness Bridge, made famous by Hugh Walpole as the home of Judith Paris, then passing the Lodore Falls and on to Rosthwaite, marvelling at the graceful beauty of the silver birches, the glimpses of sparkling lake and green mountain, fresh charms revealed at every twist and turn in the road.

'From Borrowdale comes the wad to make the lead pencils for which Keswick is most famous,' David told her. *'Crayon d'anglais.* Provided riches equal to a diamond mine in its day. The area was rife with illegal digs and smuggling on secret paths and trods across the fells. I shall take you to see the pencil museum another time.'

They exchanged smiling glances, each reading more into the simple suggestion than the history of the humble pencil could possibly justify.

They took lunch at the Royal Oak at Rosthwaite, opting for spicy Cumberland sausage which David claimed was his favourite local fare. Laura told him about the Carrs and he laughed so much he got the hiccups and she had to pat him on the back.

'I must be mad to play such dangerous games. Felix isn't the sort who likes to lose. He's bound to fight back.'

'Let him. You have your rights, and it is your house.'

'Trouble is, he doesn't always play by the rules.'

He looked at her questioningly for a moment, then took her hand between both of his. 'You know where I am. Should you need a friend.'

'Thank you.' Acutely aware of her hand being

warmly enclosed by the strength of his grip, Laura felt as tongue-tied as a young girl, and then recalling his earlier words, began to giggle. 'I thought you said I was the practical, capable, no-nonsense and non-fussy type, so surely with such attributes I should be able to cope on my own?'

'Why do I get the feeling the compliment has not come across quite as I intended?'

Laura widened her eyes in pretended innocence. 'Is that what it was?'

'I did add beautiful, charming and deliciously sexy, didn't I?'

Laura shook her head slowly. 'You were comparing me to Daisy, I seem to recall, who was almost eighty when she died, I believe.'

He hung his head. 'No, it clearly didn't come across at all as I intended.' He glanced up at her and gave his lazy smile. 'What about dessert by way of recompense for my clumsiness?' He insisted she try hot gingerbread with rum butter. 'It's a traditional dish of the Lakes so I won't take no for an answer.'

'Might as well be hung for a sheep as a lamb,' Laura laughed. 'It feels sinful enough to be out with a man other than my husband.'

'We're only having lunch. There's surely nothing very wicked about eating lunch, is there?'

Still holding her hand, he dipped his lips to her fingertips and kissed them, the glint of mischief in his eyes making her heart turn right over. 'Not that I'm aware of, no.'

'You don't sound too convinced.'

'Then don't look at me like that.' She pulled

her hand free and self-consciously tidied her hair. He helped her, tucking a strand tenderly behind one ear. 'Don't. Let's stay in neutral, shall we?'

'What a spoilsport you are. I was just beginning to enjoy myself. All right, I'll engage neutral. So, what was it you were telling me about the Carrs? Ah yes, I dare say they thought they'd walked straight into a nightmare.'

'Absolutely.' Laura took a sip of her lager, steadying the race of her heart. 'You should have seen their faces when I mentioned rats blocking the drains,' and they both set off laughing all over again.

Daisy

14

Daisy fortified herself for the day ahead with a cup of tea and a scone in Storms Lunch & Tea Rooms, then stood in the tiny market place at a loss to know what to do next. Despite it not being market day, the place was bustling with people, all dashing about and plainly with some specific purpose in mind. It made her feel quite alone in the world. Stuck on the windows of a tall building proclaiming itself to be the Moot Hall, there were advertisements for a War Weapons Week that had taken place in May, and one on the dedication of a new assembly hall at Keswick School to be held in June. A badly torn poster urged the residents of Keswick to come to see *Twelfth Night*, performed by the Old Vic Players. And yet another announced that there would be dancing every Tuesday night at the Park Hotel.

Daisy felt a lump come into her throat as she thought of the dances she'd attended with Harry. It had become a regular event for them after that first date, at least until he was posted to Silloth. Despite her better judgement, she'd fallen head over heels in love, and worrying about him was now a part of her life. Loving Harry was the last thought in her mind as she slipped into sleep each night, and the first when she woke every morning. But she didn't regret loving him. Oh dear me, no. Daisy had resolved to live for the moment. It seemed the only way to cope. So long as she got his regular letters, telling her that he was fit and well, that he still loved her, what else need concern her? The war couldn't go on for ever, and then they would be together at last. Oh, and didn't she love the bones of him? He made her head positively spin whenever he kissed her, which made it difficult not to let matters run out of control. She could remember all too clearly the last time that they very nearly had; replay every blissful moment in her head.

'Harry, I must be careful,' she'd whispered, as they'd lain together in some dappled patch of woodland, all flushed and hot and rumpled from their loving. He'd lifted her blouse to fondle her breast, and she'd made no attempt to stop him. Didn't she long for him to love her properly? In no time, lost in a riot of emotion, he'd been lifting her skirt, smoothing his hand along her thighs,

228

over her flat belly, and still she didn't protest. But Daisy hadn't wanted him to think her cheap. 'What would my mother say if she saw us like this?' Oh, but didn't she just know what Rita would say?

'You can trust me, Daisy. I love you too much to risk hurting you.' But he'd sat up and lit a cigarette, drawing deeply upon it and remaining silent for a long time as if he couldn't quite trust himself, before talking about the war and how uncertain life was. 'The worst of it is, how can I bear to be away from you, knowing some other chap might snap you up while I'm gone.'

Daisy giggled as she smoothed down her skirt. 'Nobody's going to snap anything on me, take my word for it. No one shoves Daisy Atkins around, not without my say so.' Not any more, said a small voice at the back of her head.

He'd turned to her, eyes burning with an intensity she'd never seen in them before. 'If anything did happen – between us – I wouldn't mind too much. I love you, Daisy, every hair of your head, the sound of your voice, your lovely smile, every last freckle. I love everything about you that makes you who you are, so if we were to make a child, so be it. I'd love him too.'

There was a great swell of happiness in her breast. It was all going to be all right, after all. Perhaps she should tell him now, about the baby she already had? 'Oh, Harry, and I love you too. We'll make everything good between us, war or no war, I know we will. It'll all be fine. The thing is...'

He kissed her then like he never had before,

with a hunger that made her ache with renewed longing. When they broke away his eyes were dark with need. 'I'm not sure how much longer I can be satisfied with just a few kisses. I need you Daisy girl, all of you.'

'And I need you,' Daisy said on a sudden burst of shyness.

'We could always...' But she stopped the words with the flat of her hand.

'Don't say it. Don't ask anything of me, not just yet, eh? We've only been going out together for a short while and it's too soon. Where's the fire, eh? Give us a kiss and be happy with that, for now, eh?'

And he'd groaned, tossed away the butt of his half-smoked cigarette and pushing her back down into the sweet-smelling grass, proceeded to kiss her with such a passion that it made her head spin.

Daisy couldn't bear to think that a dirty old man had attempted to touch her as Harry had. Not that she had any intention of telling Harry about Mr Chapman's fall from grace. Yet another secret to carry with her through life. It would only upset him, remembering how he'd called him a silly old cove and taken exception to his lack of trust when Harry had taken her to that very first dance.

But she could cope well enough. At least she hoped so.

But then she'd naïvely imagined that she could cope with Mr Chapman's wandering hands though really she'd got off lightly, considering what might have happened. She didn't dare let

230

herself think about poor Mrs Chapman. That was too dreadful to contemplate. Poor woman. Daisy rather thought the guilt of that moment would live with her for ever. She'd gone over and over in her head how she might have prevented the accident. Perhaps if she'd not dashed so recklessly out of the room, or if she'd tried to talk rationally to him. Yet Daisy knew that would have been hopeless. Mr Chapman had not been in a rational frame of mind. He'd had his hand up her night-dress, and God knows what he might have been about to do next.

The incident was accepted locally as a tragic accident. Daisy certainly had no intention of becoming embroiled in any difficult questions to the contrary. She would never forget her employer's grey pallor on the day she'd left, for all she'd kept her mouth shut and said nothing to anyone. His face bore the look of a broken man: the confident, self-important and slightly pompous person he'd once been had gone for ever. He'd allowed the dark side of his nature to overtake him, and now he could never get back to the sunny side.

She hadn't waited for the funeral. She'd taken the money he offered, packed her bag and walked out. It had seemed the right moment to find Aunt Florrie. Catching the bus to Keswick had been simple enough; finding where her aunt lived was proving to be more problematic.

'I've a tongue in me head. All I have to do is ask,' she'd told herself when she'd first arrived but the morning was almost over and she was no nearer to fulfilling her quest to find her aunt. With

231

increasing desperation Daisy had discovered that no one had heard of Florrie Pringle, let alone have any idea where she might live.

But she wasn't for giving up. Oh dear me, no. The last thing she wanted was to look for a fresh billet with yet more strangers, or worse, be forced to return to Salford and her mother. Nothing would induce her to do such a thing. Florrie was family, after all, and she must be around here some place. All she had to do was find her, then she could write and give Harry her new address. There must be no question of losing touch with Harry. She adored him far too much to contemplate such a dreadful prospect happening. Daisy had written to tell him that she'd moved and that her new address would follow shortly.

But if she didn't find Florrie soon, she faced a night in the open, although Daisy didn't feel particularly concerned about this. She'd decided there were worse places to sleep than under the stars. It was a warm day in August so it needn't be unpleasant, even quite exciting. There was still all the afternoon ahead of her, plenty of time in which to find her aunt.

She stopped and asked several more people but then, quite worn out with trekking around the streets, headed for the quiet of Derwentwater where she got out the sandwiches she'd brought with her.

It proved to be so pleasant sitting in the sun watching the rowing boats setting out from the landings that Daisy could almost imagine herself on holiday, and not a homeless evacuee at all. A mother with her two children was paddling about in the shallows; with skirts tucked up and fishing nets in hand they made a perfect picture of family fun, and Daisy felt a surge of envy. But then, how could you tell whether the mother wasn't grieving for a husband, or at least anxiously awaiting news. Somehow Daisy didn't think they had much hope of catching even a minnow with all the giggling going on, so perhaps all was well for them after all. Daisy sighed, as if she'd been relieved of a genuine cause for concern.

Soft white clouds bounced lightly from mountain top to mountain top and she gazed upon them with awe, ignorant of their names but marvelling at their beauty; at the way the dappled sun chased the cloud shadows across their smooth, sleek slopes, the green so brilliant it almost hurt her eyes to look upon them. There was grace in every fold; pride, majesty, and an odd sort of security. Their timeless beauty seemed to cleanse her soul of the grubby fingermarks left by a dirty old man and bring peace to a sore and fearful heart.

She felt young and strong, bursting with energy and optimism, free of all restrictions. Ever since she'd left Salford, Daisy had discovered that she'd become quite adept at standing on her own two feet, as well as solving whatever problems the war, or other people, threw at her.

Look at how she'd cared for Megan and Trish: how she'd found food for them when poor Miss Pratt had unexpectedly died without them knowing, stood by them as they were moved from pillar to post. Thinking of her two friends,

Daisy modified her boast ruefully because, sadly, she'd failed to help them this time. She'd believed she could persuade Mrs Marshall to let them stay but, in the end, the poor woman's ill health had changed everything. The children had been taken to yet another strange home where they were at least safe and well cared for.

Daisy felt cast adrift, as if they'd all been buffeted about like tiny ships on the open sea, caught up in a storm not of their making and left with no one but each other to depend upon. She could only hope that they weren't too unhappy, or missing her too much. She certainly missed them. Before leaving the village, Daisy had gone into Penrith and talked to the billeting officer who'd given her the address where they'd been sent.

They'd both burst into tears at the sight of her. Megan had at once begged, 'Have you come to tek us home, Daisy?' It had near broken her heart to have to say no.

'You are all right here, aren't you?'

Silent nods had indicated that they were, Trish's mouth turned upside-down in the familiar U-shape, and Megan was clearly doing her best to be brave. 'But we miss you, Daisy.'

'And we miss the dog,' Trish added.

Daisy had given them both a hug and a kiss, smiling to herself that at least she'd been put before the dog. 'Soon as I find Aunt Florrie, I'll write. I'll keep in touch, I promise. I'll let you have my new address so that if ever there's anything wrong, you can let me know.' She didn't make any other promises; that maybe she could persuade Florrie to allow them to join her, which was what she hoped to achieve. That was far too risky.

'You'll come and see us again?' Megan wanted to know, hanging on tight to Daisy's hand while Trish wrapped her arms about Daisy's waist as if she might never let her go.

'Course I will. We're bosom pals, right? The three musketeers.' And then they'd all wept, for how could they not when parting was so painful?

Life, Daisy had discovered, at the ripe age of seventeen, was desperately uncertain and insecure and you never knew what might be waiting for you around the next corner. She was forced to admit that really she'd had very little control over what had happened to her thus far, only in the decisions she made to deal with it.

Now she was in a strange town she didn't know, looking for a woman nobody had ever heard of. Daisy had knocked on the door of every fine house which seemed a likely candidate, remembering how her mother had never stopped complaining over how her sister had got above herself, living in grand style in Keswick.

'Too posh to talk to us now. Thinks she is someone. Always did give herself airs, that one.' Just as if Rita would never dream of doing such a thing.

Several of the imposing terraced houses with their dark slate walls and bright windows looking out over the fells, had turned out to be boarding houses with landladies grumbling about the war ruining the holiday trade. Daisy had even rung the bell at the Keswick Hotel, mistaking it for a private house which looked fine enough for an aunt who had gone up in the world. Instead, she learned that some posh school called Roedean had been evacuated into it. Several other equally grand houses and hotels nearby had suffered the same fate. She didn't envy these girls in their smart uniforms, all cooped up together like chickens. Daisy valued her freedom too much.

She'd called at the station to make enquiries there, and found herself in the middle of a geography lesson in the waiting room. Daisy had begun to feel like Alice-in-Wonderland in a world gone mad, where everything was topsy-turvy and not at all what it should be. Even those houses which had not turned into something entirely different, whose doors were opened by smiling maids or the lady of the house, knew no one of the name of Florrie Pringle.

Daisy tossed the last few crumbs to the ducks swimming about on the water's edge. The sun was hot on her neck now, making her feel quite sleepy but she couldn't allow herself to succumb to a desperate need for rest. She must do her utmost to find her aunt. Focusing her mind on the problem, Daisy recalled that the last time she'd wanted help and information, on that occasion over Miss Pratt, she'd gone to a corner shop. So that's what she'd do now. Aunt Florrie must do her shopping somewhere. She'd visit every shop in town till she found the one she patronised.

A few miles outside of Keswick, living on the side of a mountain and chaffing over a life which

236

didn't suit her, Florrie pegged out her washing thinking how she longed for a bag of fish and chips and a dish of mushy peas soaked in vinegar, followed by an afternoon at the flicks with her friends. How she would love to put on her glad rags, doll herself up and go to Benson's Dance Hall. This year she would turn forty, surely young enough to still hope to find a bit of fun and romance, in place of this living death up here in the middle of nowhere?

She'd soon been disabused of any hopes for a lively social life amongst the country set. No hunt balls or harvest suppers for Florrie. A church coffee morning or rummage sale, and occasional visits to the Alhambra Cinema in Keswick with her nearest neighbour, Jess Jenkins, were the limits of her delights, and then only in the early days of her marriage. Florrie couldn't remember the last time she'd been out with Clem, probably when they were courting and he'd still been trying to win her. He never had time for such treats nowadays, couldn't bear to tear himself away from his precious farm.

The second shock had come when she'd learned that she was expected to help with the animals on the farm, feed the hens and calves, make milk and butter, and when a pig was killed, do all kinds of dreadful things with the bits that came out of it. She'd been thoroughly alarmed. 'What, me?'

'Aye, why not? Mam did.'

'I dare say your mam was born to it. But I'm a city girl, Clem, a townie. I haven't the first idea where to start. Oh heck, why did you choose me for a wife?'

And his eyes had darkened as they'd rested upon her. 'You know why.' And he'd taken her upstairs.

Oh aye, there'd been compensations at first, at least within the confines of the bedroom. But then in those halcyon days the expression in his dark eyes whenever he'd looked upon her had made her heart beat faster, filled as they were with intense interest and admiration, and a frank, raw need.

Life in the farmyard, however, was another matter. The kind of tasks that any country housewife would take for granted, were quite beyond her. Frequently she forgot to feed the hens, or to put some of the eggs in isinglass as she'd been told to, so they'd have none to eat when the hens went off laying. Once, she'd left the pop hole open and a fox finished off the lot. Then when they got new hens to replace them, she forgot to clip their wings and they all flew away. She just seemed to get everything wrong.

'They might fly back, don't you think?' she'd asked.

'I reckon Mr Todd has had them for his supper by now,' Clem had drily remarked.

'Well, why can't you see to them? The farm is your responsibility, after all.'

'Looking after poultry is allus the job of the farmer's wife,' Clem explained carefully, and would patiently go through the tasks expected of her all over again.

Florrie did her best but would get confused over when to plant the potatoes, leeks or other vegetables in the little plot behind the house, or she'd plant them in the wrong place and they wouldn't thrive and Clem would be forced to buy some from the market, which he said was a waste of money when they could easily grow their own. She was happy enough to feed the pet lambs he brought to her kitchen, while they were still small, but getting up at three-hourly intervals during the night and walking out on to the freezing cold fell to feed them as they grew a bit older, was another matter entirely. She refused point-blank to do it.

'If I look after the hens, it's surely your job to look after the sheep.'

'Not the pet lambs, love. They're your responsibility. It's not as if you have to go far, they're kept close to the house, after all.' So she'd wrap herself in several layers against the raw cold, pull on a pair of Clem's old boots and go out into the freezing darkness, tripping over her night-dress and hating every minute, wishing she'd never set eyes on Clem Pringle.

Now there was a war to trap her even more firmly, spending her days in an endless litany of dull chores. Today she'd fed and cleaned out the hens, churned the butter, dug some potatoes and earthed up the rest. Florrie had mended the roof on the outhouse, since she was tired of asking Clem to do it. She'd fetched the peat and chopped several logs, winter being just around the corner. She'd scrubbed and cleaned, mended and fixed, heaved and shifted, and the worst of it was that tomorrow, much of it would all have to be done over again, in addition to whatever tasks she generally did on that particular day of the week. The drudgery seemed endless.

'And our Rita thinks she's got it hard.'

Silence had become a way of life, conversation non-existent, save for Clem's stock phrases. Florrie served him his supper on this particular evening as on every other, which he ate without a word, without even lifting his head. Except that at the first mouthful he said, 'It's warm, bless it.' And as he lay down his knife and fork at the completion of the meal he'd commented, 'That were reet tasty,' just as he did every night.

In fact Florrie felt certain she could mark the progress of each day with these remarks. The moment he set foot out of the door each morning he'd tug on his cap, lift his face to the mountain as if sniffing the air and out would come another, 'We'll get a wetting afore nightfall,' or, 'We might escape it today,' depending on the direction of wind and density of cloud, but he always liked to prove that he knew better than the man on the wireless what the weather was going to do.

And when he returned, after a long day out on the hills, dog at his heels he'd say, 'It's cowd enough up theer to freeze a brass monkey.'

He never failed to go to chapel on a Sunday. Afterwards he would read his bible and, as the clock chimed ten, climb into bed in his long nightshirt, pull the covers up to his chin and remark quietly, 'A Sunday well spent brings a week of content.'

Sometimes Florrie felt she might scream as she waited for the next predictable response. She hated the dull repetition of her life, the grinding routine, the habitual treadmill of the farming year, and the knowledge that if something didn't happen soon, she'd go quite mad.

His favourite remark was to look at her, shake his head and say in his droll way, 'Nay Florrie lass, it's seeing you so cheerful what keeps me going.'

It was almost as if he enjoyed her misery.

She told herself that it didn't matter any more what she did, nor that she often saw no one from one week's end to the next. Florrie had no desire to walk into Threlkeld and seek out friends, not any more. She knew she should be grateful for small mercies: a roof over her head, food in her belly. What else need concern her? Anyone she did meet at chapel or market, would see only the superficial picture of a couple disappointed by life but giving every appearance of getting along in a contented marriage. They went through the motions of living together, doing chores, eating meals, sharing a bed even, although more out of habit than for any other reason. Clem didn't bully her, hit her or order her about, rarely in fact acknowledged her presence. He asked only that she put food on his table as and when required, keep his clothes and home in reasonable, though fortunately not pristine good order, and work every daylight hour as he did himself.

Florrie understood that this was the only way he knew how to cope. It was simply not an answer so far as she was concerned.

Rarely a civil word had been exchanged between them in years, not since that terrible

241

day. The promise of their early love affair had withered and died, killed by grief, she supposed, and she had neither the will nor the facility to resurrect it. But she mustn't think of little Emma just now, not so late in the day. She'd never sleep.

Florrie took a moment to bring her emotions back under control before plunging her hands into the soapy washing-up water. Wallowing in self-pity did no good at all, it simply leaked away the last remnants of her strength, and she needed every ounce of that, oh indeed she did.

'It's ten o'clock. I'm off to bed, Florrie.'

Lips pressed together tightly, she didn't trouble to nod or acknowledge his words in any way. Hadn't she heard them a hundred, nay a thousand times. She'd once used to ask him if he'd locked up, barred the back door, but against who or what? There was no one fool enough to come up this mountain at dark of night.

Left to herself, Florrie gave a small sigh of relief then stirred the ashes of the fire, pulling the few remnants of unburnt logs together to kindle a flame. Over a comforting mug of hot, sweet tea, she pulled out an old Christmas card she'd kept, safely tucked into her knitting bag. It was from Daisy. The childlike, cursive handwriting informed Florrie that she'd recently been evacuated to the Lakes, was being forced to change billets but had failed to find her aunt, not knowing where she lived or even her married name and could she please let her have the address. The girl had sent the card via Salford, and Rita, for reasons best known to herself, had forwarded it on. She'd added a postscript, as dry and cutting as ever.

'I'm sending you this from our Daisy, though I don't suppose you're interested in your family now that you've got so high and mighty.'

But it was the last sentence which cut to the heart of her: *'Don't worry, we got rid of the encumbrance.'*

Such a heartless remark, and so typical of Rita. This presumably meant that she'd given up the child for adoption whether Daisy agreed or not. Florrie thought of Daisy, of how she must have felt at only sixteen to give birth to, and lose, a child. Devastated! Florrie, more than most, could well understand what the poor girl must have gone through. The weight of such pain and sadness bowed her own shoulders each and every day, and kept her awake night after night till she felt crippled by it. She too was not to be allowed anyone of her own to love which proved that her marriage had been a terrible mistake; the whole enterprise cursed from start to finish. But Florrie had always believed that to go back home would be an admission of failure. She'd rather die than see her sister gloating over her misery. Heart of stone, had Rita. She certainly would not understand a fraction of what her poor lass was suffering now.

Perhaps, Florrie thought, she should have agreed to help, after all. Would it have been so impossible? Guilt gnawed at her. She could at least have let Daisy spend the months of waiting here, safe from Rita's machinations. Wasn't there enough anguish and pain in the world, what with the war and all, without creating their own?

As Florrie sat watching the fire flicker and die and the last of the wood turn to ash, she came to a decision. Reaching for pen and paper, she began to write a letter. It was to Daisy, and she meant to send it to her via Rita but halfway down the first page she screwed up the paper and tossed it in the fire. She pulled out another sheet and started again. After four more sheets of paper had been woefully wasted in this way, Florrie stopped writing. This wouldn't do at all. Paper was a precious commodity. Weren't they supposed to be conserving resources, not tossing them away in the fire? There must be another way.

The next morning Clem milked their two shorthorns, did his few chores about the yard and ate a substantial breakfast of bacon and eggs, as always. Then he stood at the kitchen door tugging on his boots and cap. 'We're in for a bit of a wetting afore nightfall, I reckon. Them clouds don't look good.' So saying, he called up his dog and went on his way, shoulders slumped, head thrust forward and knees slightly bent in the characteristic gait of a man used to walking on hills.

Florrie watched him go till he was no more than a speck on the mountainside, then she buttoned on her coat, picked up the overnight bag she'd packed while he was out of the house doing his morning chores, closed the door and walked away. In her mind she could already smell the smoke and tar of Salford Quays. For the first time in years, she felt something akin to excitement. War or no war, she was going home. Daisy had given her the very excuse she needed.

15

Having spent the night huddled on a bench by the lake, and a second day knocking on doors, finally Daisy discovered that Florrie in fact lived at Lane End Farm by enquiring at a small grocer's shop on the edge of town. She managed to hitch a lift out in a milk lorry heading back to the village of Threlkeld, and now it was almost eight o'clock, the day's warmth fading as Daisy toiled up the seemingly endless lane to the farm. She was half dragging her suitcase, a stitch in her side and dripping with sweat from the exertion. She doubted she'd have had the strength to climb this mountain in the full heat of the day after her long, exhausting search.

When she reached the gate, a dirty, chipped board bearing the name Lane End, she stopped to catch her breath. The house was certainly old, a typical Lakeland farmhouse so far as Daisy could tell with its lime-washed stone walls, thick enough to keep out the worst of the mountain weather and dark, narrow windows peeping out from beneath a heavy, slate roof. Behind was a cluster of outbuildings in varying stages of decay, and some short distance from the house, half hidden in a copse of tall trees, stood what appeared to be a small stone barn, the roof partly crumbled away. A line of washing hung across a green sward of grass, beneath which hens pecked about, their soft cackling making a surprisingly comforting sound.

She set down her suitcase in the porch and hammered on the front door. 'Hello! Anyone in?'

When no one answered and the door remained firmly closed, she walked round to the back and tried again there, with the same result. It would be just her luck if Florrie had gone down into town shopping. Or perhaps she was out in the fields, tending to the sheep, or whatever farmer's wives did. Daisy didn't know what she'd expected but not this. Somehow she must have got it all wrong. It was perfectly clear that her aunt had not gone up in the world, as they had all imagined. No wonder no one had heard of Florrie in Keswick. She wasn't a fine lady living in a grand mansion. By the looks of it she was nothing more exciting than a humble farmer's wife.

And yet where was the harm in that? None at all. Daisy marvelled at Florrie's good fortune at being able to spend her life in such a wonderful place. It seemed an incredible place to live. With the mountain at its back, the farm looked out across the most magnificent countryside Daisy had ever seen. A wide valley, to the right of which could be seen the grey cluster of houses which was Keswick, and the glint of the lake where she'd sat and had her sandwiches just behind the town. Following the railway line from there led her gaze to a scar in the land which looked like a quarry, and ranged behind and beyond this seemingly endless common, were the mountains. Daisy knew none of their names, save that the highest was Helvellyn, but the scene took her breath away and she made a vow, there and then, to learn them all.

The pity of it was that Florrie had never told them about this enchanting place, never given them her address, or allowed them the opportunity to visit. Why hadn't she? Why had she lied?

Daisy fell in love with Blencathra on sight. The mountain seemed to hold out its arms to her, its softly rounded folds like an embrace and, tired though she was, she could barely restrain the urge to climb it there and then, to explore its buttresses, crags and water courses, to reach its lofty summit and look out across the whole of Lakeland. Wouldn't that be a sight?

'Noo then lass, were thoo wanting our Florrie?'

The voice broke into her thoughts, making her jump and Daisy turned to find herself gazing into a face as round, red and wrinkled as an old, well polished apple. It possessed a hawk nose and a firm, square jaw, but this was no gentleman farmer in his flat cap, made from checked woollen cloth and tugged well down over his brow. The fustian trousers had seen better days and the waistcoat, worn over a blue and white striped, collarless shirt, gaped open with not a button in sight. He wasn't smiling but he seemed to Daisy more shy than solemn, reserved in his manner rather than deliberately unfriendly, and studiously polite to this stranger who had appeared on his doorstep. If this was Aunt Florrie's husband, yet

247

again he was not at all what she'd expected. She swallowed her surprise as best she could and held out a hand in friendly greeting.

'You must be Uncle Clem.' Daisy patiently waited while he seemed to consider the out-stretched limb, wiped his own hands on the backs of his trousers then thought better of it, all the while continuing to study her with a keen, sharp-eyed gaze. When still he said nothing, she continued, 'I'm Daisy, if you remember? Florrie's niece.' She struggled to recall if she'd ever met him before when she was a child, and gave up.

Clem walked past her to push open the door. 'I know 'oo you are. Thoo'd best cum in. By leuk of you, thoo's in need o' summat to wet thi whistle.'

Why would anyone choose to build a farm on the lip of this awesome giant of a mountain? Daisy wondered as she gratefully drank the glass of cold milk and ate the cheese sandwich he provided. And how had Clem himself come to live in this remote, magical place?

'Did your family build this farm?' she asked.

'Aye.'

'Why here particularly?' Daisy waited patiently, hoping he might add something more but he continued to placidly chew on his sandwich. The room in which they sat evidently served as both kitchen and living room and had developed a warm fug, not simply from the lingering heat of the day, but also from the smoky fire. They were seated by the great inglenook which incorporated an ancient bread oven, well blackened by age and usage. Despite it having been one of the hottest

248

days of the year, it was necessary to have a peat fire burning in order to boil the kettle that swung from a crane over the fire, its own blackened surface revealing it had served this purpose for many years. On the scrubbed flags before the hearth lay a pegged rug and against one wall stood a large deal table and a cupboard with four doors, all of which stood open wide, just as if Clem might need to reach for something at a moment's notice.

He'd removed his cap carefully, she noticed, and set his boots with a line of others by the door. In their place he'd put on a pair of carpet slippers. Daisy found it hard to believe that this quiet little man had so captured her aunt's heart that she'd up and left her family and the home she loved. Perhaps she now loved the fells more.

'How is she then, Aunt Florrie?'

'She's gaily weel.'

'Has she popped out to do a bit of shopping?'

'She's away just noo, aye.'

Again they fell silent and Daisy was beginning to find the conversation hard going. She'd already run the gamut of the weather, his health and her being evacuated to the Lake District, tactfully making no mention of her need for a new billet. It seemed somehow premature to venture into those sort of details. She felt nervous of explaining more fully how and why she needed a bed for the night, for several nights in fact. Where was Aunt Florrie? If only she'd come, then they could sort everything out, woman to woman. The old man seemed lost in thought and Daisy didn't like to interrupt.

She was wilting in the over-warm room, half asleep in the chair when finally he spoke again, 'Because it always was here, and always will be.'

Daisy blinked, struggling to concentrate and recollect what they'd been talking about. 'What was?'

'The mountain.'

'Oh.' She'd forgotten that she'd asked him about how he came to be here. She rubbed the sleep from her eyes and sat up, ready to listen. 'Was the farm left to you by your father then?'

'Aye.' Clem didn't say that he loved it, or stayed here because it was beautiful, nor did he wax lyrical about its serenity or its grandeur, yet all of that seemed implicit in the simple explanation which followed, and in the pride and contentment in his faded, grey gaze. 'It's a challenge, d'you see, living here? It takes sturdy stock wi' some Norse blood in thee veins to cope wi' life on these harsh fells. The first men o' my family to farm here decided the low lying pastures was guddish ground, but they'd build a bit higher up, so's they could see who were cummin like. Them were troubled times, and no one can approach this farm without us being aware of it.'

'I can see that. It must have been hard work, building right in the teeth of the wind? It will get very windy this high up, I suppose? Won't it blow the house to bits in the end?'

Clem seemed unconcerned by such a possibility. 'Whatever thoo does the house'll be gone in the end. Four – five hundred years is but the blink of an eye when you set it against the life of a mountain. One day the slate will be wiped clean like, by nature, though Blencathra will remain.'

Daisy couldn't help thinking that it was perhaps this philosophical approach to house maintenance which explained the poor state of the property. She'd noticed dry-stone walls falling down, several outbuildings in dire need of repair and a number of slates missing on the house. Even inside it looked in a sorry state with one of the hinges on the front door missing and several window panes cracked. And the chimney must be in dire need of sweeping, judging from the cloud of smoke that hung low in the room. The whole place gave the appearance of being about to fall apart.

The old man, seemingly oblivious to all of this, was well into his stride, speaking of a subject dear to his heart. 'There's a stone circle not far off at Castlerigg. Put there hundreds, if not thousands of years ago by the first men who ever come to these hills. There's no sign of the mud huts they must hev lived in once, and the stones themselves are toppling over. Man has done his best to tame this mountain, fed his flocks on it, drained the marshes at its foot, mined deep within its belly robbing it of its secret wealth, and building cottages on its face to live in while they did so. But none of that lasts. Nothing does, save for Blencathra himself. You can't fight him, d'you see, great giant that he is. Love him or hate him, thoo has to learn to live with him because he'll outlive us all.'

Daisy had not, for one moment, expected to hear the old farmer speak so movingly, or so fully, about his home. But she understood precisely what he was trying to say. He was telling her that the mountain gave him a sense of belonging, a permanence, made him feel one with the soil, a part of the fabric of his environment. And Daisy rather thought she could easily come to share that view.

Having said his piece, suddenly he stood up, lit a tilly lamp and with a jerk of his head urged her to follow him. 'Thoo can sleep up in t'loft. Theer's only the swallows and house martins to disturb you up theer. But I'll show you wheer t'petty is fost.'

He led her outside into a clear moonlit night, almost but not quite dark, along a stony path which trailed back as far as the wooded copse, Daisy following the circle of light from his lamp. 'Here it is. Allus tek a light with thoo to t'petty, so's we know it's occupied. It shows through th'hole like.'

Cut into the front of the door, at eye level, was a small diamond shaped hole. As well as serving the current incumbent to make his presence known, it also gave the next visitor the opportunity to peep in and check for a vacancy. Taking a lamp inside sounded like an excellent idea though. 'What happens in daytime, when you don't need the tilly lamp?'

'Can you whistle?'

'No.'

'Then sing. Watch out fer t'nettles on yer way back.' He handed her the lamp without another word and left her to make her acquaintance with the ramshackle building. Daisy sat on the

252

wooden seat laughing till the tears ran down her cheeks. Why couldn't the silly old man fit a bolt on the inside? She could always try fixing one herself. In the meantime, she'd best learn how to whistle. It couldn't be any worse than her singing.

Back in the house, he was waiting for her at the foot of the stairs. Daisy dutifully picked up her bag and clattered up after him. They were surprisingly fine and wide with a carved banister rail and panelling on the walls, all sadly scratched and pitted with dirt, but beautifully crafted. She felt a knot of excitement somewhere deep inside. Something good was going to come out of finding Lane End Farm, she could sense it.

Daisy said. 'What time do you get up?'

'Early.'

'Will you wake me?'

'If you like.'

'Yes please. I'd like to help. I don't know anything about farming, but I feel sure I could learn. I want to pay me way. If you'll let me stop on for a bit, that is.'

He'd paused at a turn in the stairs to listen to this breathless little speech, lamp held high so that he could consider her with his keen-eyed gaze. She thought he might be about to say that he didn't want her to, or ask how long she intended staying, but whatever he saw in her face must have satisfied him for he simply nodded and continued to climb. Clearly a man of few words.

The loft bedroom was tiny, containing a narrow

bed, a chest of drawers and nothing else. But from its tiny window under the eaves came again that breathtaking scene, fold upon fold of mountain in a landscape that seemed to stretch into infinity.

'That's Skiddaw over there,' Clem pointed out. 'And over theer, beyond Mungrisdale Common and Coombe Height you can see the Scottish Hills and the Solway Firth, in daylight that is. The light's fading fast right now.'

Daisy felt quite certain that she'd chanced upon heaven, and who knew what tomorrow might bring? She washed her face, scrubbed her teeth in the bowl that sat upon the chest, then quickly undressed, pulled on her nightgown and stretched out between the clean sheets, toes curling with excitement.

Tomorrow she'd explore further, take a peep in all the other rooms and outhouses, perhaps climb to the top of Blencathra, this friendly giant, just to see what it felt like to stand on top of the world. Daisy knew she wouldn't sleep a wink. It was all far too wonderful and thrilling. But with two long days' exercise behind her, the fresh air and a soft feather bed to sink her tired body into, her eyelids were drooping in no time. Her last conscious thought was that she hoped Aunt Florrie would be back tomorrow, from wherever it was she'd gone.

And deep in her heart Daisy knew that whatever happened, she'd be all right here at Lane End Farm. She was quite certain of it. It almost felt like coming home.

Florrie walked up Liverpool Street with hope in her heart, revelling in the familiar smells of smoke and tar, dust and grime, the crowds of people bustling about, grim-faced and unsmiling admittedly but that was the fault of the war, not Salford. She looked with pleasure upon the rows of back to back houses, the lines of washing blowing in the breeze, and the tall chimney stacks. She heard the shunt of trains, the sound of children's laughter, the clatter of clogs on the setts. She was home.

It was only as she neared the entry leading to Marigold Court that her pace slackened and doubt crept in. What reason would she give for choosing this moment to come? Why had she only now, after nearly a year, concerned herself with Daisy?

And what sort of a welcome could she expect from Rita after the years of silence?

And then on a rush of pain came the memory of the last occasion she'd visited her home city. Oh dear God, why had she done that? What had possessed her to abandon her child, even for only two days, just so she could have a bit of fun?

She stopped walking to lean back against a wall, gasping for breath and found, to her horror, that tears were rolling down her cheeks as the memories rushed in, forcing her to confront them. Convinced she'd made a terrible mistake and still deeply homesick when she had discovered she was pregnant, Florrie had cried throughout the entire nine months. Looking back now it filled her with shame and remorse how she'd longed to be free of the *encumbrance* of

255

a baby, so that she could escape the chains of a bad marriage and life on the harsh, unforgiving fells. She'd felt that way until her beloved child had been born. Her darling, sweet, adorable Emma. The months following had been the happiest of her life, filled with joy and happiness. She'd even managed to cope better with her chores, and Clem, besotted by his new daughter, had been happy to relieve her of as many of them as he could.

But then one sunny day in April, all that happiness had crumbled to dust. Every single day of her life since, she'd longed to turn back the clock, to unwind her life like a piece of bad knitting so that she could change the pattern of it and stay at the farm. Had she done so, then surely her child would have been alive today?

Clem had made no objection when she'd asked to spend a couple of days with her family. On the contrary, he'd been pleased. 'Aye, it's long past time you went to see them, and they'll be glad to see our Emma, I'm sure. Just take care, love.'

Florrie knew he was telling her not to go out dancing or anything foolish of that sort, to be sure and come back safely to him, but she was still suffering deeply from homesickness, the quietness of the fells. She felt desperate for some fun, a bit of life and laughter. Her intention was to visit some of her old haunts, have a drink or two with friends. If she took baby Emma then Rita would be on at her the whole time not to go out, insisting she should stop in and mind her, as well as criticising everything she did for the child. Where would be the fun in that? What harm would it do to give herself a day or two away? 'I feel in need of a break, Clem. Couldn't you manage her on yer own, just fer once?'

He'd looked a bit nonplussed but had rallied quickly. 'Aye, course I can love. The rest will do you good,' he assured her, beaming proudly as he glanced over at his sleeping child in the pram standing out in the sunshine, 'and we can't both go away together, now can we, what with the lambing well under way?'

So Florrie had put on her glad rags as Clem called them, and set off with a light heart for a much-longed-for taste of city life. Her family had been surprised to see her, had chided her for not writing to warn them to expect her, and for not bringing the child. But Florrie had successfully kept up the fiction of being comfortably off. In her best frock and with the smart new coat Clem had bought her to wear at chapel, she'd certainly looked the part. They'd all been most impressed.

She'd had a good time showing off in front of her best friend, Doris Mitchell, too; performing a tango with her husband Frank and flirting outrageously with him.

It'd all been taken in good part, everyone just having a laugh but in the end Doris had butted in, told her to stick to the husband she'd got and leave hers alone, thank you very much. Florrie's was rich and Frank had nowt, only her, and she meant to keep it that way. Amused by his wife's jealousy, Frank had climbed up on to the bar counter, dragging Doris with him and done the tango with her there, tiptoeing between the glasses and sending several flying in their merry state.

It had all seemed so different from life on Blencathra, Florrie had been reluctant to leave and return home, save for her eagerness to see her child.

She'd returned to find Clem waiting for her at the station, standing forlornly by his farm truck, the expression on his face saying everything. Florrie had stopped short some twenty yards away, her heart in her mouth as fear crept through her like a black tide.

'What is it? What's happened?'

He told her then that their precious daughter was dead. On his way to the milking he'd taken a peep in at her and his shepherd's instinct had told him something was wrong.

'She didn't look right Florrie, so I went to pick her up. But it were too late.' Florrie felt as if she'd turned to stone, as if the world had stopped turning, as if everything inside her had been emptied out and destroyed. She stood listening but his words meant nothing, failing to penetrate her profound sense of disbelief. 'Theer were nowt I could do. I've brought any number of lambs back from the dead, but I could do nowt for me own lass.'

She saw the sobs well up in him, spill over, even in this public place and he an intensely private man. His whole body was shaking with the effort to control them but Florrie could do nothing to ease his distress.

She railed at him, beat him with her fists, fought him tooth and nail, screaming that he should have looked after her properly, while he struggled calmly to hold her, tears running

258

silently down his cheeks. Florrie accused him of handling her roughly; demanded to know if he'd left her to choke on her bottle, or carelessly smothered her with a blanket? How could her precious child simply fall asleep and not wake up? Deep in her heart she knew that that was what had happened. It was nothing more than a terrible misfortune, the kind of thing that occurred all the time with babies, but why to them, why to their child? Didn't she deserve one piece of happiness in her life?

How he had got her home in that state she couldn't afterwards remember. The days following were a blur, but against all reason her anger needed someone to blame and Clem was the most likely candidate.

Florrie instructed her sister not to come to the funeral and Rita wrote back tartly informing her that God had taken the child away as punishment for her own wickedness, for her immoral behaviour in the past. Deep down Florrie believed this to be true. Hadn't she once considered her own child an *encumbrance*. It took all of her will-power not to scream at the undertakers when they'd carried away the tiny coffin. She would never get over her child's death. Never.

From that day on, everything changed. Florrie knew Clem must blame her too for he'd barely looked her in the eye since, nor had she ever let him touch her again. Never. She didn't dare take the risk, in case the same thing happened to another child.

She never went out, rarely stirred from her

259

chair. If she did, she would forget what she had gone for and end up trailing from street to street as if searching for something, someone. Florrie became convinced that Emma was only just out of reach and if she searched hard enough, she would find her. She had only to glimpse a pram to be drawn to it like a magnet. She would stand and gaze upon the child within, drinking in the sight of a soft cheek, fluffy fair hair and tiny star-like fingers, seeing not an unknown child but her own precious Emma. She knew, in her heart, that it was not Emma, yet her longing was such that Florrie attempted by sheer will-power to conjure her own child in its place.

On one terrifying occasion, the baby was crying and needed a cuddle, and some part of her brain lost track of reality and she'd lifted the child from the pram. The mother came running from out of a nearby shop and shouted at Florrie. Bemused, she'd handed the baby over without a word and walked blindly away.

The pain had been so bad following that occasion, that Florrie rarely ventured far from the farm again. There were times when she chided herself for not making more of an effort to at least visit her nearest neighbours in the huddle of houses in the valley below, but Florrie shied away from the pity she saw in her friends' eyes, the sound of it in the special tone of voice they adopted whenever they spoke to her. Her loss was hard enough to bear. She'd no wish to be constantly reminded of it. Besides, she didn't trust herself. What if one of them had a baby, or her feet took her searching again? She couldn't take the risk.

Jess had clung on longer than most, trying to persuade her to continue with their Thursday afternoon outings into town, a bit of shopping, trip to the pictures followed by tea and cakes. They tried it once or twice but somehow Florrie had lost the ability to take part in small talk or chit-chat so that, in the end, Jess too had stopped coming. Florrie hadn't seen her in years.

Now she wondered what had brought her back to this place. Why put herself through all of that pain again? Hope, and dreams, Florrie had discovered, were things of the past. Her child was dead and each and every morning when she woke, she too longed for that same state of oblivion. Which must surely be a sin too. Why had she come here? She didn't belong. Not in Salford, not in the Lakes. She had no real home, no family, no one at all to love her.

Perhaps things would have been easier over these last years if she'd been honest with Rita and Joe from the beginning about her situation; if she hadn't tried to hide the truth of her disappointment in Clem, or the situation she'd faced as a young bride in a strange setting. But then she'd hoped to make a go of her marriage, despite everything. She sometimes fooled herself into believing that she might well have succeeded, had Emma lived. But there was no proof of that.

She wiped away the tears, drew a lipstick from her handbag and applied it carefully. She would put on a brave face at least.

16

He woke her early, as he had promised, and again Daisy wondered where Florrie had gone but didn't like to ask, despite her curiosity. Clem would no doubt tell her when he was good and ready.

At breakfast, which he ate largely in silence while nodding sagely at Daisy's endless chatter about her adventures and worries over Megan and Trish, there'd been no mention of a missing wife. The nearest he came to referring to Florrie's absence was when he got up from the table, paused a moment, looking slightly perplexed then quietly remarked: 'Florrie generally sees to all this.'

Daisy glanced at the already full sink and hastily offered to wash up.

Clem nodded. 'She usually fills that girt box wi' peat morning and neet, an' all. The coup cart is in t'shed.'

'Right, I'll do that too, and should I stoke up the fire to keep it going?'

'Aye, pack it wi' peats and scatter a bit o' coal on top, only a tidy bit mind. That'll see it reet fer today. I dun't know what else she does in the house. Washing and such like. I know she meks bread on a Friday, gingercake and apple pasties usually; allus thrang she is on that day. Other than that, I can't say fer sure. I could show you the yard.'

It was almost as if, Daisy worried, he wasn't expecting Florrie back. But why would that be? Where could she have gone?

His pride was evident as he showed her around the farm, not seeming to notice the way an outbuilding leaned perilously as if about to tumble over, loose guttering hung from a roof, or the way an unhinged door banged to and fro in the wind. He was too busy explaining how the calves needed feeding morning and night, on something called oilcake poddish, and the pigs mainly on household scraps. 'We likes 'em fat.' Then he told her how he used to 'butch' a bit at one time. 'After the war that were, the last one that is. Ah've gin it up now, save fer us own use.'

He instructed her on how to care for the hens, showing her the correct quantities of mash and corn. 'Awk'ard things, they are. More trouble than theer worth but we need the eggs. They 'as to be kept clean, d'you see, or you'll get problems. It's stinky in theer now. Leuks like they happen could do with a muck out. Florrie's bin a bit tekken up wi' other things lately like. Anyroad, it's not her favourite job to tackle.'

'I'll see to it.' Daisy said, eyeing them with nervous apprehension. The closest she'd ever come to a hen before was at Miss Pratt's. She supposed she could manage but would her aunt object? 'Aunt Florrie won't mind if I do a bit of tidying up, will she?'

'Nay, she'll niver notice,' and he walked away to indicate the subject was closed.

Was something wrong between them? Daisy

263

wondered. Surely not. This set up wasn't at all the kind of life she'd been led to believe her aunt was living in the Lake District. No fancy house. No servants. Yet why would she lie? Why be ashamed of this? It surely couldn't be the fault of this harmless little man who clearly still adored her, despite his main passion undoubtedly being his precious farm, and the mountain, of course.

Could that be it? Daisy wondered shrewdly. Did Florrie hate the farm? Did she not feel that she fitted in, or was she jealous of her husband's love for it? Only time would answer that puzzle, and she certainly didn't have any to spare to stand about pondering the problem. If she finished her chores by early afternoon, she could take a walk on Blencathra and see it for herself, and then write a postcard to Harry.

Rita was standing at the wash tub in the back kitchen, elbow deep in soap suds when Florrie walked in, and in that moment it was as if she'd never been away. She could smell the familiar, eye-watering odour of washing soda, feel the warm dampness cling to her hair in the steamy kitchen. Rita stopped rubbing the collar of a shirt against the rubbing board to stare at Florrie open-mouthed.

'By heck, which ill wind blew you in?'

Florrie walked over to the stove. 'I'll put t'kettle on, shall I? I'm fair parched with thirst and I dare say you need a cup of hot sweet tea for the shock.'

The tea was drunk largely in silence, Florrie having decided not to give any explanation about why she was there. She asked about Daisy but

264

Rita only shrugged her shoulders.

'Don't ask me, I'm only her mother. We've no idea where she is. She's left her billet. Gone off in a sulk somewhere, I shouldn't wonder. Allus was independent to a fault. Cut off her nose to spite her face, that one. We offered her the chance to come home but she refused. Getten hersel' another chap up there in the Lakes, so she's running true to form, no better than she should be and we know where she gets that from, don't we?'

Florrie didn't rise to the jibe. 'Have you been to see her recently then?'

'Me? No, why should I? I sent our Joe.'

'But it's been near a year.'

'She doesn't deserve no namby-pambying from me.' And then the whole sorry tale was told from start to finish, Rita savouring every word as if to justify her actions. Florrie listened in silence. What was there to say? 'Poor girl,' was all she managed in the end.

'Poor girl?' Rita looked affronted. 'What about us, her mam and dad? What about the shame, the immorality of it all? We're the ones who have to live here, amongst all the sly looks and behind-hands gossip. Poor girl my foot. She doesn't deserve one jot of sympathy, nor will she get one, not from me.'

'I shouldn't imagine she expects to,' Florrie remarked drily. Draining her cup, she set it down for Rita to refill it. A small silence followed as each sister took refuge in their own thoughts by way of defence, as if wary of confrontation. It was Rita who, itching to know what was going on, gave in first. 'So, to what do we owe this unexpected pleasure? How come you've landed up here, doing a bit o'slumming?'

'I can come and see me own family, I hope, without needing to say why?'

'I don't know about that, not after – what is it now – near twenty year? Tha's a niece tha's never seen for one thing.'

'That's not true, I have seen her. I saw Daisy when she were little, that time I paid you a visit before – before we lost our Emma.'

'Oh aye, I forgot about that. You acting daft as a brush wi' Frank Mitchell. You didn't have another then?'

'No.'

'Thought not. Too busy living the life of Riley I suppose, to want it spoiled with kids.' Rita's tone didn't soften in the slightest, not even noticing as Florrie flinched at her words. She poured some of the hot tea into her saucer, blew on it, then slurped it up from there. Florrie watched the performance in silence but the disgust must have shown in her face for Rita said, 'Don't look like that. We don't all have your chances to learn how things are done proper. We do what we wants to here. Anyroad, it's still a fair while since you come, so, what's fetched you now? Has he run off and left you?'

'Don't be daft. I found that letter of Daisy's and I was wondering how she was, that's all, sorry I didn't offer to help when perhaps I should've done. What happened to the baby?'

'What d'you think? It's getten a good home, and nobody can pin it on us. What else matters?'

'Daisy's feelings perhaps. I'd like to see her. Where was she evacuated to, and why is she moving billets? Don't you know?'

'Nay, I've no idea. She fell out wi' her dad and took herself off, happen wi' this new fella of hers.' Rita started to laugh. 'It's a bit of a turn-up, you being here when she's somewhere in your neck of the woods. Up in the Lakes.'

'Yes, I saw that she was from that Christmas card you sent on to me. I meant to write to ask exactly where but – but I've been so busy I – I forgot, and then I bethought mesel to come and see you all instead.'

'Tha should have let us know fost. I'd've put out the flags.'

Another silence, time enough for Florrie to reflect that her coming back home had been a complete waste of time. It was far too late to help Daisy, even if she could be found. But now that she was here ... Florrie cleared her throat. 'I was wondering about stopping on for a bit. You'd have no objection, would you?'

Rita's eyes flew wide and Florrie could see that her head was buzzing with questions, that she was itching to know what on earth had happened to make her sister walk out on her fancy life and rich husband. 'Well, strike me down with a wet kipper, what's getten into thee? We've no maid-servants nor butlers here, that's for sure.'

'If you're just going to be rude to me, p'rhaps it were a mistake me coming.' Florrie got up as if to go, but Rita wafted a hand at her to sit down again.

'Allus jumping on yer high horse. I niver said

tha couldn't stay, I were just making the point that I'll not wait on you hand, foot and finger. Tha's still family so I reckon there's no reason why you shouldn't stop on fer a bit, but you looks after yersen and thee hands over your ration book.'

Florrie slapped it on the table. 'Can I go and have a wash now? Or does hot water come extra?'

After a wash and a bite to eat, Florrie took a chair and went to sit at the front door, as she had used to do years ago. From here she could see people going about their business. Women carrying their shopping baskets in search of 'a bit o' summat fer tea', or 'camping' in doorways, having a 'sup o' tea' afore their men get home from the mills.

She wondered how often these conversations had concerned herself and Clem, speculating on this grand life she was supposedly living in the Lake District, or Daisy and her sudden disappearance. What a family they were although Florrie doubted they were any more unfortunate, or less moral than any other. These were hard times, always had been to Florrie's way of thinking.

She saw her old friend Doris Mitchell go by, arm in arm with Milly Crawshaw. Florrie called out a greeting but when Doris glanced in her direction, she didn't wave or come galloping over for a gossip, she looked quickly away again, chin high, as if she didn't want to know and the pair strode on up the street, faces set in a mirror image of contempt.

'And to think she was once me best friend. We

went everywhere together,' Florrie complained.

Rita, coming to join her on the doorstep at that moment, gave a loud sniff. 'If you act all toffee-nosed wi' folk, why should they bother about you? Anyroad, she doesn't trust you with her husband.'

Florrie made no reply, more hurt than she cared to admit by the rebuff. This wasn't at all what she'd hoped for. She hadn't expected it to be easy to pick up her old life where she'd left off but she'd hoped that her friends, at least, would welcome her back. Apparently she was wrong.

The muffin man came along next, calling out his wares. 'Muffins and pikelets. Buy 'em while they're fresh.'

Tempted by the prospect of hot crumpets with a dab of marg running through the holes, and needing something to cheer her, Florrie ran to fetch her purse and bought a couple for each of them. Rita didn't thank her. 'Think I can't afford to buy me own food now, do you?'

'Don't be daft! Course I don't. I just reckoned they'd be a treat.' She stowed them away in the bread jar to keep fresh till supper and went back to sit in the chair. But all the happiness she had felt when she'd decided, on impulse, to come at last to Salford, had quite evaporated. It had been a mistake. First, it had reminded her of that last visit and her subsequent loss. Secondly, Rita clearly wasn't going to make things easy for her, and last, but by no means least, she didn't seem to have any friends here either.

Florrie wondered what Clem's reaction would be when he found her note. Happy to have a bit of peace for a while, or glad to be shut of her? How long did she mean to stay, and where else could she go? Where did she belong? She'd give it a couple of weeks or so, and make up her mind then.

Daisy came to like Clem more and more with each day, each week that passed, recognising his dry wit and warming to it, his solid strength and unflappable personality. She knew he wasn't yet sixty, though he looked older, and that her aunt was considerably younger than him but she couldn't help wondering what had driven Florrie from her home? Why had she chosen to leave, and where had she gone? According to the wireless, September had been a terrible month with raids in many major cities, so that even the King had gone to see how the people were faring. Where was Florrie, and was she safe?

The year was passing quickly and Daisy knew that here in the Lakes, the back end, as they called it, was actually the start of the farming year, war or no war in a few weeks' time the tups would be put to the ewes. Would Florrie be back by then? At length, curiosity got the better of her and Daisy resolved to find the answer.

She found Clem in the barn one morning, mixing a dose for his sheep. It smelled dreadful but, determined not to be put off, she held to her purpose and asked her question. 'I was wondering about Aunt Florrie. How she was and that. Will she be back soon, d'you reckon? And where was it, exactly, that she went? I'm curious to know.' She felt all fluttery and nervous inside,

270

fearful of hearing bad news. 'I'm so looking forward to meeting her. We've never had a chance to get to know one another proper.'

'Tha's only a li'le lass, tha wouldn't understand about married foalk.'

'How will I know, if you don't tell me?'

He stood stock still to consider her, then he took off his cap and scratched his head while he gave the matter more thought. 'If anybody had telt me as being wed were so difficult, a feather would a felt me. Once I'd see'd her, I thowt I'd be in clover but she's not easy i'n't Florrie. Not an easy woman at all. 'Afe the time she leuks like she's swallowed a shilling and f'un' a penny.' A shaft of sunlight coming through the door glinted on his silver-grey hair and Daisy got the feeling that he wasn't usually so forthcoming, that in some way he was opening his heart to her. But what could she possibly say in response to this mild criticism of the absent Florrie? And if she really was an old misery-boots, as he seemed to be implying, perhaps she had good reason.

Daisy sat down on a bale of hay and waited, vowing that if she had to wait all day, she'd get to the bottom of it. She couldn't go on living in another woman's house, or start making changes to it unless she knew how she stood. It took no more than twenty seconds before he carefully replaced his cap and sat down beside her. Then he stunned her by saying that odd as it may seem, while Daisy was here in Lakeland looking for her aunt, Florrie was in Salford looking for Daisy.

Daisy's mouth dropped open in shock. 'Why didn't you tell me that in the first place?' And

271

then she saw why, reflected in the sadness of his faded grey eyes. 'You thought I'd go after her, if you told me, didn't you? And you didn't want me to go. You wanted me to stay.'

'It gets a mite lonely up here. I like the quiet but...'

'You can have too much of a good thing, eh?'

'Florrie allus says I talk more t'yows than I do to her. I used to say it's because they don't moan all the time.' He gave a shamefaced smile. 'Happen she's right.'

Daisy pressed her lips firmly together to stifle a giggle at this entrancing picture of Florrie talking to Clem and getting no answer, while Clem talked to his precious sheep because they didn't nag him or moan. But then his next words wiped the smile from her face. 'It might've been different, if 'n we hadn't lost the bairn.'

'What bairn?' Daisy edged closer, all ears, and then it was as if a plug had been drawn and Clem, once having started talking couldn't seem to stop. He told her all about the joy he'd felt when Florrie had given him a daughter, her trip to Salford to see family and friends and how he'd been left in charge of the infant, only to wake and find her dead in her cot. 'It fair shattered us both, I don't mind telling you.'

'I can imagine.'

'And she didn't have any more children?'

'Florrie weren't keen.' Clem looked away and Daisy realised she'd accidentally trodden on tricky territory.

'I see. The pain would have been terrible, of course. I can see why she would be afraid of it happening again.'

'Can you? It's not generally summat folk can understand, unless they've experienced it fer themselves.'

'I had a baby,' Daisy said, surprising herself as much as him by the sudden need to reveal her secret. He turned to stare at her wide-eyed, bushy brows raised in open curiosity. 'Didn't you know? I thought Mam wrote to Aunt Florrie.'

He shook his head. 'Nay, I wouldn't know about that. Women's stuff. Nowt to do wi' me.'

Daisy told him anyway. He'd been honest with her and she was equally so with him. He didn't judge her, or tell her she was a bad lass but by the time the tale was told, Daisy knew they were going to be firm friends.

'Leuks like we've both been in t'wars then,' and they smiled shyly at each other in perfect understanding and acknowledgement of the other's pain. Somehow or other it seemed in that moment as if they had forged a special relationship, an empathy that Daisy had never experienced with anyone else, certainly not with her own father.

'You won't tell, will you? I'm supposed to keep quiet about it. It's meant to be a secret. Mam says I've to say nothing to anyone, because of the shame.'

'And how do you feel about that?'

'I don't know.' Daisy frowned. 'I have a fella, Harry.'

'And you haven't towd him like?'

'No, I haven't told him. Not yet. Do you think I should?'

'Nay, it's not fer me to advise.'

'He's asked me to marry him.'

'Then happen, when thoo's ready to wed him, tha'll be ready to tell him about the bairn. Do you know where it is?'

Daisy shook her head. 'Mam said he's gone to a good home.'

'It were a boy then?'

Daisy nodded, quite unable in that moment, to speak, as they both considered the implications. Daisy knew instinctively that he was wishing he'd known sooner, that he would willingly have given her baby a good home and loved it with all his heart, yet for reasons best known to herself, Florrie evidently hadn't felt the same way. Daisy couldn't bear to think about how grand it would have been to have come here to have her baby, to see it brought up within her own family. And yet, if she couldn't have him all to herself, perhaps that would have caused jealousy between herself and Florrie. Perhaps Mam was right, and it was better not knowing where he'd gone, or whose arms held him.

'How about a cuppa?' Daisy offered, fiercely blinking the unshed tears away. 'Usually I have a brew about this time, do you?'

'Aye, if I get chance.'

Later, he said: 'You'll have to forgive Florrie for not offering to help. Happen Rita didn't write after all. I'm sure she would have done, had she known.'

'I'm sure she would,' Daisy agreed, and didn't tell him that Rita most definitely had written to her sister, months ago, and cursed her when she'd got no reply.

It had taken only a matter of weeks in Salford to convince Florrie that this couldn't be considered a permanent arrangement. Rita was constantly dropping hints that she'd like to see the back of her with such comments as, 'You can't feed three as cheaply as two, tha knows,' and 'There's some what can just sit on their backside and let others get on with all the work and worry.'

Florrie considered both charges to be unfair and uncalled for and would valiantly defend herself. 'I've not been well.'

'You and the rest of the flamin' army,' would be Rita's stinging response. 'You need to give yoursel' a good shake, you. Start by doing more around th'house.'

'I can't lift anything heavy. I've a bad back.'

'Don't try that one with me. You're as healthy as they come and I've told thee, there's no flippin servants to fetch and carry for thee here.'

No one could win an argument with Rita.

Certainly Joe never attempted such a thing. Florrie had at first felt some contempt for the mild mannered little man, and then a reluctant sort of affection. Joe would sit with his head buried behind the *Daily Herald*, saying nothing throughout his wife's rantings, then he'd quietly put on his cap and go off to the pub. He claimed to be full of ideas for his rag and bone business, going from strength to strength he said, with the price of scrap metal being what it was, which would help him to stash away enough savings to get them out of Marigold Court once hostilities were over. Yet he never seemed to get round to

275

putting these plans into effect. The money went out as fast as it came in. Each evening he'd go off to place a bet, or for a pint or two with his mates. Then he'd stagger home the worse for wear and from the upstairs back bedroom, Florrie would lie listening to the row coming from down below. She'd hear the crash as something was knocked over as he slumped into his chair, or if Rita flung his supper at him. She'd pull the covers over her ears to avoid listening to the furious argument which followed between husband and wife. When he was in drink, was the only time Joe had the courage to answer her back.

In a way, he reminded her of Clem and yet there was a difference. Clem might have little to say but even Florrie recognised his strength. Clem was a worker. He put everything he had into his farm and there was rarely a penny left over to squander on betting or going down to the pub despite his enjoying a half-pint now and then after an auction. Joe, on the other hand, would readily take a morning off if he was suffering from a hangover. Florrie decided that unlike Clem, who had time only for stark reality, Joe was a man of dreams, but he'd never fulfil those dreams, not in a million years. Joe was weak. He was too henpecked by a carping wife and too hell-bent on self-preservation and escape, as a result.

Yet he alone offered Florrie some sort of a welcome. 'Just think of it as yer own home, lass,' he told her.

'Nay, we're not half grand enough for that,' Rita commented drily. 'How long are we to be honoured with your ladyship's presence then?'

'I haven't decided yet.'

'Ooh, hoity-toity!'

'Nay, leave t'lass alone,' he remarked bravely. 'How can she go anywhere when t'bloody Germans are bashing our boys to bits in the skies every night. Have you noticed, Rita, that there's a war going on outside your front door? It says in the *Daily Herald* here that the East End is taking a licking, and Liverpool was bombed for four nights on the trot at the end of August. Manchester won't escape. Mark my words.'

'Never!' Rita snorted, as if even the Germans wouldn't dare to cross her, or bomb her city. 'The worst we've had is when that policeman were hit on the head by that bundle of propaganda leaflets.'

'Well, just in case, I'd best mek sure that Anderson shelter is sound and waterproof.' And off he ambled, any excuse to make his escape, as usual.

17

Joe was soon proved right. Large-scale bombing was taking place in every major city from London to Liverpool, from Bristol to Coventry. 'Britain can take it,' rang out from everybody's lips. Nobody was ready for giving up, not yet, not ever. Hadn't Winston Churchill himself urged them 'to dare and to endure' in his speech at the

Free Trade Hall only last January. Words which were to prove prophetic, for Manchester suffered its first air raid at the end of December 1940.

Rita paid not the slightest attention to the siren when it went off on the evening of the twenty-second. She was too busy moaning about how she was going to manage to feed an extra mouth all over Christmas, and berating her sister over something and nothing, as usual.

Rita was notoriously mean when it came to food, and thoroughly self-righteous. She'd ladle a pitifully small quantity of meat on to Florrie's plate together with a pile of cabbage and happily tell her that green vegetables were better for her anyway. She could make a two-ounce weekly ration of tea go further than anyone Florrie knew, mainly by scalding the leaves over and over till there was no flavour left in them. She'd once saved up her sugar coupons for weeks in the hope of having enough to make jam, but then the grocer had told her that if she could manage a month without her regular supply, she could go on doing without it. Florrie had been so pleased to see Rita put in her place, she'd laughed like a drain.

That's what the argument was about now. A spoonful of sugar.

Florrie was badly missing her own kitchen, a place where she could put on the kettle without feeling as if someone was standing over her counting how many spoonfuls she used, or whether or not she'd spilled any precious grains, which is what she'd accidentally done on this occasion. 'I need lots of sugar, to keep my

278

strength up,' she'd defended herself when Rita had flown at her with fury-filled eyes. 'I'm so tired all the time.'

'Hard luck! Thee can have saccharine, like the rest of us.'

'Damn you Rita Atkins. Can't you think of anything but food, of anyone but yourself, anyone else's needs but your own? You're that flamin' selfish you turned your own daughter out because of *your* shame, not *hers*. And God knows where she is now, poor lass.'

Somewhere, not too far off there came a loud explosion and the small house shook, scattering powdered plaster dust over both women. Neither seemed to notice, or moved an inch as they stood, almost nose to nose, hands on hips roaring and shouting at each other above the din.

'Don't you preach to me, Florrie Pringle! You could have helped our Daisy but you were too high and flamin' mighty to even write back.'

Because this was dangerously close to the truth, if an unfair distortion of it, Florrie turned her back and swung away, feeling sick to the heart at her own callousness, knowing it was too late now to do anything. The baby had been adopted and there was an end of the matter. And it was all her fault. 'I wish you'd just sent her to me, instead of writing.'

'What difference would that have made, if I had?'

'I don't know. Everything, perhaps. You know how afraid I am of getting too fond of children in case ... but if I'd been faced with it, I might've managed to get over that. You never know.'

'Oh, put away the violins.'

Florrie flushed. 'Why do you have to be so heartless? You're her mother, for God's sake. You should have done more.'

'What? What could I have done? Don't you put the blame on me. Why would I send my daughter to a sister who never visits, never writes and can't even be bothered answer a cry for help. Well? What do you say to that? What's wrong wi' us that we don't warrant more than a Christmas card?'

Once more Florrie attempted to leave, oblivious to the dust and mayhem outside, the fires that had started up and down the street and were even now being fanned by a stiff breeze. But before she reached the door, Rita made a grab for her sister's hair and yanked her back, making her scream out in agony. 'Don't you dare walk away from me, not when I'm talking to you. There's summat tha's not telling us and I want to know what it is. What fetched thee here in the first place? Why asta left your precious husband, all your riches, your posh house and servants. What is it you're after?'

Within seconds the pair were rolling on the floor, scratching and tearing at each other while countless incendiaries and high explosive bombs dropped on the city all around them. The two sisters simply raised their voices and screamed and yelled all the louder as the argument raged on, so that it looked as if one might surely murder the other before ever the war settled the matter for them. Nobody, certainly not Mr Hitler, was going to interfere with this, Rita's

280

most important mission in life.

When Joe stuck his head round the door minutes later, looking frantic, he took in the scene at a glance. 'Flamin' Nora, what's got into the pair of you? This is no time for a fisticuffs, the world's coming to an end out here,' and he bundled the pair of them under the stairs, Rita protesting loudly that she didn't want to be anywhere near her dratted sister.

'Well put your mind to it, or you'll be sharing a coffin instead.'

The following night when the siren sounded, Rita was the first to head for the shelter, Florrie and Joe hot foot behind. The three of them ran through the rushing crowds of people, some shouting for loved ones, others shrieking in fear, children crying and explosions going off everywhere. They sat huddled together in silent misery until the 'all-clear' sounded some twelve long hours later. When they finally emerged, bleary eyed, black-faced and badly shaken, it was to discover that bombs had fallen on the bus and tram depot on the corner of Eccles New Road and even a tram had been hit, killing all the passengers inside.

'We're lucky to be alive,' Florrie said, appalled by the destruction that met her eyes.

'Aye,' Joe said. 'So I'll have no more squabbling from you two. Think on, let's have peace between our own four walls for Christmas, at least.'

Back home, they moved blankets and pillows under the stairs, and since all the glass had been blown out of the windows, Joe nailed black roofing felt to the frames. 'And no more locking the doors,' he warned them. 'Just in case we need to be rescued.'

'We could be murdered in our beds,' Rita complained hotly.

'Save Hitler a job then.'

It was a grim thought. And so they spent a cold and miserable Christmas, with neither electricity, gas nor water, only a meagre fire for comfort, and cold corned beef sandwiches to eat since they couldn't cook. Nor did they take any pleasure in each other's company by way of consolation. But even Rita was too frightened to object loudly.

When Laura had taken the booking for a single room from a Mr Beazley, she'd thought nothing of it, assuming him to be a walker. Strictly speaking she wasn't open for business until next week as she still had one or two tasks to finish off but she'd decided it would be good practice before the rush started, so had gladly accepted it. Now Felix was standing on her doorstep smiling his devilish smile and admitting that Mr Beazley was none other than himself, that he'd made the booking in an imitation Scots accent and looking thoroughly pleased with himself for having taken her in.

'Well you can't possibly stay. That's trickery.'

'I don't see why not. Even if you hadn't just let me a room, I'm still your husband, so stop being hysterical, Laura, and let me in. We have things to discuss.'

This was certainly true. 'You stay in the room that you booked, then. No prowling about making a nuisance of yourself, imagining you can

282

turn back the clock.'

'Of course not,' he commented mildly, as if the thought had never crossed his mind.

To say they enjoyed a pleasant evening together would have been stretching the truth somewhat. She'd explained her plans to him in a civilised fashion at last, outlined recent conversations with her solicitor and warned him to expect papers to sign soon regarding the divorce. He'd taken all this in without argument, in fact they hadn't disagreed about a single thing. Had Laura not been quite so thankful that the evening had passed tolerably well, and that he was leaving first thing in the morning, this might have troubled her more. As it was, she carefully locked her bedroom and went straight to sleep.

She was woken at six by the sound of an engine throbbing loudly right outside her window, and the hiss of air brakes. Climbing sleepily out of bed she went to the window to investigate. What was going on? A removal van stood at her front door. She could quite clearly see the top of it but because of her bedroom window being so high up in the loft, she could see nothing more. She could, however, hear Felix's voice issuing instructions, the words unclear at this distance.

Laura splashed her face with cold water and dressed as quickly as she could, desperate to know what was happening downstairs. By the time she got there, three men were already struggling to get the carved oak court cupboard out of the front door.

'What the hell are you doing?' Flushed with fury, she stood rooted to the spot in shock. Felix turned and gave her a lopsided smile.

'Just taking my cut, darling. My share from the inheritance. There are one or two choice items of furniture here which will fetch a good price at auction and since you were too busy to deal with the matter, I organised it myself. It will partly compensate me for your intransigence over the matter of the sale. Of course, should you change your mind about that then I'll call a halt, since antique furniture of this quality left *in situ* would hike up the property value quite a bit.'

'Property value? Auction? What is this? Some sort of blackmail? You think you can bully me into agreeing to sell by pinching my furniture? *Put that down this minute!*' She stormed up to the three removal men. 'That cupboard is mine, left to me by my grandmother, and it's going nowhere.'

Looking troubled and having no wish to become embroiled in a marital dispute, one, clearly the leader of the little trio, ordered his men to put the piece down. 'We'll leave you two to talk things through while we go and have breakfast in the van. Let us know when you've sorted it all out.' Whereupon they began to shuffle off.

'Oh no you don't,' Felix said, blocking their exit. 'I hired you to do a job and you'll do it. My wife is simply being difficult but will come around to reality any moment.'

'Oh, no she won't.' Laura informed him briskly.

'Indeed you will, darling.'

'Aye, well when she does, *if* she does, you let us know mister. We'll be in the van.' And they scuttled out before he had the chance to stop them.

'Now look what you've done by your stupid obstinacy. I've paid a fortune to get them here.' Felix was spitting his fury at her. 'I could always send in the bailiffs if you prefer.'

Laura was already on the phone, ringing Capstick who told her, in no uncertain terms, that the furniture belonged to her, not her husband, and that he could not remove it without risk of being sued. She handed the phone to him. 'Nick would like to talk to you. Be polite, we're fortunate he's the diligent sort of solicitor who believes in an early start to the day. I believe he wishes to explain the law of theft to you and how he'd have you arrested before you reached the end of the lane.'

While Felix argued and railed at the young solicitor, issuing dire threats which didn't seem to get him anywhere, Laura made a cup of tea for the removal men. It wasn't their fault after all, and they'd come all the way from Cheshire, making an exceptionally early start, and would return empty handed. Obligingly, they returned the court cupboard to its proper place, even putting back the precious pieces of china they'd taken out before moving it. 'I'm sure my husband will compensate you with a hefty tip for your inconvenience.'

'Damned if I will,' roared Felix. 'Don't think you've beaten me, Laura. This is but the first skirmish.'

'Would you like your bill, Mr Beazley, since you're checking out?' she enquired sweetly, and

285

he said something very rude to her, climbed into his Mercedes and drove away in a flurry of gravel.

'Don't worry love,' said the removal man. 'We got our money up front.'

With breakfast over, having expelled her excess of temper by beating rugs, bashing pillows and scrubbing baths, Laura had got her heart rate back down to normal and thankfully made herself a welcome cup of coffee. If this was a skirmish, she didn't care to think what the next assault might be. Felix really was the most objectionable man. It made her wonder what she had ever seen in him. Couldn't he understand that the more he bullied her, the more stubbornly she clung to her rights? She would not be driven into selling this place, no matter what tricks he tried.

Laura reached for Daisy's letters as she often did when she needed to feel close to her grandmother. Sometimes her presence was very strong, almost as if she were here beside her, which was somehow a comfort in the grieving process.

She handled the precious love letters with care, some quite hard to decipher in tiny, crabbed writing as if to save paper, others she'd read several times and almost knew by heart.

Laura glanced at one which was simply a diary of events finishing with, *'Yet another boring day in the post room, you will come on Thursday as usual, won't you?'* Had that been when she was working for Mr Chapman? she wondered. And then one

286

marked with a later date said: *'I love it here at the farm, not that I'm much good at anything yet. I cleaned out the hen house this morning and tried to put mite powder under all their wings. Only caught about three of them but you should have heard the racket! I've probably put them off laying for weeks. Oh, and our day out in Silloth was smashing. I can't wait for the next.'*

She must have written to Harry several times a week for one bundle contained a flurry of letters all dated within quite a short period of time, full of amusing snippets of all that had been involved in getting the boarding house ready.

Another said: *'Florrie was cross with me today because I've made some changes she doesn't approve of. It can't be easy for her with the way things are at present. It's her kitchen, after all. She insists that my boarding house idea is doomed to failure. Clem said to her, "Thanks for your vote of confidence, Florrie. We knew you'd be keen." He has such a droll wit at times he makes me laugh, but Florrie can never see the funny side of anything which makes him worse. What a pair they are. You will get some leave soon, I hope.'*
This one was dated September 1941. So they must have got the boarding house going by then or at least had some lodgers. But life was not entirely without problems for them either by the sound of it, and poor Florrie being her usual, pessimistic self.

Laura picked up another and read it with painstaking care, the writing even more crabbed and scribbled than usual, as if dashed off in a great hurry. She could feel the anguish in every word, like a cry from the heart. *'Oh, when do you*

287

think you'll get some leave? There's something awful happened. I need to explain and it can't be done by letter. Mother is here and she's being very difficult but I daren't say anything as we can't get married without her permission.'

The letter closed, *'Oh, do say you're coming soon Harry. I'm having such problems.'* What could have happened? What kind of problems was her mother causing now? Laura rifled quickly through the next few letters but could find no further references to Rita, no more letters to Harry after that date, only a mundane catalogue of events or everyday gossip. It was then that she chanced upon one short letter from Harry. Almost in shreds, it had been singed brown, as if someone had tried to burn it and then changed their mind at the last moment just before it burst into flames, which had made it largely un-readable. A few clear words which had escaped destruction almost broke Laura's heart: *'How could you do this to me Daisy, after all we've meant to each other? I think I might die.'*

She sat with the letter on her lap and shared his anguish. What had Daisy done that had hurt him so badly? It could only be that she'd cheated on her lovely Harry, after all.

'Oh, Daisy, how could you? And after your romantic day out in Silloth. What on earth had gone wrong?'

Daisy walked arm in arm with Harry on the West Beach at Silloth all the way along to the pier. They would like to have explored the docks as far as the lifeboat station and watch the fishermen bringing in their freshly caught flounders but Harry said that area was closed to unauthorised personnel, which reminded Daisy about the war and made her feel a bit sick and uncomfortable inside. A few families or other couples, servicemen and their sweethearts like themselves, sat huddled together, warming each other against a cool spring breeze. Once a favourite destination for holidaymakers, there were few around today and not simply because it was too early in the season. Holidays seemed to be a thing of the past, taken at a time when the sound of German bombers didn't fill the air every night, when the sky over Barrow and Liverpool didn't glow ominously red.

Evacuation was again under way and Daisy would often think of her two little friends, Megan and Trish. She wrote to them regularly and wished they were here with her now, enjoying the sunshine though the paddling pool was almost empty and the donkeys were nowhere in sight. Daisy had lost a few pennies on the slot machines in the amusement arcade but had soon grown bored. She didn't have enough in her pocket to risk losing and where was the fun in watching other people win?

But having no money was of no consequence to Daisy. She felt perfectly content. All that truly mattered was that she and Harry were together again after many long weeks apart. This had been partly because of her change of billet, but also Harry had been involved in some op with the Coastal Command.

'It's seemed like years,' she said, hugging his

arm close and rubbing her cheek against his shoulder. The fabric of his uniform felt rough against her skin but it smelled of sunshine and hair cream, of warmth and love and his gentle strength, of whatever made him uniquely Harry. It was an intensely masculine, erotic scent, enough to kindle a nub of excitement within.

'How about we buy an ice cream each and go and find those sand dunes? We can shelter from the wind and maybe find a bit of privacy for an hour.'

His eyes told her that he wanted somewhere private so that he could kiss her again, and Daisy was more than willing. 'And a bottle of pop?'

He grinned. 'What sort do you like?'

'Tizer.'

They sat enjoying their treat in silence, too full of emotion to find the words to express them. Then they lay together in the curve of a dune, protected from the wind and the eyes of the world, and Harry told her over and over how much he loved her as he kissed and caressed her. He promised faithfully that he'd always come home to her safe and well, no matter what, war or no war. Daisy held him tight and offered him all her love in return, fighting back the tears, desperately striving to be brave. 'I wouldn't mind,' she said, 'if you wanted to – you know.'

'*I* would mind, very much.' He sounded faintly shocked. 'What sort of a chap d'you think I am? If there weren't a war on... No, I won't say anything, not yet. I can't.'

'Say what?' Heart in her mouth, Daisy had believed for a moment that he was about to propose, but that was foolish. They'd hardly known each other five minutes.

Harry looked down at her, his loving gaze moving over her face as if memorising every feature, but he said nothing, only shook his head, giving a sad sort of smile.

Daisy frowned. 'What's wrong? You're quiet today. What is it?' Then she put her hands to her mouth, her face going all white as the blood drained away. 'Oh, no! You've been posted, haven't you? Why didn't you tell me right away?'

'I didn't want to spoil our day.'

'Oh Harry!'

He put both his arms about her then and let her weep into the solid warmth of his tunic. 'You see, that's why I didn't tell you. I didn't want you upset.'

'I'd have been upset anyway.' After a moment or two, Daisy dashed the tears away with a determined smile. 'But you're right, there's nothing we can do about it, so we must enjoy today. Every minute of it. I want you to think of me smiling, not blubbering all over you.'

He kissed her mouth, a soft, sweet, lingering kiss that held a promise of so much more. 'That's why I love you.'

'Why?'

'Because you're so strong, so full of life and joy, so – so thoroughly nice.'

Daisy giggled. 'If you like nice girls, you picked a wrong un here.'

'I don't believe that. I picked the best.'

Daisy swallowed. 'Oh Harry. You say such lovely things.'

They each had difficulty resisting the emotions that were running high between them as they kissed and cuddled, but it was Harry who pulled away first, his face filled with guilt and pain. 'We leave the day after tomorrow. Don't ask me where to, because I don't know, but you can be certain, Daisy love, that I'll write to you at the first opportunity I get.'

And she had to be satisfied with that. She had to send him on his way with love and hope in her heart, after which she got back on the train and cried all the way home.

18

A winter of bombing gave way to yet more fears of invasion and finding themselves in more danger in their billets on the coast, many evacuees returned to their home towns. Megan and Trish were allowed no such luxury. Their new guardians, a Mr and Mrs Carter, were at pains to point out how very fortunate they were to be billeted with them, and what a mistake it would be for them to go back to their mother and their drab city lives.

They burned all the clothes the children had been given by the Marshalls. 'Just in case,' Mrs Carter told them, barely touching them with the tips of her dainty fingernails. Megan wasn't sure what she meant by this exactly but when their mam came on her next visit and all three of them were expected to sit in the garden and not come into the house, she said it again. 'You all stay out there. Just in case.' The fact that it was bitterly cold and starting to rain didn't seem to strike her as a problem.

Megan suggested it might be because a bomb could drop on the house while they were sitting having tea, but her mam said they didn't get bombs in Penrith, which was why she felt safe to leave them there, so the mystery remained. Not that it greatly mattered. The children were too thrilled to see their mother to care one way or the other where they sat, or whether or not it was raining. Daisy had visited them once or twice but it was a long way for her to come now she was in Keswick and without their best friend they were desperately homesick. Trish had been sick twice recently, just from crying too much, and Megan hated her new school with a fierce loathing. They tried once more to persuade their mother to let them come home but, sadly, she was having none of it, telling them horrifying tales of the blitz, and what lucky girls they were to be missing it.

'Don't I love the bones of you both? What would I do if owt happened to you two? I'd be fit fer nowt. I'd die of a broken heart, I would. No, no, you stop here, warm and snug, till it's all over.'

But the mystery deepened when, on discovering new scabs between Trish's fingers, Mrs Carter moved them out to what she called the summer house, little more than a large shed at the bottom of the long garden. 'There,' she said, 'won't this be exciting, sleeping here in your own little house?

Think of it as your very own air-raid shelter.'

'Why, is Penrith going to be bombed after all?'

'No, no, of course it isn't. Now be good little girls and don't ask quite so many questions.' She appeared flustered as she began to fetch blankets and pillows. No sheets, Megan noticed with some relief. They weren't expected to die out here then.

Trish spotted a spider and began to cry. 'I don't like it. I want Daisy.'

Megan said, 'Have we to stop in this shed all the time?'

'It's a summer house, dear.'

'Whatever it is, it's a bit draughty,' giving a little shiver to prove her point.

'Nonsense! Good, healthy temperature. If necessary I could always send Trish to a hostel for problem children. That might be for the best. Just in case.' So there it was again, those same words.

'In case what?' Trish asked in a panic, when camp beds had been made up for them and Mrs Carter had vanished indoors, leaving a trail of Attar of Roses in her wake. 'What are problem children, and why have I to go to hospital?'

'A hostel,' Megan corrected her, cold fear gathering about her heart.

'I'm not going nowhere without you, our Megan.'

'No, course you aren't. I don't expect either of us is going anywhere. We'll stop here in this nice shed – er, summer house.'

Tears gathered in Trish's eyes as she glanced anxiously about her, on the lookout for more spiders. 'Why can't we go indoors then? Why does she want to send me away? What have I done wrong, Megan? I haven't been naughty, have I?'

'No, love, course you haven't,' and Megan hugged her little sister tight. The whole thing was a puzzle beyond her comprehension, but her small mouth was a tight curl of anger and misery. She'd quite lost patience with the war, with do-gooders who took in vacees when they really didn't want them. With Mr Churchill who kept prattling on about everyone needing to be brave and strong and pull together, and with Mr Hitler who had started all this mess in the first place. When adults fell out, they caused a whole lot of bother for everyone, in her opinion. And she'd take a guess neither of them was living in a garden shed.

The new year brought no let-up. Eighteen-years-olds were now liable for call-up and also, for the first time, women between twenty and thirty years old. They were obliged either to register for war work, or join the women's forces. Daisy's occupation at the farm was accepted as 'doing her bit', however, since that day on the beach at Silloth, an idea had been growing in her head. One that refused to be dislodged all winter.

It came to the fore again one wet day in late January when a Miss Geraldine Copthorne came to the door. She was a tall, ungainly woman in her mid-forties, not in the least out of breath from the long walk up the hill, to politely enquire if they had rooms to let.

Daisy was flabbergasted. 'Well, that didn't take long for the local jungle drums to start beating. I only mentioned in passing to the fishmonger the other day that I'd have no objection to taking in a lodger.'

'It's enough,' Clem remarked drily, eyeing the newcomer with wary rumination.

'I need to be close to the children.'

Miss Copthorne informed Daisy that she was unmarried because of a tragedy to her fiancé during the First World War, and had no intention of ever being so. She had devoted herself to teaching, and was in the area in charge of a group of children from her home city of Newcastle. 'It really is most unsettling and often distressing to see some of these youngsters missing their homes and families so dreadfully. They're coming and going all the time, and don't always fit in well with the village children. One does what one can, of course, but it never seems enough.'

Over a cup of tea and a scone, Daisy told Miss Copthorne all about Megan and Trish. 'I tried recently to contact them in their new billet but was put off going to see them. The woman seems a very pleasant, no-nonsense sort but she explained in her letter how they've been a bit homesick and it would only upset them more if I went. I haven't had a letter in ages and I suspect they may be wanting to go back home. They did run away once, as many evacuees have. But their mother sent them back again.'

'Poor things, they sound as if they've had a remarkably tough time. I could always try and find out something about their situation, if you like. I do know the right people to ask.'

'Oh, that would be lovely. How very kind.'

Miss Copthorne went on to explain her dissatisfaction with her current lodgings, since the landlady had taken to denying her the right to sit in the front parlour, or to have a fire if she did. 'Would that be allowed here?' she enquired.

Daisy assured her that it would. It was not a room that they used, except on rare occasions, so it would be for the exclusive use of their guests. 'Coal is extra, mind,' she was careful to explain.

'Of course.'

In view of their getting along so well, Daisy had not the slightest hesitation in offering her the room and it was agreed she would move in the following Sunday, her day off.

'Are you asking for references?' Clem wanted to know later as they sat discussing the matter over supper.

'No, why should I? She didn't ask for references from me. We'll either suit each other or we won't. We'd better spruce the place up a bit, don't you think?'

'Happen,' Clem admitted, looking glum.

By February, Daisy had turned the house upside down. Miss Copthorne was warned of the impending chaos but didn't seem in the least perturbed. 'Don't fret, Daisy. I'm sure we'll get by. What right do I have to complain when there are so many far more inconvenienced.' She was a remarkably placid and unflustered sort of woman. Probably this was necessary if you were in charge of children. 'And I'm still making enquiries about your young friends. I haven't forgotten.'

The spring cleaning proved to be a mammoth task but at least served to keep Daisy's mind from worrying too much about the two children, and about Harry. Just remembering that lovely day they'd enjoyed together by the seaside was enough, for now at least. Each night, cuddled up in bed in her loft bedroom, she would replay every moment of that magical day.

She was doing it even now as she scrubbed and cleaned and tidied.

'This place will be like a new pin when I'm done,' she said. Clem was backing out the door, anxious to be off up the fells before she found him a job to do. She'd really got the bit between her teeth. Wanting to please her, he told her that he'd never seen his kitchen look so clean.

'Of course it isn't clean. It only looks better because there are no dirty dishes in the sink. There's a deal of work to be done yet.'

The kitchen cupboards filled one entire wall and it took half the morning to simply empty them. By the time Clem returned for his midday meal, Daisy was standing in the middle of the floor surrounded by every pot and pan, ladle and colander, every dusty utensil and item of crockery.

'By heck, we could feed an army here, if we had to. Thoo's enjoying this, eh?' Clem challenged her, and Daisy giggled.

'I suppose I am in a funny sort of way. I've never lived in a place like this before. It's marvellous to have so much space to live in, as well as all this light and fresh air.' She handed him a plate piled high with sandwiches. 'Only cold today, I'm afraid.'

'Leuks gradely.' There wasn't an inch of table free so they ate their meal perched on stools, munching companionably. After a while, Clem said: 'Florrie didn't take to country life quite so well as you seem to be doing.'

Daisy didn't know what to say to this but confined herself to platitudes about how the long holiday with her sister would probably help Florrie to see things in a different light. 'Anyone spending several months with my mother would be bound to view anything as an improvement,' and they both laughed.

'Happen we should let them know that you're here like, safe and sound,' Clem said, giving her a sidelong look.

It was some long moments before Daisy acknowledged the remark with a half shrug of agreement, reluctant to do anything which might bring the forces of Rita bearing down upon her. 'There's no rush is there?'

'Happen not.'

Clem again considered the array of crockery and cooking utensils stacked on the kitchen table. 'Much of that stuff must be my mother's. Haven't set eyes on it in years.'

Daisy stared at it too. 'It was right what you said earlier. We could feed an army here, at least, not literally an army but several other people besides ourselves and Miss Copthorne. If we wanted to, that is. And she's been no trouble, has she?'

'Out with it. What are you getting at?'

'Nothing, only...' Daisy took a deep breath. 'I was thinking mebbe we could take in more lodgers. We've plenty of room, what with all those unused bedrooms.'

Clem looked dumbstruck by the suggestion, which Daisy didn't wonder at.

'What sort of lodgers?' he asked, ever cautious.

'Oh, I don't know. Evacuees maybe.' She cast him a sidelong glance, wondering if she dare risk making her request to have Megan and Trish with her, but thought better of it. It was too soon. She didn't want to rush him. But she could perhaps plant the start of the idea in his head. 'Aren't you supposed to take one for every spare bedroom you have? It's something we might have to consider later.

'As for guests, well, I know this isn't Windermere or Silloth, and there's a war on so the holiday trade is pretty slack, but there are so many people looking for accommodation and we have it here in plenty.' She began to get excited as the ideas tumbled out of her head. 'Those who've been bombed out of their homes, young married women who are coming to visit their sweethearts, or sons, stationed nearby. Folk who don't want to risk living in the city. Oh, there must be loads of people. And we have – er, you still have plenty of empty bedrooms, which seems such a waste. I know folk would have to go out the back for the privy but I'm sure they wouldn't mind. It doesn't trouble Miss Copthorne, does it? And in time we could perhaps put in a proper toilet and bathroom in that little boxroom on the first landing. Oh, and it would be fun, don't you think?' Daisy finally stuttered to a halt in order to draw breath.

Clem was chuckling, entranced by her enthusiasm. 'Thoo's getten it all worked out, eh?'

'I've been thinking about nothing else for ages, and then when I started counting plates it all came pouring out.' Daisy giggled. 'Oh, do say we can. Mebbe it would do Aunt Florrie good to have a bit of company around the place.'

'It'd mean a lot of work.'

'But I must do something to earn my keep.'

'Thoo's no need to worry on that score,' he said, his face closing into that all too familiar tightness. 'Thoo may only be my niece by marriage, but so far as I'm concerned thoo's family, and I'll not have you feel beholden. I'm sure I can afford to feed one li'le lass.'

Daisy, regretting her tactlessness, hastened to soothe his hurt pride. 'I didn't mean it that way. I'm used to working, and we're all expected to do our bit, we women, what with the war and all. And if I don't pull my weight here, I'll have to join up as soon as I turn twenty. Which would you prefer?'

'Nay, heaven help us. We've come to a pretty pass when we has to get women to fight us battles fer us. Do as you wish, lass. I won't stand in yer way. But if we're going to tek in lodgers, I reckon we should clean t'chimley afore you wash all them pots. It's fair thick wi' smoke in here.'

This seemed like a wise precaution to which Daisy swiftly agreed. 'Ooh, you're right Uncle Clem. Best get on with it then.'

'What, now?' In a voice high pitched with astonishment.

'Why not now? No time like the present, as they say.'

It might well be true, but for Clem this was a revelation. Work on the farm moved at the measured pace of the changing seasons. Being rushed into a job went against the grain, particularly one which would be of no benefit to his animals. But already he had learned to recognise the light of determination in Daisy's eye. Besides, he was quite taken by the idea of taking in lodgers. He'd no objection to Miss Copthorne, a quiet sort of body who wouldn't say boo to a goose, and he found he quite enjoyed a bit of company about the place. So with a resigned sigh, he went to fetch the necessary equipment.

Chimney sweeping was a complicated task which involved Clem climbing up on top of the house via the outbuildings and dropping a rope, weighted by a stone, down the chimney. Daisy waited at the bottom to tie on a sack filled with an old pillow to plump it out. Once it was secure, she gave a couple of tugs to indicate that all was in place and Clem pulled the sack up the chimney. The result was predictable. Daisy had forgotten to properly block off the chimney opening and as Clem tugged the sack up and down, a great whoosh of soot and dust came roaring out into the kitchen, covering not only the unwashed pots and pans but also Daisy from head to foot. By the time he arrived back in the kitchen, it was to find huge swathes of the stuff billowing over every item of furniture, and Daisy equally black with it.

'Well, we might have a clean chimney and have come up with a brilliant idea,' she said, wiping a smear of soot from her face along with the tears of laughter. 'But I reckon we've put hours more work on to the spring cleaning.'

Intermittent but regular air raids continued throughout January, February and March of 1941. The Docks, Ship Canal and Trafford Park were obvious targets and naturally suffered the worst of the bombing, which made local housing vulnerable. Several shelters were available close to Marigold Court, including one behind Ariel Street, another on a piece of spare land near Guide Street and a third on the corner of Weaste Road provided by Winterbottom's Book Cloth Company, which was the one Joe preferred as it was larger than the others, with more trenches to sit in. All had reinforced concrete slabs by way of a roof with earth piled on top, walls that were at least fourteen inches thick well protected by sandbags, and designed to hold forty or fifty people. In Joe's opinion it was little enough protection against a German bomb, but better than nothing. Better than cowering in their back entry under a makeshift shelter but, proud as the city fathers might be of these facilities, Rita was scathing.

'I'll die in me own bed thank you very much.'

'That's all right. You do that love, if you must. Just don't expect me to be with you.' Joe was taking no chances. Just inspecting the damage wrought upon his beloved city was terrifying. The marketplace had turned into a heap of rubble, though he was pleased to note that the Wellington Inn was still largely intact, which proved to Joe there was some justice left in the world. The Victoria Buildings and the Bull's Head, among others, had vanished off the face of the earth. Even the Royal Exchange had been hit. The smell of cordite was in the air, and fear was in his heart.

'Why don't we all go back wi' our Florrie to the Lakes? We'd be a lot safer there,' he said one morning as he viewed pictures of the damaged Cathedral in his morning paper.

'No,' Florrie said, quick as a flash. 'I've had enough of that place. We'll be all right here, if we keep us heads down.'

Rita rolled her eyes heavenwards, as if saying, didn't I tell you how impossible she was. 'Well I've certainly no wish to intrude where I'm not wanted. Not while I have a home of me own, humble though it may be, thanks very much,' she remarked tartly, determined not to appear needy.

Joe said, 'The pair of you want yer heads looking at,' and stumped off to check on the Anderson shelter as he did every morning, for all he held even less faith in it than in the municipal ones.

Joe was no hero and carefully followed all the rules, those that benefited him anyway, and obeyed all the posters, 'Your country needs scrap for shells.' Keen to do his bit he collected all the scrap iron he could, and some of it he even let the government have for free. 'Rats and pilferers, both steal rations' said one poster on Salford Quays. Joe wouldn't dream of stealing but he was not averse to getting a few bob for the odd ration book which happened to come his way. He was particularly fond of one asking if his journey was really necessary, which generally persuaded him to stop at home and not go to work after all, even though he never travelled by train or bus anyway.

And as for 'Be like Dad and keep Mum.' He was an expert on that one.

Florrie felt occasional bouts of guilt over evading her responsibility at the farm, yet not enough to make her go back. Not yet. She needed Clem to understand why she'd left, how badly he had neglected her. A part of her hoped that he might come to Salford looking for her, to urge her to come home, declaring that he missed her far too much to live without her. But these were simply fanciful romantic dreams. Clem had too much on his plate to have time for romance these days, even had he been given cause to believe that such a gesture would be welcomed. But the longer Florrie put off returning, the harder it became. Perhaps the opposite might happen and Clem find that he was quite happy living without her. Florrie couldn't quite make up her mind whether this would be a relief or not. It was all too confusing.

Throughout that long, cold and dangerous winter, she'd continued to feel like a stranger, a spare part about the place. Salford might have been her home once but it didn't feel like that now. She wasn't settling. Perhaps she'd stayed away too long, or it was asking too much for the two sisters to live comfortably together in one house but Rita was driving her barmy. She'd seek any way she could to create an argument. 'Shape thissen,' she'd say in bitter tones, the minute Florrie put up her feet for two minutes together. 'Tha's done nowt since thi come here.'

'That's only because I needed the rest.'

'What would you need rest for when you don't work?'

'Yes I certainly do work. I'll have you know...'

'What? What will you have me know? You told us that thee lives the life of Riley.'

Realising she was about to make a bad mistake by revealing more than she should about her life, Florrie desperately tried to retrieve it, putting on her posh voice. 'Clem might be well off but he doesn't believe in wasting money. He doesn't mean to be hard on me but I'm not nearly so cosseted as you seem to imagine. He doesn't really understand how fragile I am. In fact, it's been quite a hard life,' and pulling out her handkerchief, she manufactured a tear in the hope of winning sympathy.

Rita's expression was one of dubious disbelief and she pumped Florrie all the more with questions about this fancy life she supposedly led in the Lakes, about which she'd kept so quiet. 'How many maids have you got then? I bet you get breakfast in bed every morning. I've told thee not to expect owt o' that sort here. And when's your Clem going to come and see us? Or is he too grand for the likes of us now?'

Fervently wishing she'd never embarked on this

306

conversation, Florrie made all manner of excuses to fend off Rita's persistent questioning as best she could, finally blurting out some nonsense about Clem holding a vitally important job, all very hush-hush and high-up; the implication being that it had something to do with the war effort and was very well paid.

Even Rita was impressed. Utterly stunned, she asked, 'What, he works for the government? By heck, which department? What does he do?'

Irritated by her own foolishness, Florrie's tone was harsh. 'Didn't I just tell you, it's all hush-hush. Much too secret. He doesn't even talk about it much to me, and I'm his wife.' The trouble with telling lies was that one always seemed to lead on to another, and another one after that. It was all very worrying. Florrie would really like to be rid of the whole mess, wishing she'd never got herself into such a tangle and simply told the truth from the beginning. She seemed to have achieved very little by coming back to Salford. She hadn't even succeeded in helping Daisy. Desperate to evade any further questions, she made a dash for her coat, claiming she had a hair appointment. 'I'll get us a nice bit of mackerel for our tea while I'm out, shall I? And I'll cook for once. Give you a little break.'

'Ta very much, I'm sure. Dusta want me to bow and scrape wi' gratitude?'

Florrie fled. At least one good thing about being back in the city was that she could console herself by spending. Florrie treated herself to some of the new utility clothes which she found to be really quite smart, certainly a pleasant change from the dull old working skirt and blouse she wore day after day on the farm. She'd had her hair cut and waved more stylishly and bought several new hats to show it off to advantage. She could eat fish and chips whenever she'd a mind to, or go to the flicks, just as she'd longed to do when up on the fells. But despite all of these much longed-for pleasures, she was still lonely. Her old friends were conspicuous by their absence and although Rita had agreed to accompany her on the odd occasion, more often than not she made an excuse not to.

'It's safer stoppin' at home. Thee can come a reet cropper walking about in t'black-out.'

'We'll go to a matinée then,' Florrie would suggest.

'Dusta think I'm med o' brass?' Rita never failed to get in a dig at her sister's supposed wealth.

Florrie realised she was running low on money herself, having used up all the savings she'd been secretly stowing away over the years, and was forced to write and tell Clem exactly where she was staying so that he could send her some more. To her surprise he replied within a week, enclosing a postal order for her to cash and a short note expressing his hope that she was enjoying her stay with her sister, and that he would soon see her back at the farm, when she was ready to come home.

The door was still open then. But was she ready to walk through it?

19

For Daisy, preparations were going well. She scoured the house from attics to cellars, turning out every cupboard, beating every rug, scrubbing every inch of wainscot and window frame with scalding hot water and washing soda, and Clem found himself rolling up his sleeves and working alongside her. He would never have believed himself capable of getting involved in what he considered to be women's work, but there was something about this li'le lass which had captured his heart. Every pan had been scoured, every cup, saucer and plate, knife, fork and spoon in the house had been given a thorough dunking in washing soda. And when she ran out of dry tea cloths, Clem boiled kettles and washed them for her, drying them on the rack over the fire.

The house seemed to be in a continual state of siege, filled with steam and the smell of bleach, but he didn't care. More than anything he wanted desperately for her plan to work. And so he put the kettle on and, for the first time in his life, Clem brewed a pot of tea without being asked and presented a weak, milky cup to Daisy that tasted as if it had never been near a tea leaf and was indeed the washing-up water he'd used for the tea towels.

'Here, let me do it.' She refilled the two mugs with a good strong brew, and set one down in front of the old man on the now scrubbed and shining kitchen table.

When they were happy with the kitchen they started on the bedrooms.

'It's not that they're dirty,' Daisy hastily informed him, not wanting him to feel that she was insulting either his dead mother or his absent wife, 'but a good turn-out every now and then does no harm at all. Mind you, I feel in a flatspin there's that much to be done before we open properly. But it'll work out grand, I know it will.'

'I'm banking on it,' Clem told her. In his heart he knew that he never wanted this cheerful lass to leave and he suddenly had an inkling of what Florrie might have experienced when she'd first come to the fells: the empty bleakness of it all, the feeling of being overwhelmed by loneliness. All hill farmers were aware of the threat, and the resulting depression that could creep up upon them unnoticed, particularly during hard times, it was not something Clem had ever suffered from. Yet now he knew that if Daisy left, he too would feel alone, as never before.

'I've a bit of money saved up,' Daisy told him. 'It's for when Harry comes home, but that won't be for ages yet. How would you feel about getting the odd washbasin installed, and happen some new lino?' She made the suggestion with diffidence, wary of causing offence, and Clem seemed to consider the idea with a worried frown.

'Eeh, I wish Florrie were here. She'd know what to do fer t'best.'

'But she isn't here, is she?' Daisy reminded him quietly.

Clem was silent for a moment and she could see by the bleak expression in his faded eyes that he was remembering her, perhaps thinking of the early days of their marriage when everything had seemed so hopeful, so good between them. She prodded him gently back to the present.

'Don't worry, there's plenty of time for me to save up some more. I don't reckon we've seen the end of this war, not by a long chalk. But we have to get through it as best we can. So, what do you say?'

She saw how he made a visible effort to brighten. 'I'd say you were off your head, but it's your money, lass.'

'Right, that's settled then,' and they grinned at each other, well pleased with the decision, and with their burgeoning friendship.

Clem contacted a plumber friend who said he could get some second-hand basins dirt cheap from derelict bomb sites. It seemed a bit mercenary to benefit from other people's tragedies but money too was in short supply.

'Needs must when the devil drives,' was Clem's droll comment.

Daisy said, 'Think of the good that'll come of it.'

'I reckon we could afford three between us,' Clem said, determined to do his best to hold on to her.

Daisy was so tired she could hardly sip from the cup but progress was being made, so she had not one word of complaint to make, except in a

311

good-humoured way. 'I'm fair powfagged,' she laughed, resting her head on her aching arms, and suddenly found her eyes filling with tears as she remembered joking with Megan and Trish about silly words.

'What's up lass? Not fretting about your chap, are you? Go and see him, if you want. Ask him over, I don't mind.'

Daisy wiped away the tears. 'I'm fine, a bit tired that's all. But I wouldn't mind asking Harry to come over, if that's all right. I'll drop him a line.'

'That's the ticket. Life's too short for tears.' He beamed at her, well pleased with his suggestion and, seconds later, jumped to his feet and began rummaging in the pantry under the stairs to reappear carrying a number of rather battered tin trays. 'These might cum in useful. What d'you reckon? I suddenly bethought mesel that they were there.'

Daisy couldn't help but laugh. 'Clem, you're a treasure. You've put new life into me. We'll be ready by Easter, I swear it.'

Clem had begun to wonder if they ever would be ready. When he came in each night after a long day on the fells, he'd be presented with the sight of Daisy in a flowered apron, her hair tied up in a turban, and 'leftovers' for his tea. She rarely had time for cooking these days so it was hard to know what these were left over from. No doubt she made a bit more of an effort for Miss Copthorne. Clem considered himself fortunate if he got a plate of fried spam and tomatoes, a chip buttie, or a cold cheese sandwich. Yet he made no complaint. Perhaps because she would so often pop a kiss on his forehead and promise him wonderful meals every day, once they got under way. Nor did the ever-patient Miss Copthorne object to the mess and disruption but was full of praise for the improvements, and delighted that her own room was also one to be fitted with a washbasin.

'We're not done yet,' Daisy warned her.

A shortage of sheets proved to be a problem, so a trip to Preston market was planned to buy good Lancashire cotton to make more. Daisy watched, open mouthed in amazement, as Clem ushered a sheep into the back seat of his little Ford car.

'Why is that ewe coming with us? We aren't stopping off at the auction mart, are we?'

'Nay, but we can't get no petrol coupons if we don't prove we're on farm business.'

Giggling uncontrollably, Daisy cuddled up on the back seat with the sheep, just to keep an eye on her and see she didn't fall over on the bends, and off they went. 'I hope she's a good traveller.'

On their return Daisy got down to the task of cutting up and hand sewing several yards of unbleached cotton into sheets. She washed out the size which was put in during the process of manufacture, dipped them in dolly-blue to whiten them, and finally dried them in the sun till they were fresh and soft enough to sleep on.

Wandering Winnie, as the ewe came to be affectionately known, was getting on in years and surprisingly tame. She accompanied them thereafter on many such expeditions to sales and auctions for bits and bobs that they needed.

Daisy became convinced that she actually enjoyed these little outings. One trip was to Kendal in order to buy off-cuts of lino, since the original had to be ripped up for new pipes being laid for the washbasins. The friendly salesman at the warehouse took one look at Daisy and offered to deliver, even to help lay it.

Clem accepted readily, explaining how they'd no room in the old car. 'I'm delivering this yow,' he said, studiously not explaining where to, or why anyone would want such an ancient creature. Daisy stifled a fit of the giggles.

Last, but by no means least, he rooted out a variety of old curtains from the attics. 'Mam allus liked thick wool curtains for t'winter and chintz for summer, so we've plenty.'

'Oh, they're wonderful.' Some were badly moth-eaten, but whichever ones appeared sound Daisy washed, ironed, and hung up on poles at the windows. They at least made the black-out blinds look less formidable and brought warmth to the rooms. The bits left over she fashioned into make-do-and-mend bedspreads in a patchwork of colours. It took weeks of work but Miss Copthorne gladly helped and, in the end, Daisy felt it had all been worthwhile.

At last the day came when there was nothing left to clean or wash, nothing to cut, sew, mend or repair. 'That's it, work finished, all done and dusted.'

Clem said, 'It'd be more accurate to say that this is only the first peck of work. Thoo's now ready to actually start. So until we get us first customers, tek t'chance to get some well-earned rest. Where is thoo going to find them, by the by?'

'Who?'

'Our first customers?'

Daisy's face was a picture of dismay. 'Lord, I hadn't even given that a thought. Where *will* we get them from? This isn't Blackpool, is it? They aren't going to come wandering along the prom looking for somewhere to stay for a few nights, or book through the town tourist office. Oh, hecky thump. And there is a war on.'

'You'll have to advertise.'

Eyes alight again, Daisy rushed to find paper and pencil. 'You're right. We'll put an advertisement in the *Westmorland Gazette,* that'll bring 'em rolling in.' But the wording had to be just right, she decided. They didn't want riff-raff, nor to make it sound expensive or beyond ordinary folk's means. A task which proved surprisingly difficult but, tired as she was, Daisy sat up for hours writing and rewriting until finally she fell asleep with the pad on her knee and pencil still in hand.

The effort paid off as the advertisement worked. She got not one, but two letters of enquiry.

'Oh bliss! We're in business.'

'Chrissy?' Laura stared in stunned surprise at the dejected figure standing in a dripping puddle on her doorstep. 'You're the last person I expected to see.' At least she was an improvement on the last visitor.

'Thought I'd pay you a visit. Got a problem with that?'

'No, no, of course not. Come in. You look

315

soaked to the skin. Sorry about the rain. One of those Lakes days, as we call them round here.' Laura led her into the warmth of the kitchen and put on the kettle, privately thinking that the girl would have withstood the weather better had she been dressed more appropriately. In her baggy cotton trousers and skimpy T-shirt, revealing a sparkly navel stud, the only sensible item of clothing she possessed were her boots, which looked as if they'd done service in at least one world war. Certainly they would come into their own on this terrain although, strangely, they didn't even show a speck of mud, and if she carried a waterproof in the rucksack slung over one shoulder she hadn't bothered to use it. But the most startling thing about the fourteen-year-old was her hair. Not only did it hang in damp rats' tails about her neck, but was also a bright purple streaked with yellow.

Knowing better than to comment upon this radical change from her usual mouse brown, Laura handed her stepdaughter a towel to dry it, then turned her attention to making coffee. 'Does Felix know where you are?'

'I'm not a child.'

This was a line of argument along which Laura never ventured. 'He needs to know, so that he won't worry.'

'Huh! When has Dad ever worried about me?'

Laura handed her a mug. 'Have you two quarrelled?'

Chrissy pouted. 'He doesn't like my hair. Neither does Mum, just because I was sent down from school.'

'You haven't been expelled?' Not again, she almost added, but managed not to.

Chrissy shook the offending locks, which were really quite pretty, in an alarming sort of way. 'No, I've been told to dye it back to its normal colour, and I refused.'

'I see.' Laura considered this as they drank their coffee. 'Were you expecting me to put in a word on your behalf? I mean, is the school likely to be persuaded to change their mind?'

For a brief moment an image of the vulnerable child she truly was, appeared in the hazel eyes, but only for an instant. 'They're so *old-fashioned*. Over the hill, you know? It's just a little colour, after all,' she wailed, sounding rather like a TV commercial. Laura tried not to smile. In Chrissy's opinion, the world was not yet ready for her, she being way ahead of her time.

'Why don't I ring and tell your mum where you are, then we can relax and think about what we want for supper.'

Chrissy brightened. 'Can we have garlic bread? Mum never lets me have it. She says I'm fat enough already.'

'It's only puppy fat. It'll go. I'll make you some garlic bread if you promise to speak to her and apologise for frightening her. She must be out of her mind worrying about where you've got to.'

'What, thinking I've been abducted or something?' Chrissy mocked.

'Something of the sort, yes.'

She mulled this over for a moment, then gave a sulky nod of agreement.

Julia was not best pleased by her only daughter

317

absconding but tempers were finally soothed, tears mopped, bridges built and an agreement reached whereby Chrissy would stay for a short holiday at Lane End Farm, in view of her having no school to go to at present and it being almost the end of term in any case. Meanwhile Julia would negotiate terms with the headmistress. Perhaps a slight toning down of colour could be agreed upon.

'It won't be much of a holiday in the accepted sense of the word,' Laura warned as she put down the phone. 'There's too much to do. You can help put the finishing touches to the decorating, and generally getting organised.'

Chrissy wrinkled her nose and groaned, physical labour not being high on her agenda of fun things to do. 'Why should I? That's why I did the hair thing, because I was sick of doing nothing but work, work, work. I need to chill out.'

'Well, you've come to the wrong place for that. I'm planning to open up as a guesthouse again.'

Chrissy looked slightly taken aback. 'Cool! That'll make you independent of Dad, which won't please him one bit.'

Laura solemnly considered her stepdaughter. 'You're really quite shrewd underneath, aren't you? I did hope to open by the Spring Bank Holiday but kept getting sidetracked by other issues. Now it's the middle of June and I already have bookings for this weekend. So, an extra pair of hands would be most useful.'

They spent the afternoon doing nothing more taxing than putting wrapped miniature bars of

318

soap together with sachets of shampoo and shower gel in all the new shower rooms, then counting out tea bags and making up hospitality trays. The telephone rang several times and Laura answered various enquiries from the local tourist office, fended off attempts to persuade her to reduce her rates on the grounds of the magnificent views she could offer from all her guest rooms, and took a satisfactory number of bookings.

'How are you with computers?'

'I'm a whizz.'

'Great. You can help me design and produce a brochure. I can't afford to pay for one to be properly printed, not until I get some regular money coming in.'

'Lead me to your software.'

They spent a happy couple of hours scanning photographs and cutting and pasting, as well as falling about in laughter over flowery phrases intended to advertise the merits of the premises, most of which sounded too hilarious and off-putting to risk using.

'Maybe we've done enough for today,' Laura said, wiping tears of laughter from her eyes. 'Tomorrow, you can help me finish painting the skirting boards and doors in room five. Then all we have to do is clean the adjoining bathroom, make up all the beds, set the tables in the dining room and we're done.'

'Sounds a snip,' Chrissy remarked drily.

Laura considered her more carefully. 'How would you feel about waiting on, and perhaps working here for the summer as a chambermaid,

319

assuming your mum agrees of course?'

'Does that involve having to clean bathrooms and make beds and stuff?'

'That sort of thing, yes. But I'd pay you well, and with your pretty face, not to mention the Technicolor hair, you might also attract quite a few tips.'

'OK, I'll give it a whirl.'

'Excellent. Let's hope your headmistress doesn't want you back till next term,' and the pair grinned happily at each other, as if sharing a private rebellion.

Chrissy's eyes were surprisingly anxious as Laura put down the phone. 'Did he go ballistic, threaten to disinherit me and cut me off without a penny?'

'Not quite, but he wasn't best pleased. Ranted and railed for a bit but I managed to calm him down. Says he sent you here to bring me home, not have me persuade you to stay.' Laura folded her arms and considered her stepdaughter with a quizzical frown. 'You forgot to mention that Felix actually drove you most of the way from Cheshire, *and* paid for a taxi up the lane.'

Chrissy pouted. 'I walked the last half-mile or so. I needed to get wet so you wouldn't be suspicious, you see.'

'Yes, I do see.'

'Sent me as ambassador.' And when Laura looked sceptical, added more truthfully. 'All right, wanted me to use my unique skills to disrupt your life, and persuade you to give up. Dad's worried about you, apparently,' she confided, licking her fingers clean of garlic butter.

'Whatever for?'

'Thinks you're having it off with someone.'

'What nonsense! Where does he get these fantasies from? I suppose it means that at least *he* doesn't think I'm over the hill.'

Chrissy shrugged. 'He's pretty old himself, so that's no recommendation.'

'No, I suppose not.'

'He says you want a divorce, and he's no intention of giving you one.'

'Does he indeed?'

'Wanted me to apply pressure, you know, all the guilt stuff of abandoning me, making me a child from a broken home. Two broken homes actually, since I've already been through one messy divorce,' said Chrissy with a hint of drama in her tone. 'Hey, that'd be one up on my friend Lucy.'

'Oh well, that's all right then,' Laura commented drily, 'if you can be one up on Lucy.' And then more seriously. 'Look, I'm sorry about all of this. I've no wish to mess up your life too.'

'He's the one messing things up.' Chrissy considered her, out of old-young eyes. 'He's having it off with that Miranda, isn't he?'

Laura winced, as much at the bluntness of the girl's language as the images the words presented. 'You must ask him that, not me.'

'He's a head-case. How will that solve anything, or help him get things back on track?'

'Sorry, am I missing something here?'

Chrissy leaned forward, dropping her tone to a

whisper as if she were relaying a secret, or exchanging a confidence. 'Dad says the business is on the skids and you're being obstinate and cruel in refusing to sell this half-derelict house, since you helped him to spend the money in the first place.'

'I did not! He's the one spending money as if it were going out of fashion, dashing all over the Continent, and wining and dining night after night, not me.' She almost added – and attempting to steal what is rightfully mine – but decided against it. Laura slapped a chocolate mousse down on the table and Chrissy's eyes lit up. 'Anyway, it isn't half-derelict. A bit run-down perhaps, but with great potential. Is that what he instructed you to do, imply he was about to go bankrupt? What else is there? Why don't you get it all out into the open, while you're at it?'

Looking decidedly sheepish, Chrissy shook her head, making the purple strands glimmer like silk in the light from the lamp, then gave a little giggle. 'Actually, he didn't tell me any of that stuff about the business, only about his not wanting a divorce. I was ear-wigging. He and Gramps were having a right old barny, trying to think of a way to make you sell. Maybe Dad really does have problems this time, I don't know.' Picking up her spoon, she tucked into the dessert as if she'd been starved for weeks.

'Gramps? Are you saying my father and Felix were having a row? What about?'

'You, mainly,' Chrissy mumbled through a mouthful of chocolate mousse. 'About whether or not you should be forced to sell the house and

322

what Gramps should do about the land. Dad suggested Gramps might like to sell that instead, and come into the business as a sleeping partner but Gramps wasn't up for it. Said he wanted to have nothing at all to do with it, though whether he meant the land or the business, I'm not quite sure. It all got a bit muddled at that point because they were shouting over each other's words. Anyway, something about it being a huge bind, and that he'd done his bit by trying to persuade you to see sense and go home. What happened next was not his concern.'

Laura sat looking bemused. 'I think I've lost the plot. What land are we talking about here?'

Chrissy was busy scraping the last of the mousse from the glass dish. 'Oh, you know – land. The kind you use for growing things, like that stuff cows and sheep eat.'

'This is no joke, Chrissy, this is serious stuff. I didn't even know that my father owned any land. How? Where? What land?'

Chrissy dragged her attention away from the dessert dish, surprised by this revelation, eyes narrowing speculatively. She always did love a mystery. 'Why, here of course. Where else? You might own the house, but your dad owns all of this farmland. So, are you going to sell it or not? The house I mean. Don't let Dad bully you into it, if you don't want to.'

'Don't worry, I won't.' Laura's reply was vague. She was still trying to come to terms with her father owning the *land*. Not that she'd paid any attention thus far as to who owned it. But her own *father?* Why hadn't he said?

'Is there any more?'

'What?'

'Chocolate mousse.'

'No, you've had quite enough already. Drink your apple juice and go to bed like a good girl.'

Chrissy pulled a face. 'Don't you start. I've enough with them two on my back the whole time. The best thing about having you as a reserve mum, as it were, is that you never go in for the nagging bit. If you and Dad – you know – split up, can I still come round? Even after these summer hols, I mean.'

Laura began to clear away the dishes, longing suddenly to be alone, to have ten minutes' peace and quiet to think things through properly. 'Of course you can. You're my stepdaughter and always will be. Look, why don't you go and watch television while I wash up?' The kitchen was as good a place as any for some private thinking, not being one of Chrissy's favourite places.

'Won't you be lonely living up on this mountain all on your own?'

'I shall be too busy to even think about it.'

'Isn't there any talent around?'

'Not that I know of, no. None at all.'

'Pity. Anyone would be better than Dad.'

20

It was one morning in early April that the letter came. With a little jump of her heart, Florrie recognised the handwriting instantly as being Clem's, but unfortunately it wasn't addressed to her, it was for Rita and there was nothing she could do about vetting it before it was opened.

Clem had very kindly written to say that Daisy had spent the winter safely at Lane End Farm, that she was perfectly well and they were not to worry. *'I thought it best that I inform you of her safety.'* He apologised for not having written sooner but had kept expecting Florrie back any day, he explained, and then the weather had been bad so he hadn't been able to get out for several weeks. He made no mention of the fact that Daisy had been reluctant to contact her mother, or that he'd no real proof of where his wife was staying until she'd written asking for money. *'Not that Florrie need hurry home on my account, if she's enjoying her stay with you. We're busy doing a thorough spring clean.'* He closed by saying that Daisy was proving to be quite handy about the farm.

Rita's jaw dropped open in stunned amazement. 'Farm, what farm? You told us you lived in Keswick, in a big fancy house by the lake.'

Florrie gave a false little laugh. 'Whatever gave you that idea? What does he say about Daisy? My word, fancy her persuading him to do a spring clean. Clem hates jobs of that nature,' she said, hoping that changing the subject would put Rita off the scent.

'Aye, that's our Daisy, never happier than when she's getten her nose stuck in other folk's business.'

'Oh, I'm sure she's not like that at all.'

'So, what's a top government official doing working on a farm?' Rita asked the question with open contempt in her tone.

'Part of his cover,' Florrie said and scuttled away, anxious to avoid any more awkward questions.

But Rita was not one to let go quite so easily. It didn't surprise Florrie in the least when she followed her out into the back yard and waved the letter under her nose.

'Are you going to explain this, or what?'

'I really don't know what you mean. Anyway, I would have thought you'd be delighted to hear that your daughter was safe. Haven't you been worrying all winter about which billet she's moved to?' Knowing that Rita had not been in the least concerned about her daughter, nor mentioned Daisy in months.

'Don't talk lah-di-dah to me, it won't wash. I'm the one what saw you with a mucky face and a snotty nose when you were little, remember? Anyroad, our Daisy can look after herself. I want to know about this 'ere farm. Is that where you've been living all these years? Is that why I'm still waiting for an invitation to visit this so-called posh house of yours?'

'It is a big house. Biggish, anyway. And life is very busy. We work seven days a week,' Florrie said, floundering for an excuse.

'Oh aye, but not for the government eh? Not a fine house by the lake, no grand estate neither but a flamin' farm. Is that the way of it?'

Florrie clenched her fists in silent fury. For years she'd managed to keep her secret, the pretence of being well-placed. Now, thanks to Clem's excessive thoughtfulness to inform Daisy's mother that she was safe, or *thoughtlessness*, depending on how you viewed it, the truth was out at last. She could spit, she could really! Why couldn't the stupid man have kept quiet? It didn't seem to occur to her that she could have evaded the issue by returning home, that perhaps he'd been allowing her time to do so. Or even that she might have precipitated the letter by begging for money to allow her to stay away even longer.

Rita, on the other hand, was beginning to see the funny side.

'So you're not Lady Muck, after all. Only Mrs Muck, the cowman's wife.' She began to chuckle. 'Nay, and you've led us nicely up the garden path all these years. Letting us believe that you were someone important. Madame Nose-in-the-air. You made out that your precious Clem were a gentleman wi' a deal of brass in his pocket and all the time he's nowt but gas and hot air? Is that the truth of it? This grand love affair turned out to be a pig in a poke, did it? Literally!' And she burst out laughing.

'It's not funny.'

'It is from where I'm standing. Aw, come on, I'm yer flippin' sister. It's time you got it all off yer chest and told us the truth. Be honest for once in yer life, lass.'

Feeling cornered, and thoroughly vexed, Florrie buckled under the pressure. 'Oh all right, yes it's true. He's just a farmer and not a rich one at that, so go on, have a good laugh at my expense, why don't you? I've had a miserable time from start to finish if you want to know the truth, which will no doubt amuse you even more.'

By the time Laura's first guests arrived, Lane End Farm Guesthouse was as ready as she could make it. Every room had been completely redecorated and refurbished. Fresh new curtains hung at the windows, new mattresses on the old iron frame beds, the solid wood furniture polished to perfection and new lamps, cushions and pictures placed wherever it seemed appropriate to put them. Laura and Chrissy had taken great pleasure in choosing these, entering into lively debates when their tastes clashed, which was fairly frequently. Laura preferred flowers or landscapes while Chrissy leaned more towards abstracts in bold, primary colours. A compromise was reached by opting for the quieter style for bedrooms and bolder colours to brighten the hall and dining room.

The advertisements she'd placed in various regional newspapers and holiday guides seemed to be working and she and Chrissy spent a lot of time posting off brochures all over the country.

Felix still rang regularly if not quite as often as he had used to, and mainly to speak to Chrissy. He would be dismissive when Laura answered, as if punishing her for being uncooperative. Not that it troubled her in the least, for whenever he did take the time to talk to her it was only to issue another lecture.

'It won't work, this nonsensical idea you have of becoming a landlady.'

'Don't be sniffy, Felix. They call them proprietors these days. And I rather think it will work. I'm fully booked for most weekends to the end of June and through July already. This is a popular area for walkers with not a great deal of accommodation in the locality.'

'And what about us?'

'There hasn't been an *us* for some time. As soon as I get a free afternoon, I mean to pop back into Keswick and see Nick, my solicitor, and get things moving on the divorce. No point in letting it drag on.'

'Don't you ever listen to a damn thing I say, Laura? *There isn't going to be any divorce.*' Quietly Laura put down the phone.

Chrissy, who had been unashamedly listening in to the conversation, said: 'You know how Dad hates to lose. Since he hasn't managed to change your mind on this over the phone, failed to make you be nice to prospective buyers, and sending me here hasn't worked either, he'll only hatch up some other plot. Be on your guard Laura. He isn't done yet.'

'There's nothing he can do to me now,' Laura assured her, wishing she felt half so confident as she sounded. Felix's attitude troubled her deeply, but not for a moment would she allow him to know that. If he imagined that clinging on to a dead marriage would help him to get his hands on her inheritance, he couldn't be more wrong.

The first breakfast was something of a nightmare. Chrissy kept forgetting to ask if they would like coffee or tea and mixed up several orders, handing scrambled eggs to one lady who had asked for bacon and tomato, and giving a half-frozen croissant to another who'd requested a full English breakfast. Laura dropped a poached egg on the floor just as she was slipping it on to the plate, and had to start all over again to cook another one. The kitchen was steaming hot and over all hung the unappetising aroma of burnt toast since Chrissy kept jamming them too hard into the ancient toaster which prevented it from popping up properly.

'I'll buy a new one. This very afternoon.'

It seemed a miracle to them both that the half-dozen guests sitting patiently in the dining room didn't walk out long before the painful ritual was over. Somehow or other, they did all get fed and went happily on their way to explore the area. Laura breathed a sigh of relief, put the kettle on and began to stack the dishwasher. 'It can only get better.'

'Or worse,' Chrissy remarked gloomily. 'Seven weeks of this? I'll go bonkers. Did you see that chap's face when I forgot to warn him how hot the plate was. I thought he was about to burst a blood vessel. Anyway, your breakfasts went down a treat, saved the day. I think the guy in number four would marry you just for your black puddings.'

'He must be seventy if he's a day.'

'Perfect.'

'Right miss, all we have to do now is clean bathrooms, tidy bedrooms, polish and vacuum upstairs and down, scrub pans and re-lay the tables for tomorrow.'

'Simple, if you say it quickly. No evening meals then?'

'Not till I feel strong enough to cope with them.'

'Which if I have any say,' said Chrissy, 'will not be for a long, long time.'

It was Laura's misfortune that a couple of nights later, David called, just on the off-chance that she might feel like popping out for a drink down at the Salutation Inn in Threlkeld. Worse, he walked straight in without even bothering to knock, it being so wet, he explained, and not wanting her to get drenched by coming to the door. All explanations stopped short when he spotted Chrissy sitting in front of the TV set, staring at him wide-eyed with disbelief.

'And Laura said there was no talent round here.'

'Sorry? Ah, you have company, I didn't realise.'

'I would have said, if you'd knocked,' Laura remarked drily. 'Still, now you're here, allow me to introduce to you my stepdaughter.'

'I'm the wild child,' Chrissy said, with some degree of pride in her voice. 'I expect she's told you all about me already.'

'Not really. Why are you wild? Were you brought up by wolves or something?'

To Laura's utter amazement, she saw Chrissy flush and give an entrancing giggle. Obviously, David's charm transcended age and, since he made her blush too, perhaps she wasn't quite over the hill after all.

It took something of a tussle but Laura finally shooed Chrissy off to bed and over a bottle of wine told David about the startling revelation that her father actually owned the land he leased. She demanded to know why he'd never mentioned it and, to her surprise, he replied calmly that he hadn't known either. Apparently rent payments were made through his solicitor to a Trust, the name of which gave no indication of ownership.

They both considered this for a moment before David murmured his thoughts out loud. 'He must have owned it for quite a while. I've been dealing with the Trust ever since I took the place on. I mean, it's fairly common practice, to leave the house to one person and the land to another but I wonder why he never told you? Why be so secretive about it?'

'Because he doesn't wish to appear beholden to Daisy, the mother he hated. What else could it be? I'm assuming that she was the one who gave it to him, perhaps years ago. Which means she didn't disinherit him after all, and he let me think that she did, the silly old man. Was that so I'd feel sorry for him, or perhaps not nag him to come to her funeral? If only there were some way I could find out more about her. If she'd kept a diary...'

David cast his eyes heavenwards, his face

332

inscrutable. Laura watched him for a moment, thinking that perhaps he had something more to say, perhaps even some quip about Daisy having better things to do with her time than scribble in a diary but he said nothing and it finally dawned on her that his silence was telling. A burst of excitement exploded within her.

'She did keep a diary, didn't she? Where is it? Tell me. Oh, I would so love to see it.'

'Sorry, no, that wasn't her style. But I was just thinking, Daisy was a member of the Local Oral History Society.'

'Oh!' All the excitement drained out of her. Although Laura appreciated that these sort of tapes were a valued method by which an older generation could pass on information on how they'd lived their lives in the days before television and computers and technology changed employment and lifestyles for ever, yet she was disappointed. 'I wanted more than snippets about how the war was won, or when rationing was brought in. I long to discover more personal, intimate details, to know and understand the woman herself; to get inside her head.'

'Suit yourself Laura, but you might find them worth a visit. I don't think you'd be disappointed. I have the telephone number of the secretary somewhere. I'll drop it in tomorrow if you like.'

The secretary, a plump, bustling lady with spectacles hanging on a chain around her neck, led Laura with a cheery smile to an impressive filing system. 'If your grandmother recorded anything, anything at all, it will be listed here.

What was the name again? Daisy Thompson.' An agonising wait while she riffled through countless cards. 'No, sorry, nothing under that name.'

'Oh well, it was just a thought.' Laura turned to go.

Chrissy, who had insisted on coming with her on this quest, said, 'Perhaps your gran was a modern woman and used her own name for personal matters. What was it?'

'Atkins. Daisy Atkins.'

The secretary tried again. 'Ah yes, well done, dear. Daisy Atkins. Not just one tape, in fact, but several. You'll need to provide references, fill in a form, become a member of the library and so on, if you wish to borrow them.'

'No problem,' Laura said. She felt as if she'd struck gold.

Daisy's own voice came over strong and clear. *'My name, for the sake of the tape, is Daisy Atkins, although I am known locally as Thompson, my married name.'*

'Lord, she sounds as if she's giving evidence in a police station,' Chrissy said.

'Hush, I can't hear.' Laura rewound the tape to listen again to the bit she missed. They were all three, Laura, David and Chrissy, sitting in the kitchen at Lane End Farm, anxious to hear whatever the tapes could tell them.

'This is my story, a part of it anyway, for those of my family who wish to hear it. An oral diary, and because of the personal nature of what I am about to disclose I hope listeners will bear in mind that I did always what I thought was for the best.'

334

David said, 'This sounds pretty private. Would you like me to go?'

'No, I want you to stay. You've heard so much of Daisy's story already, and she was your friend. You might as well know the rest. There are too many tapes to hear it all at one go, so we'll start with this one – intriguingly labelled "Robert's, Inheritance".'

'Twice I have lost a son and in neither case through death, though it might just as well have been for the pain it caused. I don't blame Robert for leaving. He was upset and cross. I hope and pray that he will not prove stubborn about accepting his due inheritance which I give to him now, as a gift, before I die. I've put it in trust for him so that he can't do anything silly in a temper, like selling it. With that in mind, I tell my story. Perhaps, in time, he will forgive me, or at least understand.'

They came to the part where she'd finally found the farm, and how Daisy had taken at once to Clem. *'Florrie was not settling back in Salford. She got caught up in the blitz, and that's when everything changed.'*

For once in her life, Rita sat quietly and listened to the tale without interrupting, so avid was she for every mouth-watering detail. She learned all about Florrie's many disappointments over the state of the farmhouse, the hard work she had to do, the loneliness of the place, even the foulness of the weather. Her sister's bitterness at the way things had turned out was all too evident.

'Oh, Rita. You can't imagine what I've gone through,' Florrie moaned, dabbing at her eyes with a fresh white handkerchief. 'I've been so lonely up there, on that mountain. And you wouldn't believe the wind and the rain we get. My nerves are in ruins.' But if she'd hoped for a glimmer of pity, or a softening of Rita's stance, she was soon to be disenchanted.

Rita folded her arms across her skinny bosom and gave a smirk of satisfaction. 'Serves you right, you daft happorth. You should've had more sense than to run off wi' him in t'first place: a man old enough to be your father, and a perfect stranger you knew nowt about. I warned you not to marry him and see how right I was.'

'I thought I was in love.'

Rita made a pooh-poohing sound. 'You fancied yer chances at lording it over the rest of us. But it hasn't worked, has it?'

Florrie glared moodily at her sister. Sometimes Rita had an unhappy knack of putting her finger right on the pulse. Of course she'd hoped that marrying Clem would take her up in the world, out of Salford and into a fine house smoothly run by a housekeeper and a bevy of servants so that she wouldn't have to lift a finger. Why else would she choose to marry such an unexciting man as Clem Pringle, fond though she'd been of him at the time? Instead, all she'd got was a lifetime of toil and misery.

'Sometimes Rita, I don't think you have a heart. I've really suffered, can't you see? Have you no pity?'

'Not when it comes to no-good little madams like you were when you were young, and like our Daisy is now. You've got your just deserts, no doubt about it. And if our Daisy isn't careful, she'll get hers an' all.' Rita was positively glowing with moral rectitude. She'd waited years for this moment. 'Ever since you walked through my front door months ago, we've heard nowt but how hard done to you are: how tired and lonely, how Clem doesn't understand you. Now you tell us your husband isn't rich, you don't live in a posh house, you've no servants and tha's overworked. You and the rest of the flippin' universe. Hard cheese. You aren't the only one to be suffering, so stop feeling sorry for yourself and get on with life.'

If there was an iota of common sense in her sister's advice, Florrie certainly wasn't in the mood to take it. Twin spots of fire burned on flat pale cheeks as she furiously sought self-justification. 'What about losing my child? You don't seem to appreciate how that has affected my life.'

'You could've tried again but no doubt a child would have got in the way, taken Clem's attention away from you.'

'That's not true. I would've loved another only I was too afraid the same thing might happen again. Anyway, you're wrong. Clem isn't the attentive sort. He doesn't like a fuss, and he's far too busy on the farm.'

'Ah, that's the way of it, is it? You were wallowing in self-pity and he wasn't fussing over you enough. So you turned into this moaning Minnie where nothing were ever right.'

'How can you be so cruel?'

'I speaks me mind, take it or leave it. There's

337

others have lost childer, them what grew up and were loved for years. Nay, not me, thank God, but plenty in this street, and there'll be more afore this war is done. They don't wallow in self-pity. They pull themselves up by their boot straps and carry on.'

'Drat you, our Rita.' Florrie's tears were all too real now, though more from anger and frustration than genuine distress. She was utterly convinced that throughout her married life she'd suffered terrible deprivation and anguish and nobody cared; not her husband, not even her own sister. 'You never did like me and I'll not stop where I'm not wanted.'

'Nobody's asking you to. You don't belong here, Florrie Pringle. So stop thee moaning, pack thee bags and go on home to your husband, even if he isn't flippin' rich. Or else batter somebody else's ears with your troubles. I can't say we care one way nor t'other where tha goes or what tha does, but we've had enough of your whining here.'

'I'll not stop where I'm not welcome.'

'And you're certainly not that.'

Florrie marched upstairs, stuffed her new clothes into her bag and stormed out of the house, making sure she banged the door shut behind her. Determined to have the last word, Rita whipped it open again to stand screaming from the doorstep as her sister strode away through the entry. 'See if I care, you useless baggage!'

When Joe came home later, he gazed with suspicion upon his wife standing quietly at the sink and asked where Florrie was.

Rita prevaricated, concentrating on peeling potatoes with short, furious stabs of the knife. 'How should I know? I'm not her flippin' keeper.'

'Why have you got that frosty look on yer face? Nay, you two haven't had another falling out? Not in the middle of all this.'

'She started it. Miss High-and-Flippin'-Mighty. Does she think she's the only one with problems? I told her: you can go and jump, you. Go and lord it over someone else fer a change.'

Joe shook his head, looking exasperated. 'Nay lass, you're a nasty piece of work at times. What else did you say?'

'I told her to go to her husband. Happen she'll listen this time.'

'It's not your place to tell her what to do. For once in your life, woman, don't interfere. Haven't you done enough damage to our Daisy? Leave well alone, why don't you?'

Rita turned on him in a fury. 'What's come over you all of a sudden, sounding off? I've done nowt to our Daisy save what was best for her.'

'What's best for *you,* you mean.'

'You agreed. You did nowt to stop me.'

'I'd need to call out the Manchester Brigade and the Auxiliary Fire Service to stop you, once you've getten an idea in yer head. And what else happened? Go on, tell me the worst.' Joe was determined to get to the bottom of this matter because he could see by the triumphant expression on his wife's face, there was more to it than she was telling.

Rita smirked. 'I were right all along, she's been

lying to us all these years. There is no fancy big house, only a flamin' farm.'

'Nay lass,' Joe said, his tone weary, 'I knew that already. Didn't you ever guess? It were fairly obvious when she never wrote to show off her new-found wealth, or invite us over to view this grand house she supposedly lived in. Why you bother to be jealous of her, I've never been able to work out. She's got nowt to write home about at all, none of her dreams have come true. No big house, no rich husband, no wonderful love-match, and she'd give her eye-teeth to have a daughter like our Daisy.'

His words seemed to inflame her rage still further. 'She's welcome to her, wittering on about that flippin' child she lost, as if she were the only one. What about me? Haven't I suffered most with our Daisy behaving like a loose woman? I told our Florrie to go home to her husband, and good riddance.'

Joe grabbed his wife by the arm, an unheard of action in this house, and gave her a little shake. 'Damn you, Rita, you can be a venomous old cow when you put your mind to it. You know she's depressed. Has been for years, ever since she lost the babby. She can't help it, poor lass, that's the way she is.'

'Well, she doesn't have to weep all over me. I've enough troubles of me own.'

'She's yer bloody sister, fer God's sake,' Joe shouted and turned to the door, his face a mask of concern and anger. 'I'll go after her. It's not safe out there. Bombs dropping all over the damned show. Didn't you hear the siren? We're in

340

for another battering. Who knows when the next one will drop.'

Rita was untying her pinny, reaching for her coat and scarf. 'Don't you try to play the hero, or stick up for that little madam, it doesn't suit you. Get down the shelter. I'll fetch her back. The silly woman can't have got far.' Rita slapped the potato peeler into his hand. 'And finish them spuds afore you go. We need us tea, German bombs or no German bombs.'

Rita caught up with Florrie at the corner of Weaste Street where she was arguing with an ARP warden. He was ordering her into a nearby shelter and Florrie was resisting furiously. 'I have to catch my train. I'm going down no shelter. Anyway, I suffer from claustrophobia.'

'You'll suffer from much worse, Missis, if you don't get off this street right this minute.'

'I'll take me chances. I'm going home, I tell you.' Florrie made to set off but the warden grabbed her arm and dragged her back to the entrance of the shelter.

'Don't be so flamin' stubborn. It's my job to see you're safe.'

A mother and two children appeared on the scene and joined in the argument. 'Nay, leave her be. She's not the only one who doesn't like bleedin' shelters. I've left a pan simmering on the hob, Bill, so I'll just nip back to tek it off afore I go down.'

Rita said, 'We've a shelter of us own in t'back yard. We'll go there, thank you very much, if we need to,' and she made a grab for Florrie,

341

capturing her in an arm lock so she couldn't run off again.

'There's no time for a flippin' mothers' meeting here, fer God's sake!' The ARP Warden looked about him in desperation, as if he might whip off his tin helmet and tear his hair out if the irate trio didn't behave. 'Women! Do as tha's told for pity's sake. Tek them childer in that shelter this minute.' Then he pushed the young woman and her two children down the steps into the crush of people already hurrying below ground for protection. As he turned to do the same with Florrie and Rita, the world exploded all around them. It came with a surprisingly dull clunk but they felt the pavement shake and open beneath their feet, smelled the acrid scent of smoke and raw fear, saw the sky itself blaze with fire as they were lifted, arms wrapped tight around each other, and thrown backwards on a blast of hot air.

21

The next guest to follow in Miss Copthorne's intrepid footsteps during Daisy's first week of business was a commercial traveller in agricultural foodstuffs by the name of Tommy Fawcett. He wouldn't be permanent, he explained, but definitely a regular as staying on farms was generally his preference; so much more convenient in his type of trade.

It was arranged that whenever he was going to be in the area, he would write and let her know his dates well in advance. 'You'll soon get used to my routine, it doesn't vary much,' he explained, tipping his brown felt hat over one eye, 'not like my dance routine which is even more imaginative than Fred Astaire's.'

Daisy laughed. 'Nobody can dance as well as Fred Astaire. I won't have folk who tell fibs in my boarding house. We might as well start as we mean to go on.'

He pulled a sad face. 'I can't resist trying to impress a pretty young girl. Mind you, my mother always told me my bragging would get me in trouble one day. If I were as good as him I'd be in the films too.' He pronounced it filums. 'All right, mebbe he has the edge, but I *am* involved in amateur dramatics. Back home in Blackburn, I'm famous for my twinkle-toes,' and he did a few steps, there and then on the lino, making such a lovely clicking noise that it brought Miss Copthorne and Clem to see what the noise was all about. In no time they were all laughing as he jumped up on to a chair, then tap danced across the kitchen table and down on to the next chair. Oh yes, he was a real card was Tommy.

Next came a widower by the name of Ned Pickles. He was a small, wiry man in his late fifties, as stiff and starched in his manner as the high collar about his long skinny neck. One glance at his tired, gloomy face, the dusty spectacles, threadbare suit and well polished, if down-at-heel shoes, and Daisy decided he

343

needed looking after. Clearly he was missing his late-lamented wife, which would mean he'd have something in common with Clem, who was still pining for the absent Florrie. Daisy hoped the two of them might get along famously. She pushed her carefully devised list of rules back into her apron pocket unread and put him in the back bedroom; the one with the blue eiderdown and a bookcase since he claimed to be fond of reading and had brought a stack of books with him when he moved in the very next day.

She informed him that breakfast was served sharp at eight, evening meal at six, and left him to it.

Sometimes, Daisy wondered at her own temerity in embarking on such a scheme. Here she was in the midst of getting a lodging house started just as rationing was going from bad to worse. The value of the meat ration had been dropped from 1s 6d to 1s 2d, a state of affairs she complained about loud and long to anyone prepared to listen, quite certain that those in power would not be struggling on such meagre rations. Jams and marmalades were also now on ration and Daisy made a mental note to dig out Aunt Florrie's recipe books and have a go at making her own; assuming she could get the sugar, of course.

But she meant to do things properly. People were already sick and tired of 'Lord Woolton Pie', 'Boston Bake', mock cream, mock marzipan, mock beef soup and mock everything else. Daisy knew that she must feed her guests well if she was to keep them. Living on a farm and being able to produce better food than was generally available in the town shops was her one advantage, the most sound reason for her lodgers to put up with the long trek up the lane every day.

They were so lucky, having this lovely place to live in.

Florrie was the first to recover. Finding herself unexpectedly clasping her sister to her breast, she pushed her away quickly and gave her shoulder a little shake. 'Are you all right, our Rita? By, that was a close one.'

Rita struggled to sit up, looking dazed as she began to pick bits of plaster out of her hair. 'Am I all in one piece? Eeh, thank God!' She began to cough, her throat thick with lime dust.

'I reckon we must have cushioned each other as we fell.'

'What, saved each other's life d'you mean, while I was hellbent on wringing your neck? There's a turn-up for the book.'

What amazed them most was the calm. People were gathering up their belongings and walking away quietly, some to wait for their bus or tram as if nothing amiss had taken place. The world appeared to be falling apart in mayhem and chaos, yet they were concerned only with whether or not they caught the 54 bus on time. A woman appeared out of a haze of dust, a tray of tea mugs in her hand.

Rita gazed at her open-mouthed. 'How long have we been out cold, or was she boiling that kettle even as the bomb dropped?'

Yet another woman appeared out of nowhere,

insisting that she sit still to have her head examined.

'Nay, me head has needed examining for years. Happen the bomb will have knocked a bit of sense into it.'

They might have laughed had it not been so awful. What remained of the shelter was a flattened pile of rubble and as Florrie and Rita sat in stunned silence contemplating the horror of it, they each realised that being thrown backwards into the street together was indeed what had saved them. The mother and her two children, along with the rest of the occupants who had dived below for safety had been less fortunate. The ARP warden was even now scrabbling at a hole he'd found in the heap of smoking bricks, desperately trying to find some sign of life within.

'Don't just sit there ladies. Give us a flamin' hand.'

With one accord they struggled to their feet, heads still spinning yet they hurried to help. All hope seemed lost and then a baby's cry was heard and they dug all the harder to retrieve it. Black with smoke and dust yet it proved to be alive and well, unharmed in any way. 'You're one of the lucky ones, chuck,' said Rita, plonking it in an upturned barrel while she got on with the digging.

'That's no way to treat a bairn.' Florrie hurried over and picked up the baby in her arms. The child rewarded her with a beaming smile but then began to splutter and cough, a dribble of sooty saliva running from its mouth as it finally let out a howl of distress. 'Oh there, there, don't take on now.' With practised ease Florrie put the child against her shoulder and began to rub its back, rocking gently. 'Poor lamb. It needs to see a doctor.'

'Oh dear God, I've found a leg here.'

Quickly, Florrie sat the baby carefully back in the half barrel and ran to help her sister while Rita vomited her breakfast into the gutter.

They dug for hours and neither felt able to stop, even though far more experienced people than them came along to help. They pulled bodies out of the rubble one after the other, many with bricks and shrapnel buried in their chest or back, limbs broken or missing. Some suffered dreadful gaping wounds, others had their clothes and skin burned off by the blast or were so covered in blood it was impossible to identify where the injury might be, if they were alive or dead. A whole group of factory girls on their way to work were found to be still clutching each other, bus tickets in hand, a pink ribbon from one fluttering merrily in the breeze as she was dragged from the smouldering ruin that had been the shelter. Of the hundred or more people who had gone in, less than a dozen survived, though whether these could be called lucky, or would ever be the same again, was another matter.

Finally, driven by exhaustion and an increasing sense of futility, the two sisters turned wearily for home, only their numbed silence and the horror imprinted in their eyes revealing what they had gone through.

Without thinking, Florrie had picked up the crying baby, an infant of eighteen months or so, and carried it on her hip. The two women still held on tightly to each other for the length of that terrible journey, not simply for much needed support but in order to find the strength to face the stark devastation that had come to their city. They stumbled over broken glass and smoking ruins, by-passed fires, turning their agonised glances away from the fallen bodies which lay like rags in the rubble. As they made their way along Eccles New Road, they could see a wall of fire on the other side of the Ship Canal.

'Some poor soul's lost the battle there, right enough,' Rita murmured, her voice sounding shaky and weak.

Whole streets had been gutted, some houses still ablaze as fire fighters did battle. Liverpool Street was thick with smoke and a never-ending line of people carrying a pathetic few remnants of what remained of their life; awesomely silent and resigned as they walked they knew not where, thankful at least to be alive for all they were homeless and leaving behind everything they owned, in some cases their loved ones as well. It seemed strange that the sun still shone, filtering through the dust and smoke like a benedict of hope for the future. Buses still ran, taking long detours to carry people to some sort of safety out of the city. There was no panic, no hysteria, only a strange, eerie silence broken now and then by a shout as someone was found buried alive under the fallen masonry, or the quiet sobbing of a mother over a child who was not.

As they reached their own entry they quickened their pace, so that as they turned the corner, Rita was actually running. Florrie didn't recall ever having seen her sister so distressed but she understood why. Where once there had been Marigold Court, a row of back-to-back tenement houses, smoke blackened and old maybe but nonetheless solid and the place they had always called home, now there was nothing beyond a burning heap of rubble. A line of nappies flapped bizarrely in the breeze; a still smoking fireplace spilling its contents into a black hole that had once held a parlour; upper floors broken open to the elements, a bed hung precariously on the edge as if any second it might plunge into the morass of destruction below. Water poured from broken pipes and over everything was an all-pervading stink of gas.

Rita stood stock-still and stared, hollow-eyed, at the scene before her. 'Dear Lord, I hope that for once in his life, Joe didn't do as I told him and stopped to peel that bloody potato.'

It was the first time Florrie had heard her sister swear.

The next few weeks proved to be the happiest in Daisy's life. She wouldn't have been without any of them, even poor, sad Mr Pickles with his constantly long face and dusty appearance, for all he claimed to be so much happier here on the farm than alone in his old home. He would explain, at length, to Daisy how he'd felt quite unable to continue in the empty house they had once occupied together. He did have a daughter but had no wish to be a burden to her, so had come to Lane End. 'At least here I am not alone, and you have made me so comfortable. I appreciate that, Miss Atkins.'

'Ooh, call me Daisy for heaven's sake, or you'll make me feel as old as Miss – I mean older than I really am,' and she hastily assured him how glad she was that he felt at home.

That first night she'd presented her guests with lamb cutlets, new potatoes, and carrots and turnips mashed together with a dab of margarine. Even this had brought not the ghost of a smile to Ned Pickles' lugubrious expression despite him declaring that the meal was delicious. Tommy Twinkletoes, on the other hand, had been effusive in his praise. On the second night she gave them fish, with oxtail soup and spam fritters on the third, all served up by Clem who moved about with surprising alacrity, carrying plates and cups with the speed of a greyhound just released from the starting gate.

'Give 'em time to enjoy their meal before you whip their plates away,' Daisy warned. Poor man. He didn't seem to know what had hit him. One minute he'd been leading a quiet life, unchanging save for the seasons, now he was the proprietor of a boarding house. Well, at least it would keep his mind off worrying over Florrie.

He returned to the kitchen with plates mopped clean of the last speck of gravy. 'The dog couldn't leave these any cleaner but what's up wi' that Pickles character? Face as long as a wet fortneet. Has his wife run off with a sailor? Mind, any woman'd run off with t'next door's cat if she had to wake up to that miserable face every morning. He makes me want to cut me own throat I feel that depressed after talking to him for just five minutes. He's as miserable as a yow on a rainy day. I towd him once: a smile costs nowt.'

Daisy had to ask, 'And what did he say to that?'

Clem sighed. '"Life is a vale of tears." Eeh, I could've wept blood.'

Stifling the inappropriate giggles, Daisy explained about poor Mr Pickles' recent loss and later noticed Clem serve him with an especially large helping of bread and butter pudding.

Ned's reaction to such generosity was to take every opportunity to enlighten Clem with his opinions about the state of the nation or his view of current military tactics, acquired by attending regular lectures, talks and lantern slide shows put on at the school hall in Keswick which he visited regularly on his bicycle. He was more than ready to share his passion for political propaganda by encouraging his fellow residents, in particular Daisy herself, to accompany him. She would politely decline on the grounds she had far too much work to do caring for her guests. Instead, she did her best to try to persuade Clem to join him. Clem always looked anxious to get away, fidgeting as if there were a million and one jobs he'd much rather be doing, like shovelling muck in the cowshed.

'Why would I want to go?' he grumbled. 'I see enough of the miserable old bugger about the house all day.'

'But he's lonely.' She didn't say that Clem too was lonely but managed, after a week or two of

351

persuasion, to get him to go along. The pair set off together one evening in a silent fug of resentment. Ned preferring to have escorted Daisy, and Clem wishing he could stop at home with his carpet slippers.

She watched them go with a fond smile on her face. If only Florrie would come home. Maybe she'd find Clem changed, ready to talk about his grief now. Sometimes you could almost accuse him of being chatty. She chuckled softly, gazing up at the bright stars and wondering where Harry was at this moment. Was that what they called a bomber's moon? Would he be flying tonight? She shivered and rubbed her hands up and down her arms, as if a goose had stepped over her grave. Best she didn't know when he was flying, or where. He rarely spoke of it but she knew he wasn't the pilot, only the gunner at the back. Surely he'd be safer there? Or would he?

Deliberately she turned her mind back to more practical, safer issues, such as what Florrie would say to having her house turned upside down by a bunch of strangers. Daisy quailed at the thought. She'd certainly have some explaining to do when her aunt finally did come home. So long as she didn't bring Rita with her, she'd cope somehow. Thinking of her mother reminded Daisy of her father, and the awkwardness of their last meeting. She really shouldn't be too hard on him. After all, he must be a saint to have lived with Rita all these years.

After a moment, she closed the door on the chill of the evening, and pulling a chair up to the kitchen fire set about writing him a letter. You only had one father after all. And keeping in touch with family was important.

By the end of the first couple of weeks, Laura and Chrissy counted themselves as experts. 'Look at that.' Chrissy held out a five-pound note given to her by one of the guests. 'This is a great job. And everyone likes my hair. Didn't I say it was only that stuffy headmistress?'

Wisely Laura made no comment.

It was as she was heading through the hall en route to the dining room that the doorbell rang and she hurried to answer it, guessing it must be the new guest for room three, a Mrs Crabtree.

A man with a clipboard stood in the yard with that special smile on his face which marked him as a salesman of some sort.

'No double glazing today, thank you,' Laura began but he interrupted her.

'We haven't met but I've spoken to your husband. It is Mrs Rampton, isn't it? Mrs Miranda Rampton?'

Laura had very nearly closed the door when these last words gave her pause. 'What did you call me? My name is Rampton, yes. Laura Rampton.'

He looked confused. 'Oh dear, I must have got the name wrong. It's in connection with the loan.'

'What loan?' She was standing before him now, arms folded. 'I know nothing about any loan.'

'The second mortgage. Your husband did say he would deal with the matter, have you sign the necessary papers. However, it's our normal practice to visit the property in question.'

'I think you'd better come in.'

Once Laura had fully appraised him of the situation, he readily informed her that Felix had given Miranda as his wife's name, his new address as Cheadle Hulme, and named Lane End Farm as a country retreat.

By the end of a most lively and enlightening half hour's chat, washed down with some of her excellent coffee, Laura and the man with the clipboard were bosom pals. He'd shared with her horror stories from his own divorce and Laura had expressed her appreciation for his diligence in the matter. Had he not called upon her, in direct opposition to Felix's wishes, she might well have simply have been presented with a wad of forms to sign.

'And, if he'd bullied or confused you sufficiently, you might well have signed them. Is he a bully, your husband, Mrs Rampton?' The young man asked with touching sympathy in his voice.

'Indeed he can be.'

'Well, no harm has been done. We, as a Society, are always most particular about ensuring all parties and property are thoroughly checked out. I shall write and refuse him the mortgage, and see that these forms are destroyed forthwith. Good day to you, and good luck with your new project.' She led him to the door and saw him on his way with one of her brochures tucked in his inside pocket.

Some time later, Laura showed Mrs Crabtree, the new guest, up to her room, helped with her

354

bags and gave out the necessary information about breakfast times and whether she would like a morning paper. She was a woman in her mid to late sixties, full of smiles, looking interestedly about her as Laura turned to go, her mind already moving on to the tables she must lay and the pile of bed linen waiting to be ironed. Mrs Crabtree said, 'I must say you've done the house up lovely.'

'Thank you.'

She gave a self-conscious little laugh. 'When I saw your advertisement in the *Manchester Guardian*, I couldn't resist ringing up and booking for a short break. It was a chance too good to miss. This is a trip down memory lane for me.'

Laura was at once all ears. The incident over the second mortgage had shaken her badly but she was determined not to give up on her dream, not only of establishing a good business, but of finding out more about Daisy. 'Why, have you stayed here before when my grandmother ran it?'

The woman's face was a picture of shock and delight. 'Daisy was your grandmother? Oh my, I assumed you'd simply bought the house. Then your father must be... Tell me dear, his name wouldn't be Robbie, by any chance, would it?'

Laura couldn't help but smile even as her mind whirled with questions, never having heard the diminutive used in connection with her father before. It didn't seem to suit him at all. 'Robert actually. Do you know him?'

'Only as a child. I was brought here as an evacuee. Daisy was my great friend, and I adored your father when he was a baby, absolutely adored him. My name is Megan, by the by. I don't suppose Daisy ever mentioned me, did she?'

Laura was staring at the woman, stunned. 'Megan? Of course. You and your sister Trish travelled with her to the Lakes on the train.'

The woman beamed with remembered pleasure then burst out laughing. 'That's us, in our overlong trailing mackintoshes and dreadful berets. Trish emigrated to Canada after she married but I used to come here quite a lot. Became quite a regular until well into the sixties, till I started a family and life got too hectic, you know how it is. Daisy and I would reminisce about old times. Quite a pair of old gossips we were.'

Laura's eyes were shining. 'I certainly have heard all about you. How wonderful to meet you in person. Perhaps, when you've settled in, you'd come and have a gossip with me. I'm always happy to learn more about Daisy.'

'Be glad to. I can tell you how she came to open this place, and how she found your father?'

'Found?'

'Didn't you know that Daisy had a son who was given away for adoption? Didn't your father ever tell you?'

'Heaven help me, what are you saying? You mean Daisy *found* him again? Could that be possible? That my father was actually her lost son?'

'Of course it could. Whyever not? How old is he?'

356

'Excuse me?'

'When was he born?'

Laura considered. 'I'm not sure. He's sixty-three, born during the war, no, just before it.'

'There you are then. Daisy's lost son. The age fits.'

A moment's silence while Laura absorbed the implications. 'How can you be sure? I've practically taken the place apart and found no sign of any birth or marriage certificates, no documentary evidence of any kind.'

'Well you wouldn't, would you? What with the adoption and the war and everything.'

'But I don't understand any of this. How did it all come about? How did she find him?'

'You could always ask him that.'

'You don't know my father. Having warned me off poking and prying into Daisy's life, he'd simply blow his top again. No, no there has to be some other way.'

'Shall I tell you what I know? It might help. I could tell you how we found Daisy again.'

'Oh, please do. Perhaps we could get together this evening, over supper? What happened after the bomb? And tell me more about how you came to know my father.'

'So what d'you think you're going to do with it then? You can't keep it. It's not yours.'

Florrie looked at the baby and began to cry. The pair were sitting on a pile of broken bricks and splintered window frames, all that remained of their home. From the harshness of her tone a stranger might be fooled into thinking that Rita

357

didn't care that her husband was probably buried somewhere beneath it all. Florrie knew different. Rita was always at her nastiest when she was most upset. Besides, her eyes were red, her nose was running and she could barely get the words out through the tightness of the pain constricting her throat. 'How should I know what we ought to do with it, but right now it needs feeding. God almighty – and changing.' She lifted the baby, wrinkled her nose and shook her head in despair. 'Aw, poor little love.'

'Never mind the baby being a poor little love, what about us? We're homeless. Bombed out. Or haven't you noticed?'

Florrie looked with pity on her sister. And you're a widow, but didn't have the courage to say as much in so many words. Between first finding the ruins of their home, not to mention all of the other houses in Marigold Court, to them arriving back here and seating themselves upon its smoking remains, the two women had trailed from one air-raid shelter to another in their search for Joe, not missing a single opportunity to ask if anyone had seen him, or check out a place where he might have taken cover.

'He's a goner,' Rita had finally admitted, not a tear in sight. 'I bet he stayed put, peeling that bloody potato. Never did know what was best for him, the silly old fool. Now what are we supposed to do? No home, no husband, no job, no money. What now?' She rooted in her pocket for a bit of grubby rag that passed for a hanky and blew her nose upon it, loud and hard.

'And we've the bairn to think about, don't forget.'

Rita shot a venomous glare at Florrie. 'Aren't you listening to a single word I've said? We've bigger problems to consider than a lost child. Anyroad, there's some nappies, over there. I reckon they'll be dry by now,' Rita's black humour seemed stronger than ever as she gazed upon the ruins of her world.

Florrie stared in horror at the washing line with its row of terry napkins. Who had washed them, and where was the child? Had it, or the mother, survived? Even if they had, she could surely spare one nappy in the circumstances. Propping the baby on her hip, Florrie picked her way over the heap of loose chunks of plaster and burning debris to unpeg the cleanest one from the line, deciding to take a second as well, just to be safe. Milk for the baby was another matter.

Back beside her sister, Florrie pointed out this problem as she cleaned up the baby as best she could and pinned on the clean nappy. 'He must be weaned by now, mustn't he, but a bairn still needs milk.'

'Never mind milk for the babby, what are we going to eat? Dirt, I suppose.'

A woman who happened to be passing by as Rita asked the question, answered it for her. 'We're to go down to t'council school. There's soup on offer from the WVS, and summat fer t'child an' all, I reckon.'

Rita didn't thank her but simply nodded, by way of a greeting when she saw whom she addressed. 'That's what I've got coming to me now, is it? A blanket and a bit of hard floor in an old schoolroom, and handouts from a soup kitchen. It'll be the flamin' workhouse next.'

'Reckon we've all come down in t'world today. Some of us with a bump.'

'How's your Percy?'

'Fair to middling.'

'It's a boy, a fine one at that,' Florrie said, quite inconsequentially, paying no attention to the conversation between the two neighbours as she buried the dirty nappy amongst the rubbish around her.

The woman stared at the baby with bleak eyes. 'At least you can be thankful he's too young to fight. Unlike my lad. Got near shot to pieces, he did. You'd think he'd be safe on a big ship like that, wouldn't you?'

'What about your Annie and the nippers?' Rita asked, but the woman only jerked her head in the direction of the destruction behind them, and even the hard-hearted Rita seemed moved by the gesture. 'Joe an' all,' she said, acknowledging their mutual loss. Both women looked away, embarrassed by their own vulnerability and not yet able to cope with pity.

'I'd best be going.' Without pausing to linger, she went on her way, dragging her feet as if the effort even of walking were too much for her, face pinched and drawn with suffering.

Reality finally began to penetrate. An entire area, all the entries and yards and courts with their fanciful names and long history of gloom and poverty had been destroyed this day. No loss, some might say, save for the number of mothers and children, old folk and loved ones who'd been lost along with them. Every one an innocent victim of war. Rita expelled her anger by blaming not only the German planes who'd dropped the bombs but the local authorities for their inadequate means of protection, the government, and even the ARP Warden who, in her opinion, had very nearly been the death of them.

Florrie was still preoccupied with the baby. 'Who does he belong to? Did you see anyone who might have been his mam? We should take him back to the ARP Warden, get him checked out by a doctor. There, there, don't cry little chap. Hush now, hush.' She sat him on her lap and began to rock him to and fro, crooning gently as she gave him a finger to suck to ease his hunger. Rita was saying nothing, only sat staring at her in an odd sort of way.

22

Daisy was enjoying herself hugely and finding them all to be excellent guests. They paid their rent on time, were perfectly amenable and pleasant to live with. And if she made mistakes with her cooking, they were most forgiving, this being a new enterprise for her and she so young. They didn't mind in the least the blackened toast, the soggy vegetables, the somewhat leathery Yorkshire puddings because they were so enchanted by her cheerful smile, her lovely face, and by her willingness to be helpful.

And she made a point of listening to their problems. It soon became clear why Miss Geraldine Copthorne had been barred from the parlour at her previous lodgings. Nothing at all to do with the price of coal. The woman was a bore. Well-meaning, stoic, hard working, but nonetheless a crashing bore. She barely stopped talking long enough to take a breath, and certainly never seemed to expect a reply.

As April gave way to May and the blossom on the cherry trees supplied a stark contrast to the dark horror that continued to fall from above, lighting the skies over the coast where Harry was stationed to a dull red, Daisy kept her mind occupied by taking great care of her guests. She worried so much about him that she was glad of the distraction. She worried too about Megan and Trish, having had no reply to her last two letters.

In addition to her regulars, there would often be a young soldier with his sweetheart sneaking off for a weekend. She would make sure they were comfortable but allow them plenty of privacy, not appearing to even notice if they didn't come down to breakfast. She might envy their joy in each other a little, but didn't begrudge them their need to escape from hostilities. One of these was a pilot by the name of Charlie Potter. Charlie and his girl became regulars during those first months, often popping in just for one of Daisy's high teas, even if they didn't stay overnight.

'There's no one like you Daisy,' he'd say. 'Most

landladies are dragons. Not our Daisy.'

Another was a Mr Enderby who came to visit his elderly mother but swore he couldn't live in the same house as her or there'd be murder done. He would put his shoes outside the bedroom door to be cleaned, just as if he were staying at the Savoy. Daisy would always clean them, and place them neatly back there the following morning.

'You're too soft for your own good, girl,' Clem would warn, but Daisy only grinned.

Daisy found herself sitting for hours with the spinster teacher in the parlour, hearing about her work, and her intention to take night-school classes in French once the war was over, which might gain her a much improved teaching post, perhaps in a girls' private school. She would offer to hold the wool if Miss Copthorne wanted to wind it. Knitting and sewing were her favourite forms of relaxation, next to talking, that is, and as she knitted socks, wound wool or hemmed handkerchiefs she would drone on and on, going over and over the same conversation night after night. Daisy felt duty-bound to listen; in truth there was little chance of escape once she'd got going. She learned more about education than she really felt the need to know; the woman's one topic of conversation being her precious charges and how difficult it was to keep up the necessary standards.

'We must still do our arithmetic, our algebra and get our school certificate,' she would declare sternly, followed by the oft-heard cry, 'war or no war.'

Miss Copthorne would discuss the relative merits of chain stitch as opposed to feather and why it was essential for each girl to learn plain sewing while the boys concentrate their efforts on running the school allotment. 'Even the children must play their part, dear Daisy, and dig for victory. However, education cannot be neglected. Oh, dear me no! War or no war.'

She was so thrifty that she would cut exercise books in half.

Daisy laughed, and said that she was just as bad with soap. 'I always think it will go twice as far if I give people half as much.'

'Ah, but is it thrift or the terrible sin of hoarding, dear Daisy, if a frugal housewife saves bars of soap, for instance, against a possible future shortage. Is it patriotic to be thrifty or are you a liability to your compatriots? A moot point don't you think?'

'I wouldn't know the answer to that one,' Daisy said, 'but I do know that anything we need to do here on the farm seems to require six sheets of foolscap to deal with it.'

'Oh indeed, I know all about forms, believe me. And you can be fined for throwing away your bus ticket in the street.'

Daisy enjoyed these lively exchanges but soon they'd be back on the same old treadmill of discussion on education and examinations, upon which Daisy could make less of a contribution. She did become familiar with the words of *The Young Lochinvar,* and *The Forsaken Merman* which Miss Copthorne was fond of reciting by heart.

Miss Copthorne was also concerned about the evacuee children who had returned to Newcastle, about whether her old school would open again to admit them despite the seemingly endless bombing, and how they would cope without her if they did.

'I certainly dare not leave these precious mites here all on their own.'

'Of course not,' and Daisy would helplessly wonder if the poor woman bored the children at their lessons in exactly the same way, by endlessly dull repetition, drumming facts into their tiny heads until they were heartily sick of it. Or perhaps her little charges brought out the best in her.

In the secret depths of her heart Daisy too worried about the evacuee children, two in particular. She still held on to her dream of having Megan and Trish come to live with her at Lane End Farm. Again she'd written and got no response and if Miss Copthorne's enquiries revealed that they were in any sort of difficulties, or the slightest bit miserable, she would take her courage in both hands and beg Clem to take them in. There was plenty of room, after all, and at least then she would know they were safe.

And then one morning there came a knock at the door. Daisy hurried to answer it, curious as to who it might be since they didn't get many visitors living so high up on the mountainside.

It was Harry, brown hair cut shorter than ever, polished boots caked in mud from the long walk up the lane, and an ear to ear grin wreathing his

365

face. Daisy leapt into his arms on a shriek of delight. 'Have you got some leave?'

'Two days.'

'Oh bliss!' She hadn't seen him for weeks, not since he was posted, and this was the first time that he'd come to the farm. It felt wonderful to have his arms around her again, to breathe in the scent of him and lose herself in the glorious power of his kisses. But he wasn't alone.

'Look what I've got here,' he said, when they stopped hugging and kissing long enough to stand apart a little, smiling shyly into each other's eyes. And from behind his back he drew out two small figures.

'Megan! Trish! I don't believe it.' Tears of joy sprang to her eyes as Daisy gathered her two small friends to her in a fierce hug. They were bounding with exuberance, like a pair of puppies wriggling and yelping with glee so that they knocked Daisy over in their excitement and all three were soon rolling about on the grass while Harry stood by, laughing in delight.

Wouldn't he do anything for his Daisy? And bringing the children to her had seemed to him the perfect way to prove that. He couldn't quite get over his good fortune at attracting her attention in the first place, him being such a homely sort of bloke and she a real looker.

'I decided it was time you three musketeers got together again,' he explained as they sat in the kitchen and Daisy fussed about heating soup and buttering bread, saying how she wished she'd known they were coming then she would have baked something special for the children. 'When you said in your last letter that you hadn't heard from them in ages, I took it into my head to call and see how they were.' He was frowning slightly as he said this, and something in his face told Daisy not to ask any more questions just then, so instead she went to him and kissed him.

'I'm so glad you did.'

Megan said. 'He just walked up the garden path bold as you please.'

'Right into the shed, picked us up out of our camp beds and carried us away in his arms. Mrs Carter said she'd never seen such cheek in her life,' Trish added, slapping her hand over her mouth to hold back her giggles.

Daisy listened to this in astonishment. She longed to ask what on earth the children were doing sleeping on camp beds in a garden shed, but mindful of the warning in Harry's eyes and of Megan's small mouth pursed into mutinous angry silence, she managed to hold her tongue.

Trish, realising she'd revealed more than she should, cast her sister an anxious, sidelong glance before adding in hushed and horrified tones, 'She were going to send me away. To an 'ospital. On me *own.*'

'Hostel, for problem children,' Megan corrected her quietly in a tight little voice.

Later, as Daisy sat cuddled beside Harry while the children played ball, he told her the full story and she was appalled to hear how they'd been treated. How could anyone put two such lovely children in a garden shed, just because they might have scabies, or some other problem which was not of their making?

Harry too had been more shocked than he could say when he'd found them like that, all huddled up together like a pair of frightened mice. He knew from his own experience, coming from a large, close-knit family, the value of a happy childhood. Didn't he go back to Halifax to visit them whenever he could? His own mother had taken in two evacuees, despite having a full house already, and treated them as members of the family.

'I know I've created a problem, broken some rules maybe, but I couldn't just walk away and leave them like that.'

'Course you couldn't. The very idea.'

'Unthinkable. I like children too much.'

'Do you?' Daisy gazed up at him starry-eyed. Perhaps she should tell him now, about her own baby? But then Trish fell down and started yelling and the opportunity was missed.

Once she'd been put back on her feet, bruised knees wiped and kissed better, Daisy looked on with concern as they played. Trish seemed even more jumpy and excitable, constantly crying out for attention while Megan was quieter, more withdrawn. The smiles and joy at having found each other again had quickly vanished and she'd withdrawn into some sort of shell, which Daisy didn't wonder at. These two had spent the entire war being shifted about from pillar to post with no one prepared to take responsibility for them. It was utterly inhuman, and settled the matter once and for all so far as she was concerned. 'They're staying here with me now, come what may.'

368

'I guessed you might say that,' Harry grinned. 'That's why I brought their stuff.'

'Oh Harry, did you really?' Her eyes were round with surprise and delight.

'I left their bags round the back, in the barn.'

'Harry Driscoll, you old softy.' Daisy leaned into his strong shoulder, curling an arm about his neck as she smiled up into his green-grey eyes and knew a moment of such all encompassing love, she felt choked with emotion.

'I am, where you are concerned, Daisy.'

'So that's how she found you again?' Laura said.

'Yes, through Harry. He was the kindest man I know. And the most patient. He adored Daisy, would do anything for her. And that was the most wonderful summer I can ever remember.' Megan Crabtree got up from the table. 'But I'm an old woman now and must away to my bed. That was a lovely meal, thank you. Perhaps tomorrow, I can tell you a little more.'

Laura said goodnight, had a slight tussle of wills with Chrissy but finally got her off to bed too. Which left her alone with David since she hadn't been able to resist inviting him along to hear more of the tale, and he couldn't resist coming. Now she turned to him with smiling eyes.

'I'm so glad Daisy was happy with her Harry. Happiness is so important, don't you think?'

'You have gorgeous eyes, do you know that? So alive.'

'I beg your pardon?'

David's mouth twisted into that irrepressible

369

grin. 'Your eyes. Did anyone ever tell you how lovely they were? All dark and mysterious. A soft, velvet brown. Most inviting.'

'David, for goodness' sake. We're discussing important issues here, important to me anyway.'

'Your eyes are pretty important to me too, as a matter of fact. Hey, don't scowl at me, it spoils the effect. OK, I find Daisy fascinating too, but...'

'You're bored.'

He pulled her very gently into his arms. 'I was only thinking that perhaps we've discussed family history long enough, and maybe it was time to move on to more personal concerns.'

'So what subject would you like to discuss?' She found she was having difficulty holding on to her scowl, it kept slipping into a smile. Could that be because of the nearness of him, the solid strength of his arms, or the mesmerising motion of his hand smoothing up and down her back?

He was kissing her nose, her throat, moving round to her ear. 'I didn't actually have talking in mind.'

Laura could feel herself starting to melt, rapidly losing control as a pleasurable sensation began to grow deep in the hollow pit inside her, a place more accustomed to despair and misery in recent months. His arms had tightened about her, his breathing shortened and there was an increasing intensity to his kisses. Laura slid her arms about his neck and gave herself up to them. Sensation rocked her, throwing her completely off balance. How long had it been since she'd properly loved a man? She and Felix had become distant strangers. Felix, oh heavens! What was she thinking of? She pushed David away, knowing her eyes were glazed with wanting, her face as flushed as a newly awakened girl.

'Look, you're a nice guy but...'

'I know, you're still married. You need time and space. This is all going too fast for you.' His voice was soft, a caress in itself.

'So you read minds too?' She couldn't take her eyes off his. They were asking a question she couldn't answer. Demanding. Compelling. Challenging her to give in to the inevitable, and filled with a quiet certainty that in the end, she would. Yet there was also in the depths of his gaze a rare understanding, a reassurance that he would tread delicately through this minefield of her emotions. Together, these produced an intoxicating combination that left her weak with need. Laura cleared her throat. 'The fact is, I'm a bit out of my depth here, and out of practice.'

'I could help you rehearse and get back into step.'

She giggled. 'I'm sure you could.'

'Perhaps I should call every day to take you through your paces. Lesson one, relax.' He pushed her back gently on to the cushions of the sofa, smoothing his hands over her bare arms, lifting them above her head while he kissed her softly, increasing the pressure on her mouth as she made no move to resist; taking his time over the kiss, savouring it, making it last as long as possible. He slid one hand beneath the silk blouse to smooth it lightly over her breast, making her groan softly. He pulled away to look unsmiling into her eyes and it was she who pulled him back to her, begging him to kiss her some more for it was much too late to protest now. One minute her fingers were wandering of their own accord through his hair, the next tugging at the buttons of his shirt.

He slid her silk blouse from her shoulders, dropping it to the floor with barely a whisper, making no comment about how her body trembled as he lay her upon the rug with reverent care. 'Are you sure about this?' was all he said as she struggled with the buckle of his jeans.

Her mind in turmoil, unable to think of anything but the touch of his fingers on her over-sensitised skin, Laura had never been less sure of anything in her life. She'd set the wheels in motion for the divorce but there was months to go before she would be a free woman, and was afraid of something going wrong in the meantime. With Felix, it felt a bit like lighting the touchpaper and standing back to wait for the explosion. There seemed to be plenty of explosions going on inside of her right now. 'I'm quite certain that if you don't take me soon, I might ravish you instead.'

'I've no objection to a bit of ravishing.'

'The only thing is,' she murmured breathlessly through several more kisses. 'You can't stay *too* much longer. I have to be up early tomorrow to cook breakfast, and there's still the washing-up to do.'

He let out a heavy sigh of resignation and finally, reluctantly, released her, albeit with a smile. 'OK, lead me to the dishwasher.'

'Do you think having a love affair was any easier in World War Two?'

'You mean everything to me, Daisy. I don't ever want us to be apart.' Even as he said these glorious words, Harry was kissing her face, her throat, her lips with such tenderness, Daisy felt she might weep she wanted him so much. Then he pulled away and smiled very tenderly into her eyes. 'But I mean us to do everything proper like. I mean us to wed, if you'll have me.' He was fumbling in his pocket, pulling out a box, and Daisy could hardly believe her eyes as he opened it to reveal a tiny, solitaire diamond on a twist of gold, glittering in the sunshine. 'I know I should ask your parents first, you being under age, but until I get the chance, we could at least get unofficially engaged. If that's all right with you?'

'Oh Harry. It's lovely.'

'I take it that's a yes? I couldn't bear it if it wasn't.'

She gave a soft little chuckle and kissed his nose. 'Silly boy, don't you know by now how much I love you?'

'And I love you, Daisy. Don't ever forget that.'

'As if I could.'

'You and me for ever girl, right?'

'For ever and ever.'

Being together for a whole afternoon was magical, over much too soon and Daisy felt all wobbly inside at having become engaged to the most wonderful young man in the world. But she didn't dare to wear the ring, not yet, not till everything had been made official between them and she wasn't yet ready to confront her mother. Carefully she wrapped it in a handkerchief and hid it in her undies drawer. Perhaps she wouldn't ever need to, if Harry was prepared to wait a year or two till she was twenty-one. It would be sensible not to rush anyway, what with the war and everything. And it would give them time to save up. Daisy gave a happy little sigh and fell asleep dreaming of wedding bells and white frocks, the scent of apple blossom in the air.

Following the intriguing information that she'd learned thus far, partly from Megan Crabtree and partly from the tapes, Laura rang her father and asked if he'd like to come and stay for a few days.

'Why would I want to?' he barked down the phone.

'Lane End used to be your old home. Wouldn't you like to see what I've done to it? See if you approve.'

'You know my opinion on the matter, Laura. I certainly would not approve. If you choose to ignore my advice, on your own head be it. You'll lose Felix, run out of money and come to regret this madness of yours in the end.'

'I hope not. It's hard work but I'm rather enjoying it. Guess who is here? Megan Crabtree. Do you remember her? She remembers you with great affection as a baby, so you must have been adorable once.' Laura chuckled. 'Sends her fond regards and hopes to meet up with you again one day. Actually, that's partly why I rang. I was wondering – well, it crossed my mind that you might like to pop up now, she's here for the week, and the pair of you could catch up on old times.

374

What do you say?'

For the first time in her life Laura appeared to have left her father speechless. The silence lasted for so long that she had to ask if he was still there.

'Of course I'm still here.'

'Have you forgotten Megan? She seems to remember you well enough: a sturdy little chap, she called you. Claims she spent a good deal of time picking up your toys.'

'I remember Megan perfectly well. She used to read me endless Beatrix Potter stories. And Trish. They were evacuees. Went home eventually, after the war, then came back again.'

'Really? She never mentioned that. Well, what do you think? A reunion might be fun?' Laura fully expected him to refuse. Robert could not be called the most gregarious of people at the best of times. However, she was wrong. He mumbled something about having to look up train times, and which days weren't suitable because of golf or bridge commitments but, in the end, a day was agreed upon. Laura told Megan Crabtree, who was thrilled with the promise of meeting up with 'little Robbie' again so soon. 'I can't wait,' she said.

Neither can I, thought Laura.

It was the most touching sight she could ever have imagined. Laura parked her Peugeot on the gravel forecourt and by the time she'd climbed out, Megan was at the front door, waiting anxiously. She took one look at her 'little Robbie', now a sixty-something grey-haired man with a paunch, and held wide her arms. To Laura's utter amazement, her father beamed and happily succumbed to being thoroughly hugged and kissed. In fact, he seemed to be doing quite a bit of that sort of thing on his own account.

Laura was stunned. Even Chrissy, standing equally slack-jawed beside her, whispered, 'Would you believe it? Soppy old Gramps.'

The pair rarely stopped talking for the entire afternoon, most of it incomprehensible to Laura, all about school friends, nature rambles and concerts not to mention numerous teachers, a Miss Copthorne being the only name she recognised. Megan held a particularly fond memory of herself and Trish dressing up as Gert and Daisy.

'Don't remember that,' Robert said. 'I was probably too young at the time.'

'It was perhaps during that first wonderful summer. Oh, but it was great fun. Trish was always a great mimic, had them off to perfection. Do you remember the Christmas carol concerts and the time Trish was the Virgin Mary and dropped the baby doll?' Roaring with laughter they were off into other reminiscences.

Chrissy slipped away halfway through the afternoon, saying she was going to meet a friend down in Threlkeld. Laura was pleased that she'd found one and made no objection, knowing it must be rather dull for her to spend all her time with boring adults. It briefly crossed her mind to ask who it was but then the telephone rang and by the time she'd taken another booking, Chrissy had gone. Laura went to put on the kettle, to freshen up the tea.

It wasn't until her father was about to leave that Laura plucked up the courage to mention the subject of the land. She knew it would be a delicate issue, with deep connotations. Helping him on with his coat she tried, and failed, to persuade him to stay overnight.

'No, no, I don't want to be any trouble. Besides, I've things planned for tomorrow.'

'Wouldn't it be nice for you to stay in your childhood home for one night? You could have your old room. Which was it?'

'Unlike you, Laura, I have no wish to revisit the past.'

'You just have, with Megan, for an entire afternoon. You mean Daisy's past I suppose, since you, personally, have scarcely mentioned her name, for all it has cropped up countless times out of Megan's mouth. For goodness' sake, why? I should perhaps warn you that I've found out about the land, about you owning it, I mean. Did you think I wouldn't? I'm not sure why you kept it from me though I'll admit it really is no concern of mine who owns it.'

He looked shocked for a moment, his usually florid face paling slightly and the mouth tightening to a grim line. 'I have nothing to do with it. Nothing at all. Never touch the rent from it, it stays in the Trust.'

Laura's mouth dropped open. 'You mean you've never used the money, and you so often crying poverty? Where's the point in deliberately depriving yourself of a decent standard of living? That's not what Daisy wanted.'

'I've not touched a penny of it. Never will. What about the way she behaved with Harry? She cheated on my father with him. Betrayed him. He deserved better. Hadn't he suffered enough as a casualty of war?'

'We don't know that for sure. We don't yet know what happened between the three of them. And there was a war on; circumstances were difficult.'

'I agree there may be some things we never discover, or fully understand. But I'll not touch her damned money. It's nothing at all to do with me.'

'But she was your *mother!*'

His gaze was filled with fury now as he turned on her. 'No, Laura. She was *not* my mother. God knows who I was, but I didn't belong to Daisy. Haven't you understood anything you've heard from Megan and from these damned tapes you've been telling us about. I wasn't Daisy's child at all. I was stolen. Florrie told me so just before she died. That's why we quarrelled. That's why Daisy never loved me.'

Her father was so upset after this declaration that he stormed off into the night, slamming the door in Laura's startled face. For a whole thirty seconds she stood rooted to the spot before being galvanised into action by the sight of his fleeing figure. Grabbing her car keys and coat, she jumped in the car and went in pursuit of him down the lane.

They were sitting outside the railway station, talking quietly now. Robert had calmed down but his eyes still looked suspiciously bright. Very gently, Laura asked him why he believed that Daisy hadn't loved him.

'She lied. She told me I was her lost boy returned to her, the one she'd thought never to see again. Then Florrie told me I wasn't at all, that she herself had picked me up out of the rubble during the blitz and they hadn't the first idea who I belonged to. All that tale about Percy's sister and brother-in-law adopting me was a complete fabrication.'

Laura listened in silence as the hurt came pouring out. So this was the reason for that terrible quarrel, the family feud. 'I can see that it must have been painful to learn such a thing, but it doesn't prove that Daisy didn't care for you. Perhaps she believed Rita's story; had been taken in by her own mother's lies. And if she had ever discovered otherwise, perhaps she kept up the pretence because she wanted you to feel secure. That's what mothers do. In any case, even if she knew all along that you might not be her son, perhaps she wanted, needed, to believe that you were.'

He stared at her, saying nothing. 'Why would she choose to do that?'

'Because she loved you, why else? She didn't want to lose you. She says on the tape how she lost her son twice and hoped you would forgive her for the hurt you suffered.'

'I was either a foundling or illegitimate,' he snarled. 'I don't know which. Not much of a start in life, is it? If the former, as Florrie insisted was the case, then Daisy only kept me out of pity, because she felt sorry for me as she did for Megan and Trish. Just another evacuee. We were her compensation for the baby she lost, not a genuine, heartfelt love. That's what has haunted me all my life.'

'Oh no, I can't believe she'd ever simply do things out of pity. She adored Megan and Trish, I can tell that from the tone of her voice let alone all the other evidence I've heard. As for you, you were special. You were her son. Whatever the truth, whether you were her own natural child or adopted, she wanted to keep you out of love for you, not pity. None of it was your fault, nor Daisy's, and nothing at all to be ashamed of. I expect she was angry with Florrie for telling you, for putting that doubt into your mind but Florrie was an old and bitter woman. You'll have to forgive her too.'

He looked at her then, his eyes beseeching her to convince him.

'Dad,' Laura said. 'I love you too,' and she put her arms around him and hugged him.

'And I love you,' he mumbled into her collar.

23

Clem had no objection to the two little girls staying on, not if it meant that Daisy would stay with them, and personally went to see the billeting officer to make it all right. 'Just what we need, to have a couple of young 'uns about the place.'

'They can help with the cleaning,' Daisy said, laughing when they both pulled mock faces of dismay, for their shining eyes were telling quite a different story.

They quickly came to love the old man and readily obeyed his every word, trailing behind him wherever he went. 'Like Mary and her flippin' lamb,' he would say with a great chortle of mirth, secretly delighted to have such adulation.

Clem showed them how to collect eggs from the hens, still warm from the nests, without getting pecked by the bad-tempered cockerel. He taught them how to cut peat and trundle it back to the shed in an old wooden coup cart. They were allowed to help him fill the paraffin lamps each evening, and to wash and carefully dry the lamp glasses, so long as they were careful, but were never permitted to use matches. The ceremony of lighting the lamps was strictly in Clem's domain.

He was quite strict with them in other ways too, making it clear they must never come anywhere near his plough, harrow or other sharp implements which he kept in the barn. 'These aren't playthings and this in't toytown, so think on, leave well alone. We don't want no chopped off fingers messing up the works, now do we?'

Trish gave a delicious squeal of horror while Megan shook her head solemnly.

But it wasn't all work. He tied a piece of wood to a length of rope and hung it from the big old ash tree behind the house. The pair of them would happily swing on it for hours. Sometimes,

381

he let them take jam sandwiches and a bottle of tea down to the beck and they'd tuck up their skirts and paddle, Daisy along with them, something they'd never had the opportunity to do in their lives before. And he bought them a tin hat each for sixpence at the church jumble sale, just like the one William wore in the Richmal Crompton books. They were rarely seen without them after that.

'Well, at least them two nippers is ready for the invasion, even if we aren't,' he quipped.

Their favourite task was to feed the calves and Dolly the old shorthorn cow. Megan loved their big brown eyes and long lashes, and Trish loved anything that made Megan happy. They'd fill a bucket with water down at the beck, and another of feedstuffs mixed to Clem's secret recipe and stand quietly by, watching while they dipped in their noses and munched away. When the bucket was completely empty the calves would lick their hands instead, their rough tongues making the children shriek with laughter.

Miss Copthorne found them a place in the village school and marched them there every morning at breakneck speed. 'Perhaps we might purchase a bicycle each,' she suggested one day, when she saw Trish having difficulty in keeping up.

Megan said gloomily, 'It would be fine riding down in the morning, but cycling back up the lane every afternoon wouldn't be much fun.' Anyway, she loved to dawdle, nibbling 'bread and cheese' from the hedgerows, as the local children called the hawthorn leaves that grew along each side of the lane.

The evacuee class used the schoolroom in the mornings, while the village children had it in the afternoon. When the children couldn't work inside, they put on their coats and were taken for long rambles to study flowers and trees, draw pictures, do bark rubbings and potato prints, or do some digging and weeding on the school allotment. And then they held a school concert and Megan and Trish pretended to be the famous music hall act, Gert and Daisy. They had the whole school in tucks of laughter, even Miss Copthorne.

It felt a bit odd to be with Miss Copthorne all day as their teacher, and then to walk home with her after school and have her turn into one of Daisy's lodgers. They tried not to speak to her much in the evenings, anyway, she was generally busy with marking homework, or filling in forms, about which she complained a good deal on their long trek homeward.

'I have to fill them in for everything: milk, clothing, national savings, not to mention dozens from the clinic and several more from the canteen. Anyone would think I had nothing else to do all day but collect information to put on these pestiferous forms.'

Megan would maintain a shrewd silence but Trish's eyes would grow round. She always loved it when her teacher used rude words.

It was an unforgettable summer, and in September while Russian pilots flying Hurricanes and Spitfires desperately defended Leningrad, Clem looped a piece of string through a National

Dried Milk tin and the pair went happily off blackberry picking, without a care in the world.

All in all, everything was going well for Daisy too. September was by tradition a month for shows. Clem had reminisced for days over how it used to be before the war, the serious discussions that would take place over whether the animal was well ribbed up, if its ears were pricked at just the right angle. And how he generally won a prize or two for the carefully bred tups and ewes he showed. Most had been cancelled, because of the war but the one Clem was attending today was going ahead, war or no war. It would be a mere shadow of its former self, of course, more of a shepherds' meet for the purpose of buying and selling prize stock, borrowing tups and returning strayed ewes; a time to have a bit of a crack and a chance to share problems. He'd wanted Daisy and the children to go with him but she'd said no, there was too much to do.

'Anyway, you don't need me getting under your feet. You have a good day with your chums.' And she'd packed him a substantial lunch box of home-made pies and home-cured ham butties.

The children returned from their expedition, faces black with juice. Daisy was up to her elbows in flour from making bread and pastry for the pies, her two small assistants helping or hindering, depending upon your perspective when the door flew open and Daisy finally came face to face with the kitchen's owner.

'Florrie?'

But it wasn't her aunt who held her sole

attention. Nor even Rita standing beside her, a look of malicious triumph on her face, as if to say: I've found you at last.

It was the sight of the child held in Florrie's arms who captured her utterly, heart and soul. Daisy walked over and gazed at him with open longing in her eyes. She took in the red-brown hair, the bright blue eyes and her heart turned slowly over inside her, just as if she were on a big dipper. No matter how hard she tried to push it to the back of her mind, deep inside the hurt had never gone away. She wanted her baby back as badly as ever, so much that it was a physical pain clamped tight around her heart. 'Who is this? Clem didn't say anything about a baby. Is he yours, Aunt Florrie?'

It was Rita who answered. 'Nay lass. Don't you recognise him? He's your son. Yours and Percy's. He's come home to his mam at last.'

Daisy heard the fear in the children's voices as she slid to the floor.

It seemed too good to be true. When Daisy came round after her faint, she half expected to find it had all been a dream but no, there he still was, sitting on Florrie's knee, happily kicking his chubby little legs while her mother stood guard over the teapot and Megan and Trish knelt anxiously beside her, their little faces as white as the streaks of flour down their pinnies.

'Are you all right, Daisy?' Trish stroked away a tear from her cheek, then patted it kindly.

'I thought you'd dropped dead too,' said Megan, in a worryingly matter-of-fact tone.

Daisy sat up quickly and pushed her hair from her eyes. A rush of blood to her head made it spin dizzily but she smiled nonetheless. 'No, no, I'm right as rain. Just had a bit of a turn, that's all. Must be the heat of this kitchen after all our cooking.'

Rita made no move to assist her daughter as she struggled to her feet, merely remarked, 'I reckoned you'd come round some time.' Just as if Daisy had deliberately allowed herself to faint and deserved to be left lying on the cold kitchen floor.

Assisted by her two small friends, Daisy dragged out a chair and heaved herself into it. 'What would I do without you two?' she said, smiling and hugging them close, and even as she offered further reassurances that she was perfectly well, her eyes were glued to the baby. Was he truly her child? He was about the right age, coming up to two years old. Heavens, was it so long? It felt like only yesterday. He had Percy's hair, brown with a hint of red if not quite so dark. Perhaps she'd got it all wrong, had indeed dreamed it in a way: wishing so hard that he could be hers that she'd misheard what her mother had actually said. She cleared her throat, feeling suddenly nervous.

'He's a fine baby, Florrie. You must be proud of him.' Best to play safe and assume he belonged to her aunt. She seemed so vulnerable with her deeply sunken eyes, purple shadows beneath, stringy bleached blonde hair in need of a wash, and yet on her feet a pair of red slingback shoes, boldly making a declaration of the woman she had once been. Oh, how Daisy wished Clem was here, but he'd warned her to expect him to be late home from his meet. Florrie looked up, a mixture of surprise and anxiety on her tired face as she flicked her gaze to Daisy and then quickly over to Rita.

Rita said, 'I told you, lass. He isn't our Florrie's. He's yours. Yours and Percy's. Don't you recognise him? He's the spitting image of his dad.'

There seemed to be a roaring sound in her head. She couldn't quite take it in. This was the second time Rita had announced this fact but Daisy was still finding it hard to believe the evidence of her own eyes and ears. Could it be true? Why would her mother lie? But wasn't she the one who wanted rid of the child? Wasn't he supposed to be a secret? Yet here he was, her own flesh and blood, or was he?

'Don't you want to hold him?' Rita asked, again with that odd little smirk on her face, thoroughly pleased with herself.

Daisy shook her head, panic washing over her. She daren't go anywhere near him. If she picked up the baby she might never let him go. She had to be sure, absolutely certain in her heart of hearts that he was hers, before she ever took the risk.

A small hand gently shook her shoulder. Megan was again offering her a mug of strong, sweet tea and Daisy smiled her gratitude at the child and took a few sips. She began to feel stronger almost at once. Something was wrong. She couldn't quite put her finger on what it was, but something wasn't right about all of this. She needed to find out exactly what was going on. Daisy turned to the two little girls. 'Why don't you go and play out on the swing for a bit.'

'What about our blackberry pie?' Megan asked, her mouth in a sulk.

'I'll give you a shout when I'm ready to put it in the oven.'

Trish went over to the baby and stroked his silky brown hair. 'Can he come and play too?'

'Tomorrow perhaps. He'll be tired just now, after all his travelling. Aunt Florrie will be putting him to bed for his nap soon, I expect.'

Florrie shot to her feet, as if a signal had been given for her to escape. 'I'll take him now. He'll need changing anyway,' and she flew up the stairs.

When the children too had gone and they were alone at last, Daisy turned to face her mother. 'I don't understand. You gave him up for adoption. Said he was to be for ever a secret. What changed? Where has he been all this time, and how come he's with you now?'

All questions Rita had been prepared for, along with several others. 'Nay lass, take a breath, will you. Give me a chance.' She settled herself comfortably at the table, poured a fresh mug of tea which she sweetened generously, with no regard to shortages, and then launched into her carefully rehearsed tale.

Rita had realised, the moment she'd clapped eyes on the remains of her home that she was done for, that there was no way her daughter would take her in off the streets. Not willingly anyroad, not after the way she'd been treated. There was too much bad feeling between them. It was a sad fact, in Rita's opinion, that today's generation didn't have the morals of her own. She'd done her best to bring up Daisy clean and decent, but the girl had let her down badly. So if she refused to be dragged down into the mire with her, where was the fault in that? But in the circumstances, it had left her in a pretty pickle.

It was finding the baby which had put the idea into her head. He could well be the key to Daisy's heart.

She'd dismissed it at first, on the grounds that it was too risky. Daisy wasn't stupid. But throughout the long weeks of trekking around vainly seeking accommodation, and with Florrie time and time again refusing to even consider returning to the Lake District or ask Clem to offer Rita a home, she'd begun to have second thoughts on the matter. She'd taken her time, letting the seed grow in her head, thinking it through from every angle till it blossomed into a fully fledged plan. Rita felt sure that she'd now examined all possible difficulties. The delay in putting it into effect had been no bad thing, as it turned out. As well as overcoming one or two minor problems, Florrie had been allowed sufficient time to grow fond of the child, even to give him a name. Robbie. So when Rita had finally put forward her plan, she'd very cleverly been able to put the stopper on further objections without any difficulty whatsoever.

'I don't really think you are in any position to argue, do you?'

'But you can't possibly let Daisy think this child is her own, when we know for certain that he isn't.'

'But we don't know that, do we? Not for certain,' Rita had remarked blithely, thin lips curling into a humourless smile. 'Since we've no idea who the lad is, he could very well be Daisy's babby.'

'It's not very likely though, is it? That would be too much of a coincidence. We found him in the shelter.'

'Who's to know where we found him, if we don't tell them? We need a roof over our heads before winter comes, and you can be absolutely certain that our Daisy won't offer one unless we make her.' Rita had given a careless shrug. 'Course, it's your house by rights, not our Daisy's, so you could happen exercise some power over that husband of yours.'

Florrie had paled visibly at the suggestion. 'Clem wouldn't listen to me. Not now. He happen won't have me in the house, let alone you. Not after walking out on him. Anyroad, I've told you already Rita, I'm not going back.'

'Oh yes you are, girl. You're coming with me. You'll do exactly as I say or else you might find yourself up for baby-snatching. Then where would you be?'

'Baby-snatching?' Florrie's voice cracked with fear. 'But I didn't snatch him, I picked him up – to nurse him, to look after him because I thought his mam had been killed, or hurt or something.'

Triumph gleamed from Rita's boot button eyes.

'So why have you done nowt about handing him back? How will you explain keeping him all this while, eh? And you know what they'll say, the polis. Didn't you lose a baby of your own once, Mrs Pringle? Sent you a bit wrong in the head, has it? Happen you'd best go into an asylum then. It'd be for the best, don't you think? Can't have you going around pinching other folk's babbies.'

Florrie had sobbed for days but, in the end, had complied with the plan, as Rita had known that she would. Simply because she had no choice. Nevertheless, it would be politic to keep a close watch on her, tighten the screws from time to time, just to make sure that she didn't defect.

None of this was revealed to her daughter as Rita calmly explained how the child she'd given birth to had been taken, not by strangers as she'd supposed at the time, but by Percy's own family. Rita had fabricated this tale as the only one Daisy would be likely to find credible; that Percy's sister and brother-in-law had agreed to take the child, because loving children as much as they did, one more was neither here nor there. 'And they wanted to help Percy. You remember Annie, lovely girl she was. The poor lass was taken, along with all her children, in the same blast what got your dad. It's a miracle this little one escaped.' Which of course meant there was no one to dispute her story, beyond the girl's mother who was unlikely to hear of it, and Percy himself of course. Not that he cared one way or the other. Like most young men, he was more interested in himself and had found no difficulty in accepting the yarn Rita had spun him too.

She was the only one who knew the truth, the only one ever likely to know.

Daisy's whole body jerked as if she'd been struck, one fact alone standing out among all the jumble. 'Dad? Dad's been killed? For God's sake why didn't you tell me?'

'I'm telling you now.'

She was on her feet, leaning over the table and banging upon it with her fist. 'You let me sit here, supping tea, and me dad's *dead?* What kind of mother are you? Have you no heart?'

'Close to him were you?' Rita asked, a challenge in the glitter of her hard eyes, and Daisy sank back on to her seat with a sad sort of sigh. 'Thought not. There's a war on, if you haven't noticed. Don't suppose you have, living here in paradise. But while you live up on t'top o' world, some of us down in the gutter have had it hard and lost everything. My home is nowt more than a heap of muck and rubble. Everything gone. Most of our neighbours in Marigold Court copped it.' She stabbed a thumb against her own skinny chest. 'And me and Florrie would have bought it too, if we hadn't been having a barney with an ARP Warden at the time. With nowt but the clothes we stand up in, we've been like two gypsies all summer, striving to put a roof over us head. We've slept in schoolrooms and church halls, air-raid shelters, bus shelters for heaven's sake, at times.'

'I don't believe you,' Daisy interrupted, unable to keep quiet any longer. 'I know how you always love to dramatise.'

Rita leaned across the table and spat her bitter disappointment of life into her daughter's face. 'I'm telling you the truth. Would I lie about your dad? Useless lump that he was, and he left me nowt.'

'No, not even a sore heart, because you have none.'

Rita sat back in her seat on a long-drawn-out sigh of resignation. 'Well, that's a nice way to talk to your mam, I must say. Florrie and me have filled in hundreds of flamin' forms, sat for hours in council offices trying to persuade some pofaced official that we should be given priority for proper accommodation, what with the baby an' all. We might as well have cried for the moon. In the end we gave up, and here we are. It's still your aunt's home remember, madam, so far as I'm aware.'

Daisy stared at her mother in horror. 'I know it is, but don't think *you* can stop here as well. It's not on.'

'Why isn't it on? Florrie has led me to understand there's plenty of room, any number of bedrooms in fact. I only need one. And it's surely on her say-so, not yours.' Having delivered her speech, Rita levered herself out of the chair, rested her hands on her hips and gazed about her in a proprietorial way. The gesture brought a chill to Daisy's heart.

'You can't do this. I've turned it into a boarding house. At least, Clem and me have opened it up to a few lodgers. Most rooms are taken.'

'Most? Then there's some still empty by the

sound of it. Like I say, I only need one.'

The instinct to dispute any plans Rita made was still too strong in her for Daisy to let go of the argument; even when, strictly speaking, she really had no right to say who lived here and who didn't. That was up to Clem. But knowing how soft-hearted he was, she didn't want to put him in the position of having to decide. It wouldn't be fair. He'd feel obliged to say yes, simply because Rita was her mother. But the prospect of living under the same roof as Rita was too appalling, far too dreadful to even contemplate. It would be a living hell. 'No, no, we need those bedrooms too, all of them, for occasional visitors, for Charlie and his girl, and for Mr Enderby, and those who come to see relatives, forces sweethearts and the like. There are plenty of regulars who come and stay.'

'Well, they'll be unlucky in future.'

Daisy could feel herself starting to panic. She could not, would not, allow her mother to destroy this little piece of heaven she'd found, or the business she was building with such love and care. 'No, I'm sorry. We've no room.'

Two spots of feverish crimson appeared on Rita's flat cheeks as her face tightened with fury. *'No room?* So you'd turn me out into the cold, would you? Your own mother, a homeless widow.'

Daisy was struck silent by this awful truth. Put like that, her attitude did indeed sound heartless and cruel. Yet Rita had always been the cruel one, the one with a heart of stone. *She'd given away her own grandchild, for God's sake!* 'I swear to God,

394

Mother, I could never be as heartless as you.'

'I only did what I thought was for the best. If I was wrong, I'm sorry. Truly sorry.'

'Are you?'

'Didn't I just say so? What more d'you want, for me to prostrate meself on t'floor? What about this babby then? Doesn't he deserve a mam? You'd find room for him, no doubt?'

'You know I would,' Daisy said, in a voice barely above a whisper. 'If I could truly believe he was mine.'

'Well, then. Why don't you ask his father?'

'I beg your pardon?'

'Why don't you ask Percy hissel. He's coming over on Sunday, to say hello. Did you know he'd been invalided out of the navy? Got shot up, apparently.'

'No, I didn't know. I'm sorry to hear that.' This was all happening far too fast. She couldn't think, or quite take it in. 'Why would he be coming here?'

'He wants to see you.'

'After all this time?'

'He's worried about the babby. Now his sister and her family are gone, God rest their souls, he wants to be sure little Robbie is taken proper care of. I reckoned you'd be pleased to see him, in the circumstances.'

Daisy's heart was thumping like a mad thing. Dear lord, how would she feel about seeing Percy again, after all this time, after all that had happened as a result of their foolishness? There was no love between them now, no feelings of any sort, not now that she'd found Harry. But he wasn't coming for her sake, but for the baby's, and it was good of him to be so considerate, particularly when Daisy recalled how uninterested he'd been in his son when he'd been born. Perhaps fighting in the war had matured him, made him grow up a bit as he needed to, as they both had needed to do. For the first time, a kernel of hope sprang up inside. Could it really be true? Could this be the answer to her dream? 'I am pleased. It'll be nice to see him again.'

'Course it will. You was always fond of young Percy. So, I reckon I deserve a bit of consideration, don't you, for arranging it all? It would be a pity if you missed this opportunity to be reunited with your own son.'

Daisy became very still, her gaze narrowing as she watched her mother pace about the room, picking up a jar here, a plate there, as if inspecting it for any sign of careless dusting. 'What are you saying? Are you suggesting that I can't have my son back unless I agree to take you in as well?'

Rita's smile was triumphant. 'I'd say that was fair, since I found him, wouldn't you?'

24

Daisy was so brimming with fury she had to keep her mind firmly on preparing the evening meal for her guests, that way she might manage not to take a knife to her mother's throat. The whole argument had been so distressing her only refuge seemed to be in anger, otherwise she might start crying and never stop. She wanted desperately to believe that the baby truly was hers, and that she could trust her mother. Yet how could she, after all that had happened?

And if it were true, wouldn't that only present her with a fresh load of problems? What would her guests think to discover that their landlady had a child, an illegitimate child since she wasn't even married.

And then there was the question of Harry. Oh, darling Harry, why didn't I tell you ages ago when I had the chance? Daisy thought. Now it'll be a thousand times more difficult. It's all going to seem so contrived, as if I planned it all along; as if I just waited for him to properly propose before presenting him with the fact that I already have a child. He'll hate me now. Any man would. Oh, what should I do?

The blackberry pie had been baked, the two children packed off to bed but Daisy steadfastly refused to go anywhere near the baby, leaving him entirely to Florrie. Florrie had offered to hand him over, had cast anguished glances over in her direction while she bathed, changed and fed him.

'Are you sure you don't want to put him to bed yourself?'

'No thanks. You do it. I'm busy.' Still simmering from the confrontation with Rita and worrying over the complexities of her problem, Daisy was in no mood to take issue over who should care for the baby, not right then. It was all too sudden, too confusing.

Rita, content that everything seemed to be going perfectly to plan even if she had stirred up trouble, headed for the front parlour to meet her fellow lodgers. Not that she considered herself to be one of them, she being family while they were paying guests. Nor would she be eating in the dining room. She would take her meal in the warm kitchen later, with her daughter and sister, naturally.

Daisy was chopping vegetables ferociously, tossing them with such abandon into the pan that Florrie, who had offered to help once she'd put the baby down, kept a safe distance away and quietly got on with laying the tables. It was vital, she decided, that she said not a word, that she didn't get involved. Just hold your tongue, Rita had hissed at her as she'd slipped by. And indeed, Florrie was an expert in that skill. Hadn't she had long years of practice?'

When the meal was ready, Daisy felt calmer. Cooking was proving to be a good therapy, homely fare but always well received by her guests. She'd made a big pan of stew, to be followed by the blackberry pie and custard.

'We shan't ever want to leave here,' Miss Copthorne told her, as Daisy took round the pie dish for second helpings. 'You look after us far too well.'

'I certainly shan't,' agreed Ned Pickles, managing a small smile by way of reward for Daisy's culinary efforts, while holding out his plate for more. Daisy had grown used to his lugubrious air. She thought him a dear man if rather sad, so determined not to be a burden to his only daughter that he'd settled here as a permanent lodger. It was clear he still missed his wife, not least because she must have tidied up after him all the time as Daisy constantly found herself falling over piles of books he'd left on the stairs. She'd discover his scarf or hat tucked down the back of the settee or under his bed, or he'd leave heaps of lecture notes drifting all over the dining table which she had to move in order to lay it. Why he needed to collect so many, she really couldn't imagine. In the end she had taken him to task over the matter, pointing out the bookcase she had provided him with, the wardrobe cupboard, the row of hooks behind his bedroom door, and was there perhaps something more that he needed in order to keep his belongings under control? Sheepishly he'd declared himself more than content with the arrangements and thereafter made a valiant attempt to be more organised.

'Your cooking has come on a treat these last weeks, Daisy love,' he told her now. 'An absolute treat.'

'You have too, Ned. You're a new man, now that I'm around to keep an eye on you. Even your spectacles are polished,' and he grinned at her, not in the least taking offence.

'S'matter of fact, Daisy, I was thinking of signing up for the Home Guard,' he confided in a hushed whisper. 'Now that I'm feeling more settled.'

'Good idea. Do your bit, eh? Here y'are love, have the last slice,' and she slid it on to his plate

'Hey, what about me?' said Tommy Fawcett.

'You've had two already, cheeky tyke.'

'That's true. It's your wonderful cooking, Daisy. Can't resist it,' and he jumped up and tap-danced all around the dining room, just to prove how much new energy she had given him, making them all laugh.

Flushed with pride and satisfaction in her work, Daisy went back into the kitchen still chuckling, her good humour restored. 'We have a house full of satisfied customers.' Seated by the hearth opposite his wife, sat Clem.

'I heard,' Florrie said, without a vestige of pleasure in her voice.

Daisy made herself scarce.

The first thing Daisy did was to write to Harry. She needed him to come on another visit, and quickly. She needed to talk to him, to see him, to explain, just the minute he could get some leave. The last letter she'd had from him was postmarked Ipswich, so it would all depend on transport as much as anything. It was a difficult letter to write as she'd no wish to throw him into

400

a panic and it was desperately important that he come as soon as possible.

There's something awful happened. I need to explain and it can't be done by letter. Mother is here and she's being very difficult but I daren't say anything as we can't get married without her permission. Though you may change your mind about wanting to marry me when you hear what I have to say. Oh, do say you're coming soon Harry. I'm having such problems.

Yet a secret part of her was overjoyed by this turn of events. That first evening, as she'd gone up to bed leaving Clem and Florrie to talk out their differences in private, she'd crept into the children's room. Megan and Trish were fast asleep, all curled up together in their usual fashion, like a pair of spoons, cheeks flushed in sleep. Daisy smiled, happy to see them at last thriving and content. Harry had done the right thing by bringing them to her. If only she'd done the right thing by telling him, from the start, about her own child. Oh, Harry, what a pretty kettle of fish this is. What a mess!

On this thought, she moved over to the cot which Florrie had set up in the corner. This must have been baby Emma's cot. Daisy wondered how much it had cost her to bring it out and use it for a child other than her own. The baby lay on his back, arms flung up above his head, snuffling quietly, but as she gazed upon him, enthralled, fascinated by the blue veins on his eyelids, the curl of his red-brown hair, the sturdiness of him, his eyes suddenly flickered open and he gazed up at her very solemnly, just as if he could read every thought in her head.

'Hello, little Robbie. I'm so very pleased to see you again.' She stopped, alarmed by the implication of what she'd just said, almost fearful of the baby understanding. Nothing had been proved yet. No decisions made. 'What I mean is, none of this muddle is your fault, and I'm not sure how it's all going to work out but – but I *am* glad you're here, truly I am. I don't want you to feel unwanted. I hate the thought of you being abandoned because Annie has been – because she's no longer able to take care of you. Lot's of people here at Lane End Farm are in the same boat, so you're very welcome, you really are. And somehow, we'll find the answer.'

She was rewarded with a huge smile and Daisy was able to see, quite clearly, that he had eight teeth, four along the top and another four along the bottom. He was a fine baby. Annie had looked after him well. Unable to resist, she smiled back which lit up his small face still further and he gave a gurgle of delight. And then he spoke: 'Mama,' he said.

Daisy's vision was suddenly blinded by tears, and she turned and rushed out, back to her own attic room right at the top of the house where she sobbed her heart out. She felt drained after-wards, and still with no idea how she was going to set about finding any answers.

Laura switched off the tape and rubbed her eyes. She'd been listening to it far too long and her grandmother's voice had broken with emotion at times, so painful was it to relate. She was longing to hear Harry's reaction to this news when he next came to visit, and what Percy would have to say, but it was past midnight and she had to be up by seven to begin preparations for breakfast. Laura switched off the bedside lamp and settled down to sleep.

Megan had reluctantly taken her leave the previous day, having stayed far longer than she intended but promising to come again soon, and Laura realised how much she would miss the older woman. Even in the short time she'd been here they'd become great friends and she would miss their cheerful chats. And somehow, miraculously, the visit had cauterised the wound in Robert's heart and all the pain he'd stored against Daisy had come pouring out like pus from a festering sore.

Perhaps now they're own relationship might also start to heal.

Nothing else was going according to plan. It had all started so well but now Chrissy was in a sulk and being difficult. She claimed to be vastly overworked, which was true, and although Laura did her best to keep bedroom changes down to a minimum by not taking single night bookings over a weekend for instance, demand had compelled her to provide evening meals. In a way this was her favourite part of the day. The trouble was, she already felt overstretched.

Her first effort had been only this last week when she was faced with cooking dinner for three couples, requiring her to juggle a variety of starters and two different main courses. Chrissy had gone out with a friend, a more regular occurrence these days.

'I need some *fun*,' she'd declared when Laura had asked if she could change her plans for the evening. But she really couldn't expect the girl to act as kitchen skivvy as well as do her chamber-maid job.

Laura was beginning to wonder if perhaps giving her stepdaughter the job had been a mistake. She was so young and should be having fun, not feeling tied to housework all the time. And she was beginning to cut corners, be far less accommodating than at the start. On two occasions recently, Laura had discovered she'd forgotten to put out fresh towels in the bathrooms. The difficulty was that staff were so incredibly hard to find. Anyone with any go about them was soon snapped up by the larger hotels in and around Keswick. Laura had put notices in the windows of various local businesses as well as on the library noticeboard. She'd even put advertisements in the newspaper, all to no avail. A few people had rung, two women had come along for an interview, and one had gone so far as to promise to start first thing the following Monday, but had never turned up. So she'd been surprised and thankful when Megan had offered to help with the meal.

'Can't cook to save my life but I could prepare vegetables, wait on tables and wash up. How would that be? And don't say I'm here as a guest. I like to be busy and I'd be doing it for Daisy as much as you. I owe her a great deal.'

Laura said, 'I'm filled with guilt that you should

404

offer, but I'll accept with gratitude on the basis I take it off your bill.'

They'd prepared melon in a raspberry coulis, tuna salad and home-made soup for starters, followed by a choice of grilled haddock with a creamy sauce or lamb cutlets baked in rosemary. For dessert there was fruit salad, cheese, or a traditional Rum Nicky pudding. The pair worked seamlessly together, Megan proving adept with a knife and chopping board and smilingly winning over the guests, keeping them happily chatting while Laura frantically grilled, baked, boiled, tossed and generally tried her best not to panic in the kitchen.

'If you ever feel like moving to the Lakes, let me know,' Laura said as they'd sat flushed and happy at the end of the evening, enjoying a well earned glass of wine together. 'There's always a job for you here.'

Megan had smilingly made no comment, and a day or two later she'd gone back to Manchester and Laura was forced to cope on her own.

As if this weren't bad enough, they were due an inspection from the Tourist Board at any time. She'd been warned by the local office, situated in the Moot Hall, that the booking would come in the form of a single room, usually with the requirement of an evening meal.

In her blackest moments at the end of yet another long tiring day, Laura began to question her own wisdom at embarking upon this venture. She hadn't underestimated the amount of work involved, but perhaps she had overestimated her ability to carry it out on her own. And yet she loved the work, she enjoyed meeting people, chatting to them and doing her best to make them comfortable and give them a good holiday. True, there were difficult customers at times but most people simply wanted a pleasant room and good food put before them. All of which Laura took great pleasure in providing.

But she possessed only one pair of hands and there was no doubt that she needed more. How on earth had Daisy coped?

Over the next few days Daisy could hardly concentrate on what she was supposed to be doing. From not wanting to touch the baby, she'd gone to not being able to get enough of him. He was a complete and utter distraction. She would put on the soup and then start to read him a story and forget to take it off again. She'd go outside, meaning to feed the hens, and then rush back in to make sure he was still safely playing in his playpen where she'd left him, forgetting all about what she was supposed to be doing.

Wherever she went in the big old farmhouse, she felt compelled to take him with her, all the time aware of Florrie's watchful eyes upon her, silently envious of her prior claim upon him. Sometimes Daisy would abandon her work altogether, so she could take him outside to play on the grass, laughing delightedly when he went charging after the poor beleaguered hens on plump, sturdy legs only to topple over through going too fast.

'Slow down, you're not a steam train,' and she'd run to pick him up, concerned he might have hurt himself but the two-year-old would simply offer up his toothy grin and be off again, determined to explore every corner of this exciting new world.

Megan and Trish adored him too and became slaves to his every whim, constantly picking him up and carrying him about, teasing and tickling him, fetching his toys every time he dropped them out of his pram for all he was supposed to be having an afternoon nap in the autumn sunshine. He'd wait quietly till they'd put the toy back in and crept away before giving a deliciously wicked gurgle of laughter and tossing it out again.

'He's a little monkey,' Trish would say, rushing to repeat the trick all over again.

'He's lovely though, isn't he?' Megan would quietly remark, her gaze softening whenever she looked at him. Megan loved to help feed him, teaching him to use his spoon and pusher with tender care so that Daisy could only look on with pride and love. The little girl would build up his bricks into a high tower and laugh when he knocked them all down gain. Daisy could see that having the baby around was relaxing her, bringing her out of her shell and giving her a sense of security and belonging.

'And you're good for me too, little Robbie. I love you to bits already, do you know that?'

'Mama!'

'Oh yes, I can see you could wheedle your way into any woman's heart, you little rascal.'

All the same, despite a growing sense of happiness and belief in the fact that he was indeed her child, miraculously returned to her, tension was mounting within. There were so many problems to be resolved. Daisy was waiting for Harry to write and say when he might be able to get leave; waiting for Sunday when Percy would arrive. What would he have to say to her? Daisy had carefully worked out what she must say to him. She would offer her condolences over his loss, of course, then thank him for persuading his sister Annie to look after little Robbie, which she had clearly done very well. Had they paid for her to go into the mother and baby home? Daisy wondered. And most of all she would promise faithfully to keep him safe and love him with all her heart. Only then would she explain about Harry. She would say how she held no resentment against Percy for leaving her in the lurch in the way that he had, because she'd been given a second chance at love, and was hoping against hope that Harry would understand and forgive.

All in all, it would be good to see him again, and there was absolutely no reason why they shouldn't discuss the situation in a perfectly reasonable manner. What had happened between them was all in the past, over and done with now and they'd both made a fresh start, a new life for themselves.

But when Sunday came and Percy stood before her, some instinct told her that this wasn't going to be nearly as easy as she had hoped.

There was the roar of a motorbike and the spit of flying gravel as it crunched to a halt, followed by the loud blast of a horn. Chrissy tossed aside the tea towel and reached for her jacket. 'Got to fly. See you.'

'Hold on,' Laura said. 'Fly where? Who's the knight on the white charger?' From the kitchen window she could just catch a glimpse of a helmeted, leather-clad figure on a bike, impatiently revving up the engine as he waited.

'It's a quad,' Chrissy informed her with mocking sarcasm as she half backed out the door.

'What on earth is a quad?'

'Oh for goodness' sake, a sort of bike. Look, I've got to go, Gary doesn't like to be kept waiting.'

'And who is Gary?' Laura was following Chrissy out of the kitchen, through the hall to the front door, wiping her hands on a towel as she went. 'Do I know him? Is he local? Why doesn't he come in and be properly introduced?'

'Oh get real. This isn't the nineteenth century.' Chrissy's tone held all the contempt of her superior youth. But even as she reached for the door handle, Laura moved with the speed of experience.

'Not so fast. I'm quite keen to meet Gary myself, then we'll decide if you can go out with him. Have you spoken to your mum, or Felix about him? Do they allow to have boyfriends?'

The horn blasted again and a look of anxiety flashed across Chrissy's face. 'Stop hassling me, will you. I've got to go.'

'Chrissy, you have to realise that while you're living here, you are my responsibility and I can't just let you go off with a complete stranger.'

Chrissy rolled her eyes heavenwards. 'He's not a complete stranger. I know him quite well, actually.' The smirk on her insolent face was not reassuring.

Laura held on to her patience. 'I need to check him out first, make sure your parents agree.'

'Ask your precious David to check him out then, if you want to be priggish about it, but not now, right? I'm in a hurry.' And as the horn blasted a third time she thrust Laura aside, flung open the door and stalked off. Laura reached the bike just as the machine roared away down the lane, Chrissy barely having climbed astride. At least she'd protected the purple locks with a helmet. It was Laura's only consolation.

'Oh God, what do I do now?' The last thing she needed was to have to call Felix. He'd be sure to put the blame on her, accuse her of being slipshod and irresponsible with his daughter's well-being. She went and called David instead. No answer. Of course, he'd be out with the sheep. This was a busy time with the dipping and shearing under way. The summer months were hectic for farmers.

Laura spent the entire day fretting and worrying, one eye constantly on the clock, or checking her watch. Why hadn't she insisted on knowing where the girl was going? Why hadn't she instituted a curfew, or better still, arranged to go and collect her at an appropriate time from wherever it was. Who knew what might happen to her? How old was this boy? Would he behave properly with her, and appreciate how very young Chrissy was? They might crash into a ditch at the very least.

She wasn't even her true parent, so why would Chrissy listen even if she did issue a set of rules? What had possessed her to let the girl stay? She must have been mad. How could she ever be free of Felix and start a new life for herself while she was still burdened by his daughter. Because she'd never viewed her in that way. Despite her show of rebellion, Laura was fond of Chrissy, always had been, and felt rather sorry for her being stuck with two parents as useless and selfish as Julia and Felix. She'd always done her best to remain neutral, not to take sides, and to be affectionate and reliable. Now she'd made a bad mistake. Being a stepmother suddenly seemed to be fraught with problems.

At seven on the dot, Felix rang. 'Laura, how are things?' The coldness of his tone always chilled her, even though they rarely had anything to say to each other these days and more often than not it was Chrissy he chatted to.

'Felix, um, you can't speak to Chrissy right now, she's in the shower,' Laura lied, crossing her fingers. 'She shouldn't be more than ten minutes, of course if she decides to wash her hair that may be rather an optimistic estimate. Perhaps you'd like to try later?' The brightness in her tone sounded false even to her own ears.

'It's not Chrissy I wanted to speak to, it's you.'

'Oh? Well, I'm not sure I want to speak to you,' she tried to make a joke of it but her voice cracked with nerves.

'You sound rather odd.'

'Do I?'

411

'Is something wrong?'

'Of course not. What could be wrong?'

Felix made a harumph sound in his throat. 'Exhaustion, I'd say. Impending bankruptcy because of your stubbornness. Robert says you're vastly overworked. Are you ready yet to call it a day?'

'Not at all, I'm loving it.' Felix had always been far too cosy with her father. Dealing with each of their idiosyncrasies was bad enough. When they ganged up together it became well nigh impossible. 'Whatever it is you have to say to me, Felix, can you make it snappy, I have meals to prepare for my guests this evening. Oh, and if you were thinking of consulting another building society about a mortgage on this place, let me tell you that you'd be wasting your time. I'm wise to that trick now.'

'That was a mistake,' he mumbled. 'Miranda's idea.'

'Oh yes?' Laura said, in a tone of disbelief. 'I heard you were rather cosy.'

'That was a temporary arrangement only. She's moved back into her own flat now.'

Laura began to giggle. 'Not quite working out then, after all?'

'Look, what I've rung about is that I've been speaking to the estate agent again and he's found someone else who may be interested in Lane End. As you said yourself, people prepared to live so far out in the sticks are thin on the ground, so don't screw this one up, Laura. We need the money. I'll tell him to send them along, shall I?'

'Absolutely not! Felix, what do I have to do to

convince you that this is my house and I'm staying. I live in it. I've done up the place. I'm earning a living here. Of sorts,' she added more cautiously. 'What's more, I've spoken to my lawyers and you should by now have received the divorce papers.'

It was as if she hadn't spoken. 'They're from Surrey and will arrive first thing on Saturday morning. If we get a good price I can pay off the bank loan and the mortgage, then we could buy a little place in France, take more time out from the business to smell the roses. We could have a fresh start, a second honeymoon.'

There was Florrie wanting a second chance at her marriage, and Laura being offered one and wanting only to escape. 'But you don't even like gardening,' she quipped, making a point of not taking him seriously.

'It's a metaphor, Laura. I need to get my head above water to make life easier all round. Stop being so damned difficult. You can't escape reality by hiding away in the Lake District. If you don't bloody co-operate over the house, then you can deal with the debts.'

'What debts? Now who's being melodramatic? Stop exaggerating. I've got to go Felix. I have guests to see to. But if there really is a problem we should talk about it seriously, through our solicitors if necessary, but not now. OK?'

'Is Chrissy not out of that damned shower yet? I'll hang on and have a word. Might as well.'

'Oh, there's someone at the door. Sorry, try again later,' and she put down the phone hurriedly before he could say anything more.

25

Daisy abandoned her idea of a friendly chat over a pot of tea and suggested a walk instead, assuming Percy felt up to it. The question needed to be asked, as the robust young man she remembered had quite gone. In his place was a tortured soul whose eyes reflected untold pain, who walked with an awkward stiffness for all he did his best to disguise a slight limp. Even the once glorious red-brown hair seemed dull, prematurely streaked by a few strands of grey. He'd said little since he'd arrived, revealing none of the cheerful warmth Daisy remembered so fondly, and his cheeky bounce and arrogant confidence had quite disappeared. It was as if his body was still alive and functioning, but his spirit was dead.

Nonetheless he declared himself agreeable to a short trek and they set out to walk on Blencathra, the wind in their faces. The September day was undoubtedly cold but the mountain itself, barren and treeless, somehow seemed unusually forbidding this morning. The dramatic majesty of the giant's naked shoulder reared up before them, filling Daisy with an unusual sense of awe, as if it were turning its back on her and sulking, refusing to smile upon her. It was not a place that offered comfort and Daisy had to speak firmly to herself to shake off the giddiness, the brooding sense of unease.

She felt at a loss to know how to begin. They'd gone through the usual pleasantries and all that was left now was the purpose of his visit. Daisy took a deep breath and launched into her prepared explanation. Percy, unfortunately, chose exactly the same moment to launch into his.

'Sorry, you first.'

'Nay, Daisy, I like listening to you.'

'I allus did talk too much, remember?' and they both laughed. Sadly, it in no way relaxed the tension.

When he said nothing more, Daisy cast him a sidelong glance. He was frowning as if trying to work out what to say, or why he was here. She tried to think of a way to bring a smile to soften his sternness, since one of them must make an attempt to lighten the atmosphere and get to the heart of the matter.

'Heavens, what a sombre mood everyone's in this morning. The mountain, you, even little Robbie had a fit of the sulks and wasn't interested in his usual porridge,' and having finally spoken his name, nothing would stop her now. The words just poured out, her sorrow over the bomb having killed so many of Percy's family on that terrible day during the blitz, her gratitude for the way Robbie had been cared for, and how thrilled she was to have him back. Percy heard her out in silence. When he said nothing, she blundered on.

'And I bear you absolutely no ill will over the way things turned out between us. These matters have a way of coming out right in the end, don't they? I mean, we were far too young to be sensible. Mind you, we had some fun, eh?' She smiled at him fondly, wanting him to smile back and share the happy memories with her. He simply glowered. Daisy pressed on. 'Now that I've met Harry, I can see how very naïve and foolish we were, and it's probably just as well we didn't do anything rash, you know, like get married or something.'

Percy cleared his throat, the sound seeming to come from deep inside him and took a long time in the execution of it. Finally, he asked in a soft, mildly enquiring voice, 'Who's Harry?'

'He's my boyfriend, well fiancé I suppose, since we're engaged. Unofficially you understand, until I'm of age.' Daisy could feel herself blushing.

'Everything's worked out nice as ninepence for you then, Daisy. I'm glad. Some of us haven't been so lucky.'

Despite his kind words, there was bitterness in his tone and Daisy felt mortified by her own insensitivity. What was she thinking of, to go on about her own good fortune in this selfish way? Hadn't Percy been on board a destroyer when it was sunk with most of the hands lost and he himself injured to the extent that his navy career was at an end? 'I heard about your experience. It must have been terrible to see so many of your comrades die, and to think you might die yourself. I can't even begin to imagine how you must have felt. Your nerves must be all in pieces.'

He didn't respond, making Daisy feel that she'd

strayed on to forbidden territory and shouldn't have mentioned the tragedy at all. His next words only confirmed that feeling.

Without pausing in his somewhat shambling stride, he said, 'Rita told me she was fetching you the babby. I thought that were good, because you're his mam. But tha knows, I'm his dad.'

'Of course I remember, only – well – I rather thought you were the one who didn't want to get tied up in all of that responsibility. Not that I blame you for feeling that way. Like I say, we were both far too young.'

'I'm still his dad though.'

Daisy felt puzzled by this childish persistence, wondering why he felt the necessity to repeat it, and then a thought occurred to her. 'Oh, you mean even when Harry and I marry? Well, yes of course, that's true. You would still be his dad. But I don't honestly see that as a problem, do you? I mean, it's up to the three of us to make the rules, don't you think? If you want to see little Robbie at any time, there's no reason why you shouldn't. We can tell him the true facts, once he's old enough to understand. Not that I've explained any of this to Harry yet, but I will, and I'm sure it'll be all right. I'm quite certain he loves me enough to understand.' She didn't add – and forgive, though the words echoed in her head, unspoken.

A pair of steady blue eyes considered her in open disbelief. 'Dun't he know about the baby?'

Now the flush on her cheeks deepened to crimson. 'It never quite seemed the right moment, but I will tell him, I will. In fact, I've

417

written to ask him to come over. I mean to get it all off me chest. Aw, Percy, it hasn't been easy. I missed my lovely baby so much, and I missed you too at first. Then there was Mam, bullying me as usual. I felt so miserable, all alone in the world. And after I was evacuated I made myself responsible for Megan and Trish, to compensate in a way for losing – anyway, we've had no end of troubles in our billets. This is the first time since this whole sorry saga started that we've felt any sort of security. And I owe all of that to Clem. Him and me get on really well. He's a great chap, like a father to me. A better father than me own, in point of fact, and I know I shouldn't say that when he's dead and gone, but it's true.' She was talking too much but didn't seem able to stop.

Percy nodded slowly. 'Aye, he seems reet champion. A good sort of bloke.'

'Oh, he is, he is. He's made me so welcome, let me have Megan and Trish come and stay, encouraged me to take in a few lodgers to keep meself out of mischief and earn a bit towards the housekeeping and, oh, just been a friend when I needed one.'

'He says I can stay on, an' all.'

'Oh – I hadn't thought about that. I assumed you'd be going straight back home tonight. But of course you can stay. We've still a room vacant, if you can call it that. Once was a priest hole, would you believe, and little bigger than a cupboard but you're welcome to it.'

'Not just for t'night.'

'Pardon?'

418

'Clem says I can stop on as long as I like. Theer's no place else fer me to go. I've not so much as a cupboard to call me own, now t'house and family is gone.'

Daisy stopped walking to stare at him, dumbfounded. Not for a moment had she considered this as a possibility. Yet why hadn't she? He was right. He had no one, no home, nothing. He was bombed out. Dispossessed. 'Oh, but ... you wouldn't want to stay too long, would you? Not as one of our paying guests. You'd be bored out of your mind, just like Florrie. No, you'll be wanting to find yourself a job, a new home, a girl. Life goes on, as they say,' she finished on a falsely bright note.

He too stopped walking, to turn and face her. The wind was whipping Daisy's already unruly curls into a frantic halo all about her head, but she paid it not the slightest notice. Her attention was focused entirely upon Percy's face, taking in, for the first time, the tragic, almost self-pitying droop to his shoulders, the sulky downturn to his mouth, like Trish when she was in one of her moods, and an odd sort of blankness about the eyes. He wasn't simply injured but also deeply depressed, as if he was carrying the whole world on his shoulders; and confused, which she didn't wonder at after being shelled. There were many such coming out of this war, so battle-scarred they would never be the same again. She could feel herself grow quite still, a premonition of what he might be about to say creeping down her spine like ice water.

'Why don't you tell me exactly what it is you

want, Percy? What you came for.'

'I don't know which way to turn, Daisy. I know what you mean when you say you felt lost and lonely. That's how I feel now. No home, me sister and her kiddies all dead. Did Rita tell you? I don't know what I would've done without your mam.' He looked bewildered and her heart went out to him.

'Yes Percy. She did tell me. I'm so sorry.'

'And Mam's vanished off the face of the earth. Folk tell me she was spared the blast but I can't find her nowhere. I reckon she's wandered off some place and got lost. Mebbe doesn't know who she is any more. I've no home, nowhere to go, Daisy. Except here with you. And since we were sweethearts, fond of each other like, and now we have a child I've come to you. It's the answer, eh?'

She hardly dared ask the question. 'What is?'

'We can get wed now, can't we? Like we were going to once before. Then he'll have a mam and dad. Won't that be grand? Isn't that the right thing to do?'

'You can't be serious?'

'Why can't I?' The mouth set in a stubborn line. 'What else am I supposed to do? I've lost me job in the navy, the proper use of me legs and with a hole in me back that won't properly heal. We can start again Daisy. A second chance for us both, eh? You and me together, with our little Robbie.'

She gave a half laugh of disbelief, unwilling even now to accept his suggestion as genuine. There was something naïve about the assumption that she would allow him to stay, something pitiable, and also deeply worrying, for Daisy saw that he was completely serious. Obstinately so, in fact. 'But we don't love each other, not any more. What we had was a juvenile thing, all in the past. I have Harry now, and you...'

'I have Robbie. Rita says he were with my sister but she's gone now.'

'Yes, Annie's gone.'

'Well then, I must look after him. He's my, what d'you call it – responsibility. Rita says it's the law, 'cause I'm Annie's next of kin.'

'Does she?'

'Aye,' he looked pleased with himself for remembering this important fact. 'So if you want him back Daisy, you'll have to take me on too. That's fair, isn't it?' And he laughed, but for once Daisy didn't join in.

Daisy felt as if she were living through a nightmare. Rita followed her up to her room, walking straight in without knocking, just as if she owned the place. 'Well, is it all sorted? Have you and Percy made it up?'

'Made what up? We never fell out. He was simply overwhelmed by what happened, as I was. But no, if you must know. Nothing is sorted out. If anything, it's got a hell of a sight worse.'

Rita sat down on the edge of the bed, making herself comfortable. 'So go on, tell me why. What's the problem? Nothing that can't be put right, I'll be bound. You always were a drama queen, our Daisy.'

'*Me,* a drama queen?' Daisy swallowed her

421

natural inclination to do battle with her mother for she needed to get on her right side, so that she'd give permission for her to marry, assuming Harry still wanted her. Oh, what a mess! It was no good waiting for Harry to turn up and do things properly by the book in the prescribed manner. They were way beyond that now. Very quietly, and with excessive care, Daisy said, 'I want you to be honest with me. I want you to tell me if it's true. Is the baby really mine?'

She needed an answer desperately. If this was all one of Rita's cruel games, she couldn't stand it, she really couldn't. She'd pack her bags and leave first thing in the morning, and she and Megan and Trish would take their chances elsewhere. Nothing could be more important to her than her son: not Lane End Farm, not the disapproval of their lodgers, not even Clem of whom she'd grown so fond. There was only one person's opinion who really counted, and she'd have to face him when the moment came. But how could she even begin to deal with Percy and his sudden decision to lay down rules and provisos, unless she knew the facts. The long silence made her impatient for a response. 'Well?'

'Are you accusing me of being a liar or summat, your own mother?'

'I'm not accusing you of anything but I never know where I am with you. I'm only saying, are you sure there hasn't been some sort of mistake? Where did you find him? Was he with Percy at the time? What exactly happened that day, you've never said.'

'I don't like to talk about it. It were awful. Dreadful. Explosions going off all over shop. Me and your Aunt Florrie near blown to bits in an air-raid shelter. Then we got back to find us home smashed to smithereens and me husband dead. You'll have to excuse me if things seem a bit confusing after that, if I were a bit shocked like. And you'll have to take my word for it about the babby. Anyroad, why would I say he's yours, if he weren't?'

'I don't know, perhaps to get your feet under my table?'

'It's not your table, or at least it wasn't last time I looked. It's our Florrie's.'

Daisy flushed with embarrassment. This was a fact she yet had to deal with. Would Florrie be as keen for her to stay as Clem?

'Anyroad, tha's talkin' soft. He's a grand little chap. Most women would be pleased to have their child returned to them, not interrogate their mother in this ungrateful way. So, what about you and Percy? Have you mended your differences, whatever they were?'

'It's not quite so easy as that. There's something I need to show you.' Daisy sank on to the bed next to Rita, then pulling the folded handkerchief from the drawer in the chest by the bed, unwrapped it and slid the diamond ring on to her finger.

'Well, I'll go to the bottom of our stairs, has Percy given you a ring already? By heck, the sly...'

'No, he hasn't,' Daisy interrupted quickly. 'This is from Harry. We got engaged, unofficially, just a

423

few weeks ago. I love him, and he loves me, so I've no intention of marrying Percy, not now, not ever. Sorry, but there it is.'

Rita's mouth tightened into a slit of angry disapproval. 'Is this the chap your dad warned off that time he came to visit?'

'He didn't warn anyone off. He told me to stop seeing Harry, that I'd to come home and look after you because you had a bad back, and I refused. Just as well I did, there doesn't look to be much wrong with you that I can see.'

'It mended, no thanks to you madam,' Rita said tartly.

Daisy got up from the bed and walked to the window, putting some distance between herself and her mother. Perversely, Blencathra looked benign now as a westerly sun dropped lower in the sky, lighting it to gold. 'It's good that you can manage so well without me, because I'm not coming back to Salford, even after the war. Clem has made it clear that I'm welcome to make my home here, at Lane End Farm, if I want to.' She turned to Rita, her face expressionless. 'What do you plan to do, Mother? Ask the council to find you a new place, I expect. I don't reckon it would work for you to stop on here. Not that there would be room, with all the visitors we get. You must see that.'

Rita was on her feet now, glaring at her daughter and spitting her fury into her face. 'So this is the gratitude I get, is it, for reuniting you with your son? You won't make the smallest sacrifice, or give a thought for anyone but yourself. You'd throw Percy, and me, back on the slag heap, just so's you can marry your precious Harry and swank over this nice little setup you've got going for yourself here. You'd cut us off, just as Florrie did.'

'Mother, for goodness' sake, I don't swank, I just want...'

'Have me out of the way. Oh, I've got the message.' Rita stormed to the door, her face a mask of seething anger. 'Well don't you forget for one minute madam, that you're under age. I'll never give my permission for you to marry your beloved Harry. Percy's a good lad. Happen I made a few mistakes about him in the past, but all he needs is a bit of tender loving care after all he's been through. And if you want to keep little Robbie, I'd give his offer serious consideration if I were you.'

Even as Daisy struggled to find a suitable answer to this attack, something in Rita's face changed, a perceptible alteration of her mood. As she moved thoughtfully back into the room to where Daisy was standing by the window, she was almost smiling. 'You have told him?'

'I – I beg your pardon?'

'You heard. Have you told this Harry about your little indiscretion?'

'Mother, for God's sake, what words you choose.'

'Well, have you? Come on, don't mess me about. Does he know you had an illegitimate child or doesn't he?'

Daisy would have given anything in that moment to have had the satisfaction of saying that yes, he certainly did know and didn't care a

425

jot. Instead, she bit her lip so that Rita wouldn't see it tremble and said nothing at all. Triumph blazed in the boot-button eyes.

'I thought not. Kept your little secret a bit too well, eh?'

'That was your fault, you told me...'

'I know what I told you. And now I'm telling you that when your too trusting sweetheart hears the truth about you, he'll drop you like a red-hot brick. So show a bit of sense and settle for what you've got. Percy. He has the benefit of being steady, unlikely to stray with those injuries, and you get to keep your son. As for where I'll be living from now on, well, we'll see how things pan out, shall we? See what our Florrie makes of having her kitchen taken over by a mere slip of a lass.'

It was half past eleven when Laura heard the sound of a bike in the yard. She made no move to meet her at the door, deciding it was too late to start an argument tonight. Besides, she was far too relieved simply to have Chrissy safely home.

The next morning, the moment breakfast had been served and the pair were clearing away, Chrissy began chattering about a disco Gary was taking her the following weekend.

'I don't think so, Chrissy. You're gated. Grounded. Confined to barracks.'

'*What?*'

Laura explained to her quietly that because of the lateness of the hour when she'd finally returned the previous night, in addition to her general unruly behaviour, she wouldn't be going to the disco or anywhere else for that matter. 'Not without your father's permission.'

'If I don't get to go, then I'm not doing any more work for you,' she responded peevishly, tossing aside the tea towel.

'Oh yes, you will. We have an agreement. You've three changeovers this morning, so you can leave the kitchen to me now and get on with it. We'll discuss this later.'

Should she ring Felix, or shouldn't she? He wouldn't be pleased. He'd lecture her mercilessly about the purple hairdo, and as for our friend on the motorbike who may be quite a nice young man for all she knew, Felix was perfectly capable of taking him apart, limb from limb. Laura started scrubbing the grill pan and decided against it. On balance, it seemed best to give the girl a chance to come round, which she surely would do. Chrissy certainly wouldn't thank her for calling in the heavy guns at this sensitive stage. She was a young girl struggling to find who she was, and her place in the scheme of things. Didn't she have problems enough right now with the divorce and everything? She'd keep a better eye on her and cope, somehow.

An hour later David popped in. 'I always find you at the kitchen sink. I think it's time I took you away from all of this and whisked you off somewhere romantic.'

'Don't you start. I've enough with Felix nagging me to stop working. I like what I do, OK?'

David's smile vanished. 'What's happened? Something wrong?' Laura apologised profusely

427

for her shortness of temper, then confessed to being worried over Chrissy. She told him about the motorbike, about the mysterious Gary, and the late night out.

David grimaced. 'Teenage angst. I'd forgotten how awful it was. All those hormones jumping. And it must be especially hard dealing with it as a stepmother. Maybe you should try it for real next time.'

Laura turned to look at him and was shocked to find herself blushing at the impish light of meaning in his eyes. 'I don't think this is quite the moment to discuss it.'

'Perhaps not. I beg leave to return to it on a more suitable occasion. Gary Slatterly isn't a bad lad, though none too bright and he has got his wilder side. His father tends to use him as punchbag from time to time which does him no good at all. I'll have a word with him, if you like. Don't fret about the bike. It can get up a fair speed but it's not exactly a Harley-Davidson. I wouldn't worry, if I were you.'

'Yes but you're not me, and you don't have Felix breathing down your neck.'

He pulled her into his arms and kissed her long and slow. 'Oh yes, I do, otherwise I'd be allowed much more than this.' They spent a contented half-hour chatting together over coffee before David went back to his shearing and Laura to her shopping and ironing, at least feeling more relaxed and happy as a result of his visit. David was good for her. Wherever this relationship was leading, and it looked as if it might be going a long way, she wasn't in any hurry to stop it.

Laura found that she liked having him around. They'd agreed to get together on Friday evening for a drink and, as soon as the clipping was over, he'd take her out for that romantic meal. It couldn't come soon enough for her. She was ready and willing for some romance in her life.

26

Winter was approaching, Daisy's second at Lane End Farm and she was doing her utmost to make her lodgers comfortable but it was far from easy. She put a small green baize card table in the parlour so that they could play cards or dominoes, and a chenille cloth over the best mahogany one so that Tommy could use it to write out his orders or Miss Copthorne for filling in her countless forms, without causing any damage to its polished surface. She found an old windup gramophone in the attic and put that in the parlour too so that when Tommy Fawcett, or Twinkletoes, as he was more fondly known, wasn't working he could entertain them with his toe tapping. Or they could all have a bit of a dance, if they'd a mind. And Daisy always made sure there was a bright fire burning in the grate, flowers in the vase and nicely plumped cushions on the comfy chairs. She fed her guests well, despite the restrictions, and continued to take the time and trouble to be interested in their lives and their own personal problems.

Not that anyone asked after her own problems. They accepted the presence of a baby in the house, and Percy too, by politely showing no curiosity at all. What they said to each other in private over this puzzling state of affairs, Daisy didn't care to consider.

However, her aunt was a different matter. Florrie was not at all taking to having another woman in her kitchen. Whatever Daisy did, Florrie seemed to take exception to it and deliberately undermine her efforts. She folded up the card table and took it away, saying it made the small room too crowded. She complained loudly about the amount of fuel being consumed, and put an ugly oilcloth over her best chenille tablecloth, to protect it from spills of ink. As for the two little girls, she banned drawing and painting because it was too messy, as well as dominoes and tiddlywinks which she complained went all over the carpet and, more often than not, rushed them off to bed far too early because she said they were making too much noise and giving her a headache. Finally, she put away the gramophone, along with every magazine, newspaper, book, comic and jigsaw and left the parlour looking sterile and cheerless. Rather like herself.

'They weren't doing any harm,' Daisy protested, aghast at these changes.

'We shouldn't encourage them. This isn't their home and there's no point in them thinking that it is.'

Daisy felt utterly flabbergasted, at a loss to know how best to deal with this attitude. It was as if she were treading on eggshells the whole time, on the one hand with her mother and Percy, and on the other with Florrie, desperately trying not to offend her now that she was back home and taking up the reins again. Even decisions over where to site the flour bin, hang the pans or which drawer to put the wire sieve proved to be a political minefield. And yet, low on patience because of the tension still building inside her, Daisy refused to buckle under. Now she spoke her mind rather forcefully. 'I can't agree, Florrie. This is the nearest these people will come to having a home until this war is over. You surely don't begrudge them a bit of fun?'

'Why should they have fun, at my expense?'

'I suppose you mean because you aren't having any. Well, that isn't their fault, Florrie, it's yours. I'm sorry for your troubles but really it's time to put them behind you and make a fresh start. I seem to remember hearing how you were fond of a bit of fun yourself, once upon a time. Anyroad, it's not at your expense. These people are paying good money – hard-earned money, to stay here. They deserve a bit of home-from-home comfort. As for the children...'

But Florrie had walked out of the kitchen and slammed shut the door long before she reached the end of the sentence.

Two women in one kitchen was bad enough, three women in one house was impossible. Rita would follow Daisy about from room to room criticising whatever she was doing. She'd complain that the floor needed sweeping, or the

431

tablecloth in the dining room was grubby, even when it had been freshly laundered, and when Daisy gave her a job to do to get her out of the way Rita would robustly declare that she certainly wasn't going to act as skivvy for her own daughter, and that setting tables was not her line of work at all.

'What is, Mother?' Daisy would ask in near despair. 'What is?'

Rita seemed to take pleasure in being difficult with the other guests too, generally insulting them even to ridiculing poor Ned when he demonstrated his new Home Guard uniform and the fact they only had one rifle between three men. 'Why would you need more? You wouldn't know what to do with an invading German if you fell over one. Run a mile, I dare say.'

Ned glanced across at Daisy and gave her a half-smile, silently telling her he wasn't in the least offended, and urging her not to be anxious.

Adopting all the airs and graces she could muster, Rita made it plain at every opportunity that she was not one of them, availing herself of the best chair in the parlour nearest to the fire; often insisting on something different for her evening meal to whatever it was they were having. Daisy would grind her teeth with frustration but was determined not to cross her too much, not until she'd had the opportunity to talk to Harry. Oh, if only he'd hurry up and come.

Rita's self-appointed task appeared to be to issue orders and point out errors and faults when things weren't quite to her liking. She gave the distinct impression that she was the one actually in charge and running the establishment, and not Daisy at all.

'I don't know how she would've coped if I hadn't turned up when I did.'

'She seemed to be managing well enough,' Miss Copthorne mildly remarked, resenting this slur on Daisy's character.

'Ah, but she was leaning heavily on Clem, and he has enough on his plate, poor man, running this place. And certainly my sister Florrie is no help at all. She suffers from depression, don't you know.'

Miss Copthorne didn't wonder at it, with a sister like Rita finding fault from dawn till dusk. 'Still, everything seems to be in order, wouldn't you say? Daisy has made us most comfortable.'

'Ah yes, but you've never kept house, have you, you being a spinster, so how can you judge?'

Miss Copthorne flushed, taken aback by such bluntness. 'I'll have you know I kept house for years, for my dear parents.'

Rita sniffed. 'Not the same thing though, is it?' and sailed away, nose in the air, before the lack of logic in her statement could be questioned.

Daisy picked up Robbie and went in search of some fresh air.

The September sky was a glinting blue, illuminating the patches of purple heather and making the horizon shimmer with light. The day held that autumn stillness, as if the land was revelling in the last of the summer's heat before it cooled. Somewhere above, clear as bell, she

433

could hear Clem's voice echoing through the silence: 'Ga way,' he shouted. 'Ga way by,' as he worked his dogs on the higher fells.

She set little Robbie down and the child gave a shout of pure joy and began to run in his ungainly way towards the sound of this familiar voice, making her laugh out loud. Daisy ran with her son, matching her pace to his, waving to Clem as they drew nearer. He was driving the dogs forward, to have them mark the sheep who were bunching together for protection against this opposing force. Daisy reached for little Robbie and swung him up in her arms. 'Oh no, little man, we can't have you startling either dogs or sheep.'

Clem eased them into the pen, patiently waiting whenever they hesitated and then urging them forward again at exactly the right moment. Daisy watched, holding the child in her arms, marvelling at the skill required. A ewe broke away and a dog quickly cut off her escape, nose down, belly low to the ground, directing her quietly back on course till all were safely in the fold and Clem was able to close the gap with a hurdle. He turned and grinned at her, then with a quiet whistle called up his dogs and walked down the hill towards her.

'I've brought you some tea,' she held out the blue tin can with its screw lid. 'And a bacon buttie.'

'Eeh grand, I could do with a break, let's have a bit of a crack.' They sat with their backs to a dry-stone wall, enjoying the sunshine, and a moment's respite from the day's routine. Daisy

434

gave a rusk to little Robbie and he went and sat with the dogs to happily share it with them.

Clem said, 'She dun't change much, your mam, does she? She's exactly as I remember her.' And Daisy giggled, knowing it was not meant as a compliment.

'You don't have to put up with her bitchiness. It's your house. You could ask her to leave.'

'Nay, not with the war on, and everything up in the air like. There'll be time enough to mek changes when we've put all of this kerfuffle behind us. Theer's talk of the Yanks coming in with us. That's what we need, a bit of new muscle to help our tired and aching ones.'

'Let's hope so.' Daisy wrapped her arms about her knees and was thoughtful for a moment. 'What about you and Aunt Florrie, or shouldn't I ask?'

Clem pulled a wry face. 'We're like a couple of banty cocks, circling each other and tekkin a savage peck ivery noo and then. Neet afore last we had a reet ding-dong.'

'Does that mean you're talking now?'

Clem frowned. 'Nay, I joost says we'll happen get a wetting afore tomorrer, and she storms out in a reet paddy. I were asleep afore she coom back to bed. I reckon she thinks me a bit of a bore. Happen I am. But we has to mek a show of getting on.' A shadow crossed his face and some of his bravado deserted him. 'Happen I should try harder to be more entertaining like. I just want to mek her happy, that's all.'

Daisy realised that she couldn't add to his troubles by telling him of her own problems with

Florrie; or spill out all her fears about losing Robbie if she married Harry, or losing Harry if she married Percy in order to keep her baby. Harry might not want her in any case, once he'd heard the whole sorry tale. He'd probably be ashamed of her, as her own mother was. No, this was her problem, and Clem had enough of his own. She watched with sadness in her eyes as he shambled away in that familiar loping walk, back up the fell with the dogs at his heels.

As if recognising her gloomy mood, Robbie came and put his chubby arms about his mother's neck to kiss her cheek. Heart full of love, Daisy gave him a hug. 'What a muddle! What a mess we make of our lives.'

Maybe the only way was to face it, head on. She could start with Florrie, for their differences had nothing at all to do with card tables or comics. Perhaps it was time to see if bridges could be built.

From the moment the idea of taking in lodgers had occurred to her, Daisy had been nervous of her aunt's reaction. Florrie had every reason to object to some other female taking over her kitchen, even if it was her own niece. But Daisy hadn't expected Florrie to make her disapproval quite so plain. If she continued in this fashion, the lodgers would pack their bags and leave, and Daisy would feel compelled to do the same. Clearly Florrie objected to having her home turned upsidedown, taken over by perfect strangers, and all because she left to stay with her sister for a few months. While she'd waited for her aunt's return, Daisy had played over in her mind every likely reaction but this one. She'd never expected such subversive undermining of all she was trying to do.

And on top of everything else, there was the added complication of the baby, of whom Florrie had clearly grown so fond. Daisy felt under siege from all sides.

That evening as Daisy filled the sink with hot soapy water and set about scrubbing the dirty dishes, she began quietly to explain how some of the changes had come about. She told Florrie how the linoleum in the bedrooms had needed to be replaced because it'd got torn during the plumbing work. She described how the ever resilient Miss Copthorne had helped her to make new dippy rugs to put by each bed, repair curtains for the windows, not to mention running up new sheets and patchwork bedspreads on the old box Singer sewing machine. Florrie didn't try to interrupt, or make any comment. She didn't smile or nod her head. She didn't even laugh when Daisy told the amusing tale of Wandering Winnie, the ewe who'd accompanied them on their shopping expeditions.

With a heavy sigh, Daisy picked up another pan and attacked it with Vim. 'I was wondering,' she said, 'if you minded the changes I've made. If you do have any objection to my turning Lane End Farm, your own home after all, into a boarding house then you must say so. We should have this out and get it sorted now, before we go any further.'

When no immediate reply came, Daisy

437

screwed up her courage to glance over her shoulder. Florrie sat very still, like a shrunken, wizened old woman in her chair by the range, hands neatly cupped around an untouched mug of tea. She seemed to be miles away, staring dully into the fire. At length she spoke in a weary, toneless voice. 'Why should I mind? I dare say I should've done something of the sort myself, years ago.'

Daisy paused in the washing-up, took her hands from the water and turned to stare at her aunt. 'I beg your pardon?'

'That was my dream too, once. Years ago, before ever I met Clem. Only I had somewhere like Blackpool or Morecambe in mind. A place with a bit more go about it, not these empty fells. I would never have thought to do it here, as you have.'

Daisy could hardly believe her ears. Life seemed to be full of surprises these days. Hard to fathom. She sat down slowly in the chair opposite Florrie, not even noticing that her hands were dripping soap suds all down her skirt. 'You're not really against the idea then?'

She shook her head. 'That Miss Copthorne made a point of showing me the improvements you've made to the bedrooms. What can I say? It's a miracle.'

'So why all the moving and shifting of stuff in the parlour?'

She cast Daisy a sheepish glance. 'I suppose I'm a bit jealous, filled with admiration for what you've achieved but wishing I'd been the one to think of it. I did wonder if perhaps you were after

438

an easier time of it by moving in with Clem. In need of a decent billet for a change, someone to take them two young evacuees off your hands without you needing to do another stroke. But happen I was wrong. You're a worker, no doubt about that, so why should I disapprove? You and Clem should suit each other entirely on that front.'

Daisy was shocked, then gave a surprised gurgle of laughter. 'I don't want Clem. Is that what you think? He's old enough to be my father. And he's your husband. I just want to make a go of things, to be helpful and do something useful. There are so many lonely people around, so many in need these days. Oh, I know we can only take in a few, but these folk were all alone in the world before they came here.

'Miss Copthorne lost her fiancé in the First World War and has spent her entire life since nursing elderly parents, missing out on a chance to find a new man herself; only coming to teaching late in life, after their death. All right, she rattles on a bit but she means well, and you can't fault her on the way she looks after her charges. Poor Ned Pickles, well, he's still grieving for his wife but he and Clem are becoming fast friends, against all the odds, mind, for they're like chalk and cheese.' She smiled at Florrie's bewildered expression. 'As for Tommy Fawcett, you'd never think so to listen to him but he was the loneliest of the lot. His entire family was killed in an air raid, a fact he spilled out to me one night, and the dancing is only his way of coping, of putting on a front so that he can bear to get up each morning and live through the day.

'But you're right about Megan and Trish, in one respect at least. I did want a stable home for them. And why not? We all deserve a happy childhood and them two little 'uns have had a raw deal so far. But *I'm* the one responsible for them, no one else, for all Clem loves them to bits. I can tell that by the way he never stops talking about them.'

'Talk? You've got Clem *talking?*'

'Never stops. All I have to do is listen.'

'Perhaps that's a skill I should cultivate.' Florrie gave a weak smile as she shook her head in disbelief. 'You've achieved so much Daisy, know so much about them all. I can see that you really care, that you're not at all the sort to get depressed; to give up and sit about feeling sorry for yourself, as I was. Still do, I suppose. You're far more capable than me.' She fell silent again, her quiet gaze still on Daisy, measuring her up, considering the situation.

In Florrie's opinion, Daisy was not in the least bit as she had expected, or rather as Rita had led her to believe. She wasn't flighty or silly, nor beautiful in the conventional sense of the word. Not at all the sort of drop-dead beauty you'd expect men to go for. She didn't flirt or flash her eyes, or behave in the giddy way young girls often do. Her hair was soft and well washed, a lovely brown; her smooth young skin lightly tanned and freckled from a summer spent largely outdoors. She was no Betty Grable, that was for sure, so, if Clem had taken a shine to

440

her, there must be some other reason, some inner beauty that had appealed to him. And perhaps this was it, her generosity of spirit. The love that shone out of her for her fellow human beings. Perhaps he saw her as a daughter, replacing the one he had lost.

After a moment Florrie said, 'And what about the bairn? What about this little chap? Have you decided what to do about him? We mustn't forget that he needs a mother.'

Softly, Daisy said, 'Maybe he's got two, one in me, and one in you. I know about Emma. Clem told me. I'm so sorry.' There was a long, drawn-out silence which seemed to go on for ever. Daisy didn't dare breathe as she waited for Florrie's response. At length it came, spoken in the softest of voices.

'Jealousy is a terrible thing. Like loneliness, it eats into the heart of you, robs you of your soul. Seeing you with little Robbie was like losing Emma all over again. I know it's not the same, it's just ... it reminded me ... brought back all those feelings ... all that pain.'

'I can understand that. But more than one person can love a child.'

The two women looked at each other, the hope in Florrie's eyes meeting with compassion in Daisy's. 'I don't know whether I can bear it or not Daisy, but I'll give it a go. That bairn needs a young mum, not an old one. I'll settle for being his favourite aunt.' She smiled, a genuine smile this time which warmed them both. 'You deserve him, Daisy Atkins, if only for making Clem a happy man again.'

'So you and he are...'

Florrie blushed to the roots of her bleached blonde hair. 'No, no, I wasn't meaning owt o'sort. Me and Clem have a long road to climb yet, I reckon. And happen he isn't even interested in trying.'

'Are you?'

There was anguish in Florrie's gaze as she turned to look out the window on to the empty fells beyond. 'I reckon it's too late for us to make a fresh start. I've blown me chances. I very much doubt he cares enough about me now to give me another.'

That very evening, as if to make up for her sulks and misery, and to stop herself brooding over the state of her marriage, Florrie flung herself into helping Daisy with renewed energy. She laid the dining table willingly without needing to be asked, and offered to serve while Daisy dished up.

'Many hands make light work.'

'Florrie, you're a treasure.'

Daisy smiled to herself at the sound of her aunt's red slingback shoes clattering back and forth up and down the passage. In the background she could hear the strains of music coming from the front parlour. A Fred Astaire number, what else? At least Florrie didn't have time to be lonely now. If only she and Clem could talk things through properly, she'd have some chance of shaking herself free of this depression, but the distance between husband and wife seemed to be going worse, not better.

Florrie had spread the big table which the guests shared in the dining room with a bright blue check tablecloth, set out all the knives, forks and spoons and was on her way back for the cruet, which she'd forgotten, when she cannoned into Tommy Fawcett. To her utter surprise and astonishment, he pulled her into his arms and swept the blushing Florrie into a two-step to the tune of 'Lady Be Good', right along the passage and back into the kitchen just as if he really were Fred Astaire. He didn't let her go until the record had finished, by which time he'd twice circled the kitchen table, making Daisy jump out of the way to avoid his flying feet and spun Florrie around in a dizzying pirouette to finish the number. Megan and Trish, both sitting at the table eating boiled eggs, watched the entire performance goggle-eyed. Little Robbie, chortling with glee, banged his spoon on his high chair very nearly in time to the music.

'What a star she is. Did you see that step and slide? A professional couldn't have done better.'

Florrie, one hand leaning on the table while she nursed a stitch in her side with the other, burst out laughing, her cheeks flushed to an even brighter pink. Tommy doffed his brown trilby which had miraculously stayed glued to the back of his head throughout, winked outrageously, then declared himself mortified at not being in a position to take her to a proper dance that very evening but he'd promised to accompany Ned Pickles to another dull lecture on the need for new health reform. 'You could always come with us?' he suggested hopefully but Florrie hastily

443

shook her head, before finally regaining sufficient breath to actually speak.

'Some other time perhaps,' she puffed, patting her hair back into place and glancing flirtatiously up at him through her lashes. Hadn't she known all along that being over forty didn't mean she was past it; that she was still young enough to attract a man? Yet even in her wildest dreams she'd never imagined being actually asked out on a date. 'You can always ask me another evening if you like. I used to be quite good on the dance floor once over. So I might even say yes.'

'I shall hold you to that,' Tommy said, clowning a cheery salute, then with a click of his heels he looped an arm about her waist and hung her backwards over his arm in a fair imitation of a tango, or the *paso doble*, making Florrie screech with delight and the children cheer and loudly applaud.

It was at this precise moment that Clem walked in. He stood at the door in his blue work overalls, mouth sagging open in surprise to find his wife thus engaged.

All of a fluster, Florrie pushed Tommy away and pretended to scold him, though not very convincingly. 'What a card you are Tommy Fawcett. Behave yourself, do. We're just having a laugh,' she said, seeing the grim expression on her husband's face.

'So I see.' It was very plain that he didn't see at all.

Tommy stepped forward hastily, whipped off the brown trilby and bowed low. 'It was all my doing, Mr er ... um ... Dingle ... er Tingle,' he joked, just as if he didn't already know his name. 'Dear me, I've quite lost my senses over your charming wife,' and Florrie stifled a giggle while Daisy quietly groaned as she saw Clem's face darken.

'The name is Pringle, Clement Pringle,' Clem informed him stiffly, with not a trace of his usual good humour. 'As I am sure you are aware. And Florrie is my wife. Happen that'll help you remember in future,' and he lifted one clenched fist and popped it on Tommy Fawcett's nose, sending him sprawling backwards on to the floor, a surprised expression on his face and blood spurting everywhere.

As Florrie rushed to help him to his feet, Clem spoke to her in his frostiest tones. 'When thoo's finished flirting or dancing or whatever it is you were having a laugh aboot, I wouldn't mind a bit of supper. Nor, I am sure, would our guests.'

'It's almost ready,' Daisy hastily intervened, dashing to the stove. 'I'm about to dish up,' but Clem had gone and she was talking to the kitchen door.

'Sorry about that love,' mumbled Tommy, dabbing at the blood with his handkerchief. 'Must've got a bit carried away,' and hastily made his own exit.

Florrie met Daisy's eye and now they were both smiling. 'Seems you've nothing to worry about at all, Florrie. The green-eyed monster might be working in your favour for once.'

27

Harry came one damp autumn day in early October. He arrived while Daisy was still serving breakfast, taking them all by surprise. With only a twenty-four-hour pass, he'd managed to get an overnight train and had hitched a lift from the station. Just the sight of him standing there before her, beads of rain on his uniform greatcoat, his forage cap tilted provocatively at just the right angle, brought an ache to her heart. She'd longed for him to come for so long and now here he was; the moment of truth had arrived.

Daisy left Florrie to dish up the kippers and dragged him away from the house, and from prying eyes, as fast as she could. Blencathra was covered with a thick layer of mist that morning, so this wasn't too difficult a task. She took him behind the barn, certain no one would venture out on such a morning.

It was only after they'd satisfied the first flush of kisses and Daisy was cuddled within the unbuttoned greatcoat, held close against the solid warmth of his chest that Harry asked the question, 'What's all this about then? What difficulty is your mother causing?'

Daisy wished the sun was shining and they could lie in the sweet-smelling green grass together, or they were in Silloth on the sand

446

dunes. She felt a desperate need to have everything appear wonderful and perfect when she told him her news, so that it wouldn't seem quite so terrible. A wet mountain swathed in mist seemed entirely inappropriate, the least romantic place in the world, and she ached for all the missed chances, all the times she could have opened her heart to him and hadn't done so.

She glanced up at him from under her lashes, trying to judge the right approach, having gone over it a thousand times in her head. 'There's something I need to tell you. Something I couldn't say in a letter.'

Harry grinned. 'Obviously, that's why I'm here.' And when still she said nothing, he took her cold face between his two warm hands and held it in a loving caress. 'Whatever it is, remember that I love you. So come on, tell me. It can't be so terrible.'

Daisy's eyes filled with tears. Grasping his hands she held them tightly in her own for a moment before taking a step away to give herself space to think. 'I'm going to say it quickly, to get it over with, right?'

The smile faded and his expression became solemn. 'You're frightening me now, Daisy. What is it? If you're trying to say that you no longer love me...'

'No, no, it isn't that.'

'Well, thank God for that, then nothing else...'

'I have a child.'

'What?'

'He's turned two years old. I had him at the

447

start of the war when I was just sixteen.' She didn't look at Harry while she announced these blunt facts, then shot him a quick glance, noting the stunned expression in his eyes, the way his jaw had tightened but when he made no response she hurried on, explaining all about Percy not wanting to know about the baby, him joining the navy and her mother packing her off to a mother and baby home and forcing her to give him up for adoption. Finally running out of both breath and words, she fell silent.

Harry hadn't moved a muscle. He stood looking down at her for some long moments before he said, 'Well, that's a shaker. The last thing I expected.'

'I know. And I would understand if it was too much for you to accept, if it means that you no longer want to marry me, I...' She was forced to pause. There was a lump in her throat the size of a golf ball. 'I realise it's asking a lot, only I'd just say in my own defence that I was too young and ignorant to properly understand what I was doing. My mother wasn't the sort to fill me in on essential details which might have helped me avoid such an accident, if you take my meaning. Not that I'm trying to put all the blame on to her, or wriggle out of it. I was stupid, there's no denying it, all I'm saying is that I didn't make a habit of it, I'm not a loose woman. It was only the one time and...'

'Daisy, stop it. Don't torture yourself. I don't want to know the sordid details. And I don't, for one minute, see you as a loose woman.'

Now they both fell silent, Harry trying to digest

448

what she'd told him, Daisy unsure how to proceed. But she'd only told him the half of it so far, and proceed she must. 'There's more,' she said at last, in the smallest of voices.

'Dear God, what else can there be?' His face had become rigid, etched with pain.

'He's here.'

'Who is here?'

She drew in a deep, shaky breath and launched into the rest of her tale: of Rita and Florrie being involved in the bomb blast, of how they'd found Percy, the only survivor from his own family, and little Robbie who'd been returned to her after being looked after by Percy's sister all this time and not sent to strangers after all. None of it could have taken more than a few minutes to relate. It felt like an hour.

'So little Robbie's here. And Percy too, as a matter of fact.'

Harry's eyes looked like dark coals burning in the death-white ash of his face. 'Where is all of this leading, Daisy?'

'Well...' she began, giving a slight shrug of her shoulders, quite sure he must be able to hear the frantic beat of her heart, 'he still wants to marry me. Because of the baby. He thinks we owe it to little Robbie to marry and give him a proper mam and dad. Course, I said no, not on your life. It's you I love, Harry, not Percy, and I'm sure there must be some way round this.'

'You mean some way you can keep both your child, this – little Robbie – and me?'

Fear clutched at her heart as she noted the brittle hardness in his tone. 'Yes, I dare say that is

449

what I mean.'

'I think I need to think this through.' Then he turned on his heels and strode away from her, up the mountain side, hands thrust deep in his pockets, shoulders hunched. He didn't invite her to go with him, and Daisy knew better than to try.

Laura spent the evening going through her accounts to see what she could afford in the way of extra staff. 'I'm going to have to try another advert. This isn't working,' she informed Chrissy, who was lying sprawled on the sofa watching a *Star Trek* movie on television with her eyes half closed. Laura wondered whether she should say anything further about the other night and, if so, what. Chrissy had barely spoken to her in days.

'Right,' Chrissy mumbled.

Laura sighed. Where was the sparkling wit, the sharp rejoinder for which her stepdaughter was well known? She chewed on her lower lip, thinking frantically. Money was tight, tighter than she'd expected and July had been surprisingly quiet. Everyone warned her not to get too alarmed about this. August, September and October were the busiest months in the Lakes. There was time yet to make her fortune, or at least a decent income for the season. Yet the prospect of entering the busiest period of the season with no one but a recalcitrant teenager to assist her, was too dreadful to contemplate.

'Look, I'm sorry about your missing the disco, but there have to be some rules. I can't have you running wild all over the countryside with young men I don't even know. Sorry, but that's how it is. If you don't like it, Chrissy, then perhaps you'd best go back to your mum for the rest of the summer. I'm not sure I feel able to accept the responsibility of having you here, unless you are prepared to co-operate.'

Laura held her breath. Was this the right approach: firm but fair? She hadn't the faintest idea. She'd tended to leave the discipline side of things to Julia, and to Felix who would weigh in every now and then with a tirade of instructions. Right now, she had enough on her plate without having to learn the tricks of good parenting.

Chrissy didn't take her eyes off the television. Was she genuinely tired or simply sulking? Perhaps that was the problem. They were both in dire need of a break.

Laura put aside her files and papers. 'Look, what we need is a day out, an afternoon at least, to cheer us up. Where would you like to go? Perhaps for a sail on Derwentwater, or to the theatre and a slap-up dinner afterwards, perhaps pony trekking or water skiing?' Laura was trying desperately to think of ways to amuse a grumpy adolescent. 'Could I fix up some climbing instruction for you, or canoeing? This is the Lake District after all, or even a long ramble over the fells. Whatever you like. What do you think? Is there something you fancy doing? My treat.'

'Forgot to mention,' Chrissy murmured, completely ignoring the lengthy list. 'Dad rang.'

'Oh? He caught you this time then. Good. Did he have anything interesting to say?' Laura kept her smile in place, controlling the urge to comment tartly on his obstinate refusal to

451

respond to the divorce papers which had been sent for him to sign three weeks ago. She preferred not to make snide remarks about Felix in front of his daughter, or involve her in their arguments, but it wasn't easy. His long silence was beginning to grate on Laura's nerves.

'He's coming tomorrow to take me out, so you don't need to bother. Thanks all the same.'

It was one of those put-downs that only Chrissy, in her crass, adolescent ignorance, could employ. A blunt reminder to Laura that she was only a reserve parent, not a real one. No matter how fond she was of Chrissy, and despite the time she devoted to her well-being, the PTA meetings she'd attended on her behalf, the wheedling she'd done over the years with irate teachers, and even this overpaid job she'd given her, she would never be anything *but* a reserve. It was a sobering thought and, at thirty-four, Laura wondered fleetingly, and painfully, whether she ever would have children of her own; if she hadn't missed that particular boat and it was all far too late. She had hoped they could at least be friends.

'Fine. It'll be good for you to see your dad.'

'Yep.' Chrissy pulled the cushion to a more comfortable position beneath her head.

The feeling of resentment was palpable. 'If you're so tired after your late night, wouldn't you be better in bed?'

'Nope. It's not nine o'clock yet, and I don't have a telly in my room, unlike your privileged guests.'

Laura thought longingly of her own bed, soft

452

and inviting, of the small cassette recorder beside it upon which she could listen to Daisy's tapes whenever she'd a mind. She'd taken the first three back to the library, borrowed the final two, and really couldn't wait to get to them. Daisy was a good storyteller and could certainly talk. Laura felt she knew the farm, and also understood her grandmother so much better as a result. She'd also loved having the opportunity to meet and talk with Megan. The older woman's memory had remained sharp and filled with affection and joy, perhaps because she'd been a child at the time. But she'd promised to come again, having thoroughly enjoyed her visit, particularly seeing 'little Robbie' again and the pair had vowed to keep in touch.

Laura stretched and yawned. 'Well, I think this over-the-hill decrepit would be much better off in bed. I'm going to have an early night. See you in the morning, bright and early.'

'Yep,' murmured Chrissy, idly flicking between channels during the commercials. And Laura crept off to bed, leaving her to it.

Having fallen asleep listening to another of Daisy's tapes, Laura jerked awake to discover it was half past ten and the house was very quiet. She decided to check that the house was secure and locked up safe for the night, the guests each having their own key, and that Chrissy had remembered to switch off the TV. She could make herself a cup of chocolate at the same time. She'd make Chrissy one too. Perhaps they could make friends again over a conciliatory mug of hot chocolate.

Chrissy's room was empty. She wasn't watching TV either, or anywhere in the house. What's more, her jacket had gone from the stand in the hall, and on her dressing-table was evidence of a heavy make-up session with bottles and tubes and lipsticks left scattered about. It came to Laura in that chilling moment that the girl had disobeyed her and gone to the disco after all.

She tore down the lane in her Peugeot far too fast, concern and anger warring for supremacy. Long before she reached the Village Hall she could hear the pound of music. Without pausing to think, she abandoned rather than parked the car and went straight over. The room was packed with young people, steaming hot and with ear-splittingly loud music seeming to vibrate the entire building. Any hope of easily finding Chrissy faded instantly. Nor did Laura pass unnoticed in the smoky atmosphere. As she made her way between the sticky, gyrating bodies, she was made to feel very much out of place in comparison with the thirteen-, fourteen and fifteen-year-olds around her. She was seen as being thoroughly ancient and the subject of much ribald humour and laughter.

'Lost your zimmer frame, love?'

'Looking for the bingo? It's on Thursdays.'

Eventually, when she'd trawled every corner of the room, peered curiously into every face to see if she recognised anyone, which wasn't easy in the dim light, Laura gave up. Chrissy wasn't here, not that she could see.

Back outside again, she walked dejectedly to

the car. Now what? Felix was coming tomorrow and she'd have to explain all of this, explain why she had allowed his daughter to break a curfew and go off with a young man Laura hadn't even met, let alone checked out.

And then she heard the giggle. Unmistakable. Laura stopped in her tracks to peer through the semi-darkness, narrow eyed. Surely the sound wasn't coming from behind the bike sheds? They were, in fact, behind a hedge and the pair were so wound about each other it was difficult to tell which leg or arm belonged to whom. They could have been any one of a dozen youngsters in similar gear, of either sex, so identical was their appearance. But the purple hair was a dead give-away. Laura marched over and grasping Chrissy's shoulder, gave it a shake. 'Right, I think you'd best come with me. You and I have some talking to do.'

'Laura!' Chrissy looked up horrified, the dark red lipstick clownishly smudged, the childlike eyes heavily black ringed with pencil liner. What had she done to herself?

'Come on. It's a fair cop as they say. You'd best come quietly.'

Gary was on his feet in seconds, the tension in his body like a tightly coiled spring. 'Who the hell are you? Leave her alone. We've done nowt wrong.' He was older than Chrissy, perhaps nineteen or twenty. Far too old for a fourteen-year-old, in Laura's opinion.

'This is between Chrissy and me, thanks very much. She knows what she's done wrong.'

'You're not my parent,' Chrissy protested

loudly. 'You've no right to tell me what to do.'

'I do when you're living and working with me. Come on.'

'Leave off,' Gary shouted and as Laura reached out to take hold of Chrissy's arm he lashed out a fist and punched her in the stomach. Laura doubled up, gasping for breath, as much with shock as anything. 'I said leave off, will you,' and before she had time to recover, he kicked her in the shin.

Chrissy started to scream. 'Don't do that. *Stop it! Stop it, Gary!*' But Gary wasn't listening. Perhaps he'd had enough of folk telling him what to do, or being the one on the receiving end but he kept on kicking and punching Laura, long after she'd stopped resisting and lay unconscious on the ground.

Florrie had finished the washing-up and cleared the tables in the dining room by the time Daisy got back. Rita, apparently, hadn't yet risen, for which she felt truly grateful. The two girls had eaten and gone off to school with Miss Copthorne and little Robbie was happily splattering porridge all over his face as he got to grips with mastering his spoon. A perfectly normal morning.

Florrie took one look at Daisy's face and put the kettle on.

'I don't want to talk about it,' Daisy said defensively. 'Not just yet.' She took the spoon from the baby's hand and cleaned his face with it, then lifted him out of the high chair on to her lap to finish the job off with his bib. 'Did everything go all right? Did you manage breakfast on your own?'

'Just about. Mind you, Tommy Twinkletoes took his time this morning. It was near half past nine before I managed to get rid of him.' Her cheeks were flushed as she said this and Daisy couldn't help but smile. She could only hope Florrie didn't push Clem's evident jealousy too far. They'd already been given strong evidence of it and, apart from anything else, Tommy Fawcett was a good customer. Not one it would be wise to lose. She had noticed a slight thawing in relations between husband and wife. Some mornings it was almost humorous to see Clem standing on the doorstep, preparatory to making his usual departure, desperately trying to think of something witty and original say, and Florrie patiently waiting, a pained smile of alert attention on her face.

Percy walked in as Daisy was jiggling Robbie on her knee. She was singing 'Ride-a-Cock-Horse', which he loved, as much to cheer herself up as the baby. Putting two and two together, Florrie decided to make herself scarce and hurried away to make a start on the bedrooms.

'I'll be along to help when I've drunk me tea,' Daisy called after her. *'To see a fine lady upon a white horse.'*

'No rush.'

'Was that him? Lover boy?'

Daisy glanced up with a frown. 'Don't call him that.' Percy's hair had grown quite long since he'd left the navy and looked tousled and

457

unkempt, there were holes in his sleeveless pullover and his shirt had been buttoned up wrong. A rush of pity came to her, even as she sat waiting and fretting for Harry to decide upon whether or not they had a future together. Percy was a sad imitation of his former self, nervous and constantly restless, always fretting or demanding long explanations over something or other. He was like a fractious child. He would ask why he must wear a coat when he went out. Why did he have to go out at all if he didn't feel like it? And why couldn't he tear pieces about the war out of the newspaper if he wanted to, even if no one else had read it yet.

If he wanted to sleep all day, or eat all night, or walk about barefoot if it made his leg feel better; who was she to stop him?

Always, when Daisy was on the point of tearing out her hair in frustration, or ready to scold him for some grumpiness or tantrum, he would put his arms about her, kiss her gently on the cheek and tell her how much he adored her. 'I love you, Daisy. You're my very special friend, right?'

'Of course.'

'Am I being naughty? Is Daisy cross?'

'No, of course not.'

'No bombs here. Safe with Daisy.'

'Yes,' she would assure him kindly. 'You're safe here with me.'

Somewhere in his innermost being must still be the person she'd once fancied herself in love with, though now badly damaged, broken by the war. Thinking of all this her frown faded and she

458

smiled up at him. 'There's tea in the pot. Help yourself.'

'I will, I don't need waiting on.' He still sounded to be in an irritable mood.

Daisy sighed. 'I should think not indeed. You'll not get it here. Not in this kitchen.'

'Have you told your friend Harry that you're going to marry me now?'

Daisy looked away, avoiding his probing gaze, deliberately striving to keep herself relaxed for the sake of the child. 'I've told him about Robbie. Have you thought better of what you said the other day?'

'What I said?'

'Rings on her fingers and bells on her toes.' She kissed the baby's bare toes, making him squeal with laughter. 'About you not being prepared to give up little Robbie unless I agree to marry you. Because if not...' She paused for a moment, wanting to make matters abundantly clear. 'If not ... you need to understand, Percy, that I no longer love you. I'm sorry, but there it is.'

He looked nonplussed, the hurt caused by her words clearly evident in his eyes. 'But I need you Daisy. How could I make a go of things without you? You don't really mean it. You *do* love me, I know you do.'

Daisy was desperately trying to let him down gently. Surely he would see that it was all over between them. How could he not see? All she needed was for Harry to forgive her, to not mind about the baby and then everything would be right between them again, and they could go on as before. 'Perhaps I never did love you, not in a proper, grown-up sort of way. We were barely more than kids, after all. And I certainly can't agree to ruin my entire life by sacrificing the man I do love.'

He flinched, and Daisy wondered if he understood a half of what she was trying to say. Perhaps her words had been a touch too blunt, too cruel, yet she was fearful now of retracting them. Percy had to get it into his head that there was no hope. It had to be made clear because the longer she let it go on, the worse it would get. 'I was fond of you, Percy, still am, but I don't feel for you what I now feel for Harry. So you see, I could never give him up.'

'Not even for Robbie and me?' He sounded like a spoilt child being deprived of a treat, and Daisy felt a surge of annoyance. Why wouldn't he understand? Why did he persist with this nonsense?

She turned away, to smile into her son's laughing eyes. *'She shall have music wherever she goes.* I don't believe you'd be so cruel as to deprive me of my lovely child, just because I can't agree to marry you.'

'Of course you and me must marry, Daisy. What would I have to live for if you didn't?'

'Don't be silly, you have lots to live for.'

'No I don't. My ship got hit tha knows, and the navy sent me home and told me not to come back. It's all over for me. I only have you.'

'Don't be silly, Percy. Your *war* is over, not your life. You're still young. You'll find someone else to love one day, you'll see.'

'But I don't want someone else, I want *you*.' He

460

was getting agitated, as he seemed to do when crossed or if he was denied something. Daisy patted his hand, trying to calm him.

'I'm sorry, love, I know it's hard but there it is. You can't have me. It wouldn't be right. I'm promised to Harry.'

Percy stood unmoving for a moment, fists clenched like a child about to throw a tantrum, and then he sat down at the table, put his head in his hands and began to cry, terrible wretched sobs that dragged up from the very core of his being. Daisy was astounded. She'd never seen a grown man cry before and didn't know what to do, what to say or how to react. The poor man was evidently on the verge of a breakdown. 'Don't,' she said, reaching out to him again. 'Please don't upset yourself. I never meant to hurt you, Percy.'

He shook her off and jumped to his feet. *'Leave me alone!'* he shouted. 'You don't understand. You're just like everyone else. You only care about Harry. Nobody loves me.' Then he ran from the room, tears streaming down his face.

Daisy was aghast. This was the last thing she'd wanted, to see Percy so upset. Hadn't he suffered enough? Oh, what on earth should she do? Go to him, or leave him to calm down on his own? Unable to decide what was for the best, she held her baby close and did nothing. Things seemed to be going from bad to worse, spiralling completely out of control.

28

It was almost dinner time when Harry got back from his walk. Daisy had not seen hide nor hair of Percy since his outburst and presumed he was sulking in his room. Florrie was finishing off upstairs and little Robbie had been given his lunch and put down for an early nap. So she was alone when Harry walked into the kitchen. He came straight over but stopped a few feet away from her. She wanted him to gather her into his arms but he made no move to do so.

Daisy knew before ever he opened his mouth that she'd lost. His face looked pinched and drawn, a white line of anger above his upper lip and he seemed distanced from her in some way, a cold chill in his voice. She heard a roaring in her ears, felt a giddiness in her head, as if all the blood were rushing from it. Finding that her legs would no longer support her, she collapsed into a chair, shaking. She could see his lips moving, knew he was talking to her, explaining, apologising, but she couldn't make out the words. She forced herself to listen, to concentrate on what he had to say.

'So there it is. I'm sorry, but that's how I feel. I know it's stupid in a way, that I should be big enough to overlook your – your indiscretion, but I can't. You were *my* girl, not anyone else's. I can't bear the thought of ... what you might have ... I can't bear it, that's all.

'Besides, how could I risk being the one to come between you and your child. If Percy insists that he wants you *and* little Robbie, how could I begin to compete? It wouldn't be fair to expect me to.'

'But it's *you* that I love, not Percy.'

'And you love Robbie, your son.'

'Yes, of course I do.'

'Are you saying you'd give up your son for me?'

There was a long and terrible silence in which Daisy frantically sought an answer, a way to salvage this one great love of her life that she was surely about to lose. In the end all she could think of was, 'That's a silly question.'

'A very pertinent one, apparently, in the circumstances.'

'Then no, of course I couldn't give him up, not for anyone.' She leaned earnestly towards him, desperation in her voice. 'But I'm sure it won't come to that. Percy will see that it simply isn't on to expect me to.'

'And if he doesn't? I'm sorry Daisy, but I'm not getting involved in this sort of blackmail. I love you, but I can't marry you. Everything has changed.'

Tears were blocking her throat, filling her eyes, her nose, and only by sheer force of will-power did she prevent them from falling. 'Won't you think about it some more? *Please!* You might feel differently tomorrow.'

'I don't expect I will.'

'But I can't bear to lose you.'

'Nor I you. I believed in you, Daisy, and you

463

lied to me. Can't you see how that hurts? Maybe you never loved me, simply wanted a father for your child.'

'Oh, Harry, that's a terrible thing to say, and quite untrue.'

'Is it any more terrible than what you have done to me? You had ample opportunity to confide in me but you didn't, not until after I'd proposed. What am I supposed to read into that? How can I trust anything you ever told me?'

She felt stricken, at a loss to know how to convince him of her sincerity, to express her regret and sorrow at not having told him sooner. Nonetheless she tried, recognising by the closed look on his face that she was getting nowhere. After a moment or two he sank on to the old settle, elbows on his knees and head in hands, not interrupting, not saying anything, just letting her pour it all out. But in the end, she too ran out of words and fell silent.

How long they sat there, saying nothing, simply nursing the hurt of their loss, she couldn't rightly have said, but neither of them heard Daisy's name being called from some distant part of the house. Not until the door flew open and Florrie burst in, panting for breath, her face a mask of fear.

'Thank God, there you are, Daisy. I've been calling and calling. Daisy, you must come. Right away.'

'Why, what is it? What's happened?'

'It's little Robbie. I just looked in on him and he's not in his cot. He's gone. And so is Percy.'

They searched everywhere, every room in the house, the barns and outbuildings, right along the lane to the cottages in Threlkeld at the bottom and as far up the high fell as seemed feasible. They found no sign of either man or baby anywhere. Once alerted, Clem volunteered to continue searching the summit, crags and gullies while they explored further in the villages beyond.

Even Rita joined in, shamed into doing so by her own part in this sad affair. 'Where can the daft cluck have gone? What possessed him to do such a thing? Oh, don't tek on so, Daisy. He thinks the world of that child. Percy wouldn't harm little Robbie.'

'Course he wouldn't,' Harry agreed, though privately he feared they'd no real idea whether the bloke would or not. Plenty like him had gone off their heads in this blasted war.

Florrie kept wailing, 'If only I'd popped into Robbie's room sooner. If only I hadn't taken so long over the bedrooms. Oh, why did this have to happen? Not again. Not again. Why would he take the baby?'

'God knows!' Rita said.

'To punish me,' said Daisy, breaking her silence at last with an ominous resonance. 'And it's working.'

'Don't let it. We'll find him, I swear we will,' Harry assured her and Daisy shot him a look of intense gratitude. Despite their differences, he wasn't deserting her, not yet anyway. 'We need to look further afield. He's not anywhere round here. Do you know anyone with a vehicle? He

465

can't have got far with a child, not without transport.'

The rest of that day seemed unreal, reaching nightmare proportions. How could this be happening? How could one young man and a baby vanish quite so quickly in so many acres of empty space? Bill the Postie gladly offered the use of his van, driving it himself up and down countless lanes, all to no avail. When there was still no sign of the runaways after three hours of searching, they were forced to call on the local bobby, who wasted no time in ringing the station to alert mountain rescue.

'Best to take no chances. It's dangerous up there. I wish you'd called me sooner, lass.'

'I felt sure we'd find them hiding in one of the cottages or barns.' Daisy stared into the deepening hue of dusk, cold fear gripping her heart. 'I'm beginning to believe that he might well have taken the child out on to the high fells. In this weather, he must be out of his mind.'

Harry said, 'I hate having to leave in the middle of all this, Daisy. I want to go with them and help but my commanding officer would eat me alive if I didn't show up on time. I'd be listed as AWOL, court-martialled for sure. It's time for me to go.'

She turned to him and knew in her heart that this was goodbye. The way he didn't quite meet her gaze told Daisy that there was to be no eleventh-hour retraction. This was the end. It was all over between them. 'Don't you fret. I'll be fine,' she said, shaping her mouth into a brave smile. How she was managing to hold back the tears she couldn't rightly have said. Her whole body ached for him to put his arms about her one more time, to kiss her as he had done earlier today, when he had still loved her, before she'd told him her terrible secret. 'The police will find them, I know they will. Thanks for helping, for your – support. Whatever happens, Harry, those lovely times we've spent together will live for ever in my heart.'

Daisy thought, for a moment, that she detected a slight tremor about his mouth but then it tightened and he nodded, quite brusquely. 'You'll let me know if – if things turn out all right – with Robbie. You'll write.'

'I will Harry. I'll write and let you know.'

'And if anything happens to – to change things.'

She nodded blindly, unable to speak another word.

'Tha'll have to hurry,' Bill the Postie interrupted gently, 'if you don't want to miss that train.' Then Harry turned from her, climbed back into the van and away it roared, spitting and belching out clouds of smoke in its effort to pick up speed. Daisy stayed where she was, the unshed tears burning the backs of her eyes till the van had vanished from sight, then she turned on her heel and walked back up the lane to the farm.

It was the longest night in Daisy's entire life. She sat with Florrie and her mother in the big farm kitchen, quite unable to speak, not even allowing herself to think. Somehow the guests had been fed: cold spam salad which they'd eaten without

467

complaint. She'd been thankful for the activity, taking twice as long as usual over the simplest of tasks. The entire household was subdued, Megan and Trish in tears at the loss of their chum. Daisy had struggled for hours to settle them both, up and down the stairs with cups of water and soothing words but, in the end, had given up and brought the children down to sit in the kitchen with the grown-ups. There was nothing left to do now, but wait.

Around midnight, Clem returned exhausted and hollow-eyed, sent back by the rescue service to get some rest while they took over. He looked at his wife's stricken face, at the tears rolling down her cheeks and went and put his arms about her.

'Nay, Florrie love, dun't tek on. It's not your fault. None of it was your fault, not the loss of this little chap, any more than with our Emma. It were just one of those things.'

'All these years I've kept telling meself that,' Florrie said. 'But I thought you blamed me.'

'And I thought you blamed me.'

'I did, at first. It got so's I couldn't get it out of me head, couldn't do anything but think of our Emma and long to turn back the clock. By the time I realised I'd lost you, I didn't know how to get you back. Oh, I've been that lonely and miserable.'

'Nay, I'm not lost, thoo's still got me. Allus will have, so far as I'm concerned. And they'll find this little un. He's not lost to us yet, not by a long chalk.' And he sat down beside her on the settle and took a firm grasp of her hand.

Having listened to all of this, Rita turned to Daisy and said, 'And I suppose you blame me for all of this mess?'

Daisy smothered a sigh. 'I don't blame you for anything, Mother.'

'Aye you do. You blamed me for taking the babby away from you in the first place, an act of mercy for your own good. And now you blame me for losing him again, 'cause I fetched poor sick Percy back into your life when you wanted to run off and wed meladdo.'

'This isn't the time for an inquisition. Leave it, Mother. I've had enough of your manoeuvring and manipulation.' Daisy didn't know how it was she could sit here, so outwardly calm, when inside she was falling apart, the pain in her heart tearing her to pieces.

'There you are then, didn't I say that you blamed me?' looking from one to the other of Florrie and Clem as if for support. Neither paid her the slightest attention, having eyes only for each other as they chatted away, nineteen to the dozen, at last catching up on years of brooding silence.

Daisy too was still talking, taking this moment's lull to get a few things off her chest. 'I'll make my own decisions in future, thanks very much, without any help or interference from you. Whatever I decide to do, it's my choice, my life. And once this war is over, you'll pack your bags and go on your way. So bear in mind that your stay here is temporary. There'd be blue murder done if we had to suffer each other's company for too long.'

'Hear, hear,' Rita said with feeling. 'You'll not catch me stopping on, anyroad I see what our Florrie means. I reckon nowt to this wild, open country. I were thinking of going and staying with cousin Billy. He's got a place out at Irlam, and he could probably do with the company, and somebody to look after him like.'

Poor cousin Billy, Daisy thought. 'Fine. Well, there's no hurry. So long as we understand each other.'

'Oh we do, madam. We understand each other very well.' As always, Rita must have the last word.

A pale dawn was creeping into the sky before they heard the welcome sound of a police van in the yard. Daisy was the first to rush out the door, Clem and the two women close behind. Megan and Trish were curled up together on the rug fast asleep, and slept through it all.

'Your runaways didn't get far,' said the police constable. Sat the night out in a shepherds' bothy. Bit cold, but the baby has been checked over by a doctor and passed fit and well.'

Daisy gathered little Robbie into her arms, breathing in the sweet scent of him as she held him against her heart. 'Oh thank you, officer, thank you. I can't tell you how grateful I am.' The tears were coming now, fast and furious as they rained down her cheeks and she slapped them away with a hiccuping laugh. 'What about Percy? He won't be charged, will he?'

'The young man is a different kettle of fish. Seems he had it in mind to top himself.'

'*What?*'

The constable looked sorrowful and dropped his voice to a whisper so that the child didn't hear, for all he couldn't possibly understand. 'We found a rope, d'you see, hanging from the rafters of the bothy. But because of the night being so cold, we think he was too worried about the child getting hypothermia to get round to doing anything. We found the pair cuddled up together, safe and well. How long they'd've lasted like that if we hadn't found them so soon, I couldn't rightly say. But no, there'll be no charges. It's been put down to battle fatigue. Pretty common problem these days, I'm afraid.' And then in his normal, official sounding voice. 'The hospital is keeping him in for a few days' observation. They need to know he's in no danger, to himself or to others.'

'I see.' Daisy was trembling, could hardly take in what she was hearing. Had she driven Percy to this? Was it because she had rejected him that he'd stolen Robbie and run off, threatening to take his own life?

Percy came home a week later, with not quite such a clean bill of health but, as the doctor carefully explained to Daisy, 'What he needs most of all, lass, is some tender loving care from a good woman such as yourself. Your husband will settle in time, though I can't promise he'll be as he was before. Few are, who've lived through this damned war and suffered what he's suffered. He needs to believe in life again and the possibility of a future, to know that he's safe, and feel secure. He'll heal eventually, with love and care. Just give him time.'

She began to explain that she wasn't Percy's wife, that she wasn't the one to give him tender loving care, but one glance at the sheepish guilt in Percy's anguished face, the needy appeal in his eyes, stopped her in her tracks. Someone had to be responsible for him, and who else did he have? Where else could he go? And who else did *she* have, now that she and Harry were finished? Weren't the pair of them both in the same boat?

But she had her son, safe and warm in her arms.

That night, Daisy sat in her room and wrote her last letter to Harry. She'd moved the baby's cot beside her own bed, knowing she could never risk losing him again, or taking her eye off him for a moment. Harry had made his decision and she had made hers. In the letter, she told how she bore him no ill will, how she would always love him.

'You will ever be the love of my life, Harry, but I can see that I've hurt you and spoiled things between us. I never meant to, any more than I set out to lie to you, I just kept putting it off till it was suddenly too late. I shall do my duty and probably marry Percy. I hope you can find another girl one day to make you happy, so's you can start again. I shall love you always. Yours ever, Daisy.' Her face was wet with tears, her vision blinded long before she'd finished it.

Harry's reply was swift in coming, and heartbreaking in its brevity. *'I can't believe that*

472

you lied to me. How could you do this to me Daisy, after all we've meant to each other? I think I might die.'

Daisy believed she might die too, or go mad at least. She kept reading his words over and over till her head spun. The letter upset her so much she screwed it up and threw it in the waste-paper basket, then put a match to it to burn it before suddenly realising what she was doing: destroying Harry's last words of love to her. Frantic now, she doused the flame which had only caught at one corner although the paper had gone brown and scorched all over. Daisy put it carefully away in a drawer with the rest. It was over. They had both made their choices. Harry was too hurt to forgive her. If marrying Percy and giving him the care he needed won her peace of mind as well as the return of her son, then she must somehow learn to be content with that. Perhaps she'd been expecting too much to ask for love as well. She prayed that one day Harry would forgive her and be happy again. She could only hope so.

Laura

29

'Didn't I say you were quite mad? Completely off your head. It would seem I've been proved right. Not only are you quite incapable of running your own life sensibly, you can't even be responsible for a child.'

Laura looked up wearily at Felix and wanted to protest that Chrissy wasn't a child but a stubborn, rebellious teenager whom anyone would find difficult to deal with, except that she hurt too much to risk moving her head even an inch, let alone attempt to speak. Someone was beating an iron bar against her skull and lying prone in a hospital bed swathed in heaven alone knew how many bandages, wasn't the ideal place to start an argument. Her eyes swivelled to the door, willing it to open and admit David. What she wouldn't give right now to see his smiling face, and for his solid support. No doubt he was still shearing sheep and blissfully unaware of the fracas she'd caused.

'This settles the matter once and for all. You're not staying here a moment longer. This is an unsafe place both for Chrissy, and for you. The doctor says you've got off lightly. No broken bones, though with enough bruising to make you look as if you'd gone three rounds with

Mike Tyson. You're coming home with me and don't try to argue. I won't take no for an answer.'

'No.' Until the word popped out, Laura wasn't certain she'd ever speak again. Her throat felt dry and sore, and the pounding in her head was making her feel all hot and funny again. 'Water.'

Felix thrust the glass into her face, then when it dawned on him that she wasn't able to move quite yet, lifted her head and reluctantly helped her to take a sip. Laura closed her eyes in blissful gratitude.

'I intend to tell your clients to pack their bags and leave. I'm going to close the house this very day.'

'You – are – not!' Three words. She was improving.

'Enough, Laura. No more of this wilfulness. My patience has quite run out. It's a wonder Chrissy wasn't raped or murdered. What were you thinking of to let her go out with that maniac, and so late?'

'I didn't...'

'Don't deny it. Why else would she be there with him in the middle of nowhere in the dark? I simply can't believe even you would be so *stupid* as to allow it.' He was striding back and forth in the hospital room, a private one Laura noticed, wondering who would pay for it if Felix truly was on the verge of bankruptcy. She sincerely hoped it wasn't going to be her. His fury was such that his face very nearly matched the colour of Chrissy's hair.

'How – is – Chrissy. Is she OK?'

475

'Fine. No thanks to you. Dear God, Laura, what were you thinking of? You really are the most obstinate woman I ever met. Was this your idea of revenge for that little fling I had with Miranda, allowing my daughter to be ravished by a lout?'

'That's a despicable thing to say. And she wasn't being ravished.' The rekindling of the anger she always felt when Felix started ranting at her, was bringing strength soaring back into her veins like new blood.

'Doing drugs then.'

'They were talking, and kissing. Nothing worse than that, so far as I know.'

'How would you know anything, you stupid woman?'

'I've done my utmost to be the parent you've failed to be. You *and* Julia. Someone has to give Chrissy the time she needs, and neither of you ever have any to spare for anyone but yourselves.'

'Don't start on the injured wife routine again, please.' He rolled his eyes in a fair imitation of Chrissy when she was playing her exasperated-with-adults routine.

Laura drew in a deep, calming breath. 'If you dislike me so much, why do you want me back? Why not settle for the miraculous Miranda? Or has she too grown tired of your foul moods and endlessly cooking wonderful dinners for you. If so, then find somebody else to take her place. Why does it have to be me?'

'Because you are my *wife!*' he roared, inches from her face.

'And you still love me? I don't think so. Could it possibly be because I'm the one with property to sell by any chance? Because I can't think of any other reason why you would want this mockery of a marriage to continue.' Oh, she was firing on all cylinders now. 'We're getting a divorce, remember?'

'Dammit, *I'll* decide if and when we divorce, not you.'

'Which will be after my house has been sold, presumably, and you've robbed me of my inheritance. Sorry, Felix, but I wasn't born yesterday. Well, aren't I right? Isn't that the truth of the matter?'

'Yes, if you want to know. I've a right to a share in anything and everything you own, as your husband. If you want to know the truth I've been offered a golden opportunity to buy into a business, one of the best art dealers in the country. They've offered me a partnership but I need to invest some capital.'

'So that's why you're so desperate for me to sell Lane End. Nothing to do with debts after all, only a desire for a bigger slice of the pie.'

'It's a very juicy pie, and you're being damned difficult, and unco-operative as usual. I intend to take this partnership, Laura, with or without you.'

'Oh, well if I have a choice, which I most certainly do, then I'd prefer you did it on your own, without me, thanks all the same. This isn't the nineteenth century and I'm a free woman, or at least intend to be pretty soon. I'm sorry about Chrissy. All I can say is that looking after a teenager isn't easy for anyone, let alone a step-parent, and I did my best. It wasn't good enough, I can see that and I'm too fond of her not to feel some guilt on the issue. But you and I are a different matter entirely. It's time we went our separate ways. I want a divorce and intend to get one while I'm still young enough to start again, whether or not *you* agree. I believe I have sufficient grounds.'

Felix growled, 'Give me my half-share of the house and you can have one without a battle. Gladly. Otherwise, I'll fight you every inch of the way.' Then he turned on his heel and walked out the door.

Laura sank back on the pillow and closed her eyes on a sigh of resignation. If it cost her to be rid of him, maybe it would come cheap at the price. But surely not half the value of the house, he must owe her something for all the years she'd had to put up with him as his long-suffering wife? She'd speak to her friendly solicitor on the matter. Let him sort out Felix. She'd had enough.

She'd almost drifted off to sleep again when the soft touch of a hand on hers brought her eyes flying open again. 'Laura, are you OK?'

'Chrissy. Oh love, never mind about me. How are you? He didn't hurt you too, did he?'

Chrissy's eyes filled with tears as she shook her head. The hair framing the pale face glowed a warm nut brown in the stark hospital light. It had been professionally trimmed too and looked enchanting. 'I was so frightened. I've been such a fool, and you were so kind to me. Can you ever forgive me? And don't worry about the guest-house. I rang Megan and she came right over. She moved into one of the attic bedrooms and has taken charge, with my help. We're coping fine. So can we still be friends? Please.'

Laura smiled. 'I'm thrilled to hear Megan is back. I shall offer her a job forthwith and make sure she stays. But if all this is a presage to a hug, can you make it a gentle one?' And they both burst into a fit of giggles yet somehow managed it without too many cries of agony from Laura.

'There's someone waiting patiently outside longing to hug you too. Shall I call him in?'

'I think that's an excellent idea. Oh, but how do I look? Is my hair a dreadful mess? Felix says I look like I've gone three rounds with Mike Tyson.'

Chrissy studied her with a mock seriousness for a moment. 'For one who's well past her sell-by date and with a jaw well on the way to matching my previous tint, you look pretty good actually. I doubt he'll care, anyway, what you look like.'

And, surprisingly, she was right.

Daisy

January 1947

30

The severe cold had an iron hard grip upon the land. Temperatures were well below zero with every hollow, boulder and hummock covered by a thick layer of snow. Where once had been a hedgerow or dry-stone wall, now lay a smooth ripple of drifting snow, dipping only slightly in the lane buried deep beneath it. A fox picked his way gingerly through the dusting of ice and snow in the farmyard, keeping a wary eye open as it looked from right to left. Clem spotted it through the window of the farmhouse and reached for his gun. 'That's gaan for my hens, the bugger.'

Percy, watching him load, said, 'I want to see the fox. I'll come with you.'

'Nay lad. You stop here, in t'warm. I'll fettle it.'

Percy got up and put his hand on Clem's arm. 'Don't. Don't shoot it, Uncle Clem. It's hungry, that's all. I don't like guns. Call in the dogs. Send for the hunt.'

Daisy looked up from the sock she was darning. 'It's all right, Percy. Don't fret.'

'Thoo knows well enough we don't have no hounds in these parts lad, nor fancy horses galloping about a country where they'd be sure to

480

break their necks. And how can the hunt get through in this weather? It's best I tek a pot at it mesel'. Don't worry, I'm a fair shot and he's an old rogue, a bandit, nowt else. Reynard i'n't getting his jaws on my chickens.'

Percy became agitated as he watched Clem stride away, so that Daisy got up and came to put her arms about him to soothe and calm him down. It was ever the way of it when something unpleasant occurred. 'It's all right. Don't worry. The fox will be long gone before Clem gets anywhere near, frightened off by the sight of him, believe me,' and such proved to be the case. Clem stalked him as quietly as he could, but the fox dodged capture with wily skill, his sense of smell and acute hearing allowing him to live to fight another day.

Clem returned to the house later, thoroughly cross and very cold. He stamped the snow off his boots, unloaded the gun and stowed it safely away in the case, double locking it carefully afterwards. Percy watched the procedure with great interest. It troubled Daisy that much as he hated the loud bangs made when Clem went to pop off a fox or a rat, yet the guns in the case never ceased to fascinate him. Once, Daisy had found him standing by the case fiddling with the lock.

'What are you doing? You know you mustn't touch Uncle Clem's guns.' She'd taken hold of him, tried to move him away but he'd resisted her.

'Don't like guns. Want to move them. Shouldn't be in the house. Might blow up.'

'No, no Percy. They won't blow up. It's all right. They have no bullets in them, in any case. Clem takes care of that.' But the next day, he was back again, picking at the lock with a bit of bent wire. That's when Daisy made Clem put on a padlock as well, just to be safe.

Fearful of a repeat of the incident when he'd suffered a breakdown and attempted to take his own life, they all of them kept a close watch on him.

Daisy didn't believe he was any real danger either to himself or to anyone else, quite certain that her care and control had done its job. All the same, they remained vigilant: Clem, Florrie and Daisy, even seven-year-old Robbie who followed his father about everywhere. The pair were inseparable and Daisy knew her child was safe, that Percy adored his son too much to harm him.

'I like foxes,' Percy said now.

'You would, you daft bugger,' but Clem was smiling.

Daisy smiled too, relieved Percy was again settling back in the armchair with his *Hotspur* comic. She never failed to appreciate the old man's endless patience with him. Percy was not the same man he once was, had grown ever more simple-minded over these last years, as if he couldn't face being a part of the adult world any more. He'd settled in nicely at the farm and loved the quiet of the high fells so much that he rarely left them, not even when she drove the old Ford van into Keswick for fresh supplies. Nor did she encourage him to do so, knowing that he felt secure here, and safe. The very quiet of the place

482

kept him calm and happy.

The war had broken him, leaving him quite incapable of looking after himself. The ulcerous sores on his back and legs had never properly healed, and he was very nearly stone deaf. Because of these disabilities, he could easily become disoriented and panic if he strayed too far from the farm. If his routine deviated in the slightest, he would become agitated and nervous. Daisy recognised the signs and knew how to calm him, as did Robbie. Caring for him was very like minding a child, and a stubborn one at times.

Her consolation and joy was found in her beloved Robbie. She had Florrie and Clem for company, and the boarding house kept her fully occupied throughout the day as it continued to prosper, although their original guests were long gone.

Miss Copthorne was back in the North-East, presumably still teaching. Ned Pickles had gone to live with his daughter, who had decided to at last take responsibility for her elderly parent. Tommy Twinkletoes was no longer selling agricultural foodstuffs but running a grocery store in Preston. He called to see them from time to time and bore Clem no grudge at all over the thump on his nose, though Clem remained fairly cool and distant towards him.

The worst moment had come with Daisy's mother. Following the recovery of Robbie, Rita had proudly showed off her grandson to all the guests as if she personally had rescued him from the jaws of death. 'Isn't he a little marvel? And his poor dad couldn't help it, losing his senses 'cause he were such a hero blown up in that destroyer. Poor man,' she warned, tapping the side her head.

Miss Copthorne had jiggled the baby's hand, then turning to Daisy said, 'So Percy is your husband, is he? I hadn't realised.'

Daisy would never forget the intensity of the silence which followed. It probably only lasted a matter of seconds but to her it seemed like an hour: her tongue all tied in a knot so that before she'd got it sorted out, Rita had shoved her oar in, as was her wont.

'Oh indeed, yes he is. They were married years ago, before the war. All right and proper. Fine young chap he was then. Daisy doesn't like to talk about it because it upsets her too much, remembering how he used to be. But he's done his bit for his country, so no one can ask for more than that, now can they? And we'll all stand by her in her hour of need, will we not? Ours not to question why, only to do or die.' She spouted many more clichés but Daisy was too dazed to listen.

'Oh dear me yes, of course we will,' agreed Miss Copthorne. 'The poor man has given his life, in a way,' and she cast Daisy a look half of surprise, that she should have felt the need to keep her marriage to such a hero quiet, and half one of pure pity, for who knows how one might react in similar circumstances? Daisy snatched the baby from her mother's arms and ran upstairs. She could stand no more.

She'd packed a bag, put on her coat and hat, dressed Robbie in his coat and leggings and gone back downstairs. Guessing something was wrong, all the guests had gathered at the bottom of the stairs.

Daisy began with Rita. 'You've been organising me for as long as I can remember. All my life, in fact, since I first drew breath. But I've already made it clear that I'll not stand for it any longer. This is the final straw. I'm off. You can look after Percy. I've got my baby. I'm certainly not prepared to live a lie, not any longer. I've lost the only man I truly love because you made me keep my baby a secret, so I reckon it's time I faced up to the truth.'

And then addressing the assembled guests: Ned Pickles, Tommy Fawcett, Miss Copthorne, Mr Enderby and one or two others who happened to be staying, quietly announced, 'I'm not married to Percy but it's true that he is Robbie's dad. My baby is illegitimate, so you can put that in your pipe and smoke it. Mam gave him away for adoption, and I never thought I'd see him again. Now that I've got him back, I don't care what anybody thinks of me, or whatever the gossips say. I think he's smashing and he's mine. I've packed me bags, so you won't be soiled any further by my immoral behaviour.' So saying, she picked up her bags and set off for the door, balancing the baby on her hip.

Ned Pickles was the first to be galvanised into action. He dashed after her and grasped her arm gently. 'Don't go, Daisy. We'd be lost without you. We all love you, and we don't care what Robbie's status is, whether you're married or you're not. There's been a war and everything is topsy-turvy, nothing as it should be. What we do know is that you've seen us all through it. We wouldn't have managed half so well without you and we need you here. You've made a big difference to our lives. Don't leave on our account.'

'Hear-hear!' A rousing cheer went up. Tommy Fawcett was relieving her of her bag, Mr Enderby was offering her a spanking clean handkerchief and Miss Copthorne was lifting Robbie from her arms because Daisy looked in dire danger of dropping him, she was shaking so much. And Ned Pickles was holding her while she sobbed.

Rita had been the one to leave, not Daisy, if not without playing her mischief right to the end. She told Percy that, as Daisy's husband, he was the most important person in the household.

'Did we get wed then?' he asked, frowning as he struggled to remember the wedding ceremony.

'Course you did, love. Don't you recall having a drop too much bevy at the reception?'

'Aye, I usually do,' Percy agreed, eyes shining.

And somehow, the idea that they were married, once planted in his head, couldn't be shifted. He kept calling her his wife, looking pleased as punch, calling her Mrs Thompson. And somehow that stuck too. The regulars, fully understanding the situation accepted it as a game of pretence, rather like playing a game with a child. Daisy went along with it too because it kept Percy calm and content and in any case, she was quite sure it would all blow over as jokes usually did in the end.

And if anyone asked she would say no, straight

out. Percy and she weren't married at all but he liked to think that they were. It was the war, did something to his brain. That way, she wasn't telling any lies. Just playing along to keep Percy happy and well.

Only the game didn't go away. By the time the regulars had all left, gone their separate ways to get on with their post-war lives as best they could, the entire neighbourhood had quite forgotten how the fiction had all begun, had become quite convinced that Daisy and Percy were indeed man and wife. In fact, there were times when Daisy herself believed it, calling him her dear husband, and then remembering and feeling guilty, as if she'd been caught out in a lie after all. But though the union didn't have the blessing of any church, in truth she cared for him like a wife, in every way but one. It was a marriage in name only, literally. And there was no law against calling yourself whatever you liked. She'd checked that out with Mr Capstick, the family solicitor.

Daisy was happy enough. She'd fallen in love with Lane End Farm at first sight and hadn't regretted staying. Clem and Florrie would never have a perfect marriage either but were thankfully over the worst of their difficulties and got along tolerably well these days. Her aunt could even be heard singing as she went about her work. Having a regular supply of visitors to the farm for bed and breakfast after the war was proving to be good for her too and she was able to spoil Robbie dreadfully, of course, which helped to counter some of the bitterness she would for ever carry in her heart for the child she lost.

On her days off, Daisy would leave Percy in Clem's capable hands, set a pie on the dresser for them to warm in the oven later while she and Florrie went off to the Alhambra or the Pavilion Theatre to see a show. There were no evacuees now in Keswick, they too had all gone home. Even Megan and Trish had finally made a tearful and reluctant farewell, promising faithfully to keep in touch. Daisy wasn't sure which of them cried the most, it felt awful to say goodbye.

'I don't know how we'll manage without you, Daisy.'

'You must come every summer for a holiday.'

'Oh we will. We will.'

They wrote every single week, without fail, always looking forward to their summer break at Lane End Farm which sometimes stretched to months at a time when their mother wasn't coping too well. She'd married her sailor and produced several more children, so often welcomed a break from the two eldest.

And if, deep down, Daisy was lonely and longed for what-might-have-been, she gave no indication of it. She didn't blame Harry for the decision he'd made, knowing she'd hurt him badly but the longing for him was a living ache in her heart.

He came with the thaw in late spring of that year. The ice and snow had melted save from the highest peaks, and the Herdwicks were keeping the fresh new grass close cropped as a bowling green. The leaves in the hedgerows on the lane up to the farm were unfurling all pink and new and soft, the woods behind the barn an azure lake of breathtaking blue. Daisy saw the figure in the distance and knew at once it was him. Every instinct alerted her senses and long before she could see his face she was running, galloping, jumping over nettles, racing to reach him. She flung herself into his arms on a breathless cry of exultation, and he swung her round, laughing and hugging her.

She didn't take him immediately to the farm but walked him up Blease Fell, out on to the ridge of the saddle to Foule Crag looking down over Sharp Edge to Scales Tarn below; a place where they could be alone on the top of the world with a view not only over all of Lakeland but to Silloth where they had spent their courting days, to Barrow where the bombing had been at its worst and many young airmen, colleagues of Harry, had lost their lives. But also further afield, to Scotland, Ireland, the Isle of Man and beyond. It was almost like being given a vision of their past and future all in one, for both knew in their hearts that having now found each other, they could never again bear to part.

'Are you married?' he asked at last, when their first passion had been sated and he could bear for a moment to release her.

Daisy shook her head. 'Percy thinks that we are. He's not quite right in his head. Being blown up on the ship messed it all up. His needs are simple and don't include anything ... anything physical.

But he has to be carefully watched and he needs me, Harry. Apart from anything else he adores Robbie, lives for him. The pair are inseparable. I can't leave him.'

'And I can't leave you.'

'I won't allow you to.'

'I was wrong. I shouldn't have judged you so harshly. You were merely a girl, little more than a child. I'm sorry, Daisy. Can you forgive me?'

'You're here. The war's over. That's all that matters.'

They sat and talked, and loved for hours. They lay cradled in a fold of the mountain and it was here, in Blencathra's embrace, that Daisy gave herself to the man she had always loved, and would ever love. Much, much later, she took him home.

'See who's come to visit us, Percy,' Daisy said, leading Harry into the kitchen by the hand

Percy turned trusting, excited eyes in the direction of the newcomer. 'Who is it Daisy? Who have you fetched for me?'

'This is Harry. An old friend of mine I'd like you to know.'

'Are you stopping with us, Harry?'

'I am,' Harry said. 'if you'll have me.'

'Oh aye,' Percy said. 'We welcome friends here, don't we Daisy? We love 'em all, i'n't that right?'

'It is, Percy. Everyone is welcome at Lane End Farm, especially old friends. Now eat up your tea then you can listen to *Henry Hall's Music Night*. You always enjoy that, don't you? And Harry and I will sit here and talk for a bit.'

The strength of Daisy's personality came across forcefully on the tape, her clear tones bridging the years with her memories. *'And so Harry was returned to me, just as Robbie was. I have been a most fortunate woman. Percy lived with us quite happily till he died in 1956 of pneumonia. Harry and I meant to marry after that, could have done so, I suppose. At first we didn't for fear of upsetting Robbie and then as the years slipped by there didn't seem any point. It became almost a feeling between us that we might spoil our good fortune if we did. Then Harry became ill and died in June 1969, aged fifty-one leaving me a widow in my heart at least. If the gossips sometimes suspected the truth about our* ménage à trois, *I turned a deaf ear. We kept our own counsel and did what was best, for Percy, for Robbie, for each other. People must judge us as they think fit, bearing in mind the cards we'd been dealt.*

'I deeply regret that the facts were revealed to Robert in such a cold, unfeeling way. Poor Florrie, managing to cling on to the remnants of her misery to the end. And even more sorry that it forged such a wedge between us he couldn't bear to listen to my version of the truth. It's a terrible thing to accuse your own mother of being a liar but Rita was. We don't know, we shall none of us ever know for certain, if Robert was the child I gave birth to. Nevertheless, so far as I am concerned he is my dearly beloved son, and always will be. I have no regrets and no more secrets. They are all told.'

Laura was quite alone, resting in her room on her first evening home, as she listened to the fifth and final tape. Afterwards, she smiled as she wiped

491

the tears from her eyes. 'So your secrets are now all told, Daisy. Thank you for sharing them with me. Robert understands now, I think, that you loved him. And I hope *you* know that in his heart he is reconciled with you at last. Perhaps you will forgive us both now for our shameful neglect. I'd like to think my quest has achieved that at least, in thanks for all you have given me.'

The publishers hope that this book has given you enjoyable reading. Large Print Books are especially designed to be as easy to see and hold as possible. If you wish a complete list of our books please ask at your local library or write directly to:

Magna Large Print Books
Magna House, Long Preston,
Skipton, North Yorkshire.
BD23 4ND

This Large Print Book for the partially sighted, who cannot read normal print, is published under the auspices of

THE ULVERSCROFT FOUNDATION